A MAGNUS THE BLACK MYSTERY

IMAGE COMICS, INC.
Robert Kirkman—Chief Operating Officer
Erik Larsen—Chief Financial Officer
Todd McFarlane—President
Marc Silvestri—Chief Executive Officer
Jim Valentino—Vice-President

Eric Stephenson—Publisher
Corey Murphy—Director of Sales
Jeff Boison—Director of Publishing Planning & Book Trade Sales
Chris Ross—Director of Digital Sales
Jeff Stang—Director of Specialty Sales
Kat Salazar—Director of PR & Marketing
Branwyn Bigglestone—Controller
Sue Korpela—Accounts Manager
Drew Gill—Art Director
Brett Warnock—Production Manager
Leigh Thomas—Print Manager
Tricia Ramos—Traffic Manager
Briah Skelly—Publicist
Aly Hoffman—Events & Conventions Coordinator
Sasha Head—Sales & Marketing Production Designer
David Brothers—Branding Manager
Melissa Gifford—Content Manager
Drew Fitzgerald—Publicity Assistant
Vincent Kukua—Production Artist
Erika Schnatz—Production Artist
Ryan Brewer—Production Artist
Shanna Matuszak—Production Artist
Carey Hall—Production Artist
Esther Kim—Direct Market Sales Representative
Emilio Bautista—Digital Sales Representative
Leanna Caunter—Accounting Assistant
Chloe Ramos-Peterson—Library Market Sales Representative
Marla Eizik—Administrative Assistant
IMAGECOMICS.COM

BLACK ROAD, VOL. 2: A PAGAN DEATH. First Printing. July 2017. Published by Image Comics, Inc. Office of publication: 2701 NW Vaughn St., Suite 780, Portland, OR 97210. Copyright © 2017 Brian Wood and Garry Brown. All rights reserved. Contains material originally published in single magazine form as BLACK ROAD #6-10. BLACK ROAD™ (including all prominent characters featured herein), its logo and all character likenesses are trademarks of Brian Wood and Garry Brown unless otherwise noted. Image Comics® and its logos are registered trademarks of Image Comics, Inc. No part of this publication may be reproduced or transmitted, in any form or by any means (except for short excerpts for review purposes) without the express written permission of Image Comics, Inc. All names, characters, events and locales in this publication are entirely fictional. Any resemblance to actual persons (living or dead), events or places, without satiric intent, is coincidental. Printed in the USA. For information regarding the CPSIA on this printed material call: 203-595-3636 and provide reference # RICH – 748966. For international rights, contact: foreignlicensing@imagecomics.com. ISBN: 978-1-5343-0226-6

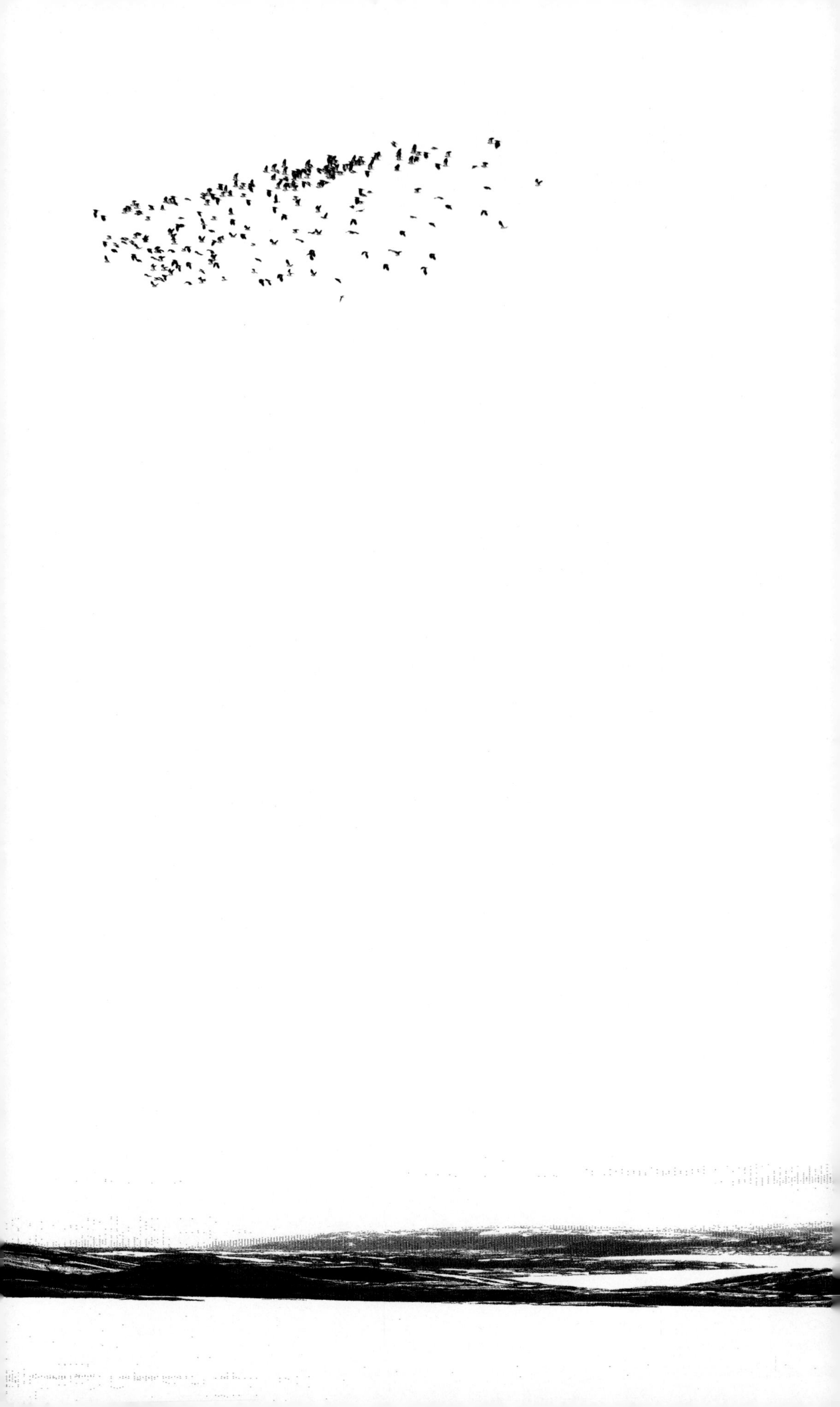

BLACK ROAD

VOL. 2

"A PAGAN DEATH"

STORY: BRIAN WOOD
ART AND COVER: GARRY BROWN
COLORS: DAVE MCCAIG
LETTERING: STEVE WANDS
PRODUCTION: BRENNAN THOME

BLACK ROAD IS CREATED BY BRIAN WOOD AND GARRY BROWN

LOGO AND TITLING CREDITS TYPESET IN HEADLINER NO. 45, © KEVIN CHRISTOPHER - KC FONTS

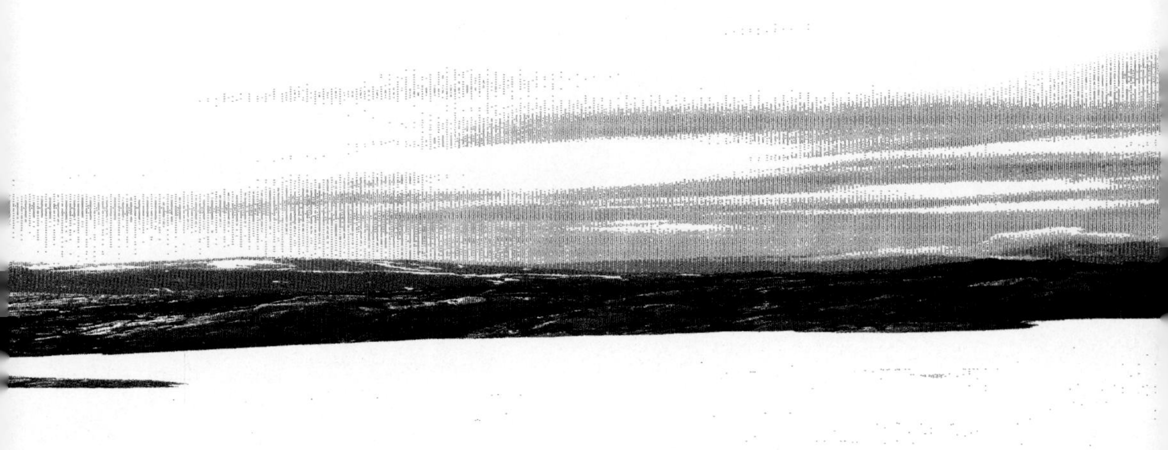

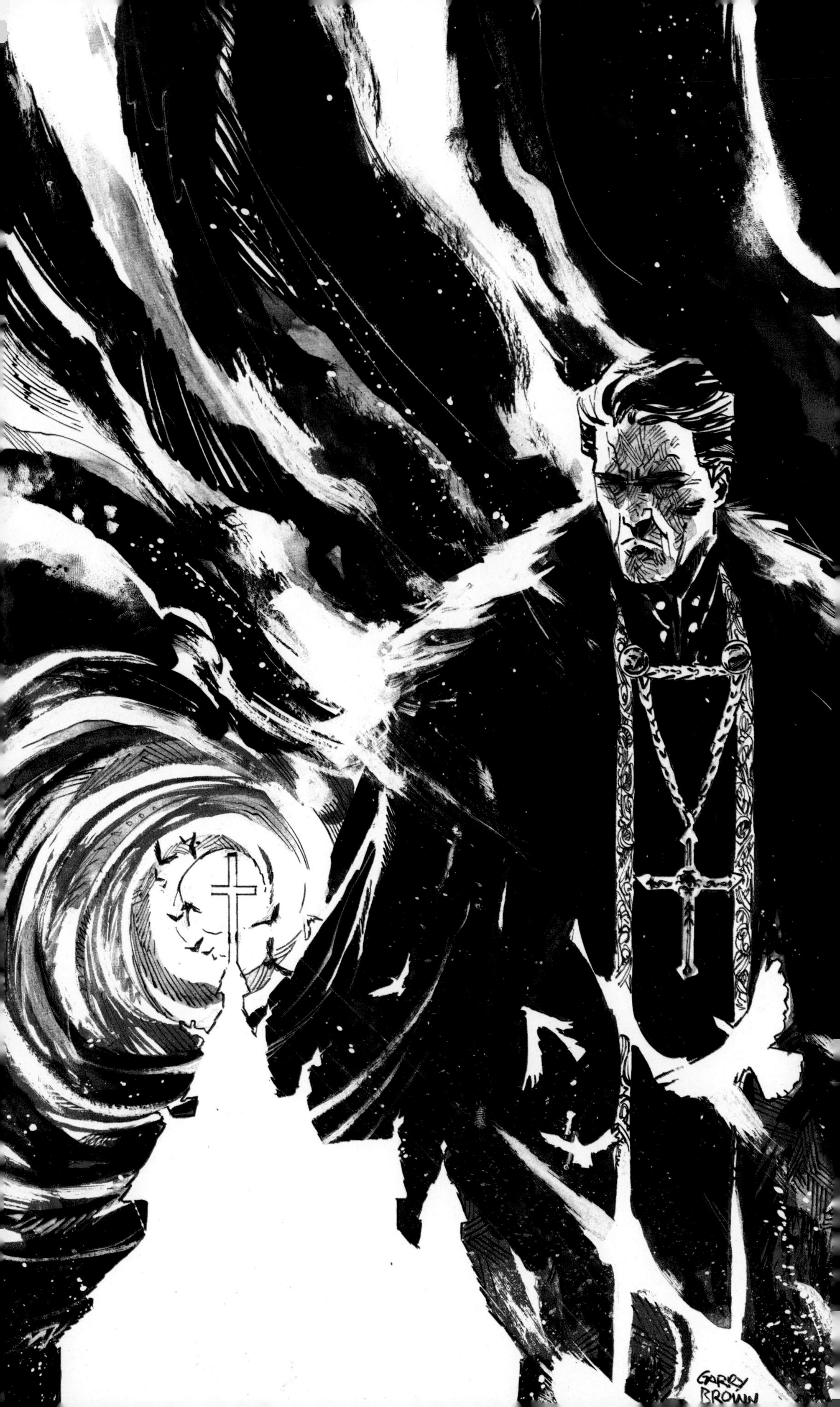
GARRY BROWN

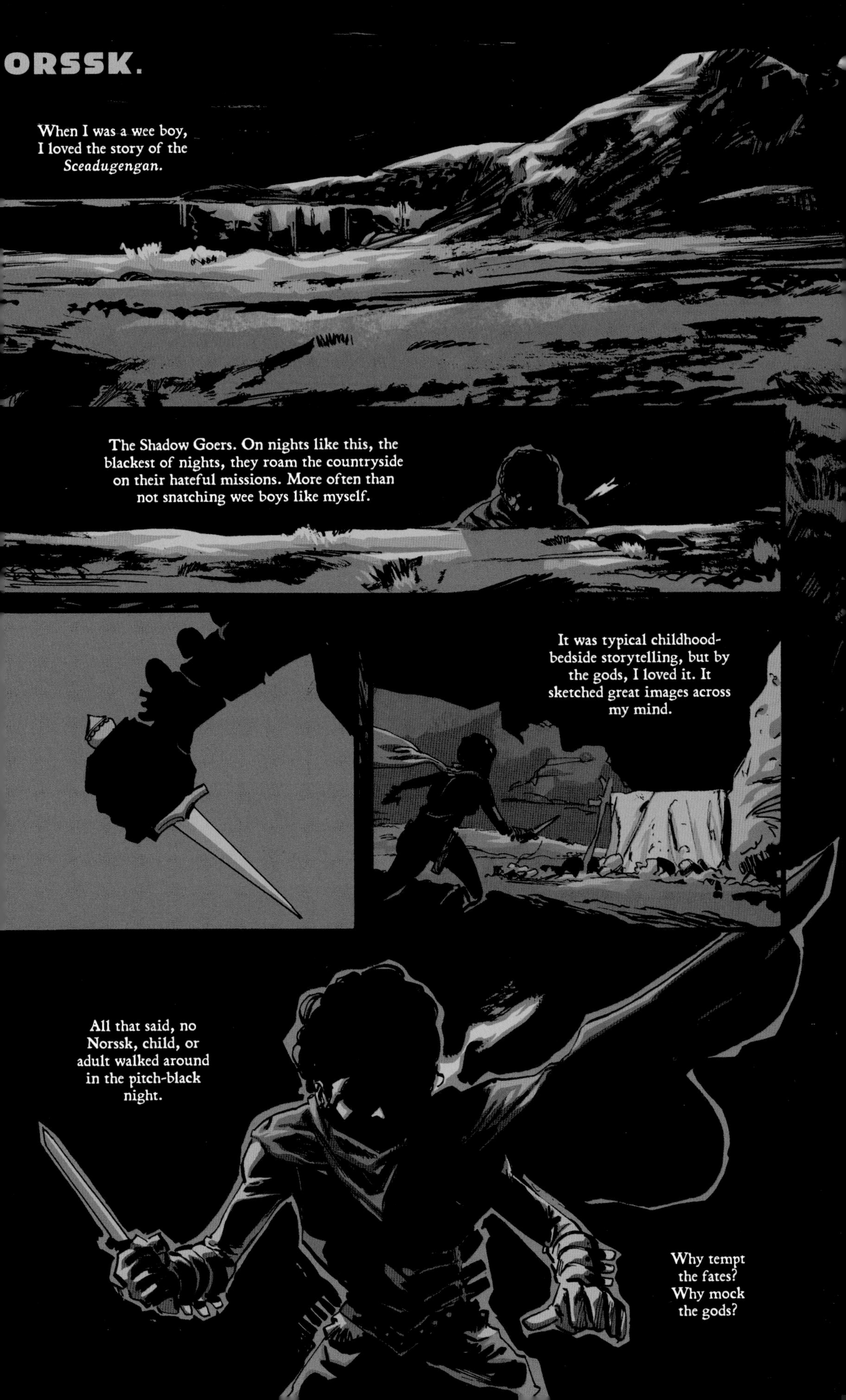
ORSSK.
When I was a wee boy, I loved the story of the *Sceadugengan.*
The Shadow Goers. On nights like this, the blackest of nights, they roam the countryside on their hateful missions. More often than not snatching wee boys like myself.
It was typical childhood-bedside storytelling, but by the gods, I loved it. It sketched great images across my mind.
All that said, no Norssk, child, or adult walked around in the pitch-black night.
Why tempt the fates? Why mock the gods?

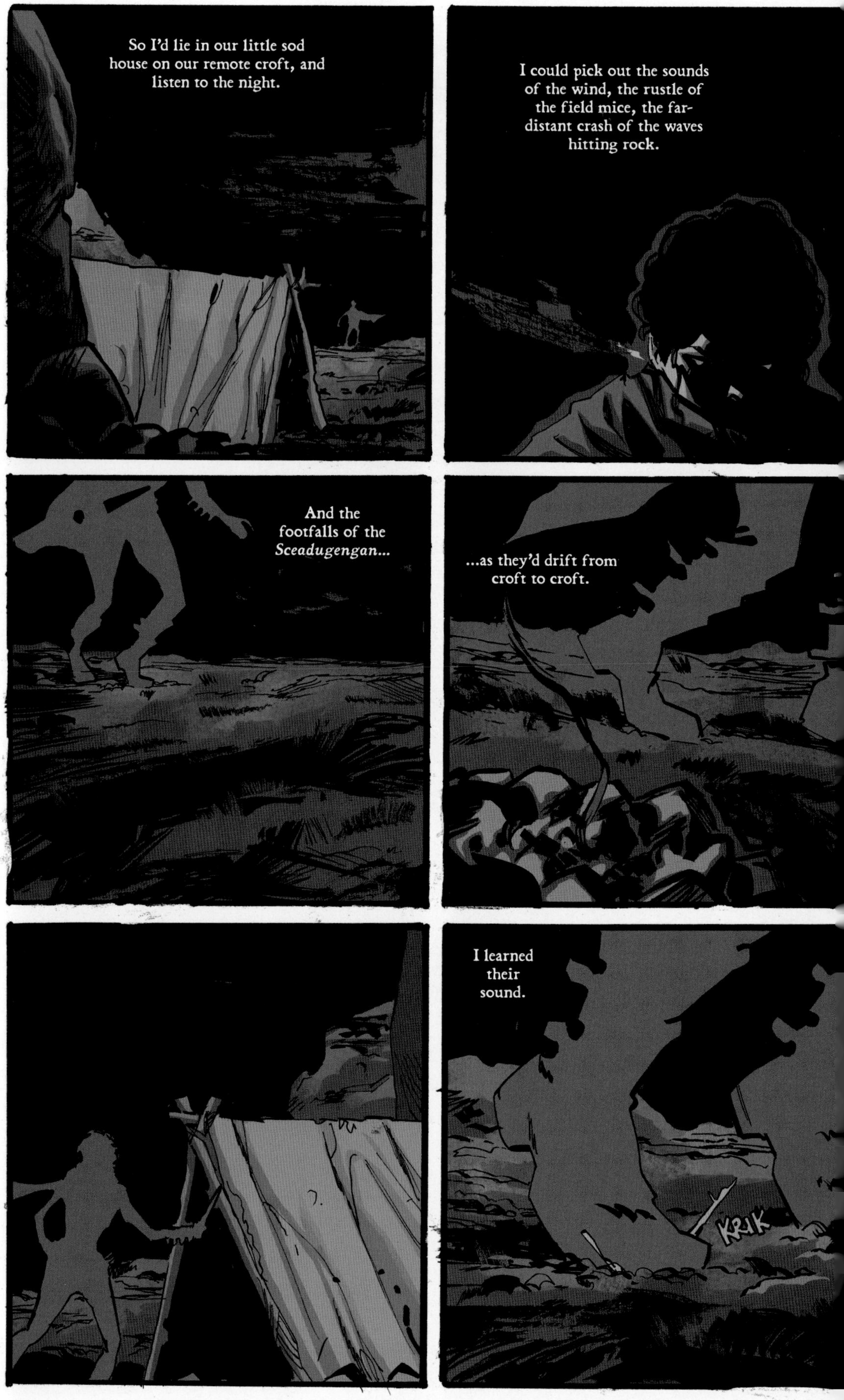
So I'd lie in our little sod house on our remote croft, and listen to the night.
I could pick out the sounds of the wind, the rustle of the field mice, the far-distant crash of the waves hitting rock.
And the footfalls of the *Sceadugengan*...
...as they'd drift from croft to croft.
I learned their sound.
KRIK

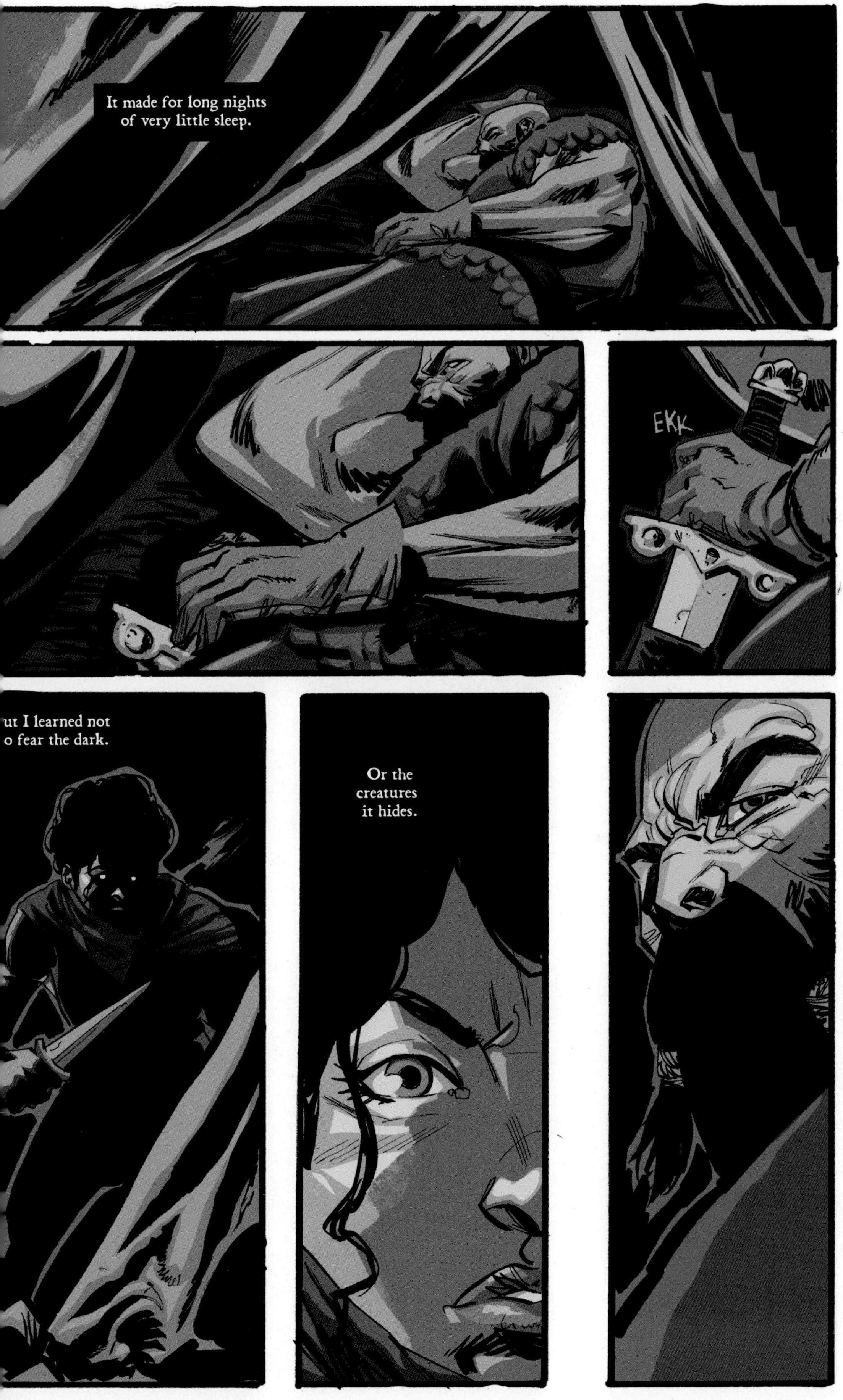
It made for long nights of very little sleep.
EKK
ut I learned not o fear the dark.
Or the creatures it hides.

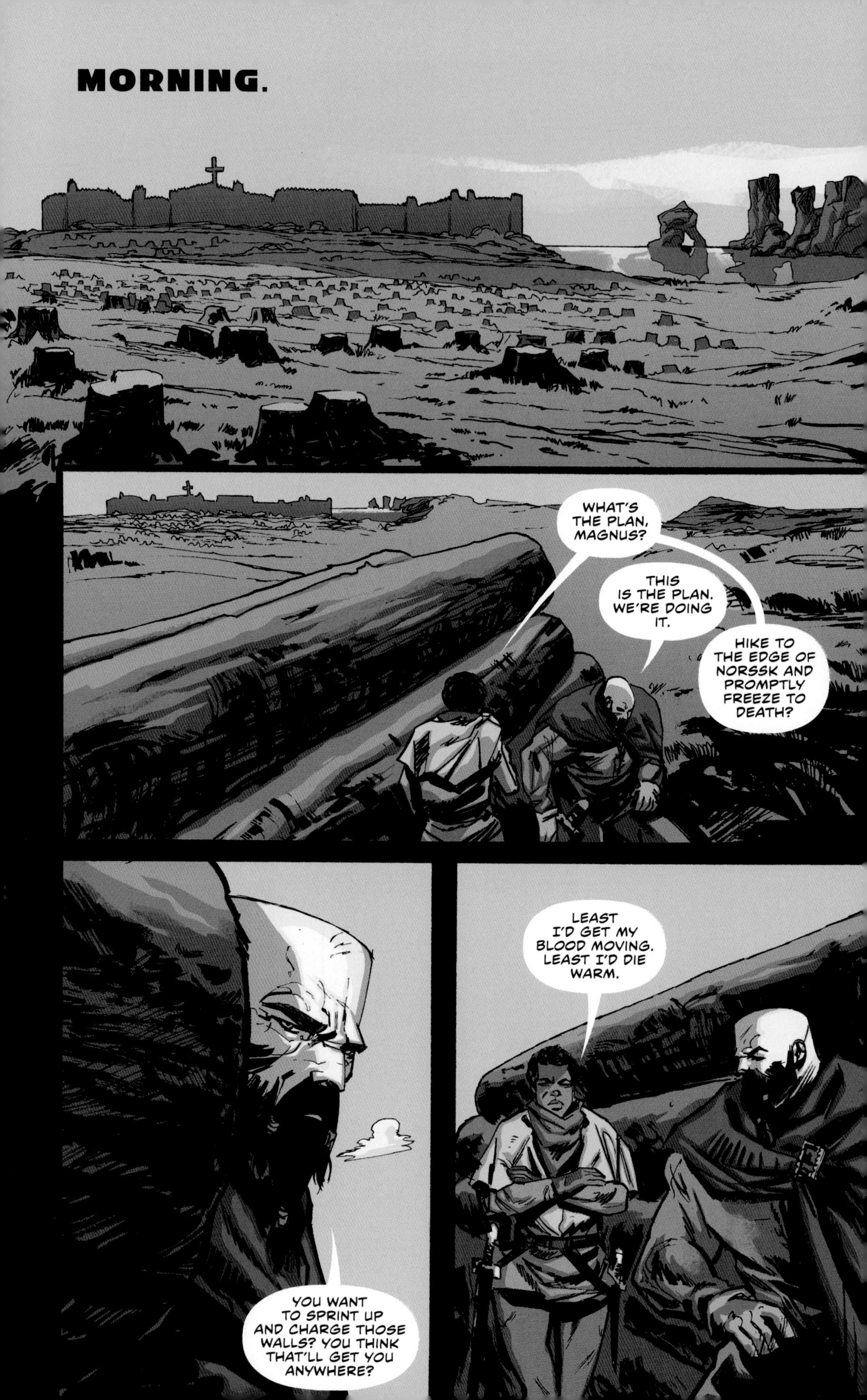
MORNING.
WHAT'S THE PLAN, MAGNUS?
THIS IS THE PLAN. WE'RE DOING IT.
HIKE TO THE EDGE OF NORSSK AND PROMPTLY FREEZE TO DEATH?
YOU WANT TO SPRINT UP AND CHARGE THOSE WALLS? YOU THINK THAT'LL GET YOU ANYWHERE?
LEAST I'D GET MY BLOOD MOVING. LEAST I'D DIE WARM.

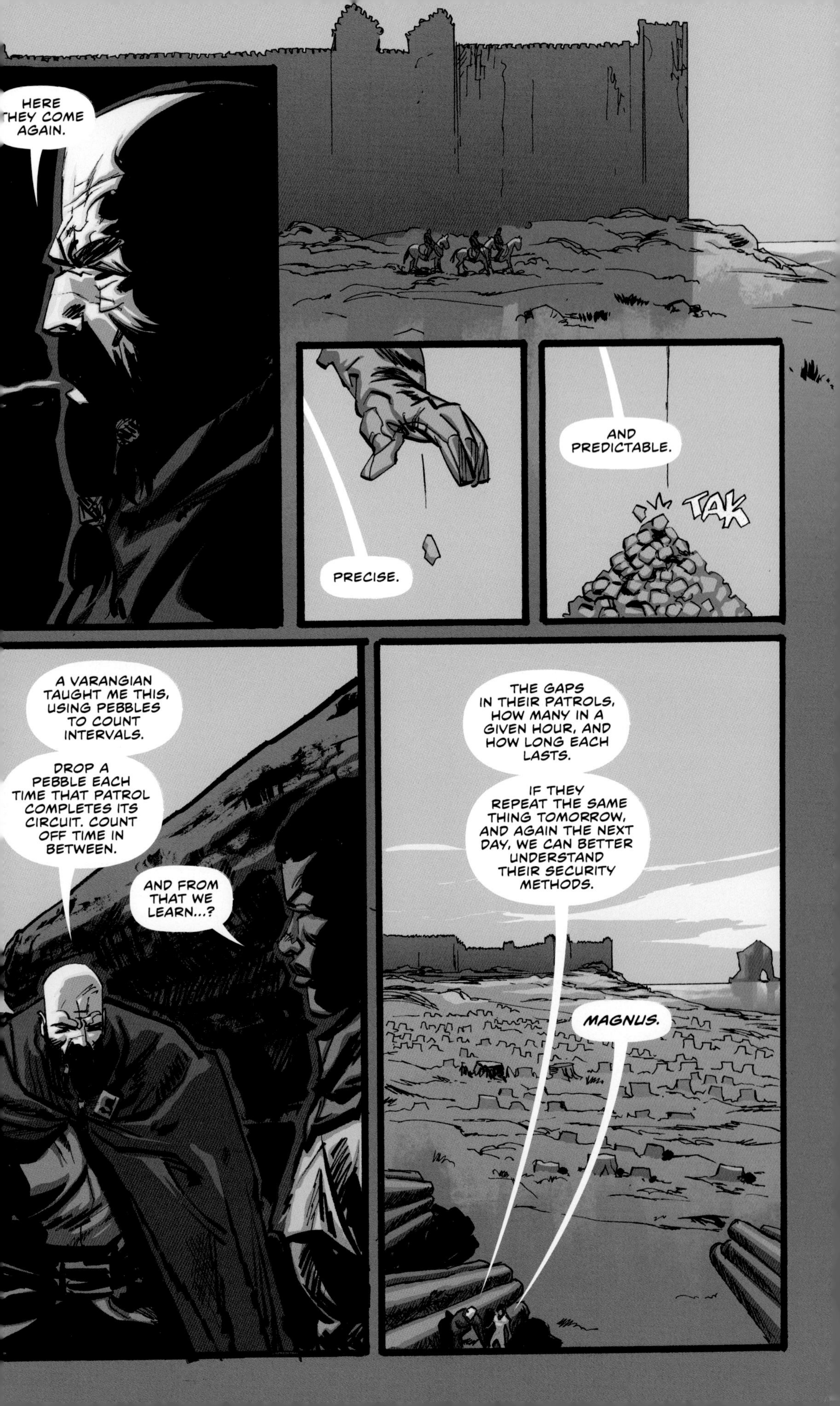

HERE THEY COME AGAIN.
PRECISE.
AND PREDICTABLE.
TAK
A VARANGIAN TAUGHT ME THIS, USING PEBBLES TO COUNT INTERVALS.
DROP A PEBBLE EACH TIME THAT PATROL COMPLETES ITS CIRCUIT. COUNT OFF TIME IN BETWEEN.
AND FROM THAT WE LEARN...?
THE GAPS IN THEIR PATROLS, HOW MANY IN A GIVEN HOUR, AND HOW LONG EACH LASTS.
IF THEY REPEAT THE SAME THING TOMORROW, AND AGAIN THE NEXT DAY, WE CAN BETTER UNDERSTAND THEIR SECURITY METHODS.
MAGNUS.

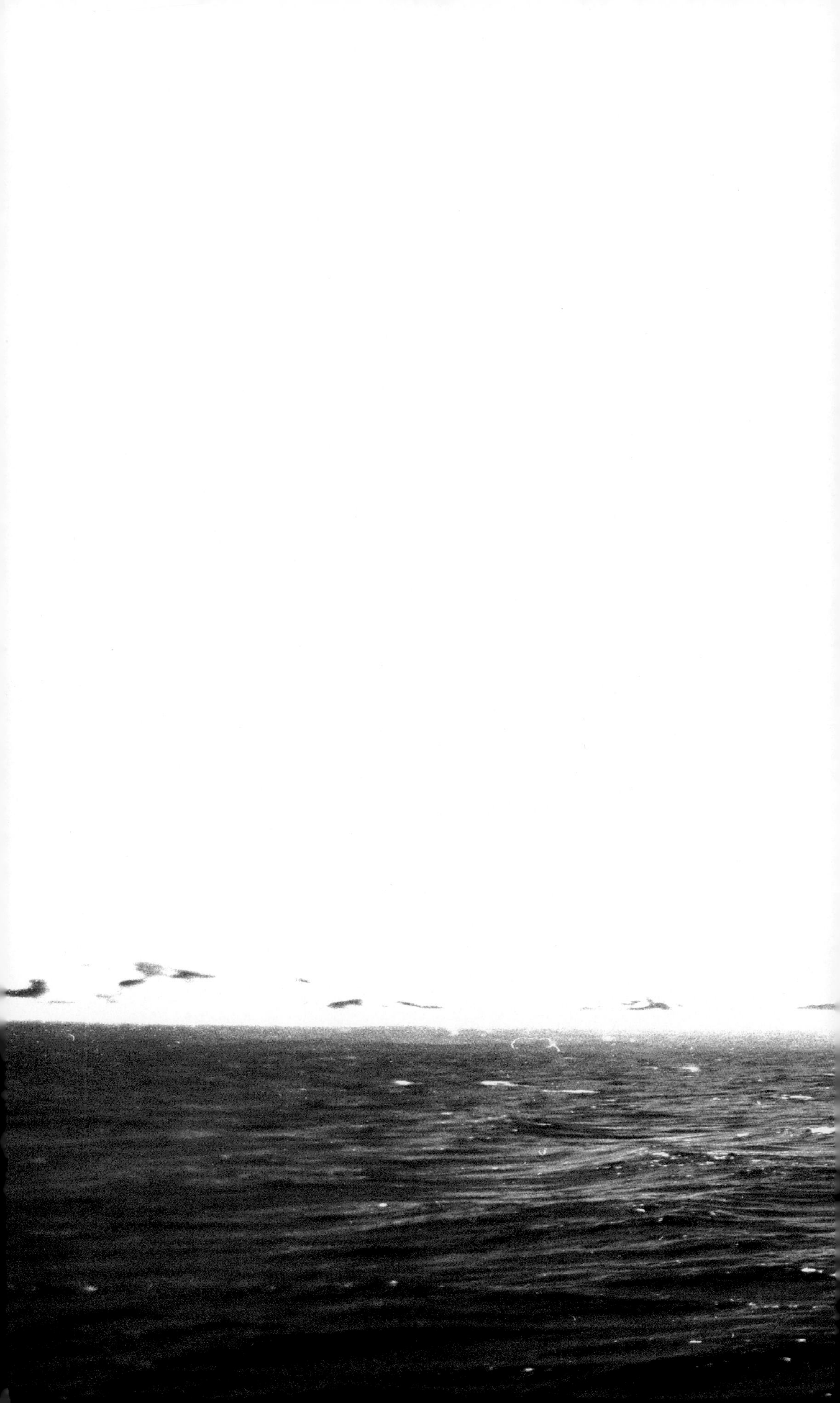

BRIAN WOOD / GARRY BROWN / DAVE McCAIG / STEVE WANDS

BLACK ROAD

#6 - "A PAGAN DEATH"

A MAGNUS THE BLACK MYSTERY

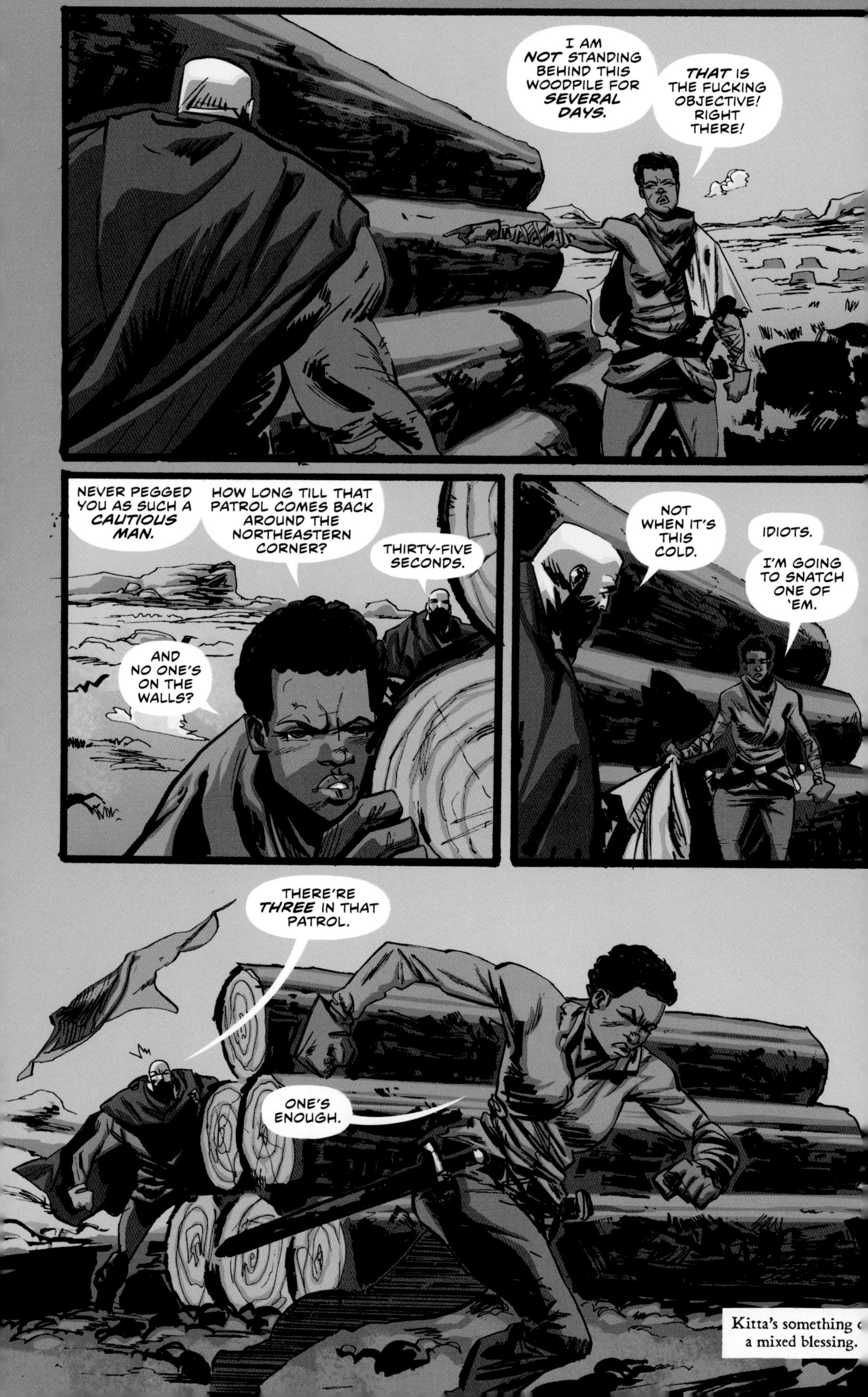
I AM *NOT* STANDING BEHIND THIS WOODPILE FOR *SEVERAL DAYS.*
THAT IS THE FUCKING OBJECTIVE! RIGHT THERE!
NEVER PEGGED YOU AS SUCH A *CAUTIOUS MAN.*
HOW LONG TILL THAT PATROL COMES BACK AROUND THE NORTHEASTERN CORNER?
THIRTY-FIVE SECONDS.
AND NO ONE'S ON THE WALLS?
NOT WHEN IT'S THIS COLD.
IDIOTS.
I'M GOING TO SNATCH ONE OF 'EM.
THERE'RE *THREE* IN THAT PATROL.
ONE'S ENOUGH.
Kitta's something o
a mixed blessing.

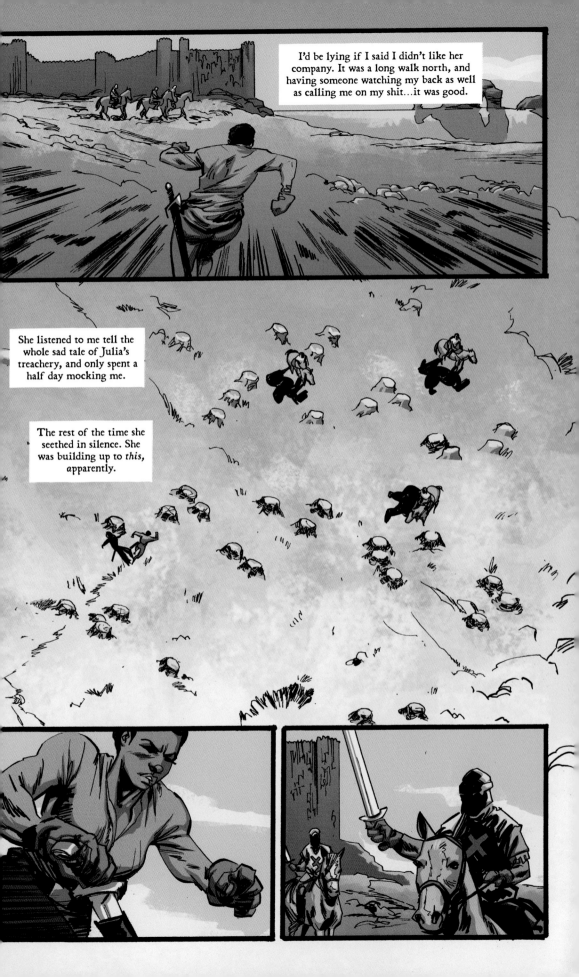

I'd be lying if I said I didn't like her company. It was a long walk north, and having someone watching my back as well as calling me on my shit...it was good.

She listened to me tell the whole sad tale of Julia's treachery, and only spent a half day mocking me.

The rest of the time she seethed in silence. She was building up to *this,* apparently.

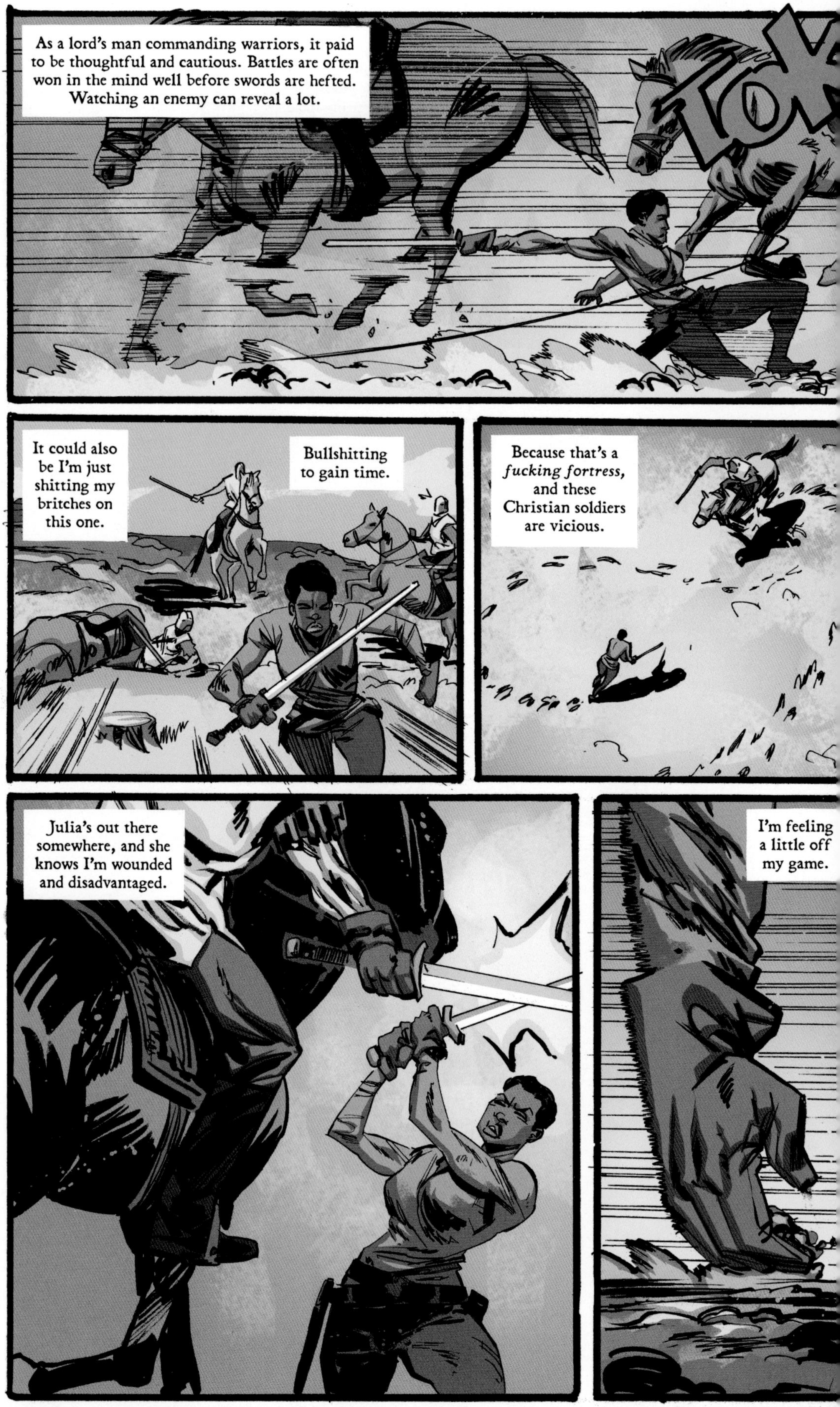
As a lord's man commanding warriors, it paid to be thoughtful and cautious. Battles are often won in the mind well before swords are hefted. Watching an enemy can reveal a lot.
TOK
It could also be I'm just shitting my britches on this one.
Bullshitting to gain time.
Because that's a *fucking fortress,* and these Christian soldiers are vicious.
Julia's out there somewhere, and she knows I'm wounded and disadvantaged.
I'm feeling a little off my game.

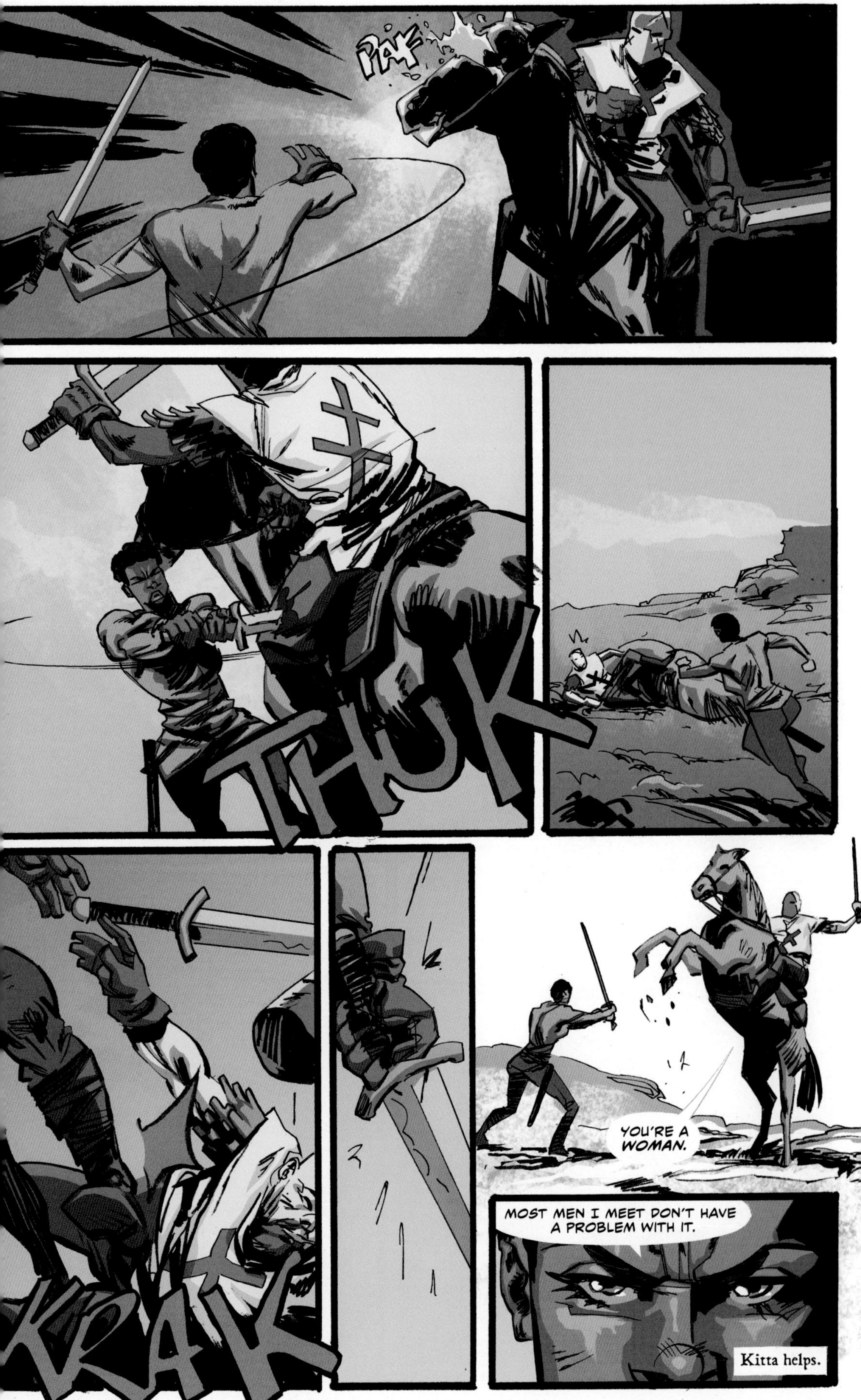
PIAF
THUK
KRAK
YOU'RE A WOMAN.
MOST MEN I MEET DON'T HAVE A PROBLEM WITH IT.
Kitta helps.

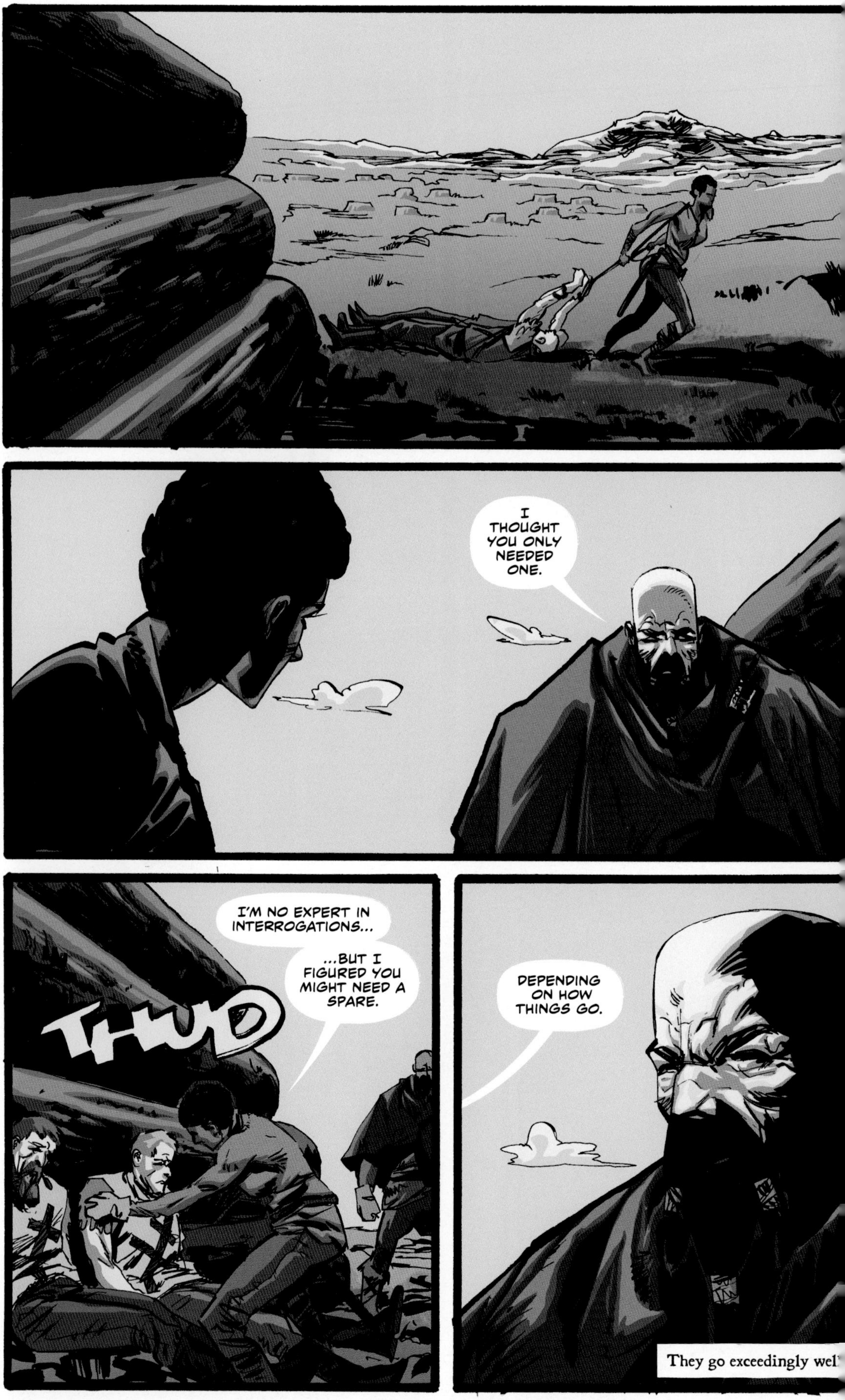
I THOUGHT YOU ONLY NEEDED ONE.
I'M NO EXPERT IN INTERROGATIONS...
...BUT I FIGURED YOU MIGHT NEED A SPARE.
THUD
DEPENDING ON HOW THINGS GO.
They go exceedingly wel

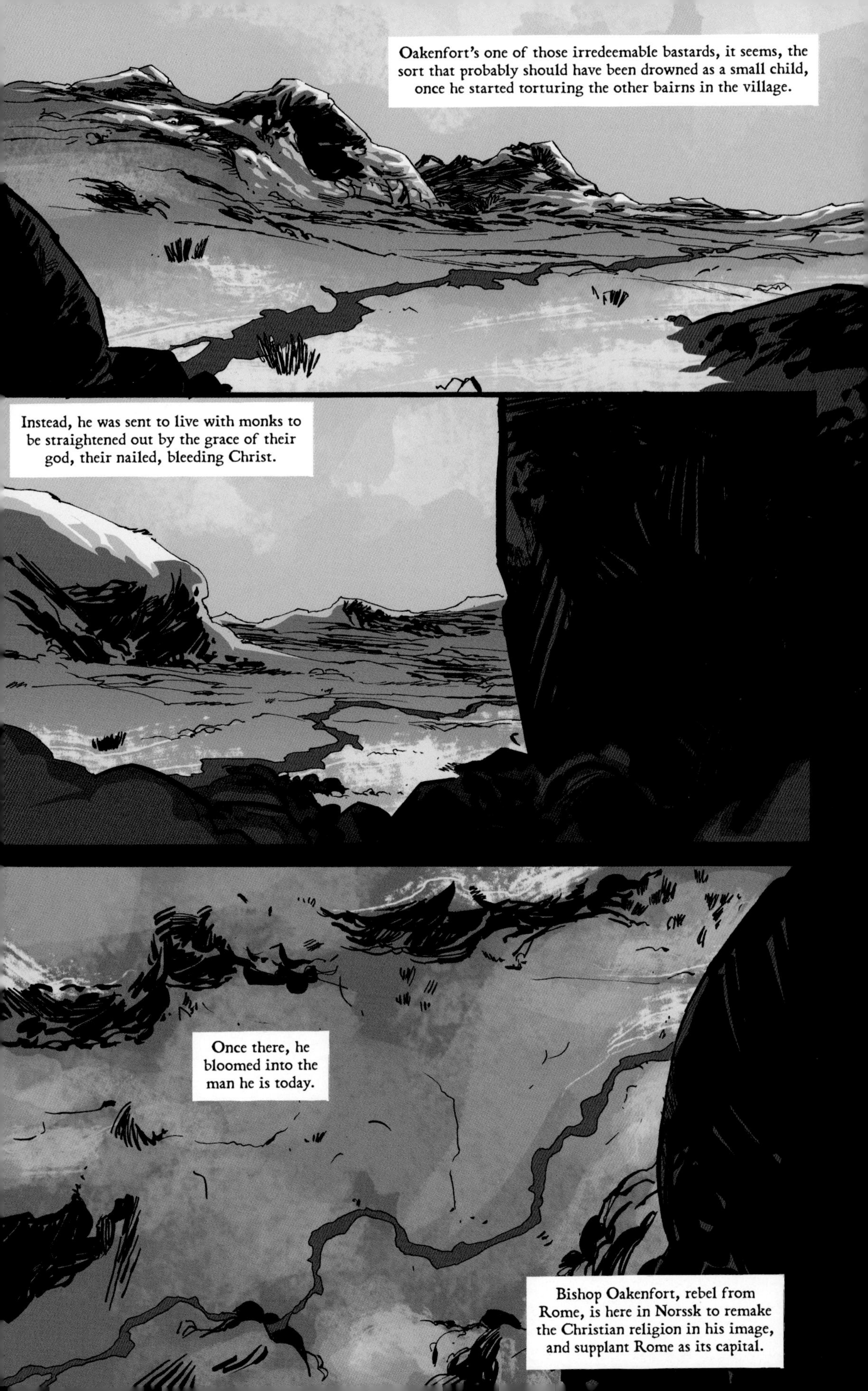
Oakenfort's one of those irredeemable bastards, it seems, the sort that probably should have been drowned as a small child, once he started torturing the other bairns in the village.
Instead, he was sent to live with monks to be straightened out by the grace of their god, their nailed, bleeding Christ.
Once there, he bloomed into the man he is today.
Bishop Oakenfort, rebel from Rome, is here in Norssk to remake the Christian religion in his image, and supplant Rome as its capital.

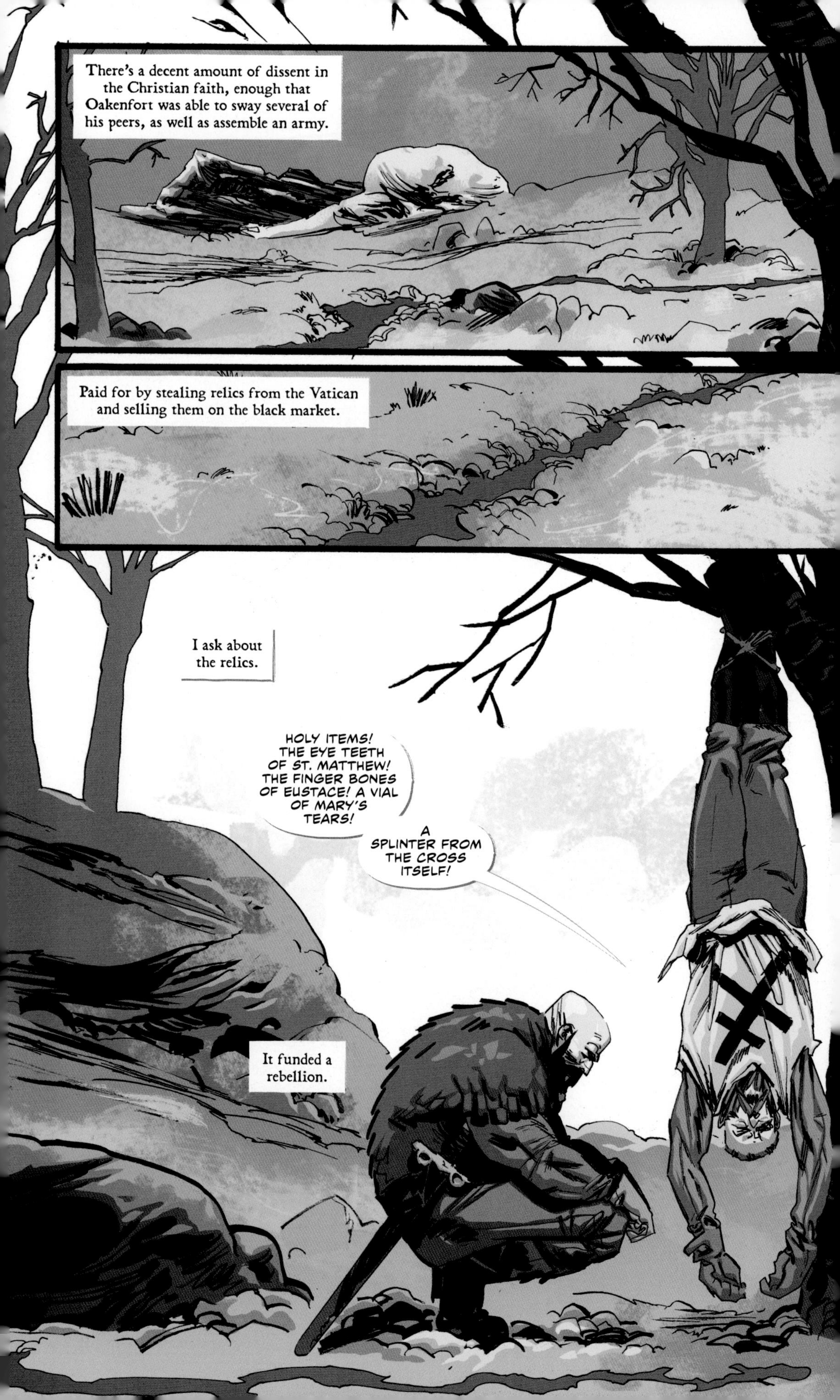
There's a decent amount of dissent in the Christian faith, enough that Oakenfort was able to sway several of his peers, as well as assemble an army.
Paid for by stealing relics from the Vatican and selling them on the black market.
I ask about the relics.
HOLY ITEMS! THE EYE TEETH OF ST. MATTHEW! THE FINGER BONES OF EUSTACE! A VIAL OF MARY'S TEARS!
A SPLINTER FROM THE CROSS ITSELF!
It funded a rebellion.

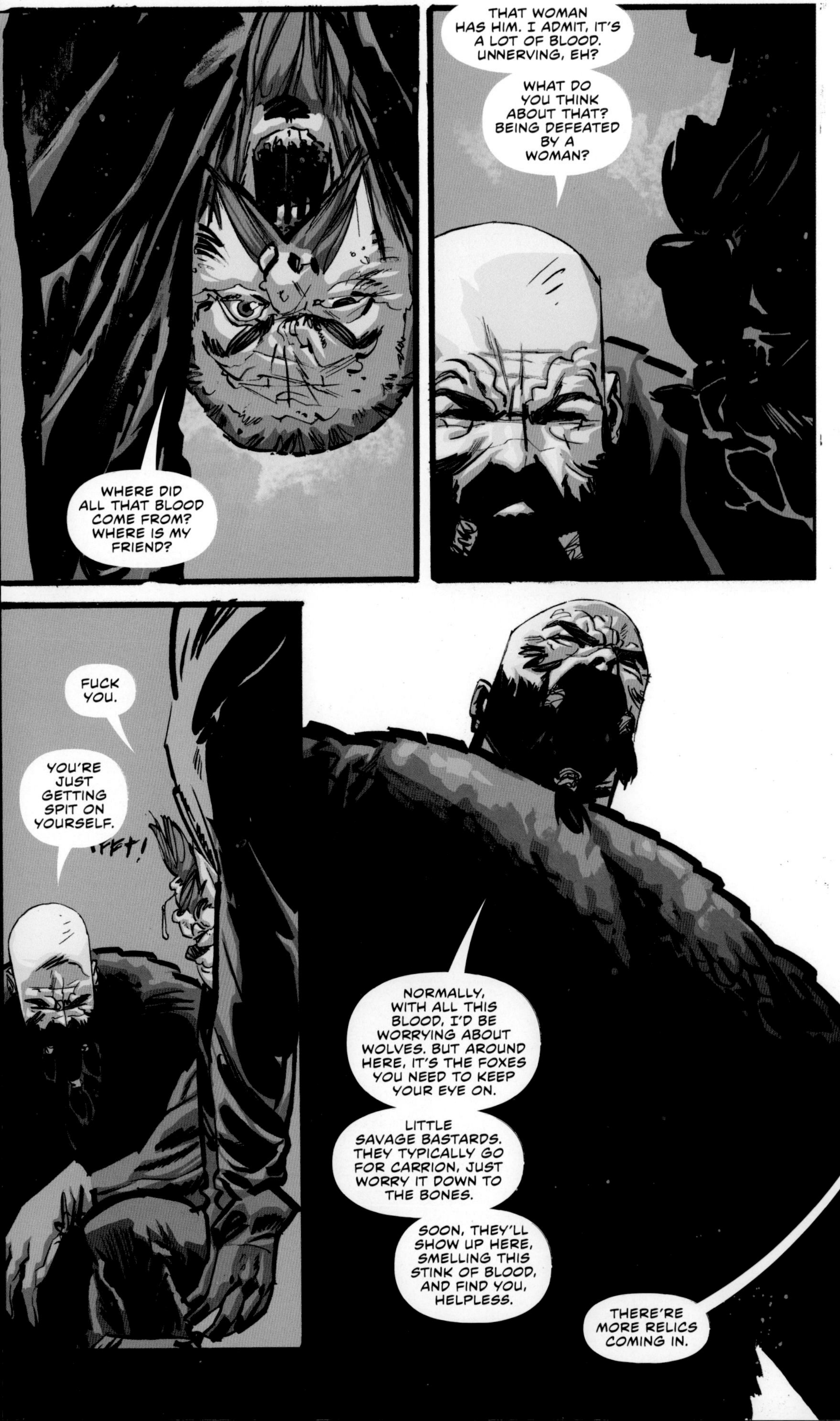
WHERE DID ALL THAT BLOOD COME FROM? WHERE IS MY FRIEND?
THAT WOMAN HAS HIM. I ADMIT, IT'S A LOT OF BLOOD. UNNERVING, EH?
WHAT DO YOU THINK ABOUT THAT? BEING DEFEATED BY A WOMAN?
FUCK YOU.
YOU'RE JUST GETTING SPIT ON YOURSELF.
NORMALLY, WITH ALL THIS BLOOD, I'D BE WORRYING ABOUT WOLVES. BUT AROUND HERE, IT'S THE FOXES YOU NEED TO KEEP YOUR EYE ON.
LITTLE SAVAGE BASTARDS. THEY TYPICALLY GO FOR CARRION, JUST WORRY IT DOWN TO THE BONES.
SOON, THEY'LL SHOW UP HERE, SMELLING THIS STINK OF BLOOD, AND FIND YOU, HELPLESS.
THERE'RE MORE RELICS COMING IN.

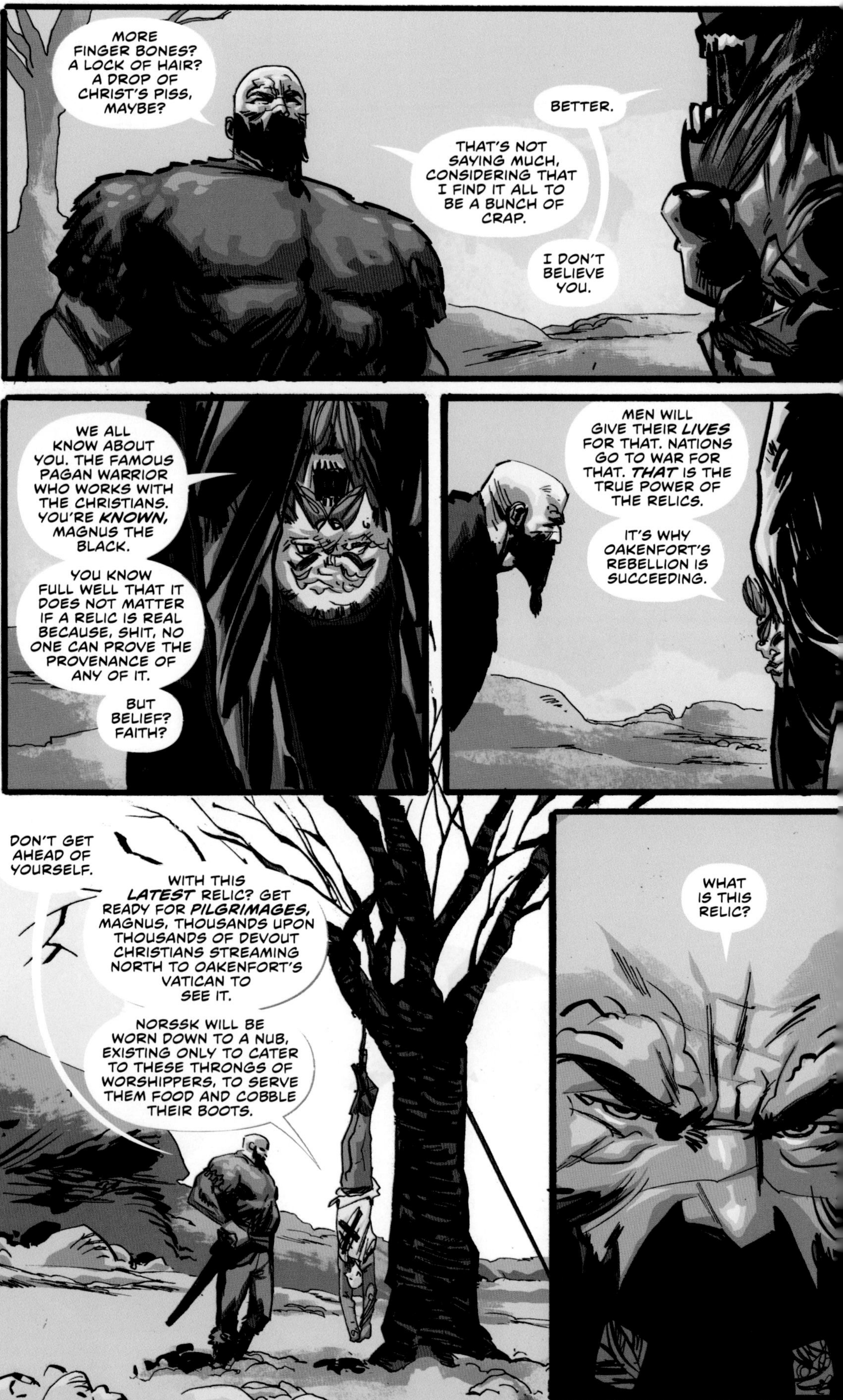

MORE FINGER BONES? A LOCK OF HAIR? A DROP OF CHRIST'S PISS, MAYBE?
BETTER.
THAT'S NOT SAYING MUCH, CONSIDERING THAT I FIND IT ALL TO BE A BUNCH OF CRAP.
I DON'T BELIEVE YOU.
WE ALL KNOW ABOUT YOU. THE FAMOUS PAGAN WARRIOR WHO WORKS WITH THE CHRISTIANS. YOU'RE *KNOWN,* MAGNUS THE BLACK.
YOU KNOW FULL WELL THAT IT DOES NOT MATTER IF A RELIC IS REAL BECAUSE, SHIT, NO ONE CAN PROVE THE PROVENANCE OF ANY OF IT.
BUT BELIEF? FAITH?
MEN WILL GIVE THEIR *LIVES* FOR THAT. NATIONS GO TO WAR FOR THAT. *THAT* IS THE TRUE POWER OF THE RELICS.
IT'S WHY OAKENFORT'S REBELLION IS SUCCEEDING.
WITH THIS *LATEST* RELIC? GET READY FOR *PILGRIMAGES,* MAGNUS, THOUSANDS UPON THOUSANDS OF DEVOUT CHRISTIANS STREAMING NORTH TO OAKENFORT'S VATICAN TO SEE IT.
NORSSK WILL BE WORN DOWN TO A NUB, EXISTING ONLY TO CATER TO THESE THRONGS OF WORSHIPPERS, TO SERVE THEM FOOD AND COBBLE THEIR BOOTS.
DON'T GET AHEAD OF YOURSELF.
WHAT IS THIS RELIC?

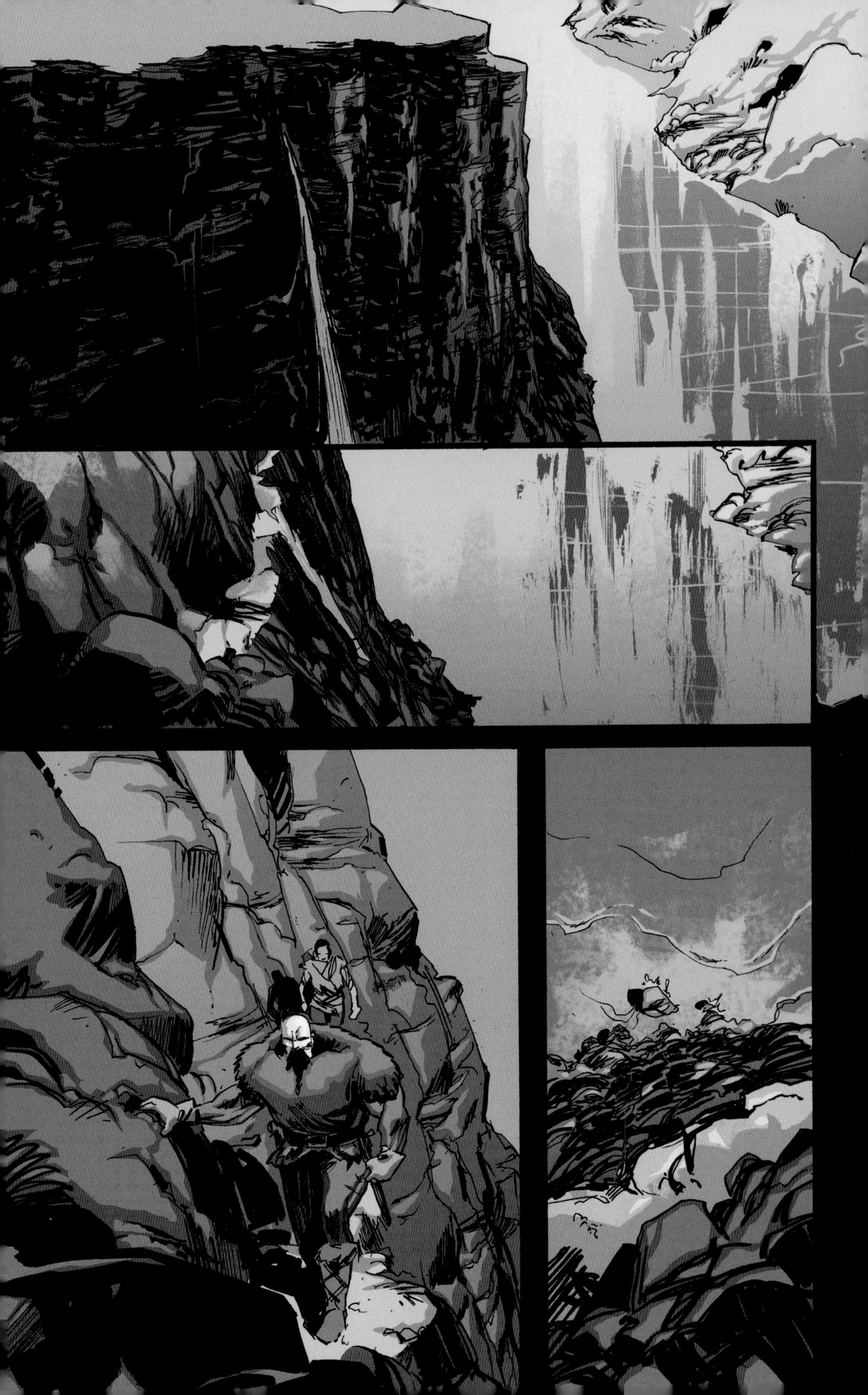

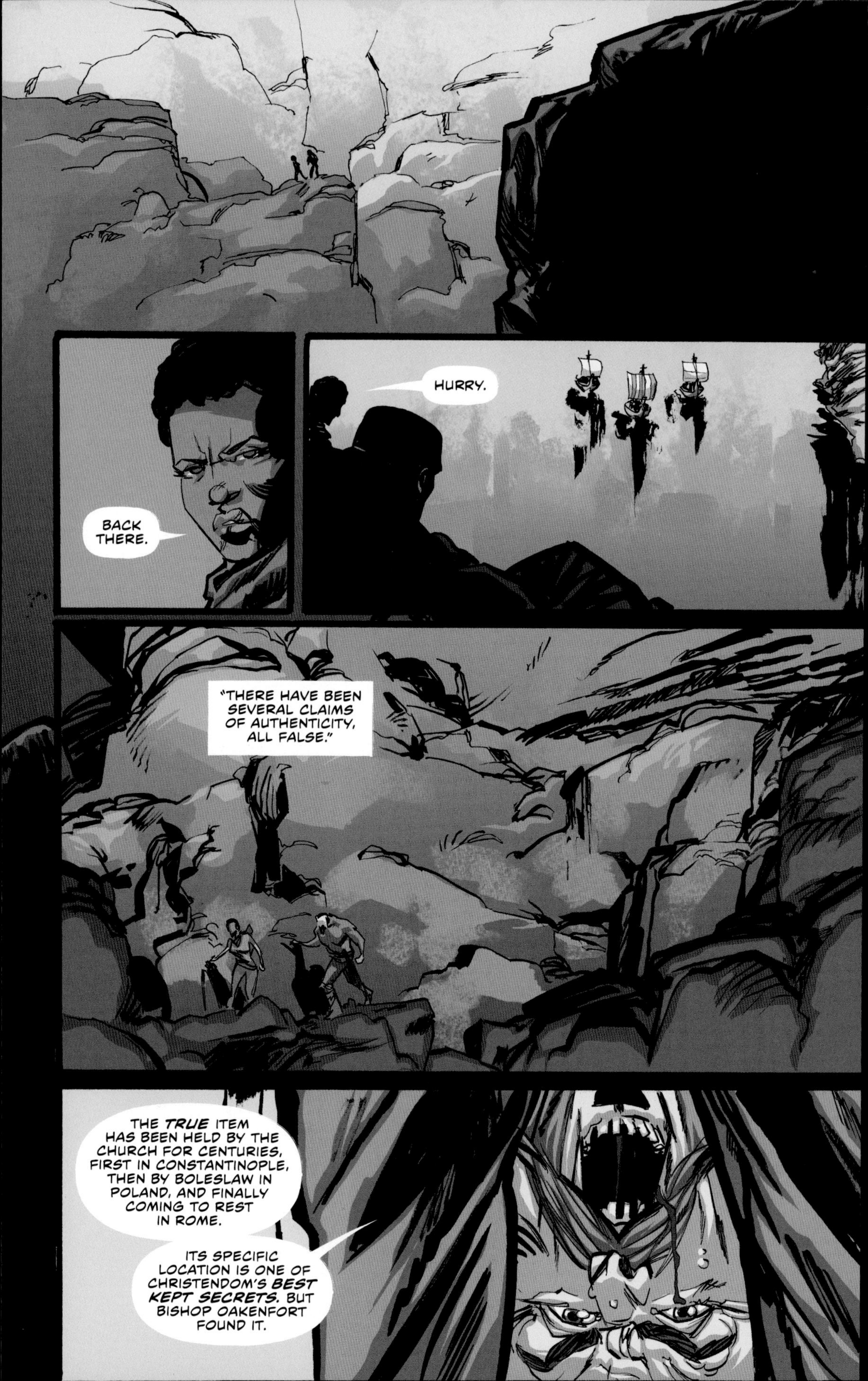
BACK THERE.
HURRY.
"THERE HAVE BEEN SEVERAL CLAIMS OF AUTHENTICITY, ALL FALSE."
THE *TRUE* ITEM HAS BEEN HELD BY THE CHURCH FOR CENTURIES, FIRST IN CONSTANTINOPLE, THEN BY BOLESLAW IN POLAND, AND FINALLY COMING TO REST IN ROME.
ITS SPECIFIC LOCATION IS ONE OF CHRISTENDOM'S *BEST KEPT SECRETS.* BUT BISHOP OAKENFORT FOUND IT.

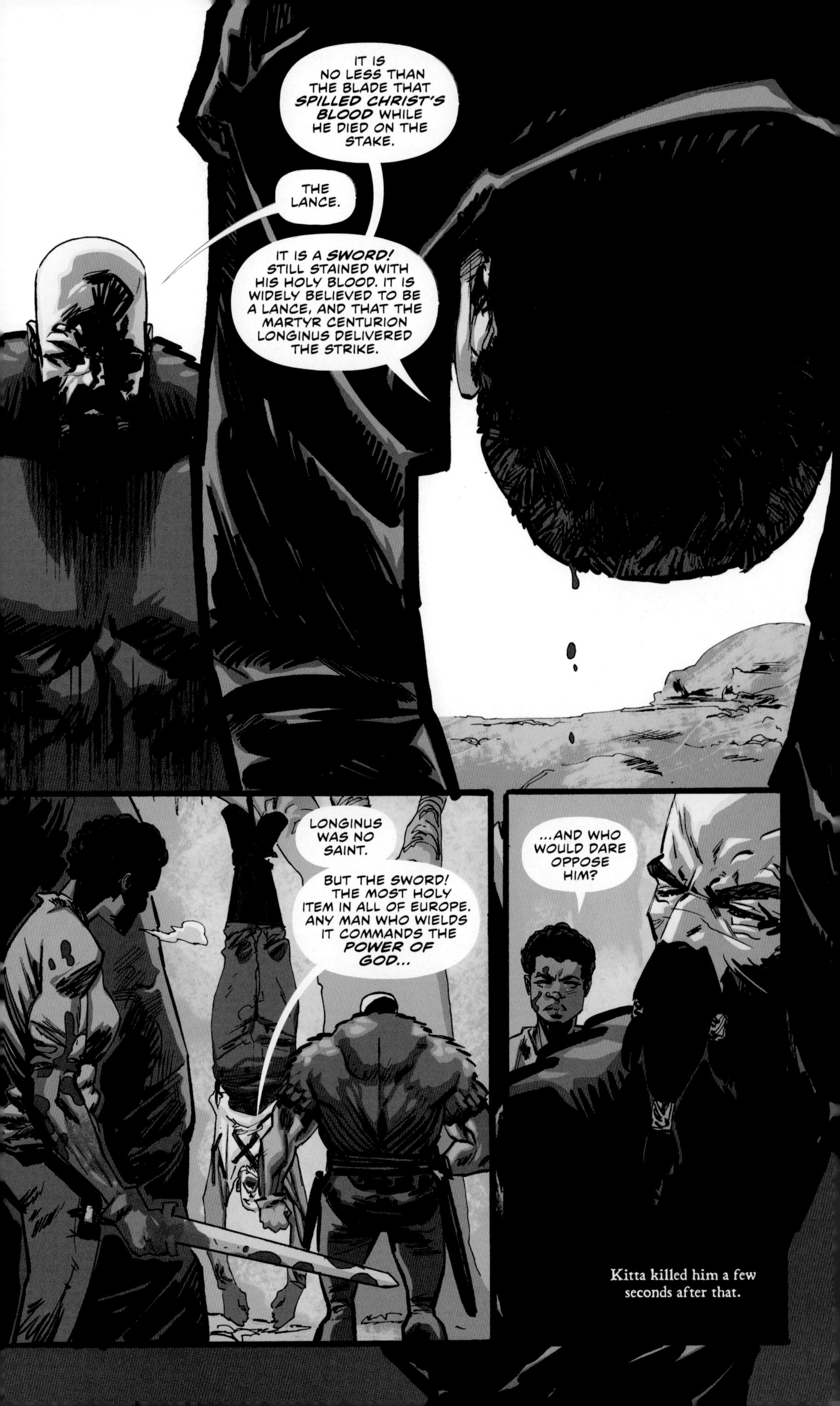
IT IS NO LESS THAN THE BLADE THAT SPILLED CHRIST'S BLOOD WHILE HE DIED ON THE STAKE.
THE LANCE.
IT IS A SWORD! STILL STAINED WITH HIS HOLY BLOOD. IT IS WIDELY BELIEVED TO BE A LANCE, AND THAT THE MARTYR CENTURION LONGINUS DELIVERED THE STRIKE.
LONGINUS WAS NO SAINT.
BUT THE SWORD! THE MOST HOLY ITEM IN ALL OF EUROPE. ANY MAN WHO WIELDS IT COMMANDS THE POWER OF GOD...
...AND WHO WOULD DARE OPPOSE HIM?
Kitta killed him a few seconds after that.

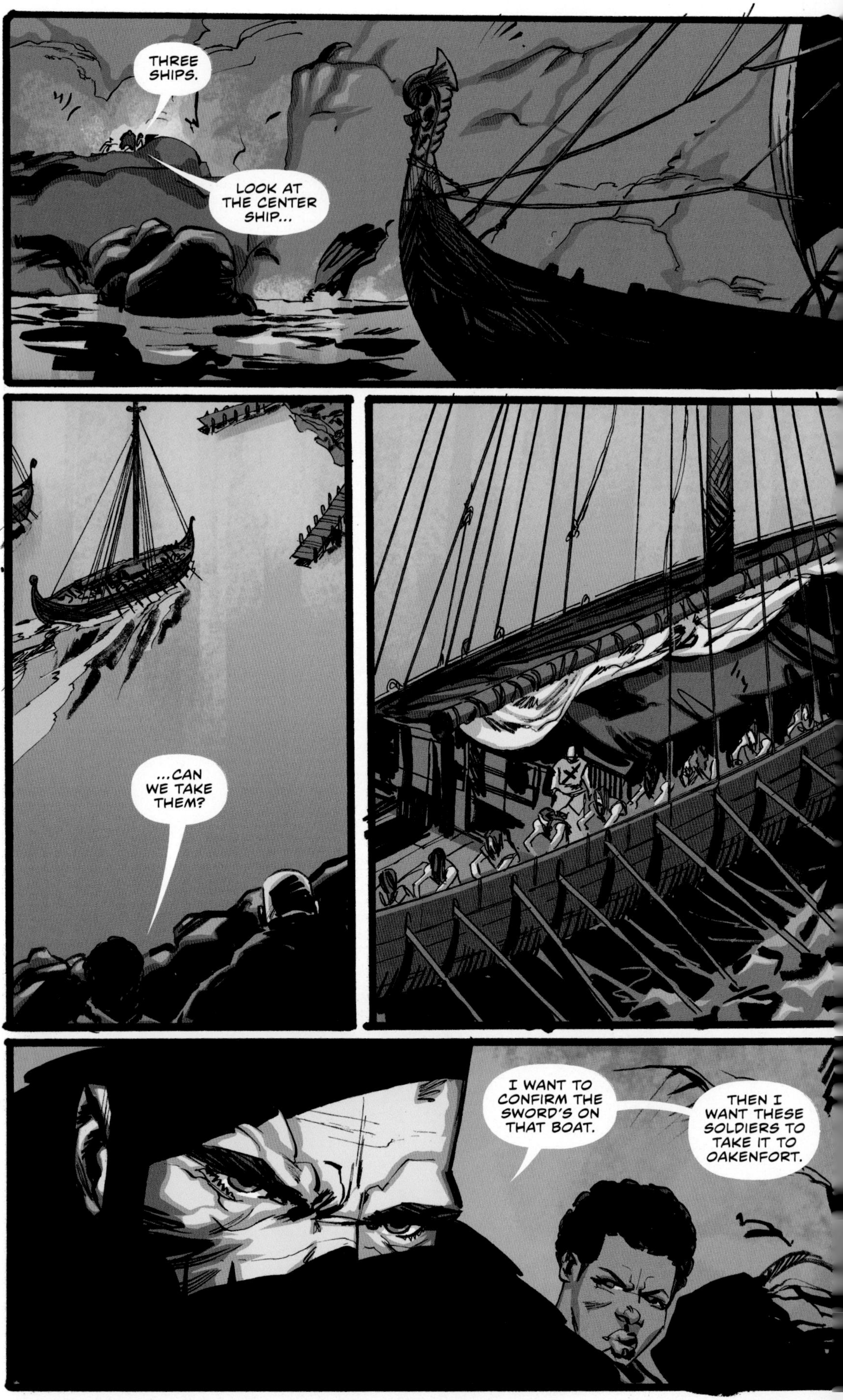
THREE SHIPS.
LOOK AT THE CENTER SHIP...
...CAN WE TAKE THEM?
I WANT TO CONFIRM THE SWORD'S ON THAT BOAT.
THEN I WANT THESE SOLDIERS TO TAKE IT TO OAKENFORT.

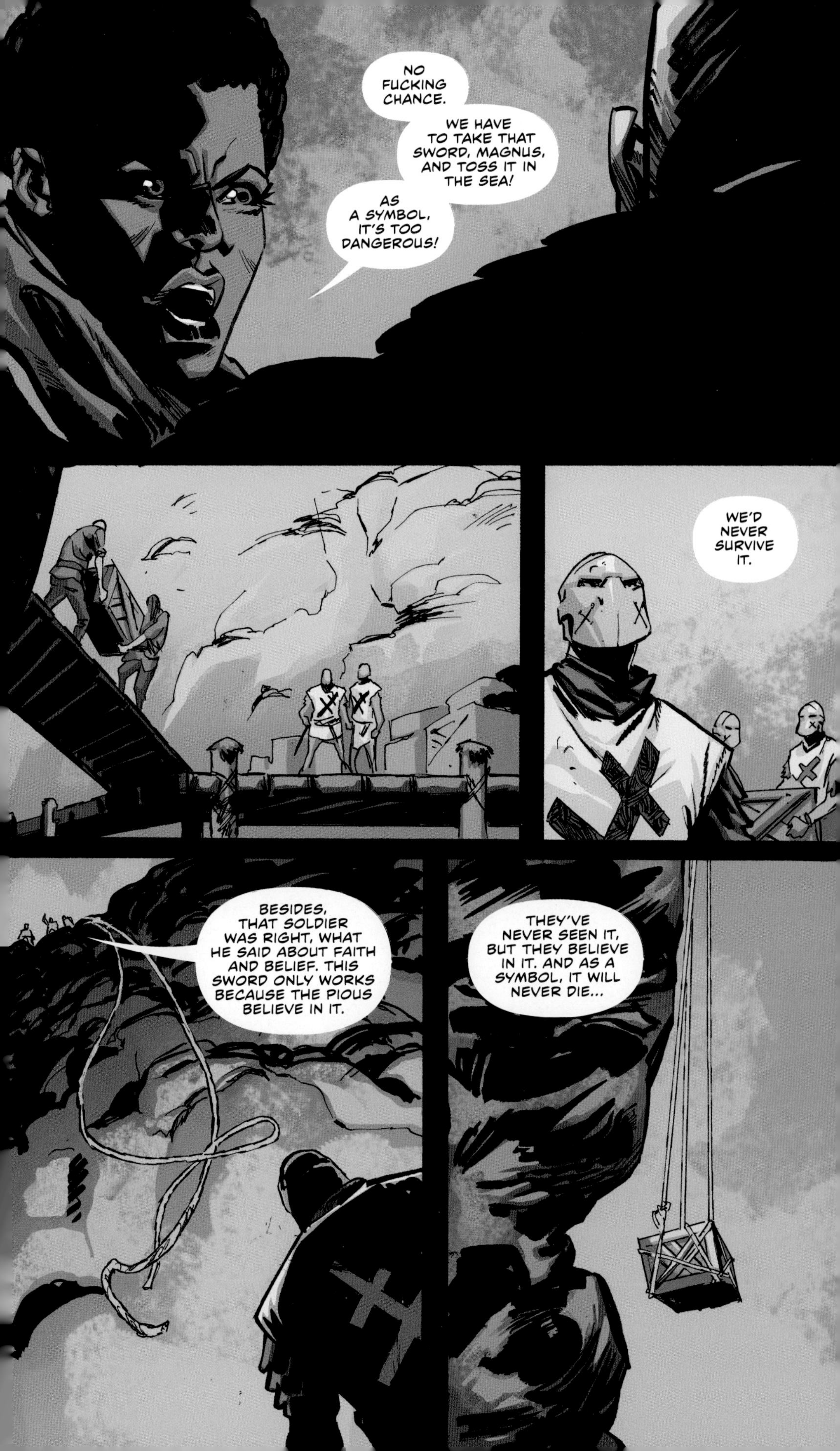
NO FUCKING CHANCE.
WE HAVE TO TAKE THAT SWORD, MAGNUS, AND TOSS IT IN THE SEA!
AS A SYMBOL, IT'S TOO DANGEROUS!
WE'D NEVER SURVIVE IT.
BESIDES, THAT SOLDIER WAS RIGHT, WHAT HE SAID ABOUT FAITH AND BELIEF. THIS SWORD ONLY WORKS BECAUSE THE PIOUS BELIEVE IN IT.
THEY'VE NEVER SEEN IT, BUT THEY BELIEVE IN IT. AND AS A SYMBOL, IT WILL NEVER DIE...

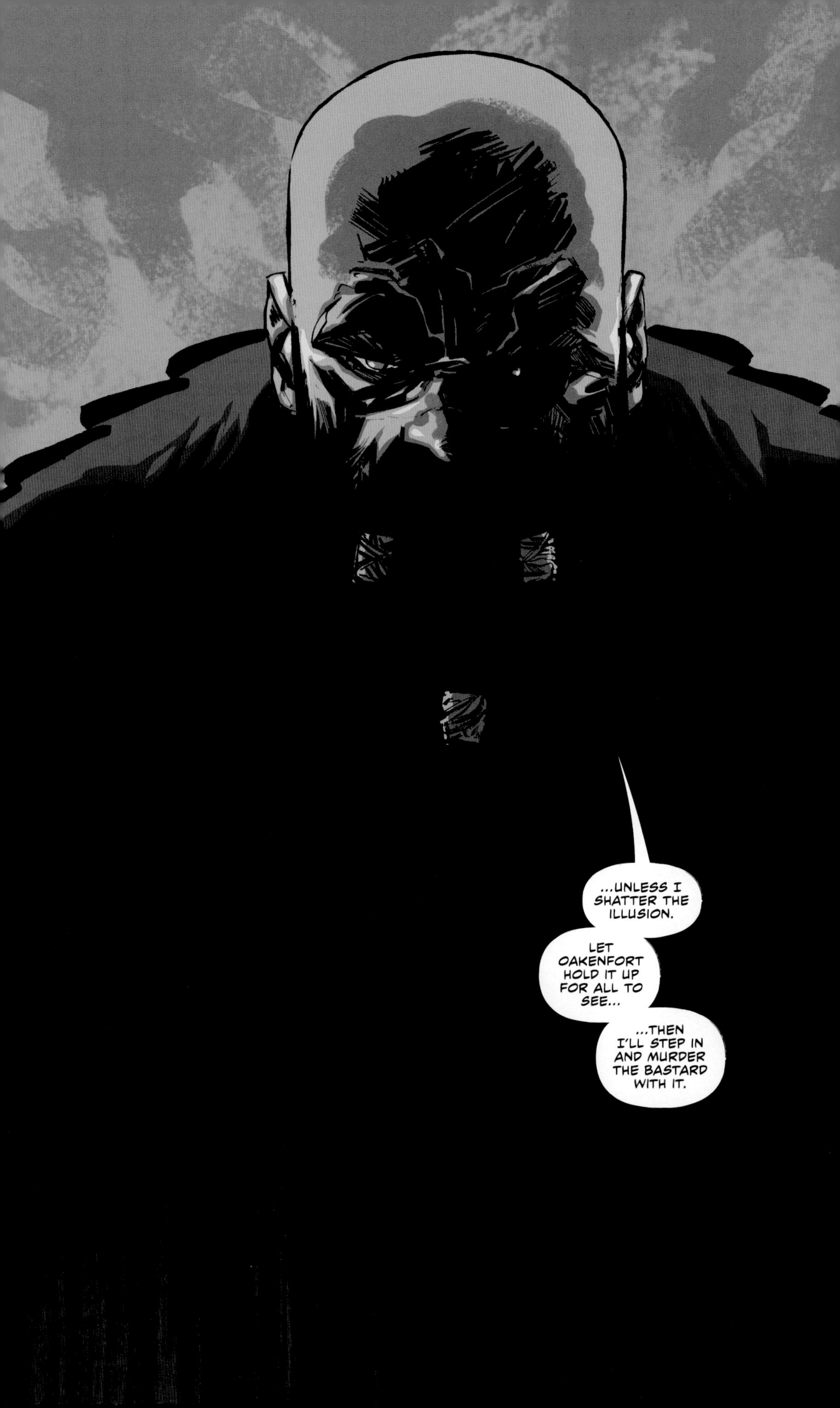
...UNLESS I SHATTER THE ILLUSION.
LET OAKENFORT HOLD IT UP FOR ALL TO SEE...
...THEN I'LL STEP IN AND MURDER THE BASTARD WITH IT.

A MAGNUS THE BLACK MYSTERY

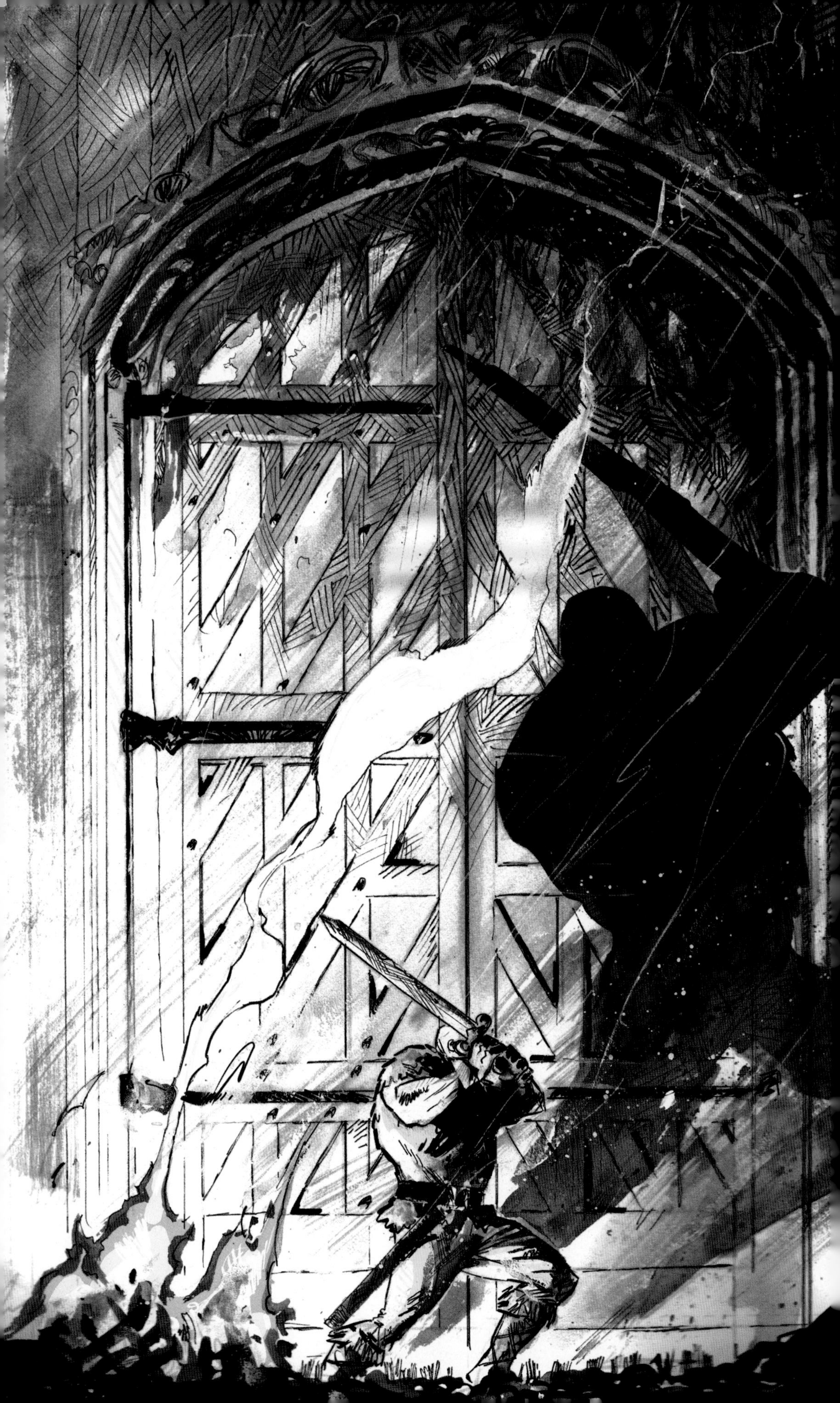

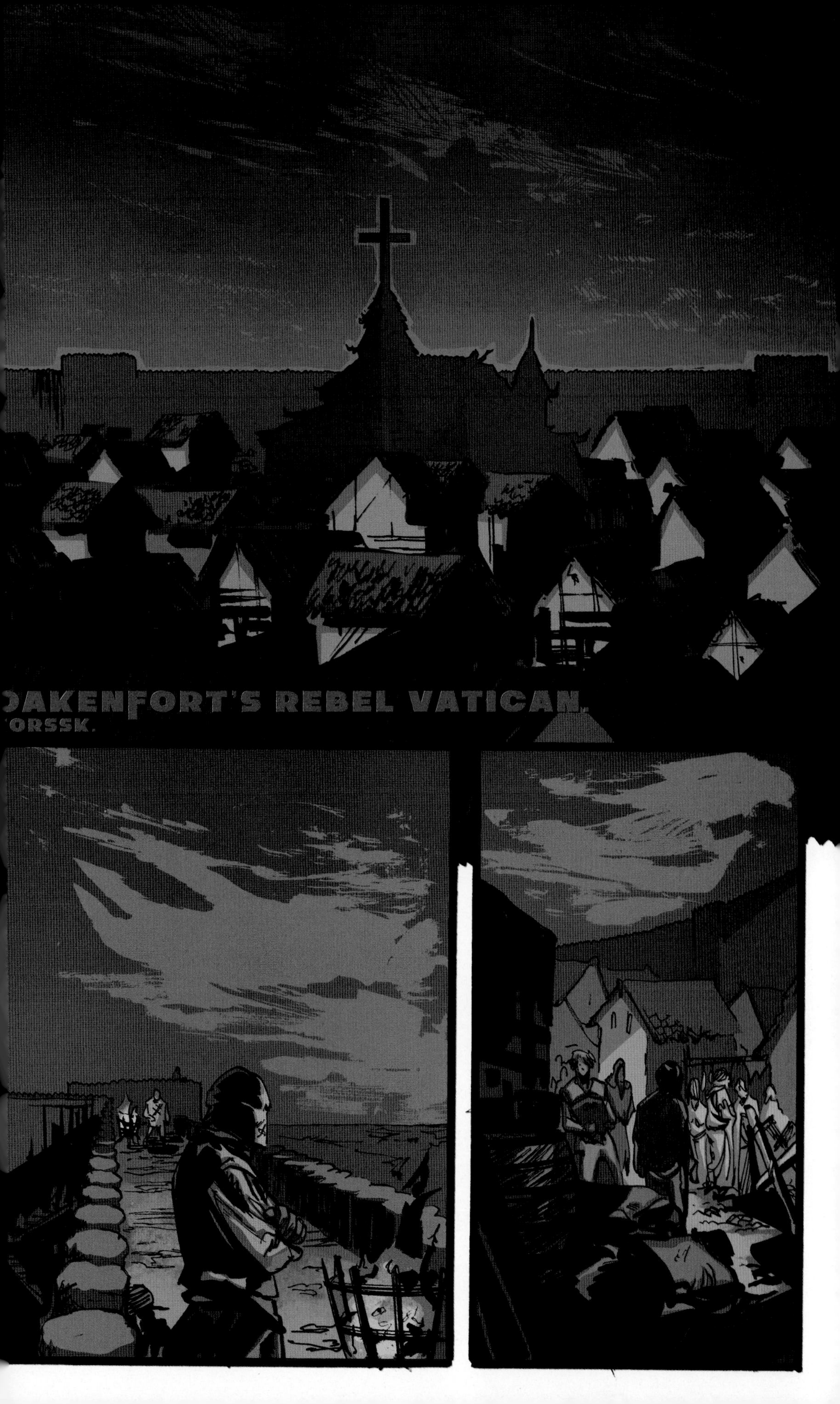
OAKENFORT'S REBEL VATICAN.
ORSSK.

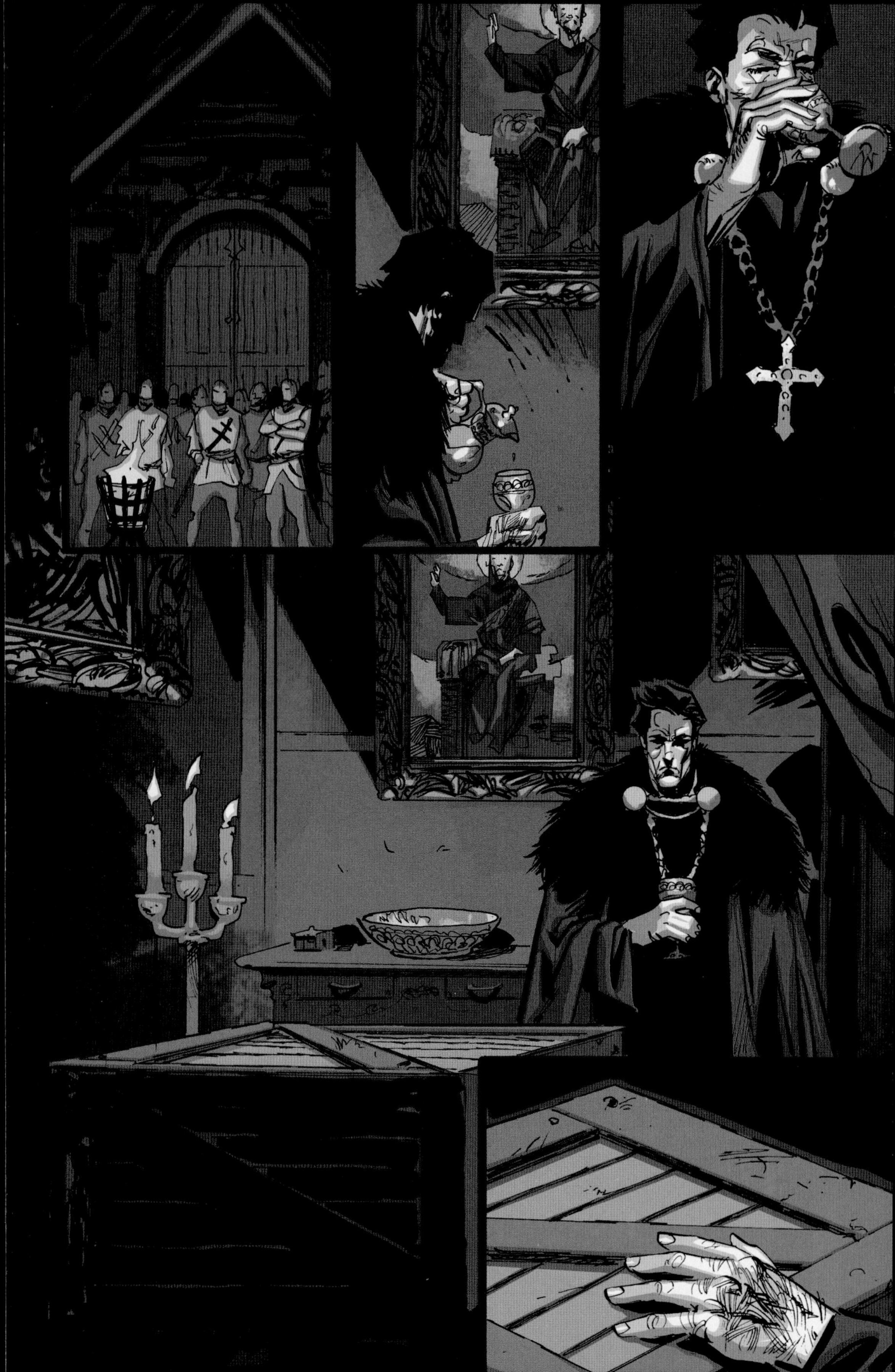

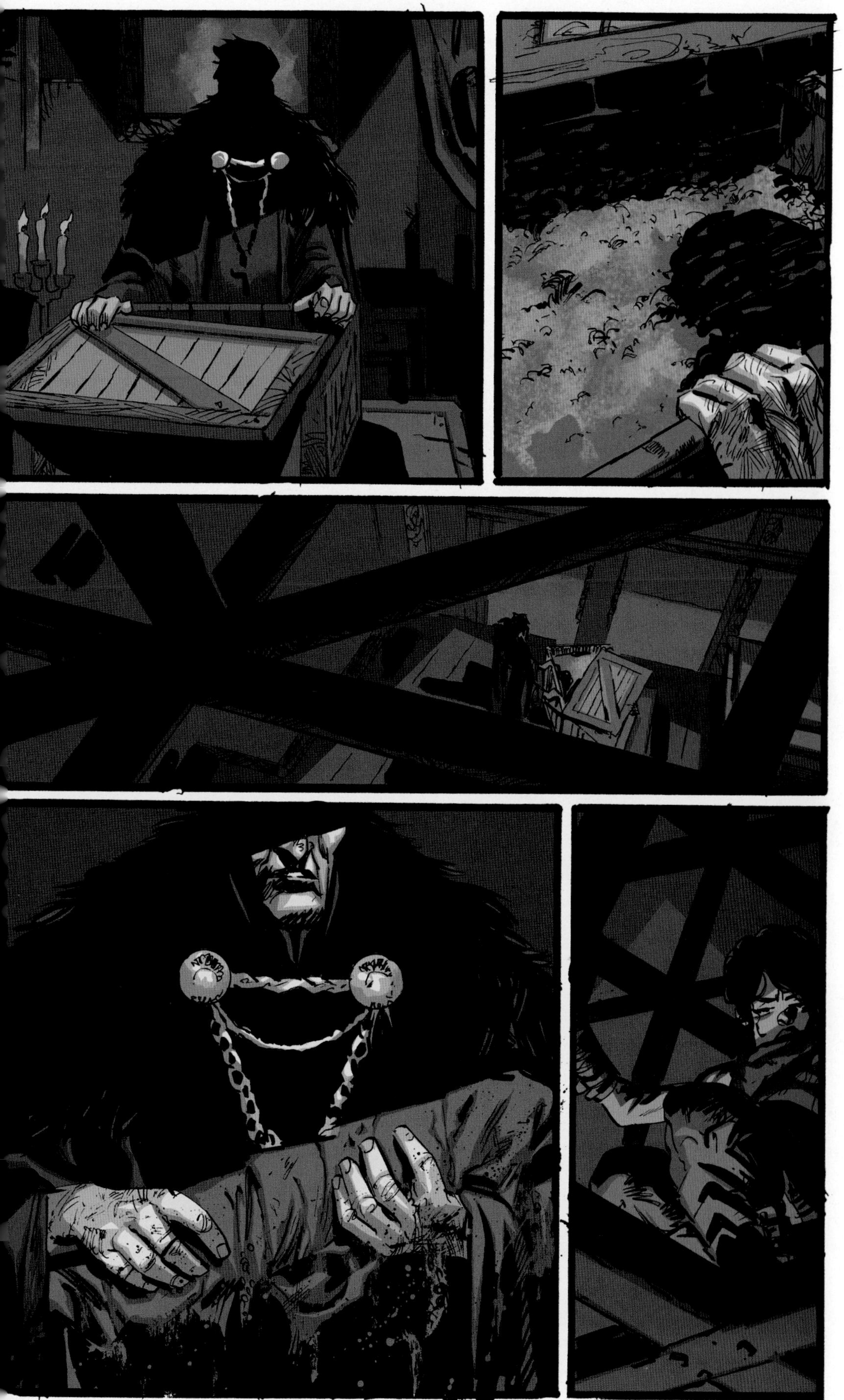

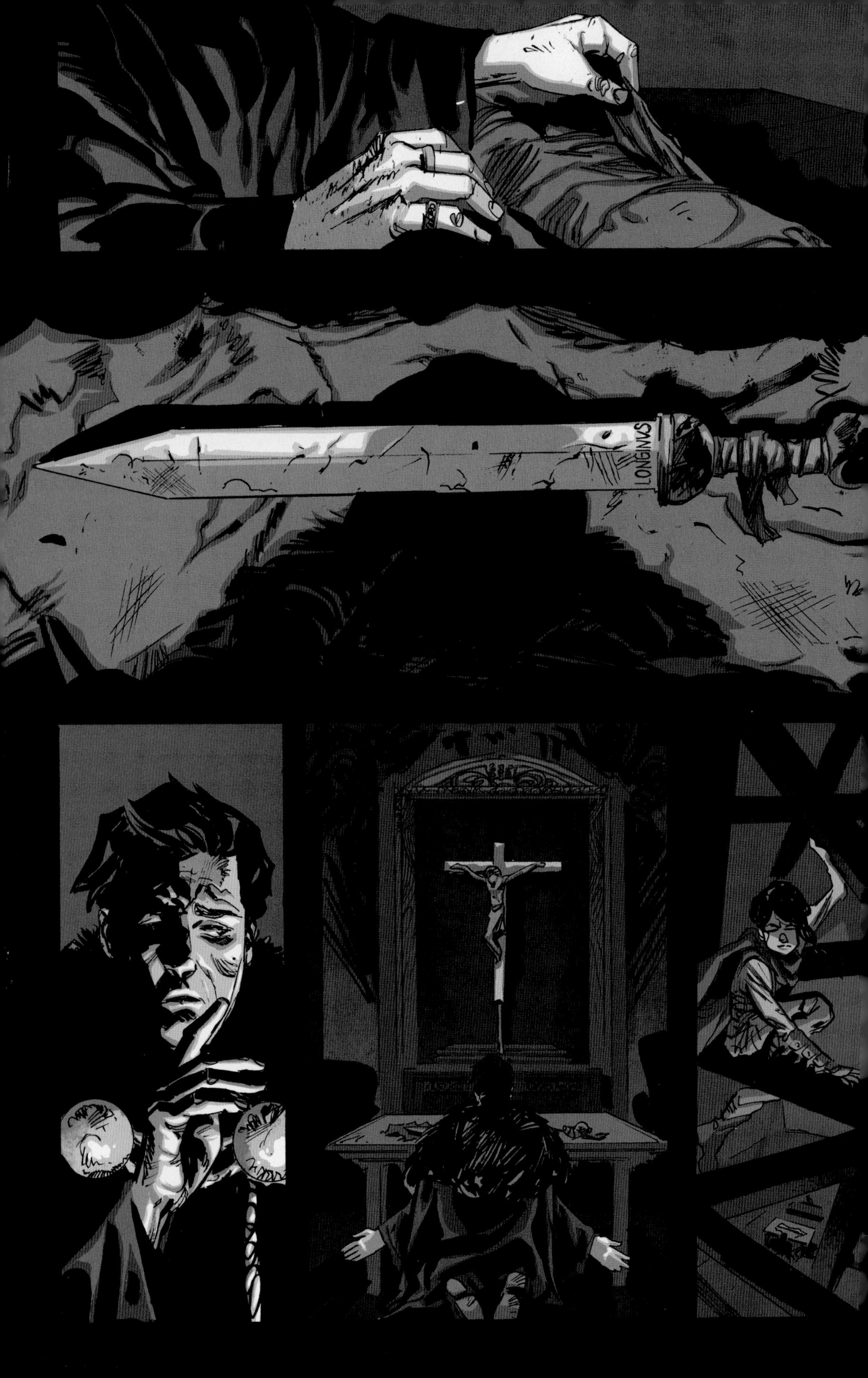LONGINVS

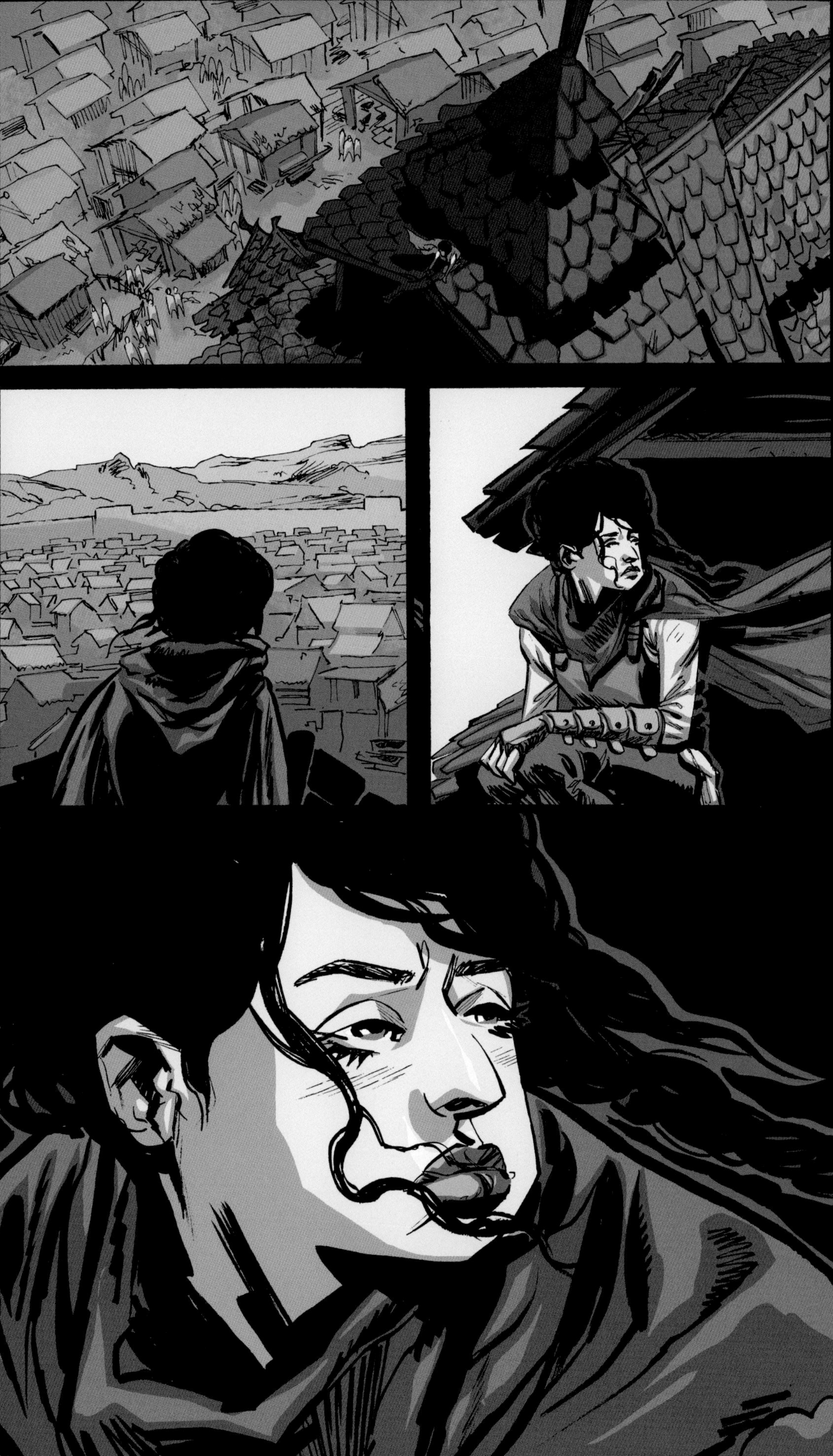

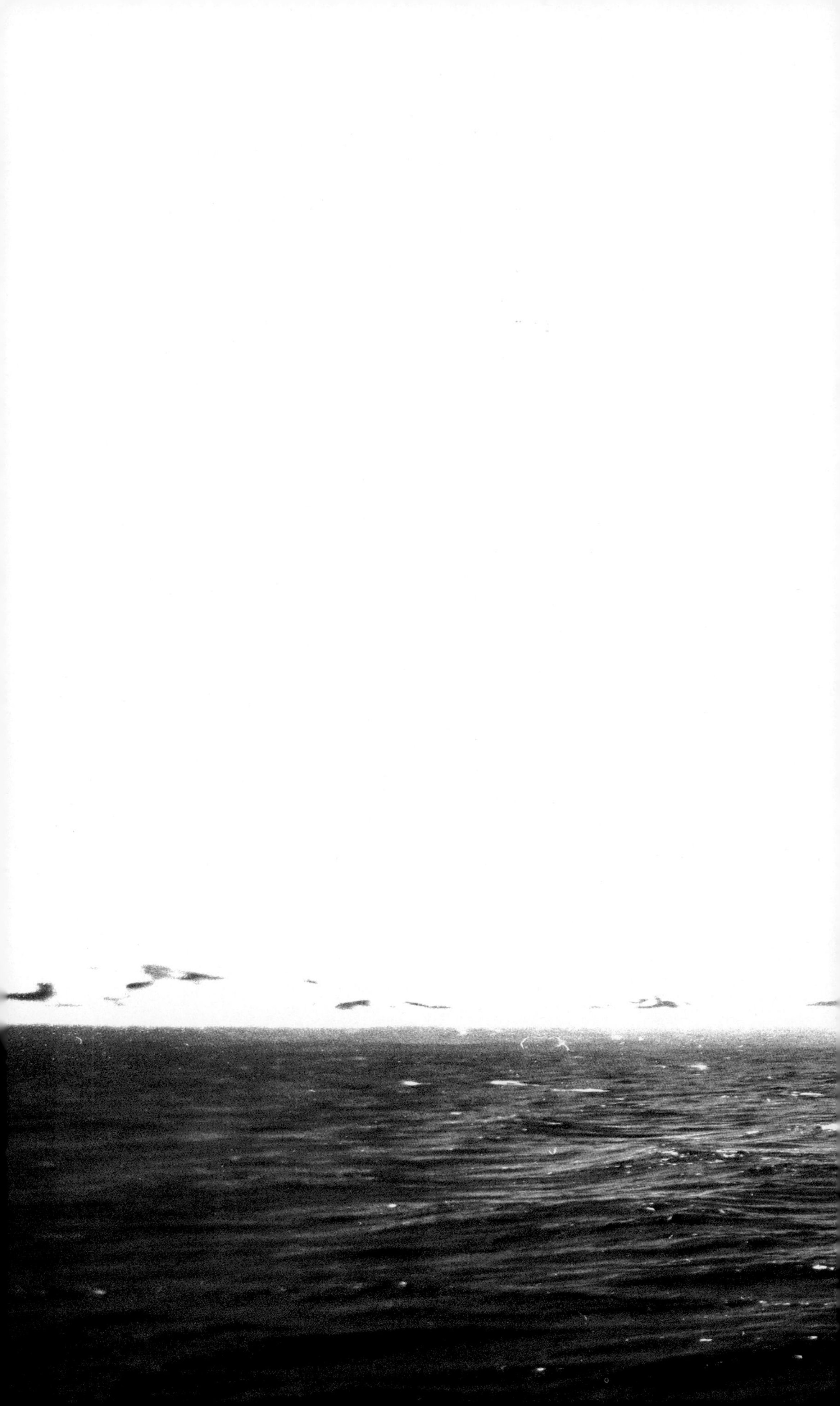

BRIAN WOOD / GARRY BROWN / DAVE McCAIG / STEVE WANDS

BLACK ROAD

#7 - "GOD'S POWER ON EARTH"

A MAGNUS THE BLACK MYSTERY

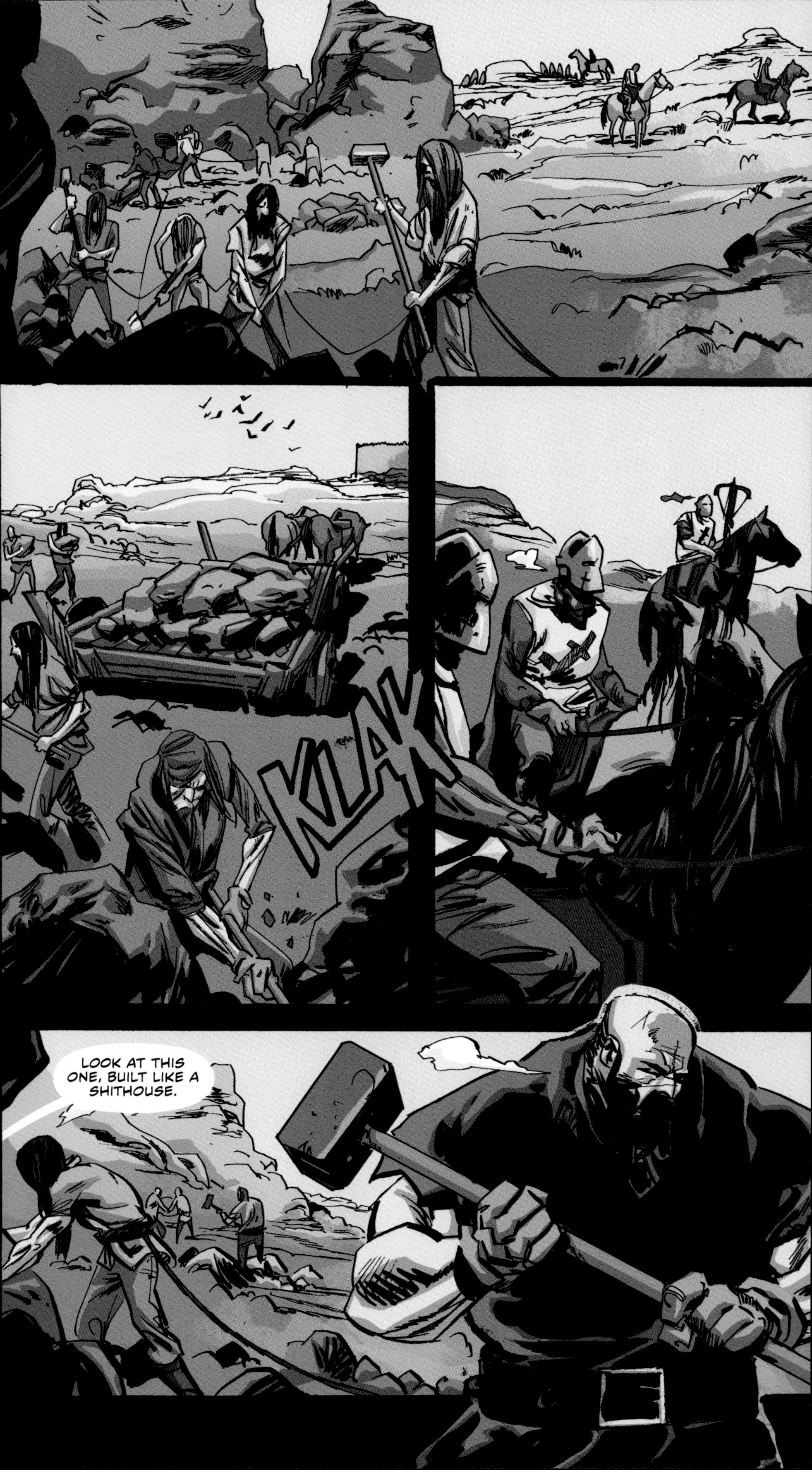
KLAK
LOOK AT THIS ONE, BUILT LIKE A SHITHOUSE.

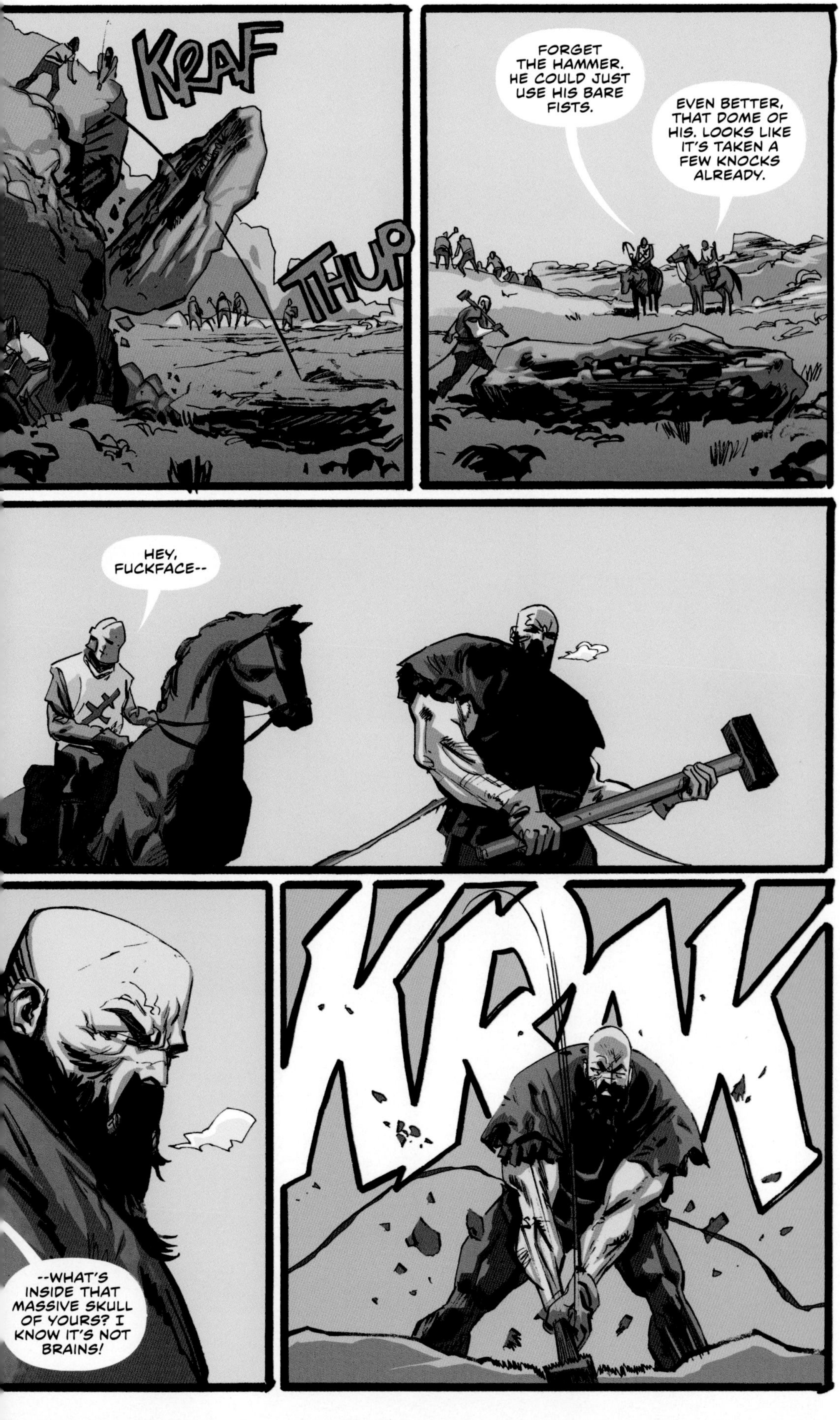
KRAF
THUP
FORGET THE HAMMER. HE COULD JUST USE HIS BARE FISTS.
EVEN BETTER, THAT DOME OF HIS. LOOKS LIKE IT'S TAKEN A FEW KNOCKS ALREADY.
HEY, FUCKFACE--
--WHAT'S INSIDE THAT MASSIVE SKULL OF YOURS? I KNOW IT'S NOT BRAINS!
KRAK

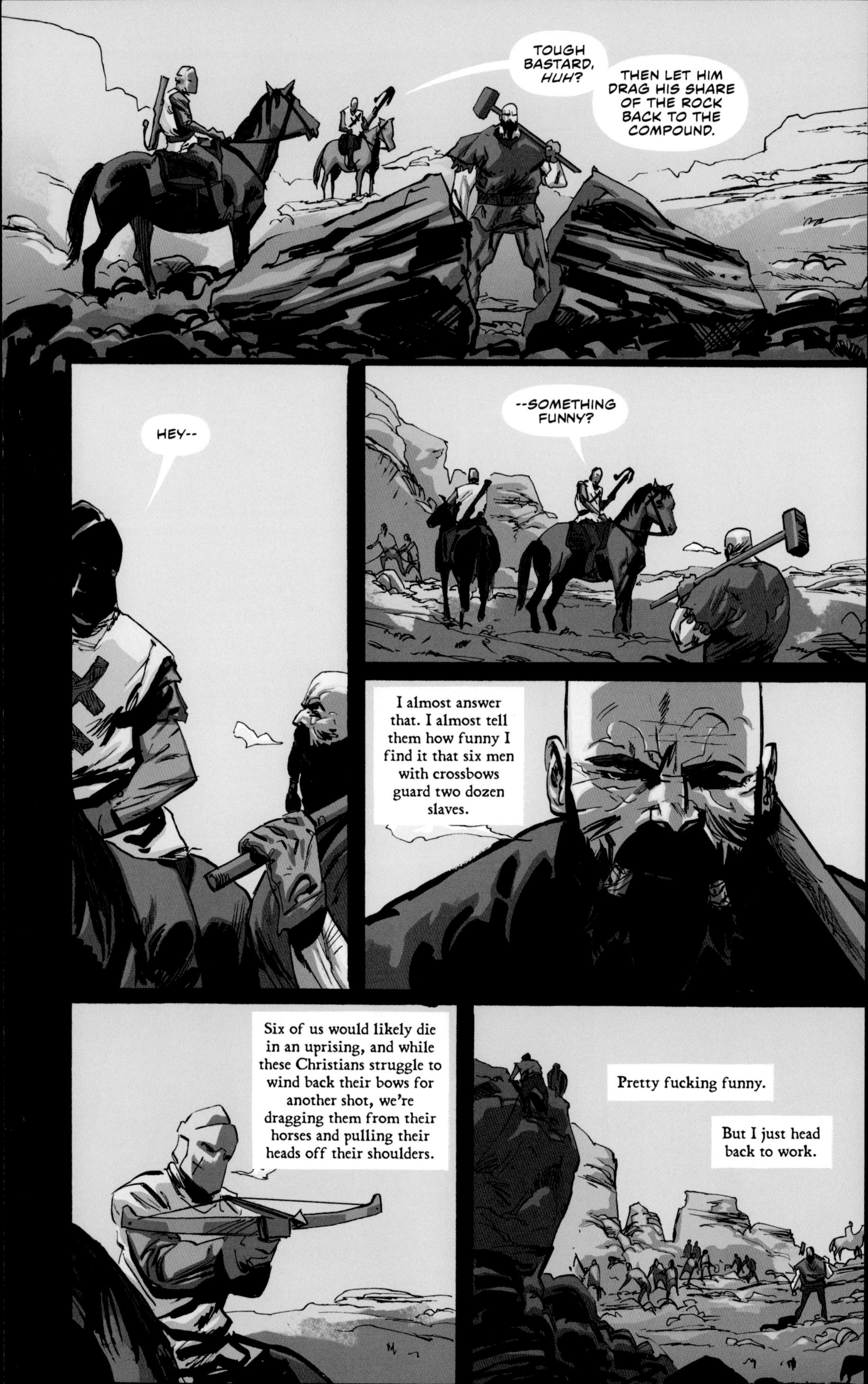
TOUGH BASTARD, HUH?
THEN LET HIM DRAG HIS SHARE OF THE ROCK BACK TO THE COMPOUND.
HEY--
--SOMETHING FUNNY?
I almost answer that. I almost tell them how funny I find it that six men with crossbows guard two dozen slaves.
Six of us would likely die in an uprising, and while these Christians struggle to wind back their bows for another shot, we're dragging them from their horses and pulling their heads off their shoulders.
Pretty fucking funny.
But I just head back to work.

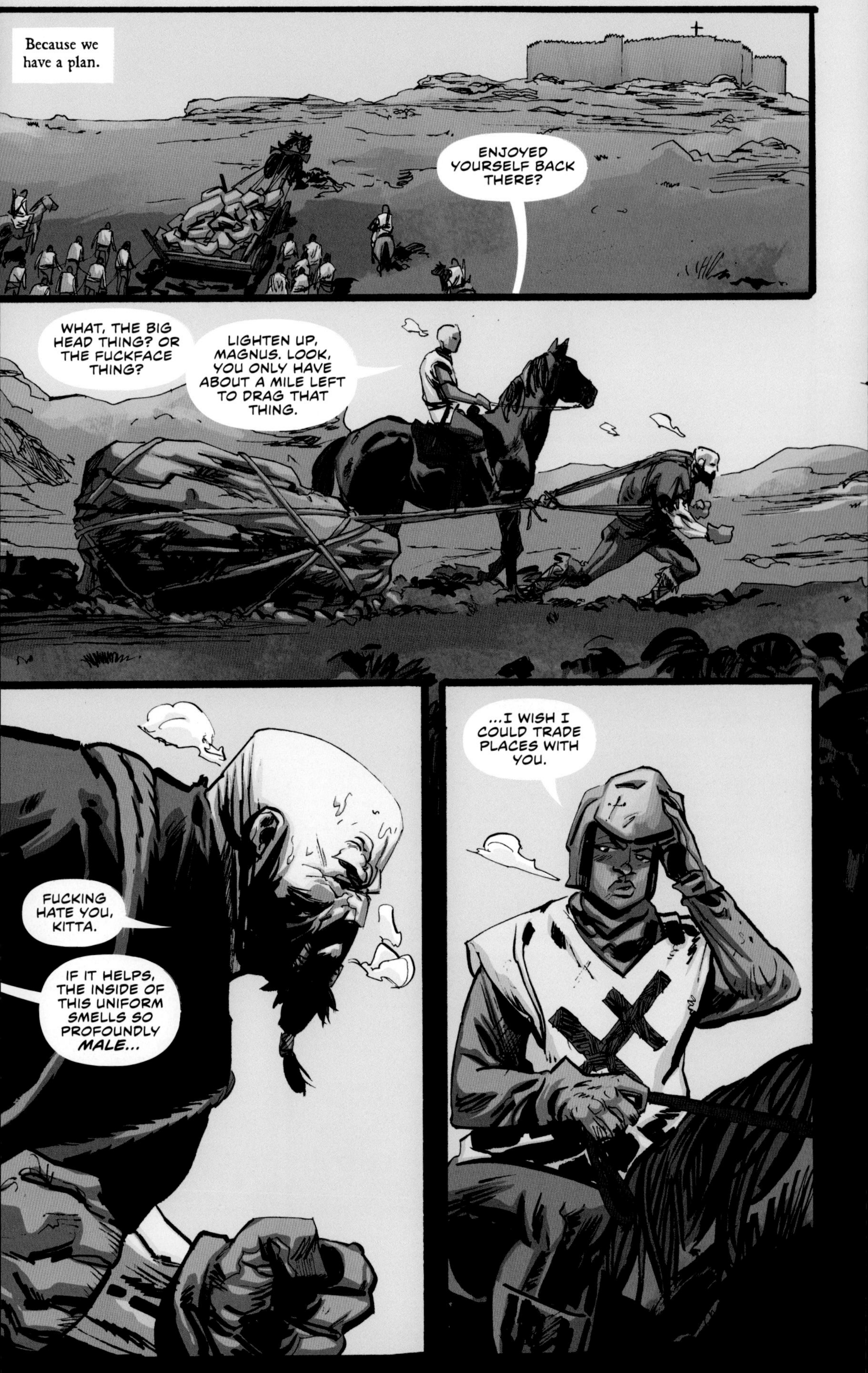
Because we have a plan.
ENJOYED YOURSELF BACK THERE?
WHAT, THE BIG HEAD THING? OR THE FUCKFACE THING?
LIGHTEN UP, MAGNUS. LOOK, YOU ONLY HAVE ABOUT A MILE LEFT TO DRAG THAT THING.
FUCKING HATE YOU, KITTA.
IF IT HELPS, THE INSIDE OF THIS UNIFORM SMELLS SO PROFOUNDLY *MALE*...
...I WISH I COULD TRADE PLACES WITH YOU.

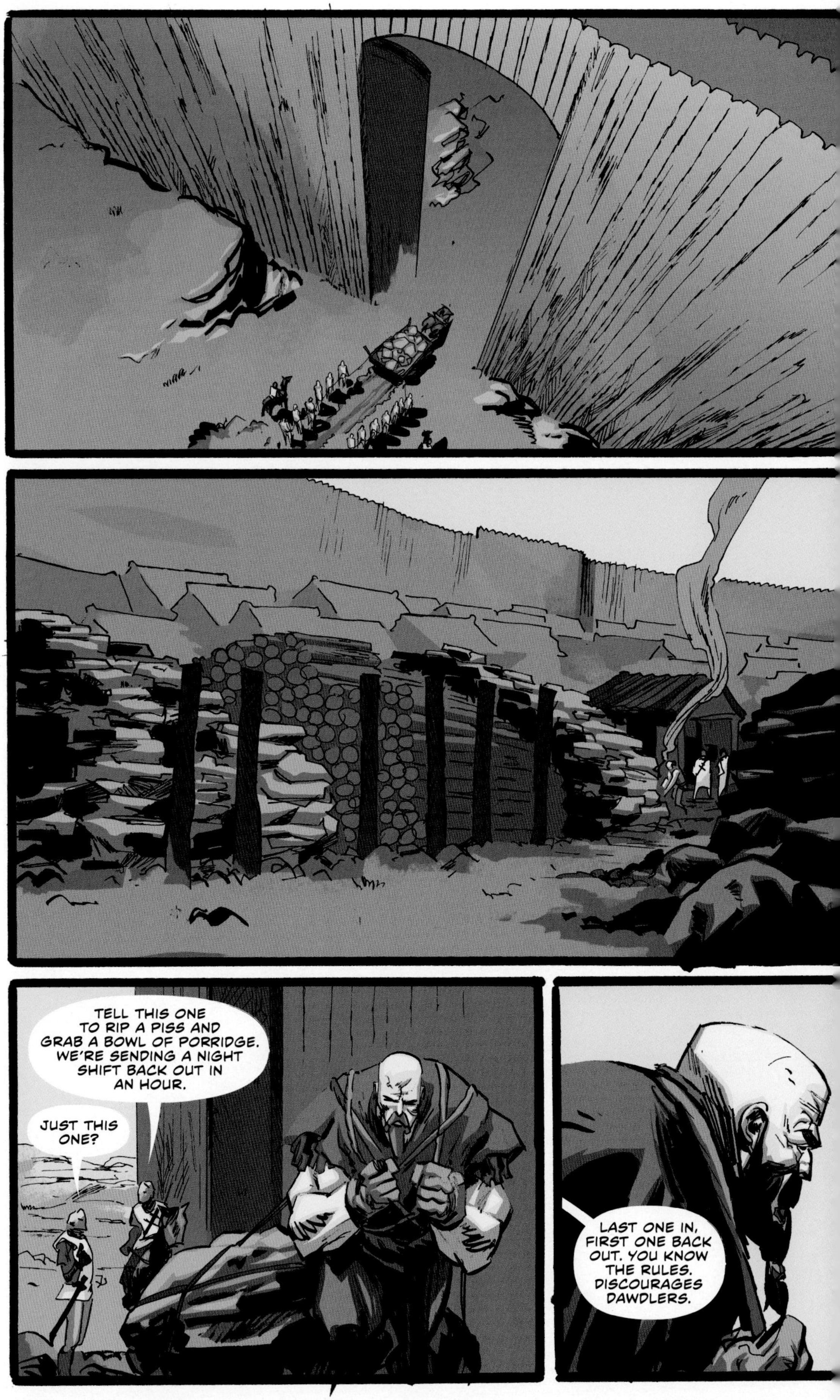
TELL THIS ONE TO RIP A PISS AND GRAB A BOWL OF PORRIDGE. WE'RE SENDING A NIGHT SHIFT BACK OUT IN AN HOUR.
JUST THIS ONE?
LAST ONE IN, FIRST ONE BACK OUT. YOU KNOW THE RULES. DISCOURAGES DAWDLERS.

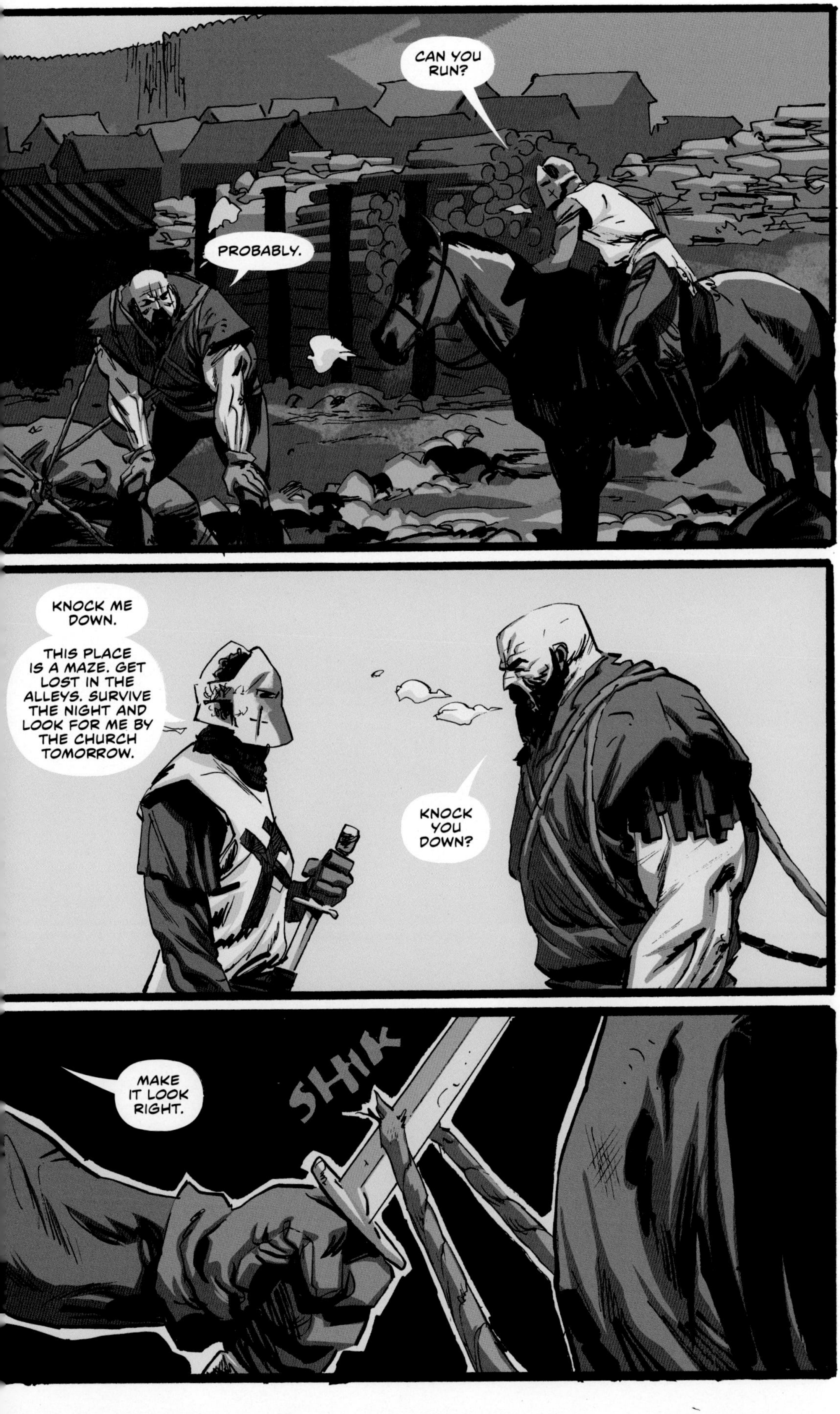
CAN YOU RUN?
PROBABLY.
KNOCK ME DOWN.
THIS PLACE IS A MAZE. GET LOST IN THE ALLEYS. SURVIVE THE NIGHT AND LOOK FOR ME BY THE CHURCH TOMORROW.
KNOCK YOU DOWN?
SHIK
MAKE IT LOOK RIGHT.

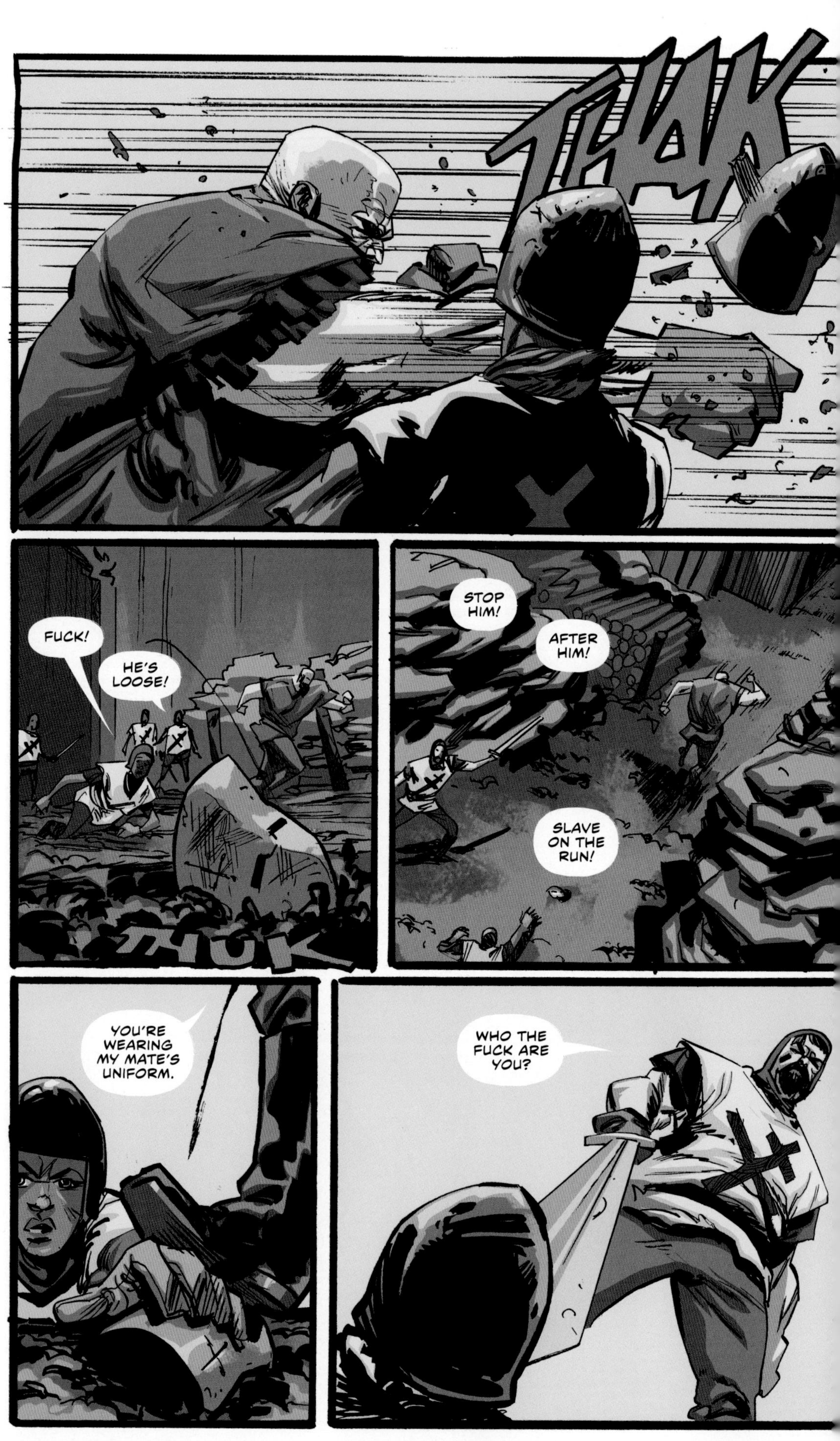
THAK
FUCK!
HE'S LOOSE!
THUK
STOP HIM!
AFTER HIM!
SLAVE ON THE RUN!
YOU'RE WEARING MY MATE'S UNIFORM.
WHO THE FUCK ARE YOU?

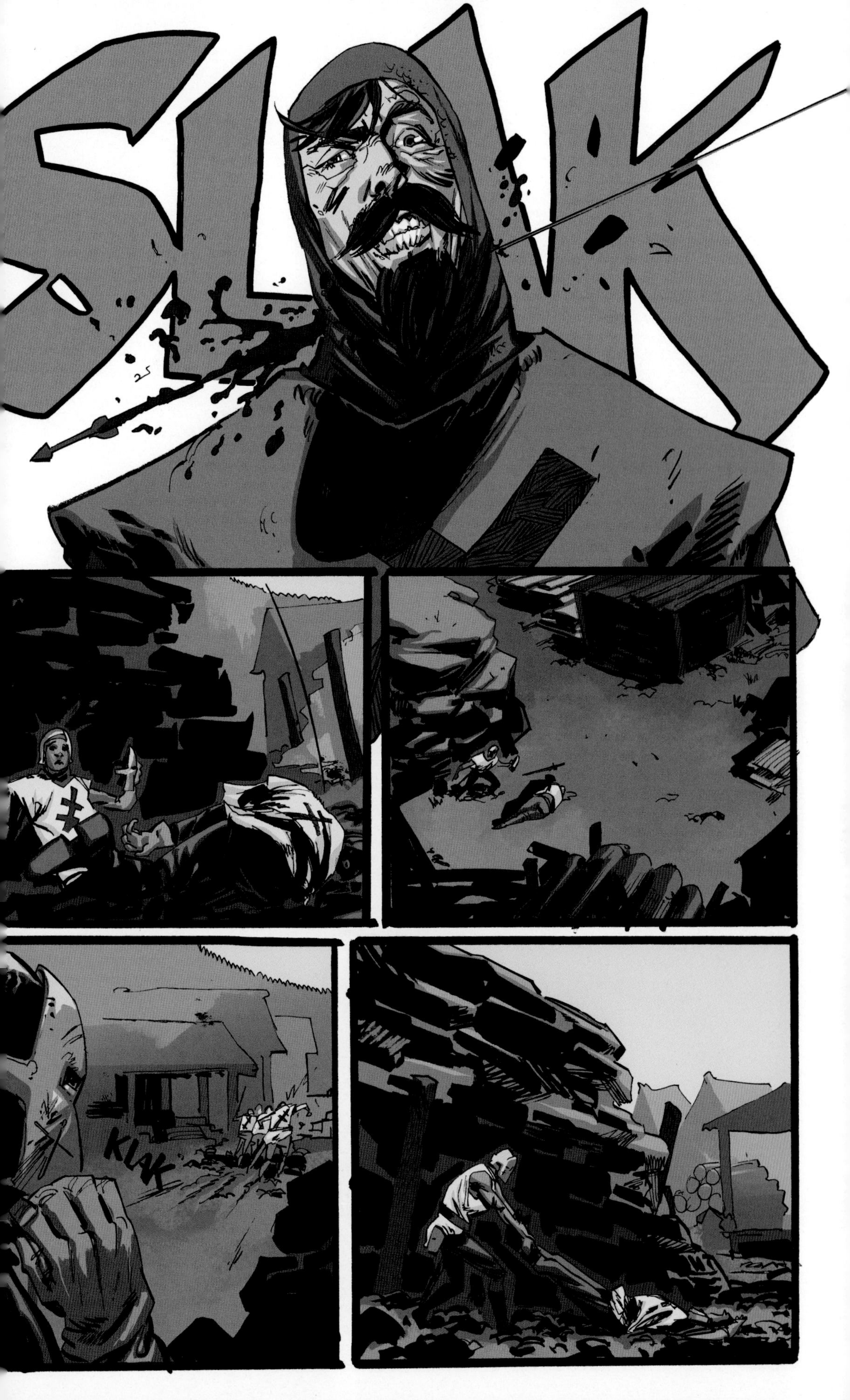
KLAK

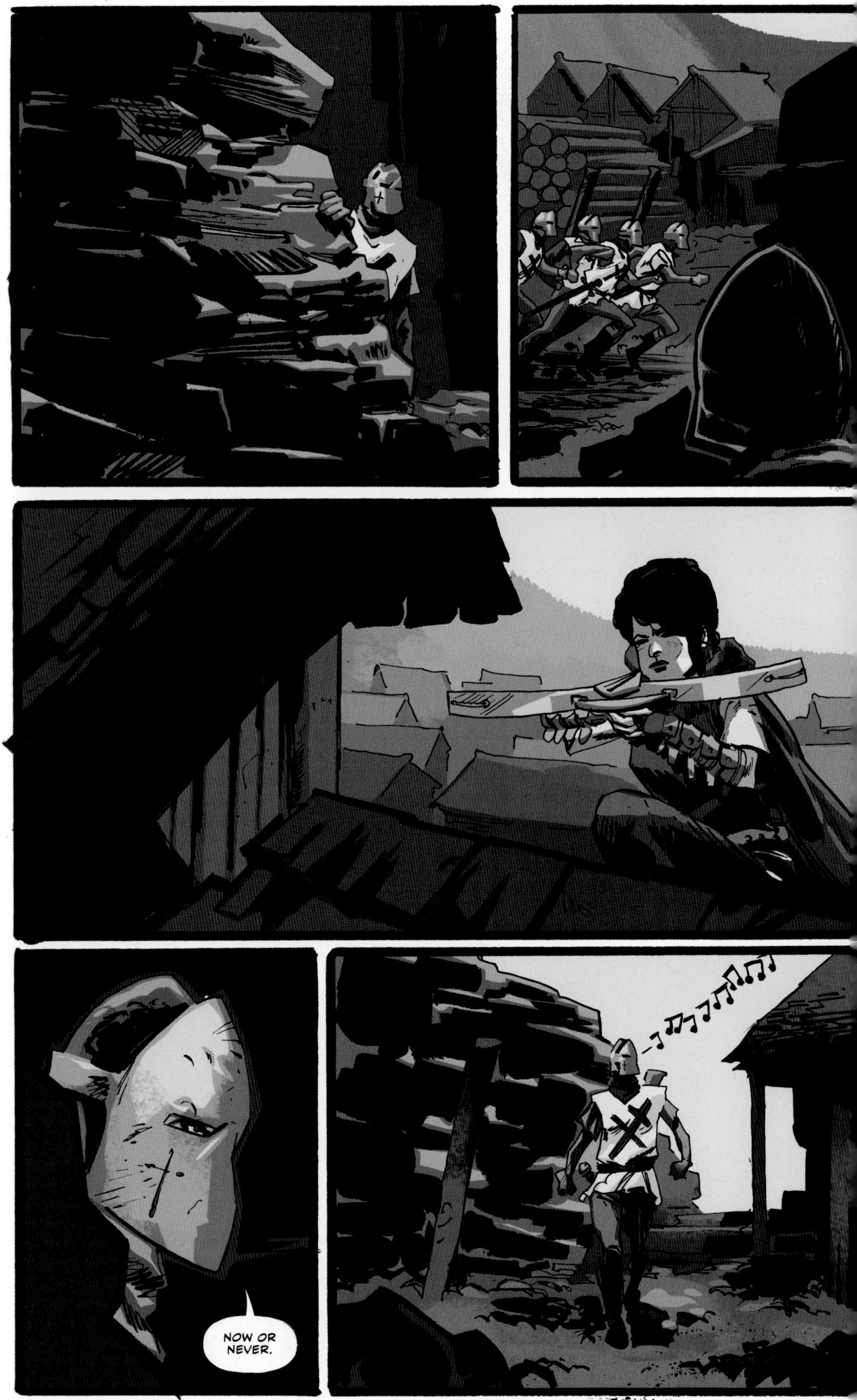
NOW OR NEVER.

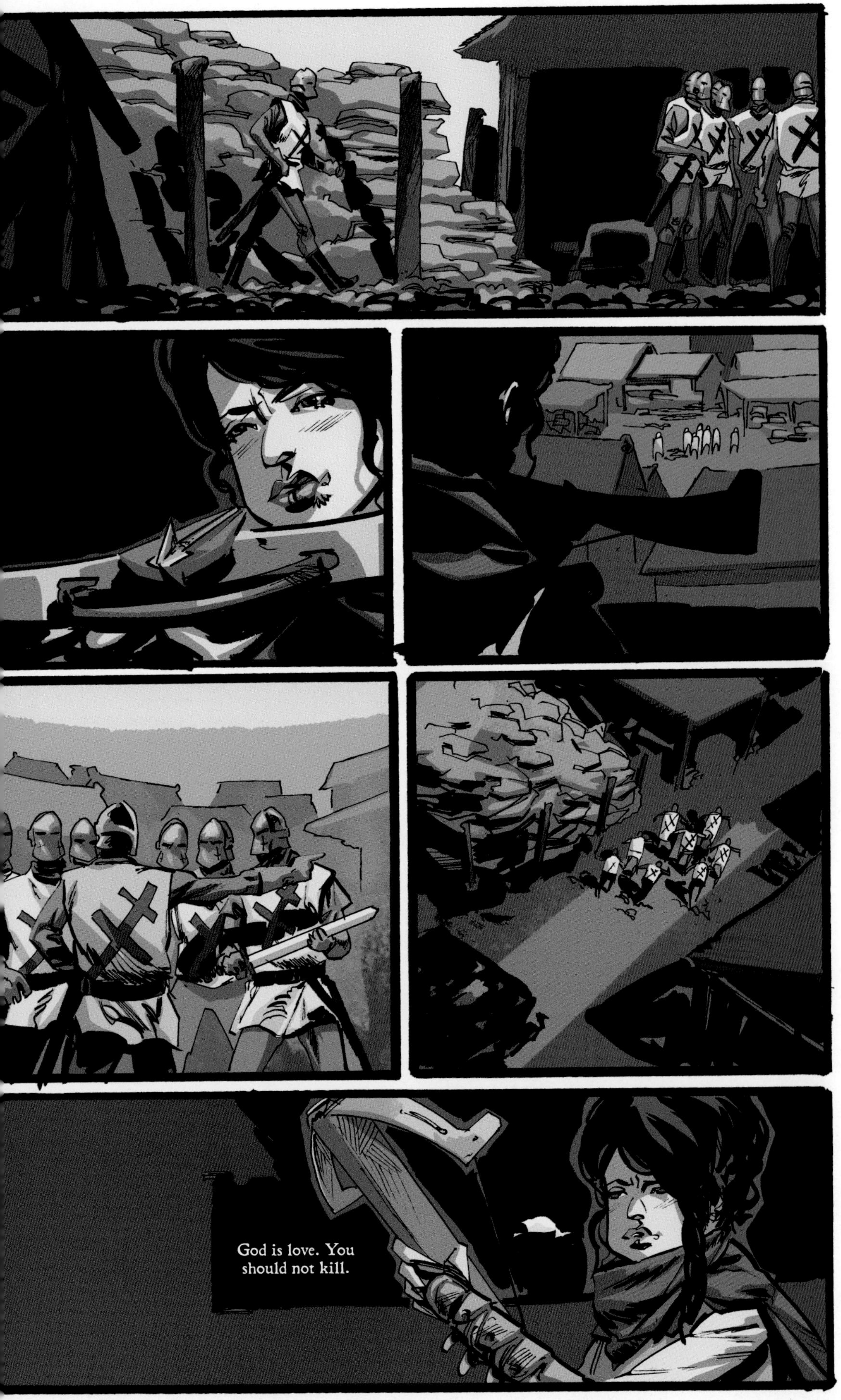
God is love. You should not kill.

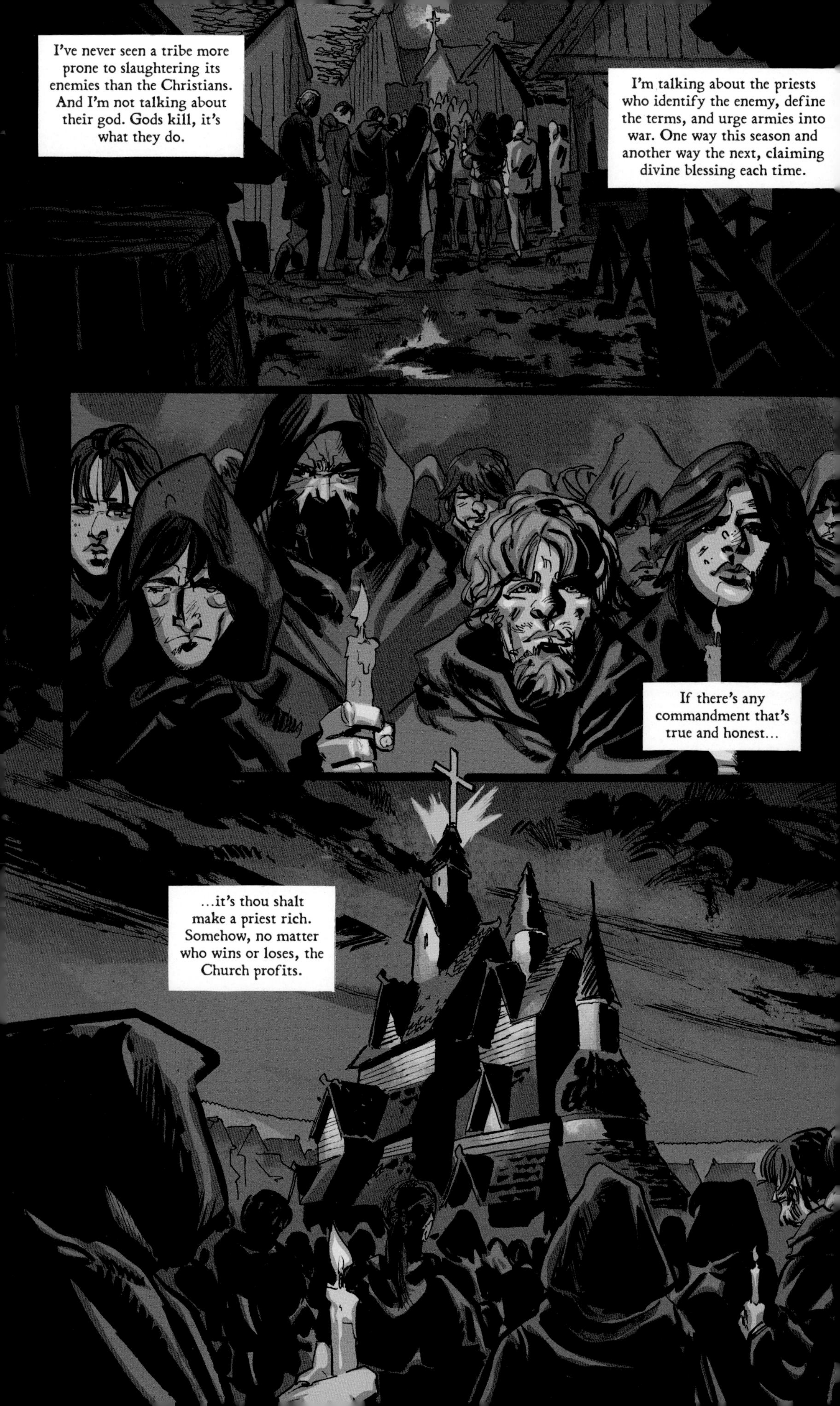
I've never seen a tribe more prone to slaughtering its enemies than the Christians. And I'm not talking about their god. Gods kill, it's what they do.
I'm talking about the priests who identify the enemy, define the terms, and urge armies into war. One way this season and another way the next, claiming divine blessing each time.
If there's any commandment that's true and honest...
...it's thou shalt make a priest rich. Somehow, no matter who wins or loses, the Church profits.

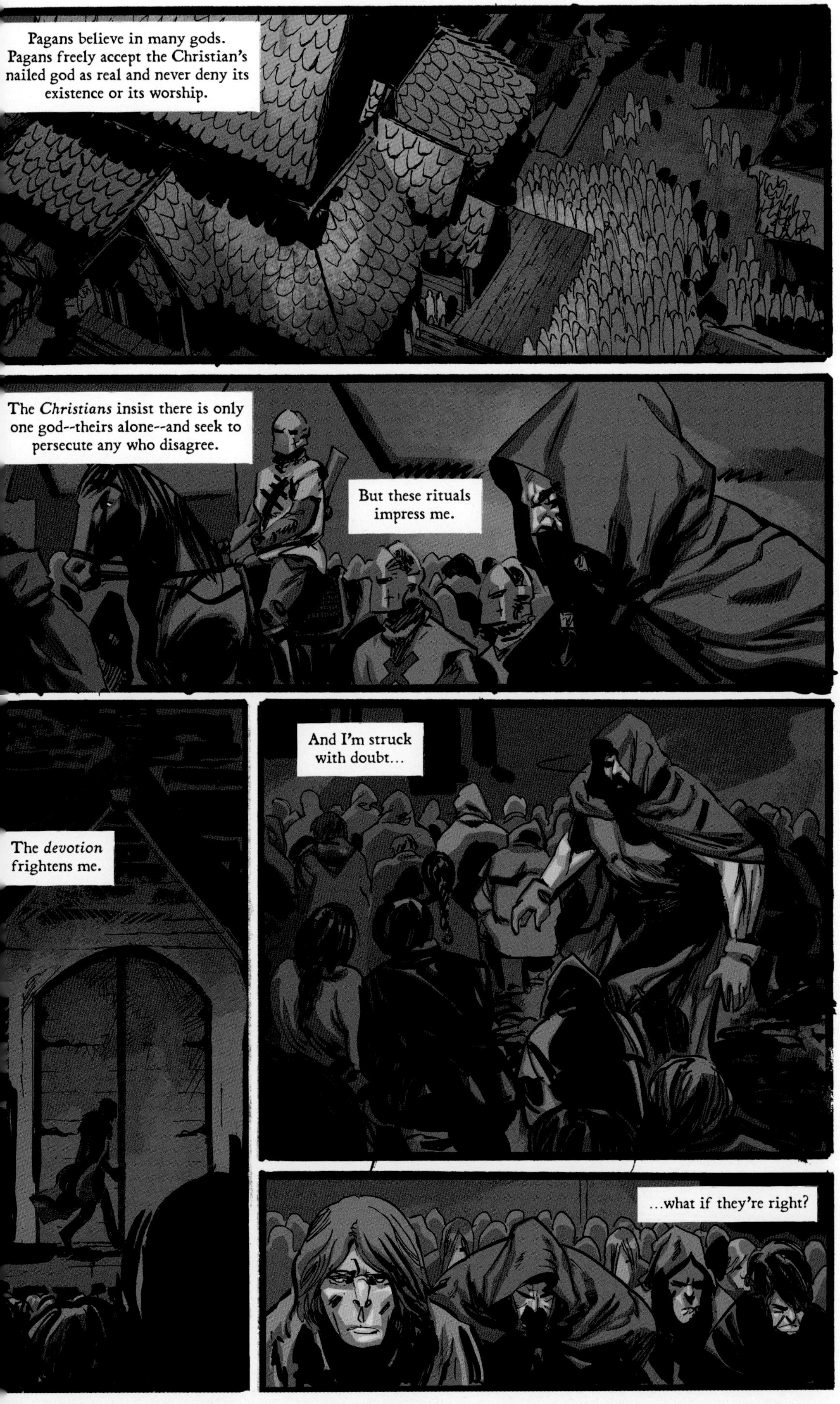
Pagans believe in many gods. Pagans freely accept the Christian's nailed god as real and never deny its existence or its worship.
The *Christians* insist there is only one god--theirs alone--and seek to persecute any who disagree.
But these rituals impress me.
The *devotion* frightens me.
And I'm struck with doubt...
...what if they're right?

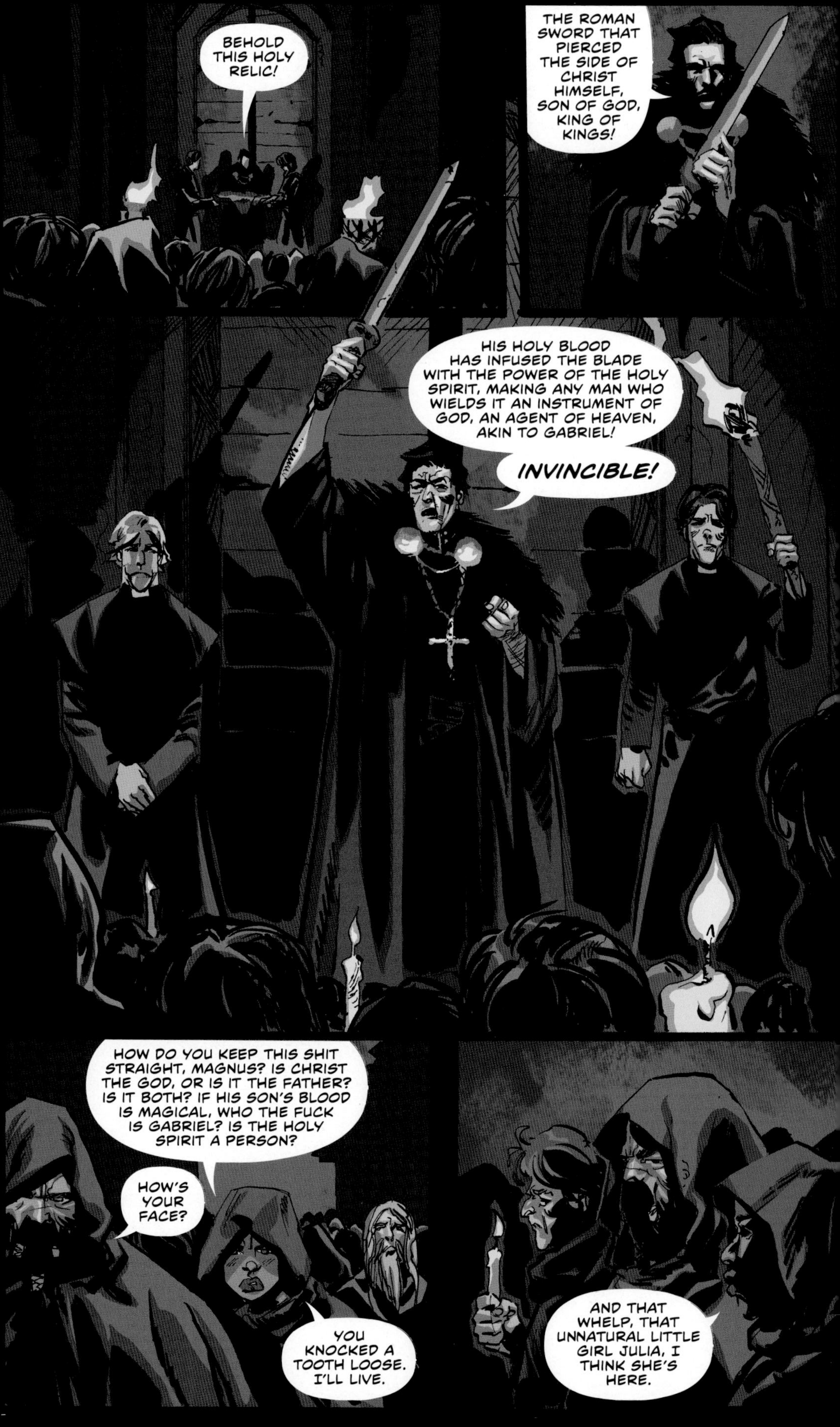
BEHOLD THIS HOLY RELIC!
THE ROMAN SWORD THAT PIERCED THE SIDE OF CHRIST HIMSELF, SON OF GOD, KING OF KINGS!
HIS HOLY BLOOD HAS INFUSED THE BLADE WITH THE POWER OF THE HOLY SPIRIT, MAKING ANY MAN WHO WIELDS IT AN INSTRUMENT OF GOD, AN AGENT OF HEAVEN, AKIN TO GABRIEL!
INVINCIBLE!
HOW DO YOU KEEP THIS SHIT STRAIGHT, MAGNUS? IS CHRIST THE GOD, OR IS IT THE FATHER? IS IT BOTH? IF HIS SON'S BLOOD IS MAGICAL, WHO THE FUCK IS GABRIEL? IS THE HOLY SPIRIT A PERSON?
HOW'S YOUR FACE?
YOU KNOCKED A TOOTH LOOSE. I'LL LIVE.
AND THAT WHELP, THAT UNNATURAL LITTLE GIRL JULIA, I THINK SHE'S HERE.

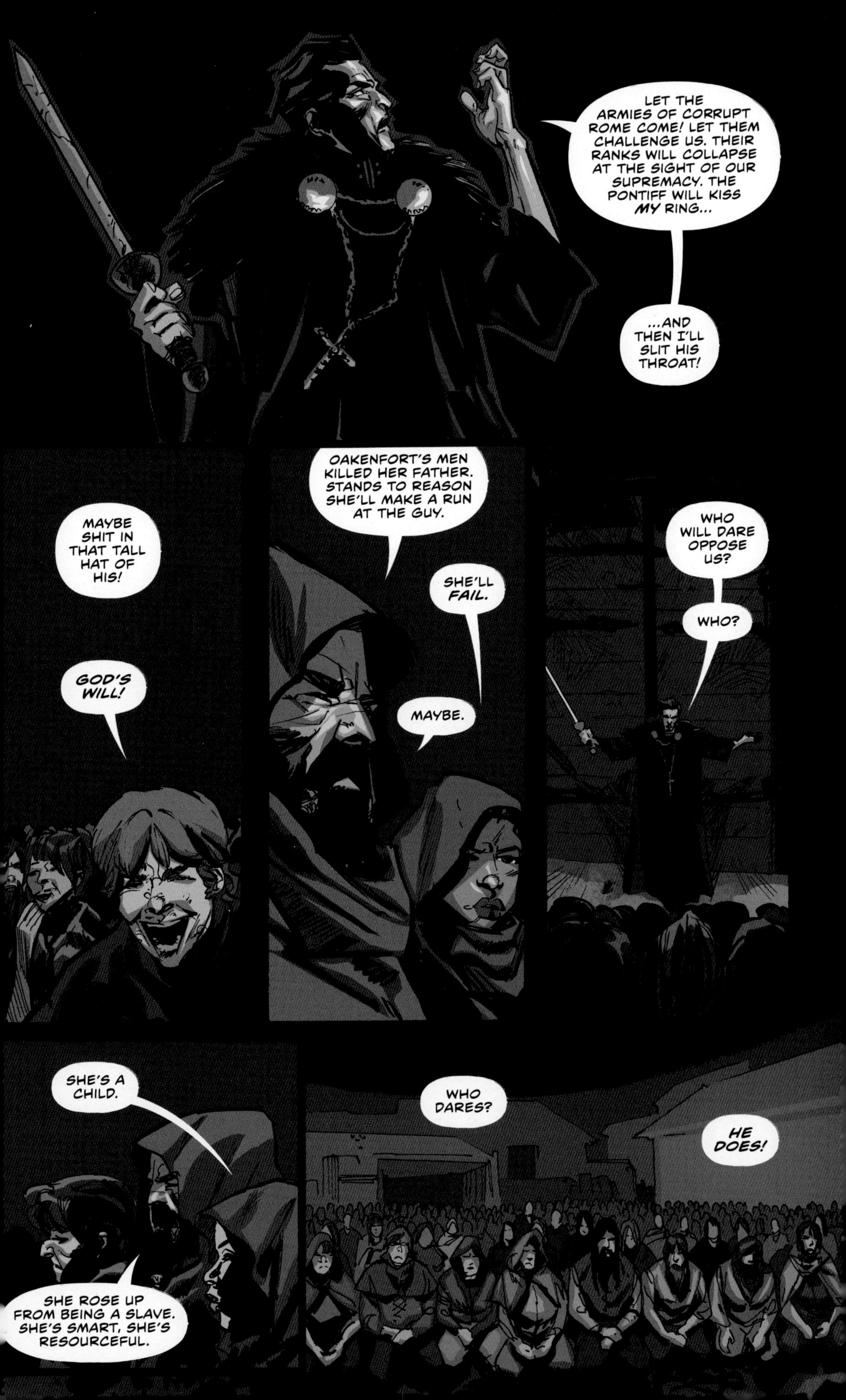
LET THE ARMIES OF CORRUPT ROME COME! LET THEM CHALLENGE US. THEIR RANKS WILL COLLAPSE AT THE SIGHT OF OUR SUPREMACY. THE PONTIFF WILL KISS *MY* RING...
...AND THEN I'LL SLIT HIS THROAT!
MAYBE SHIT IN THAT TALL HAT OF HIS!
GOD'S WILL!
OAKENFORT'S MEN KILLED HER FATHER. STANDS TO REASON SHE'LL MAKE A RUN AT THE GUY.
SHE'LL *FAIL.*
MAYBE.
WHO WILL DARE OPPOSE US?
WHO?
SHE'S A CHILD.
SHE ROSE UP FROM BEING A SLAVE. SHE'S SMART, SHE'S RESOURCEFUL.
WHO DARES?
HE DOES!

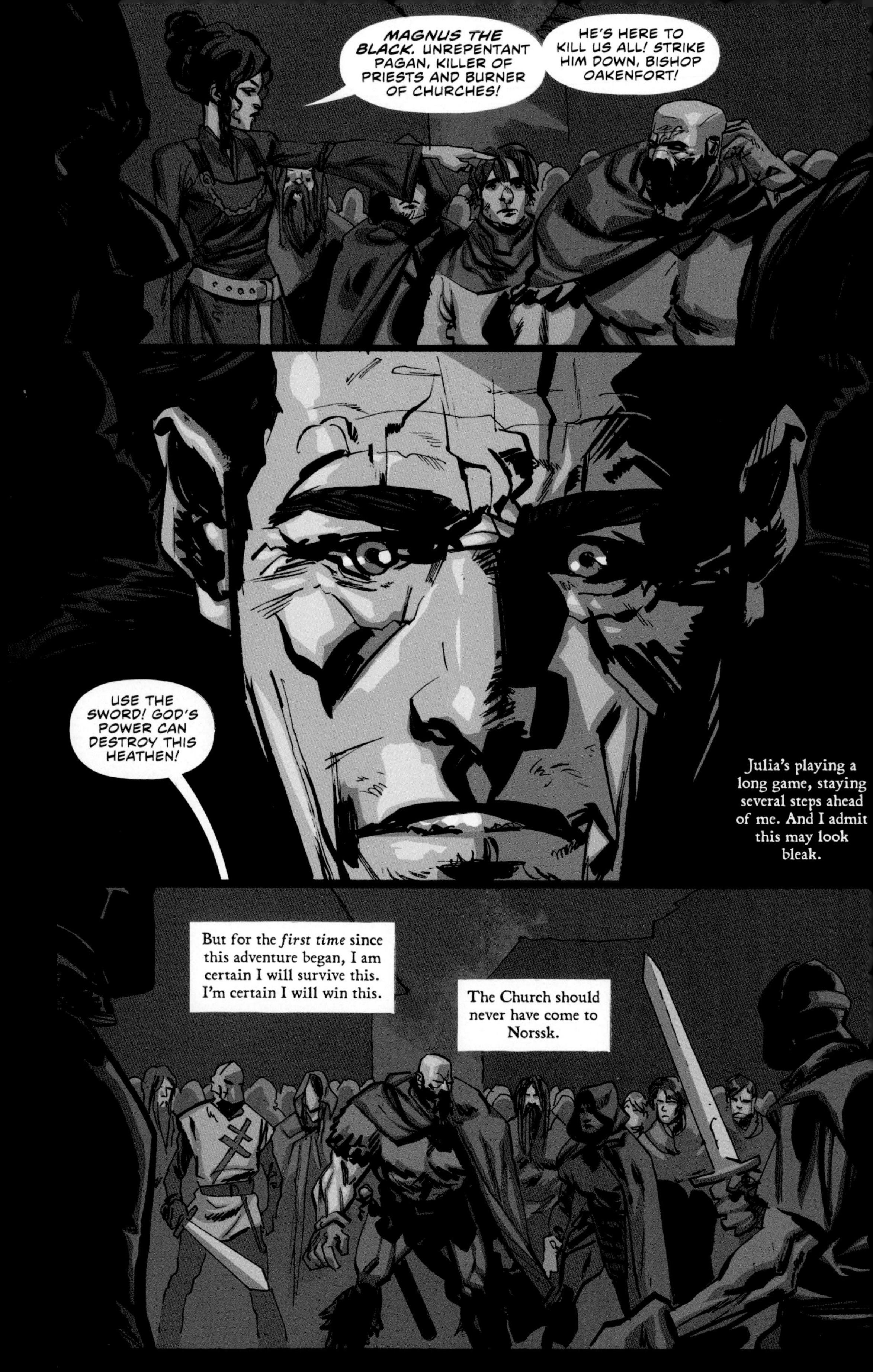
MAGNUS THE BLACK. UNREPENTANT PAGAN, KILLER OF PRIESTS AND BURNER OF CHURCHES!
HE'S HERE TO KILL US ALL! STRIKE HIM DOWN, BISHOP OAKENFORT!
USE THE SWORD! GOD'S POWER CAN DESTROY THIS HEATHEN!
Julia's playing a long game, staying several steps ahead of me. And I admit this may look bleak.
But for the *first time* since this adventure began, I am certain I will survive this. I'm certain I will win this.
The Church should never have come to Norssk.

A MAGNUS THE BLACK MYSTERY

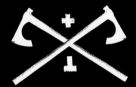

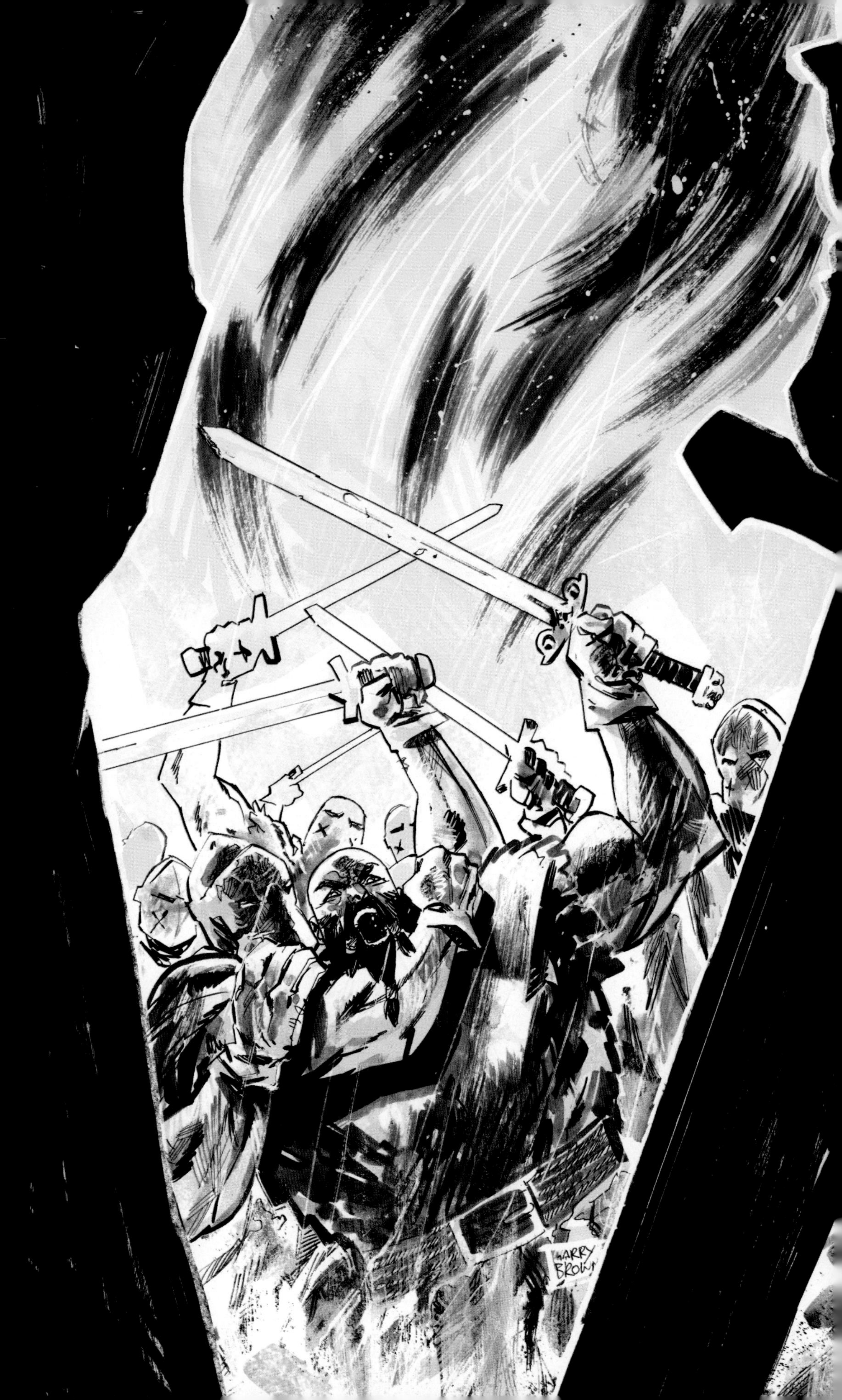

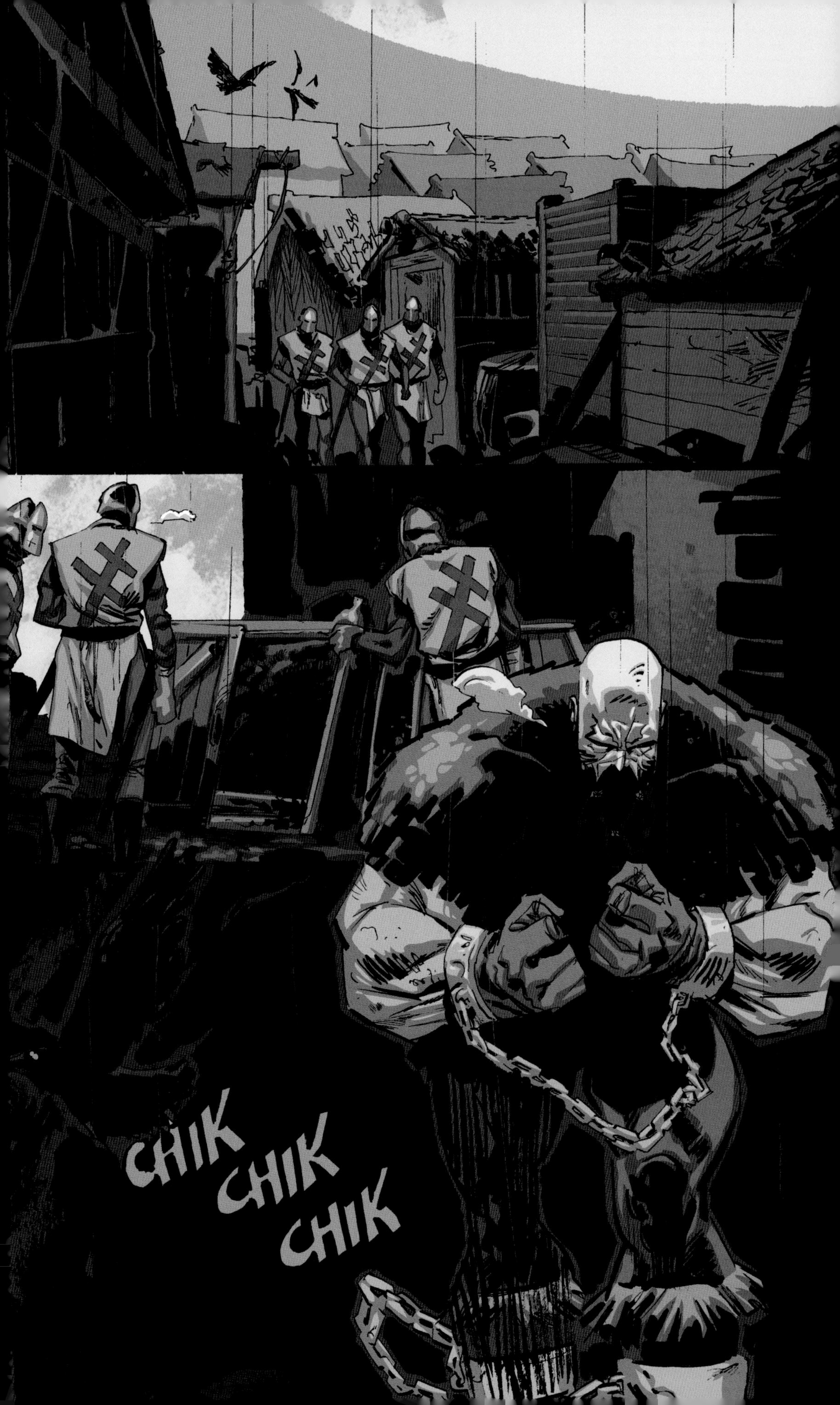
CHIK
CHIK
CHIK

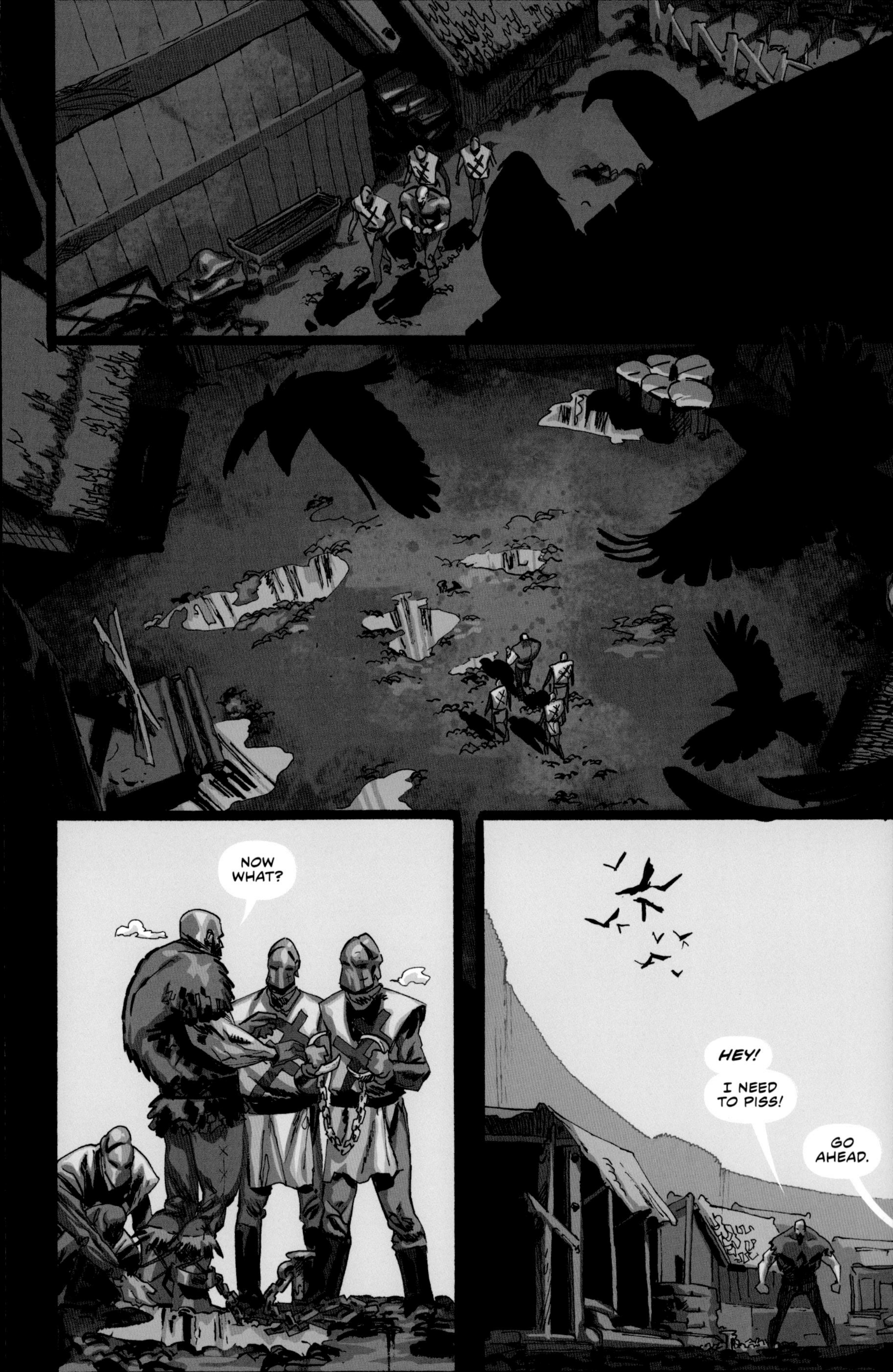
NOW WHAT?
HEY!
I NEED TO PISS!
GO AHEAD.

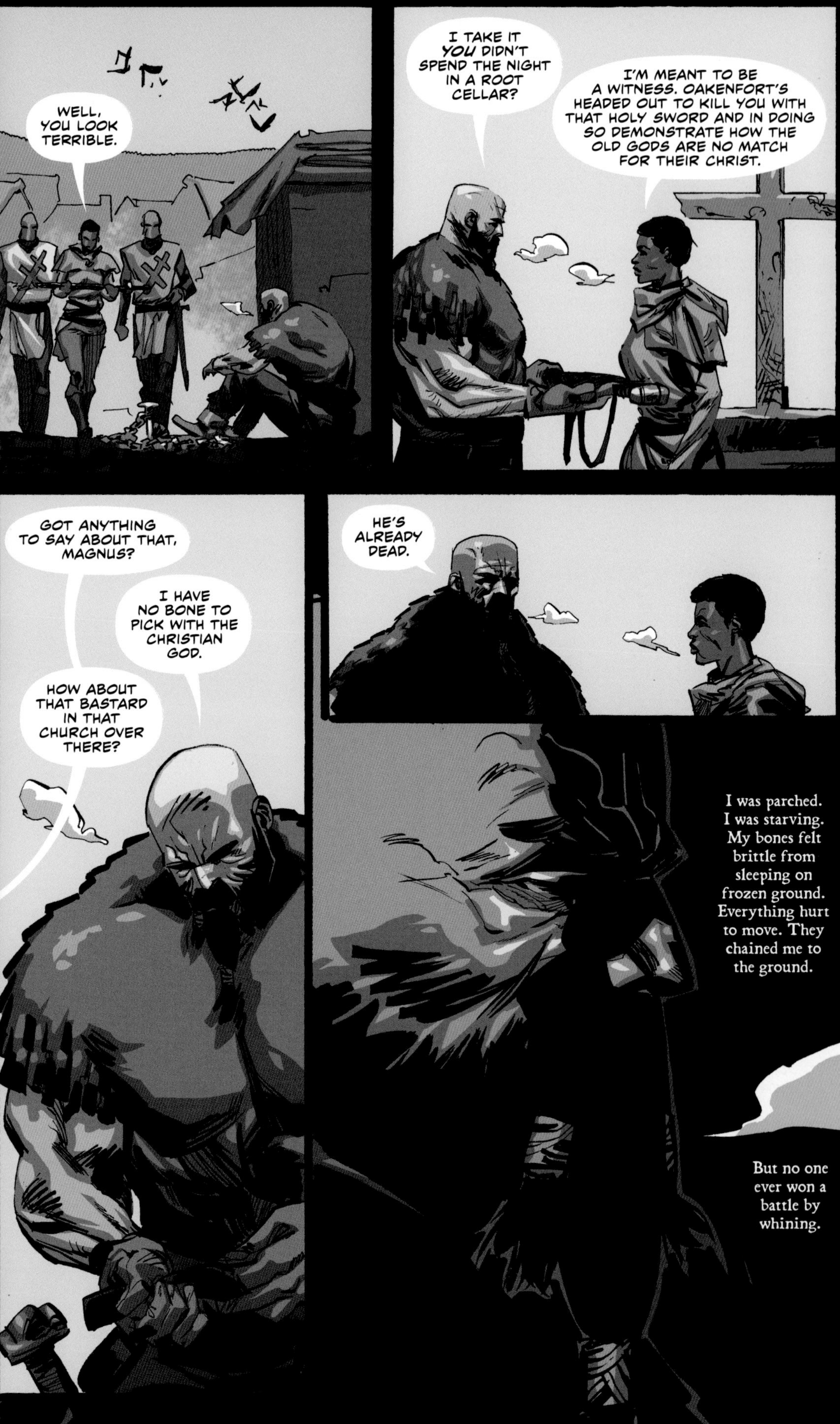
WELL, YOU LOOK TERRIBLE.
I TAKE IT YOU DIDN'T SPEND THE NIGHT IN A ROOT CELLAR?
I'M MEANT TO BE A WITNESS. OAKENFORT'S HEADED OUT TO KILL YOU WITH THAT HOLY SWORD AND IN DOING SO DEMONSTRATE HOW THE OLD GODS ARE NO MATCH FOR THEIR CHRIST.
GOT ANYTHING TO SAY ABOUT THAT, MAGNUS?
I HAVE NO BONE TO PICK WITH THE CHRISTIAN GOD.
HOW ABOUT THAT BASTARD IN THAT CHURCH OVER THERE?
HE'S ALREADY DEAD.
I was parched. I was starving. My bones felt brittle from sleeping on frozen ground. Everything hurt to move. They chained me to the ground.
But no one ever won a battle by whining.

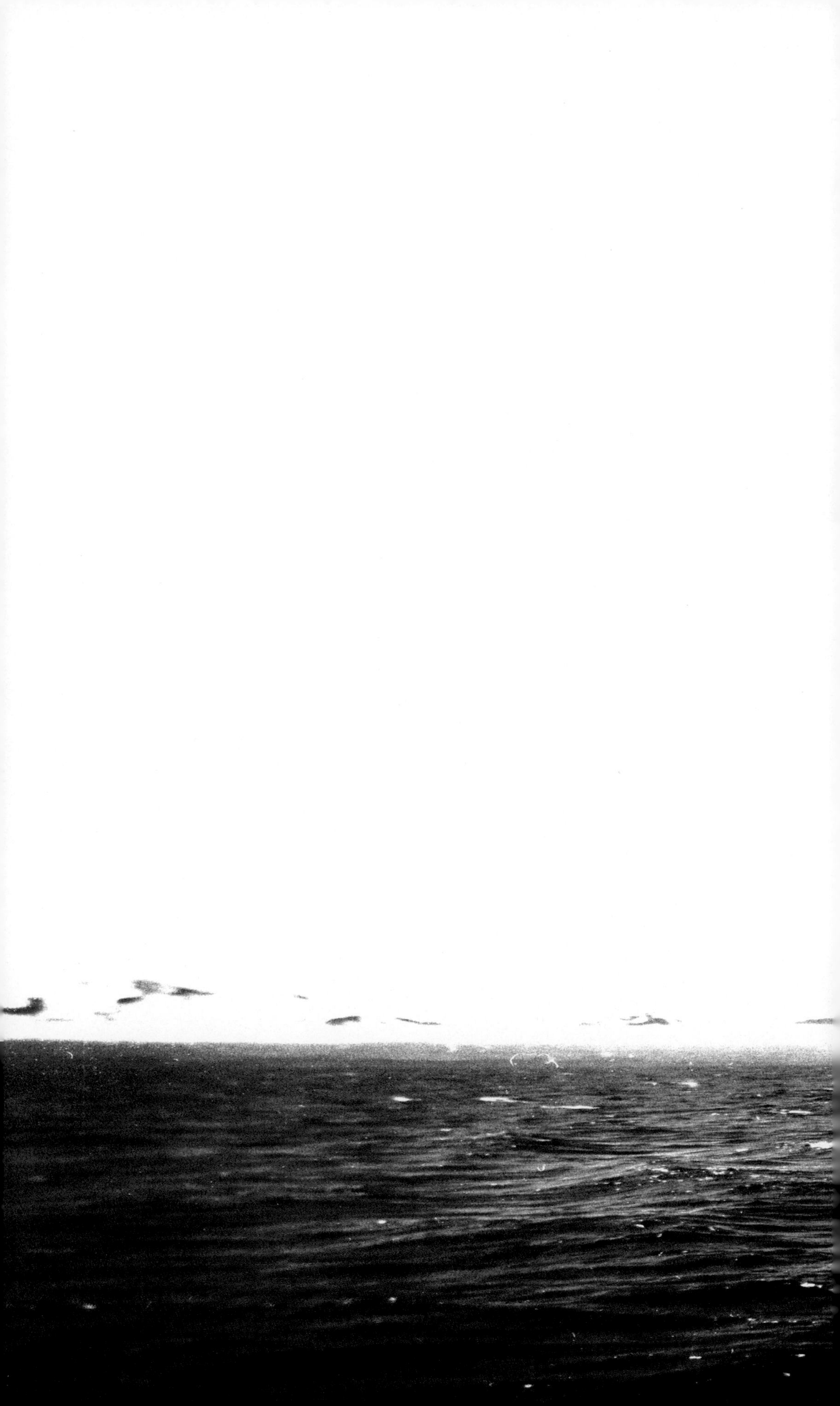

BRIAN WOOD / GARRY BROWN / DAVE McCAIG / STEVE WANDS

BLACK ROAD

#8 - "SWORD-NORSSK"

A MAGNUS THE BLACK MYSTERY

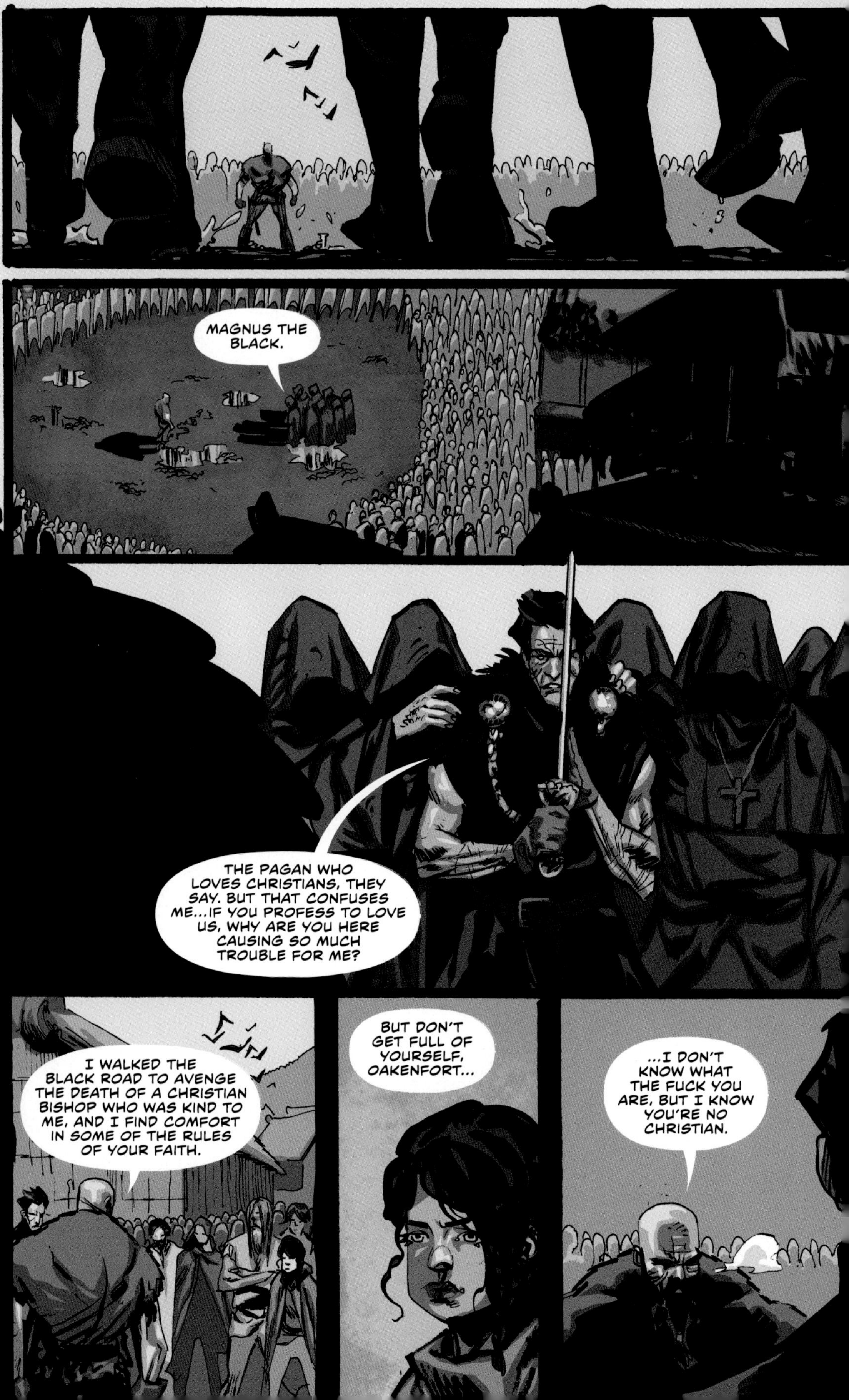
MAGNUS THE BLACK.
THE PAGAN WHO LOVES CHRISTIANS, THEY SAY. BUT THAT CONFUSES ME...IF YOU PROFESS TO LOVE US, WHY ARE YOU HERE CAUSING SO MUCH TROUBLE FOR ME?
I WALKED THE BLACK ROAD TO AVENGE THE DEATH OF A CHRISTIAN BISHOP WHO WAS KIND TO ME, AND I FIND COMFORT IN SOME OF THE RULES OF YOUR FAITH.
BUT DON'T GET FULL OF YOURSELF, OAKENFORT...
...I DON'T KNOW WHAT THE FUCK YOU ARE, BUT I KNOW YOU'RE NO CHRISTIAN.

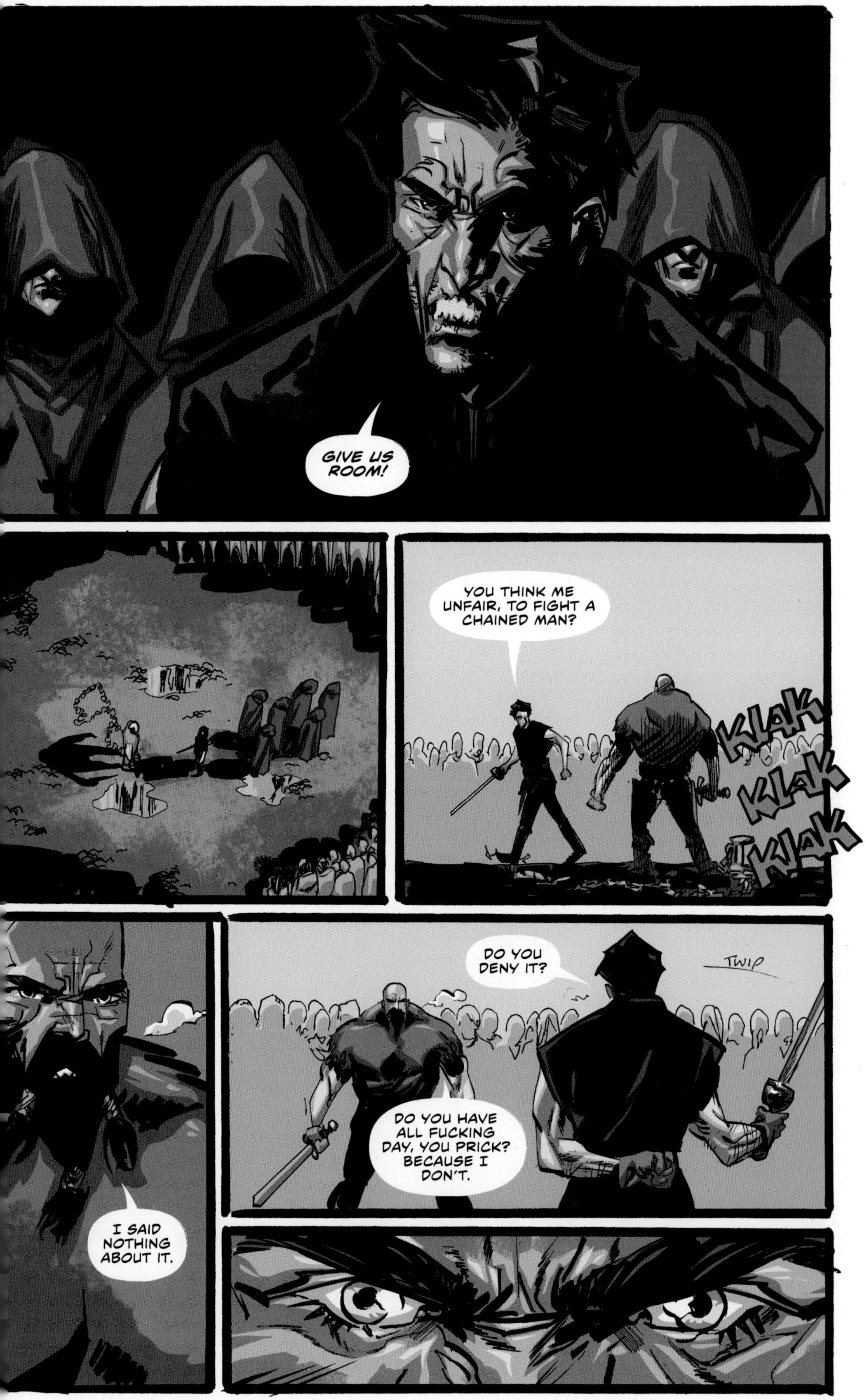
GIVE US ROOM!
YOU THINK ME UNFAIR, TO FIGHT A CHAINED MAN?
KLAK
KLAK
KLAK
I SAID NOTHING ABOUT IT.
DO YOU DENY IT?
TWIP
DO YOU HAVE ALL FUCKING DAY, YOU PRICK? BECAUSE I DON'T.

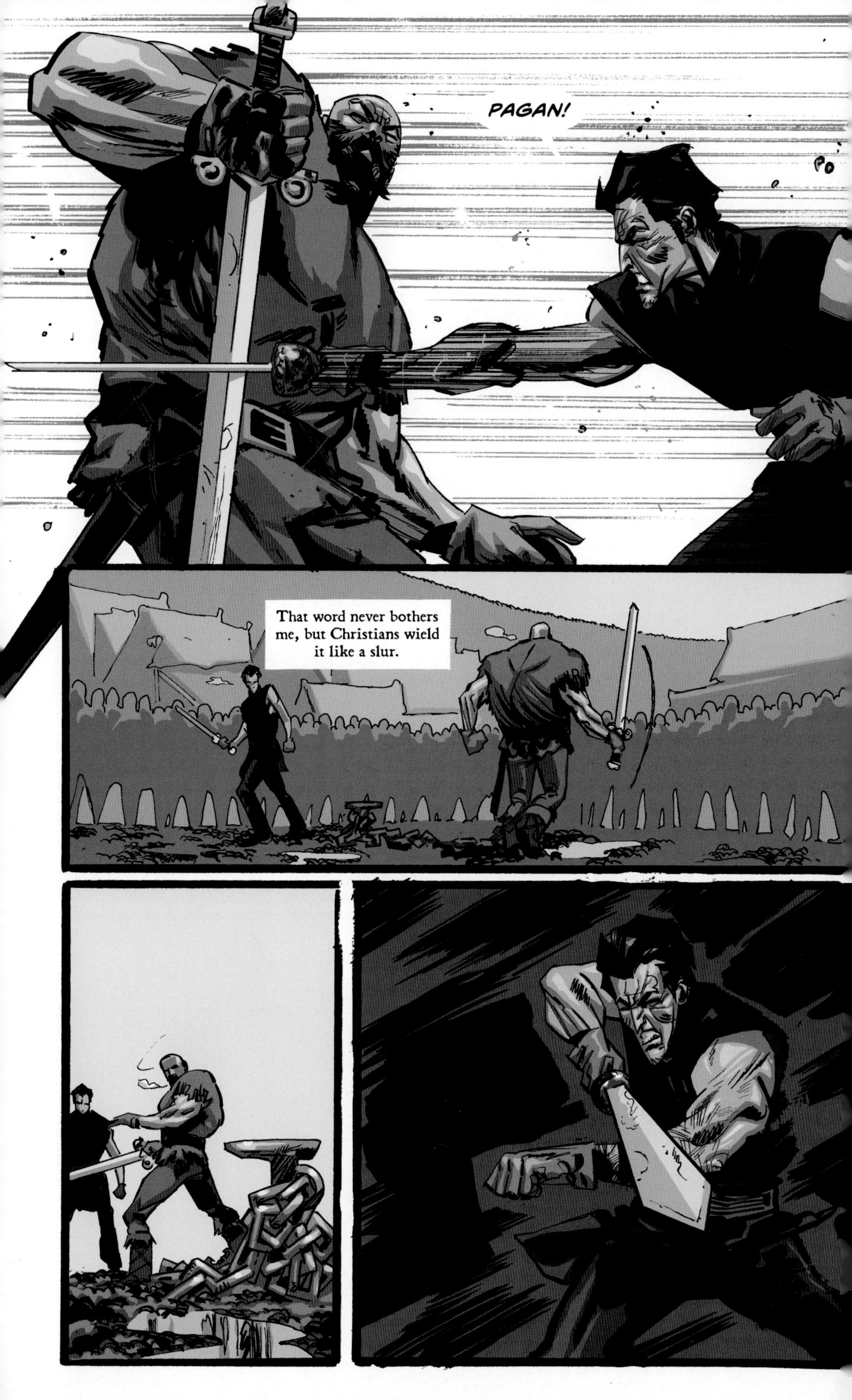

PAGAN!
That word never bothers me, but Christians wield it like a slur.

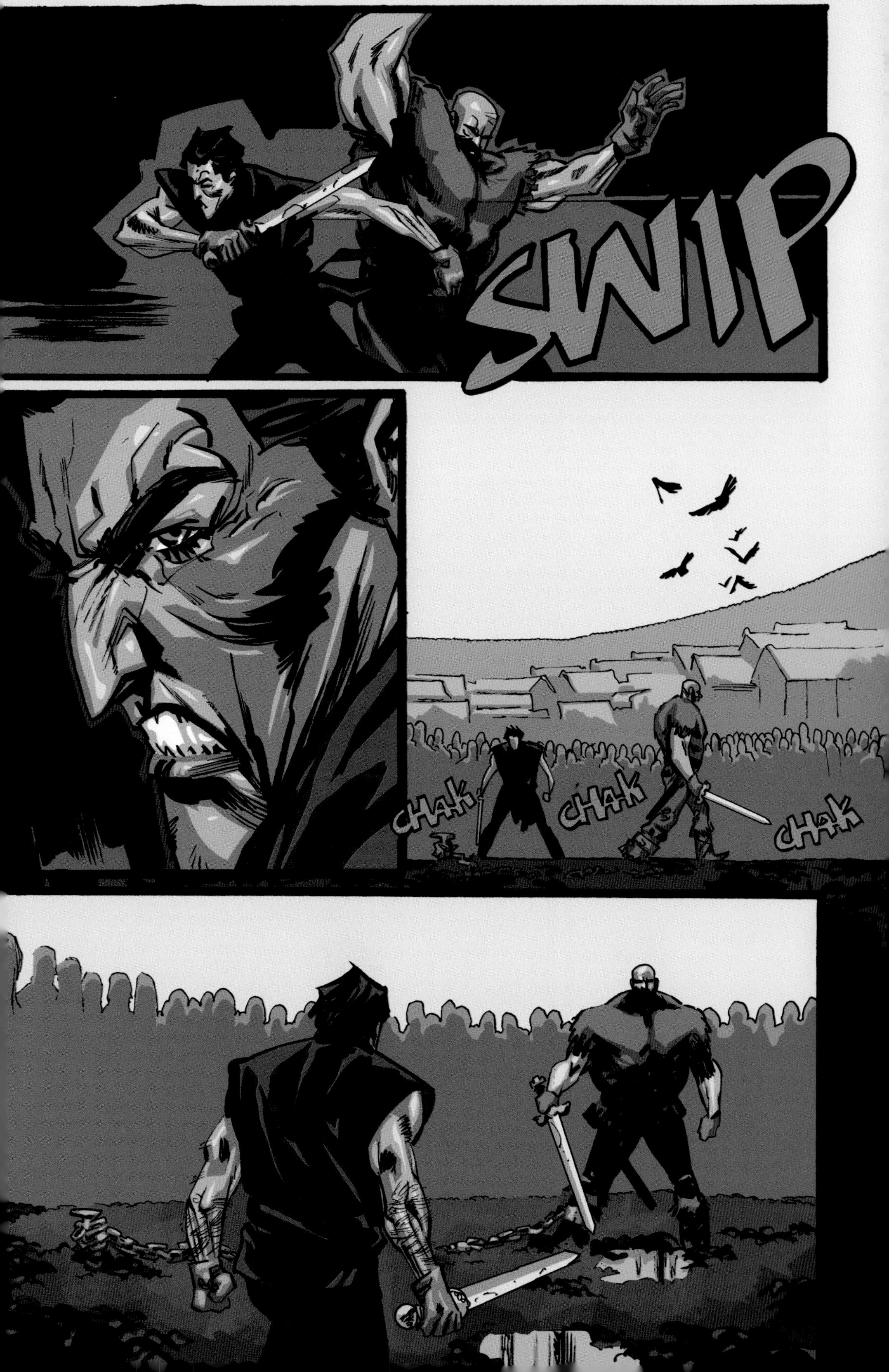
SWIP
CHAK
CHAK
CHAK

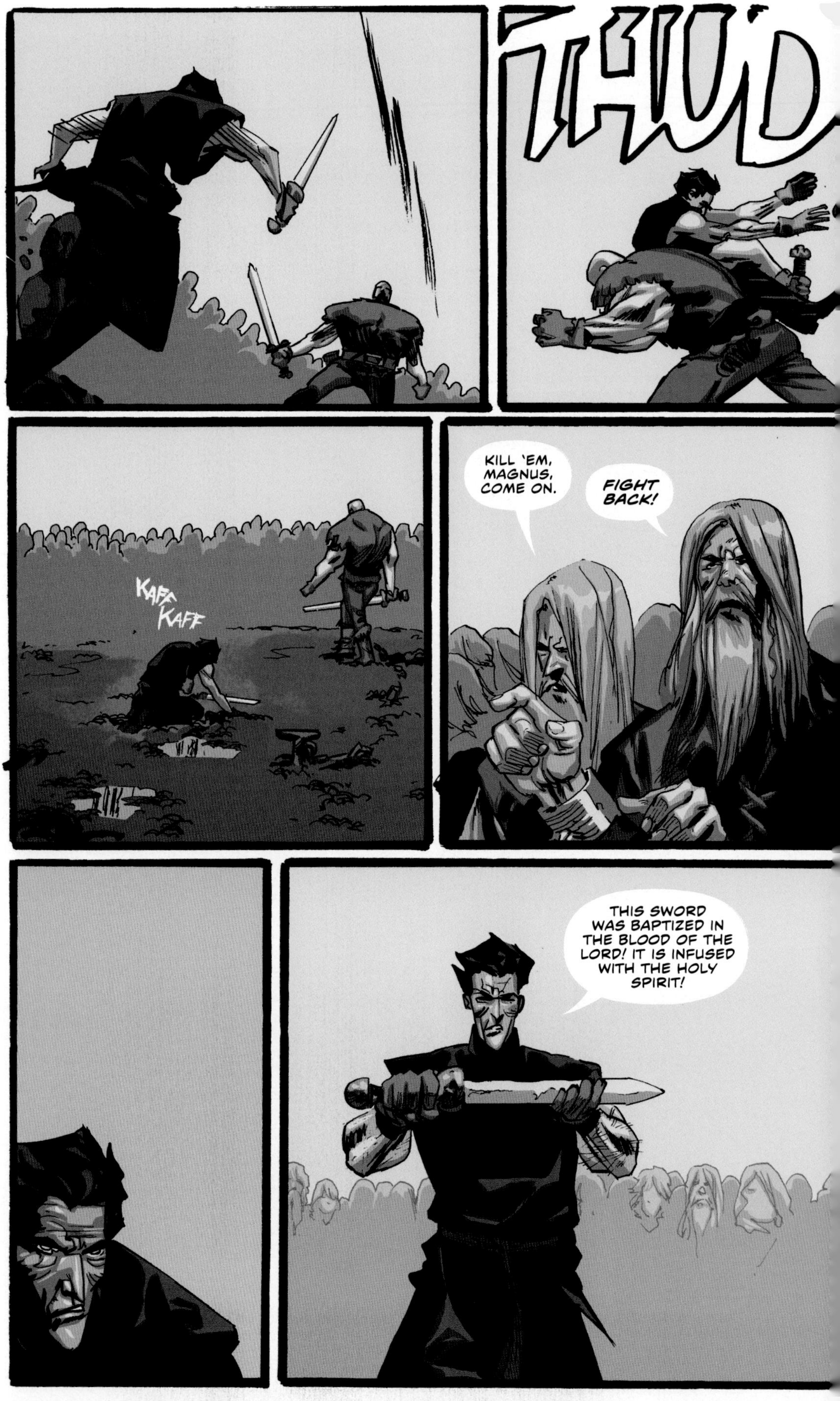
THUD
KAFF KAFF
KILL 'EM, MAGNUS, COME ON.
FIGHT BACK!
THIS SWORD WAS BAPTIZED IN THE BLOOD OF THE LORD! IT IS INFUSED WITH THE HOLY SPIRIT!

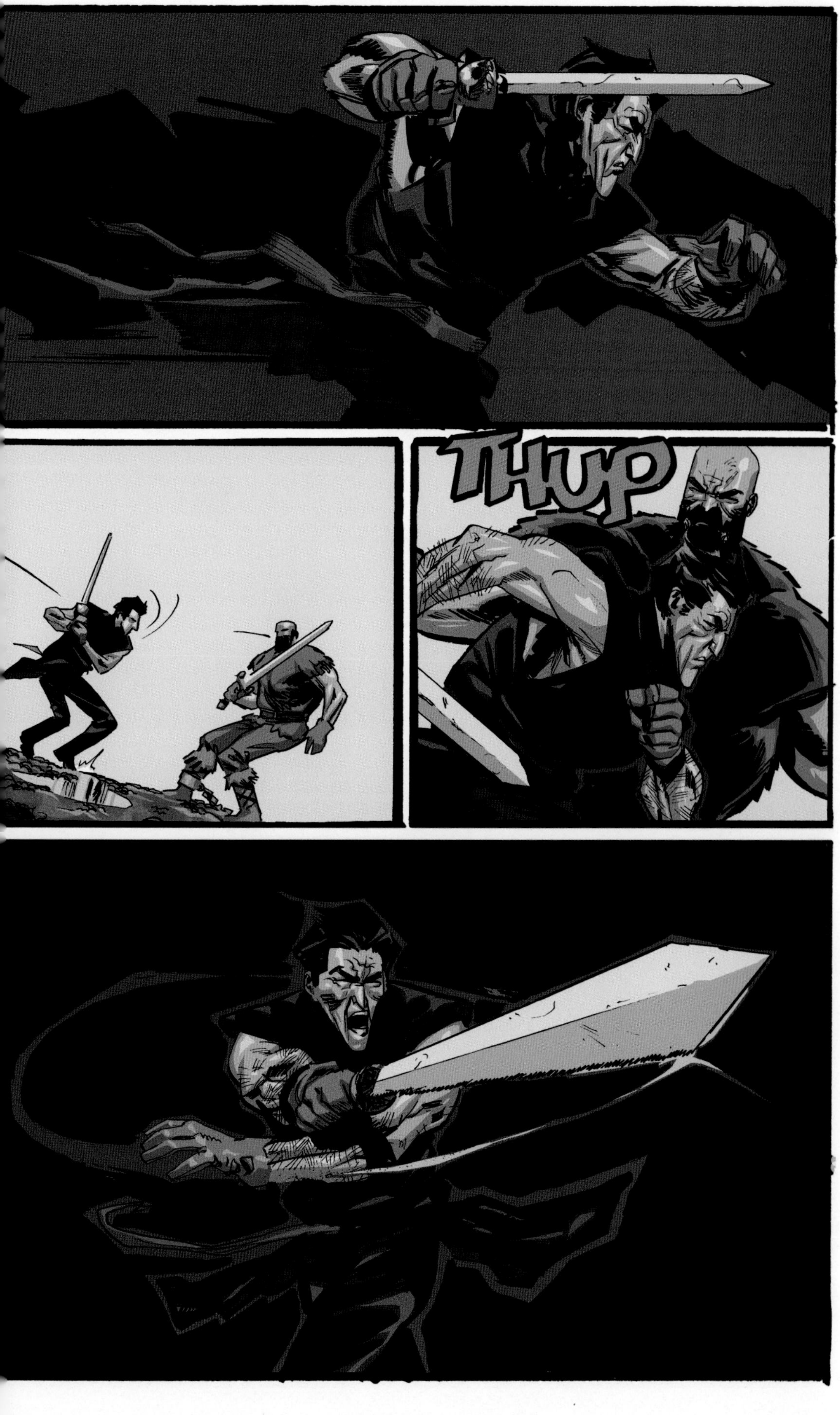
THUP

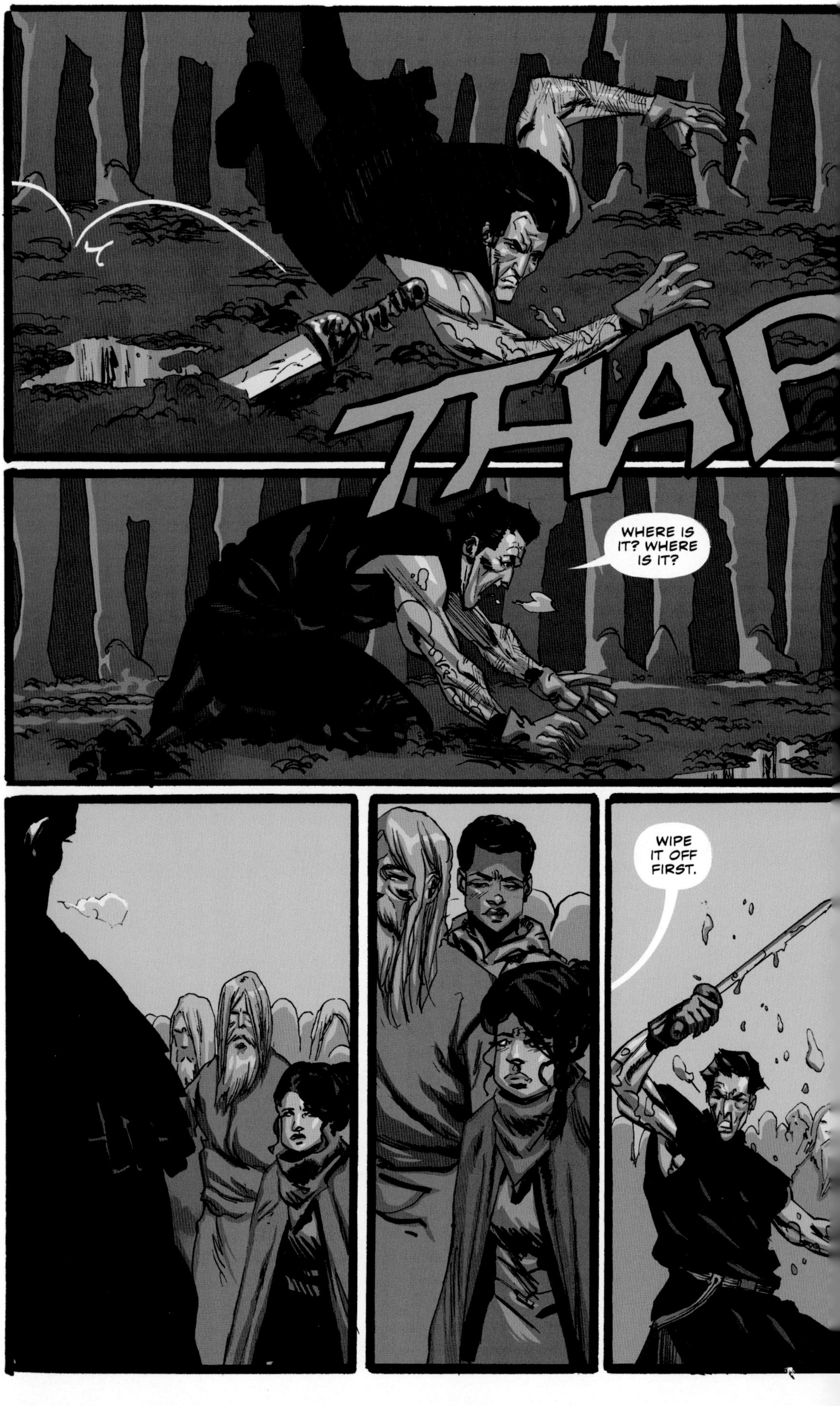
THAP
WHERE IS IT? WHERE IS IT?
WIPE IT OFF FIRST.

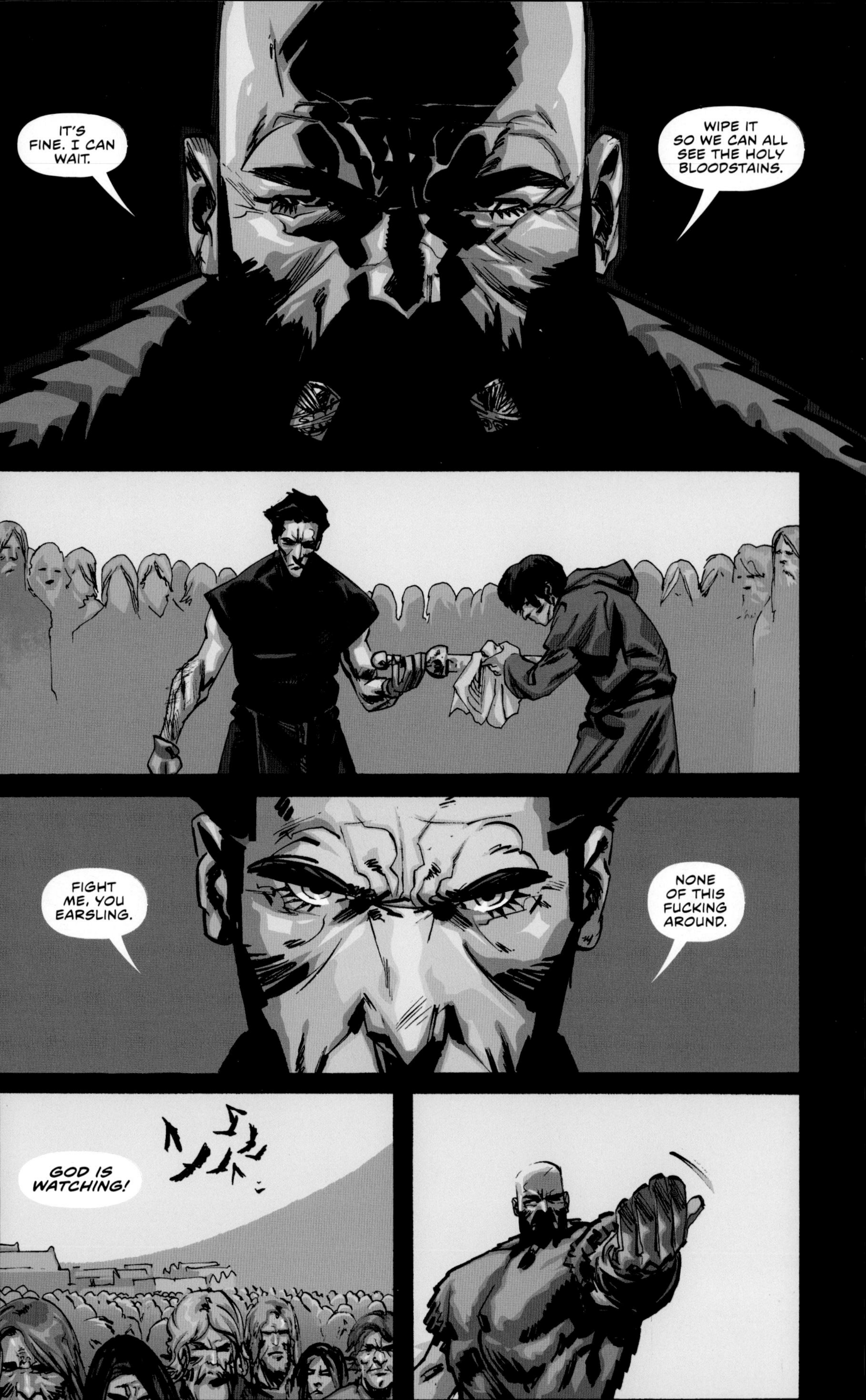
IT'S FINE. I CAN WAIT.
WIPE IT SO WE CAN ALL SEE THE HOLY BLOODSTAINS.
FIGHT ME, YOU EARSLING.
NONE OF THIS FUCKING AROUND.
GOD IS WATCHING!

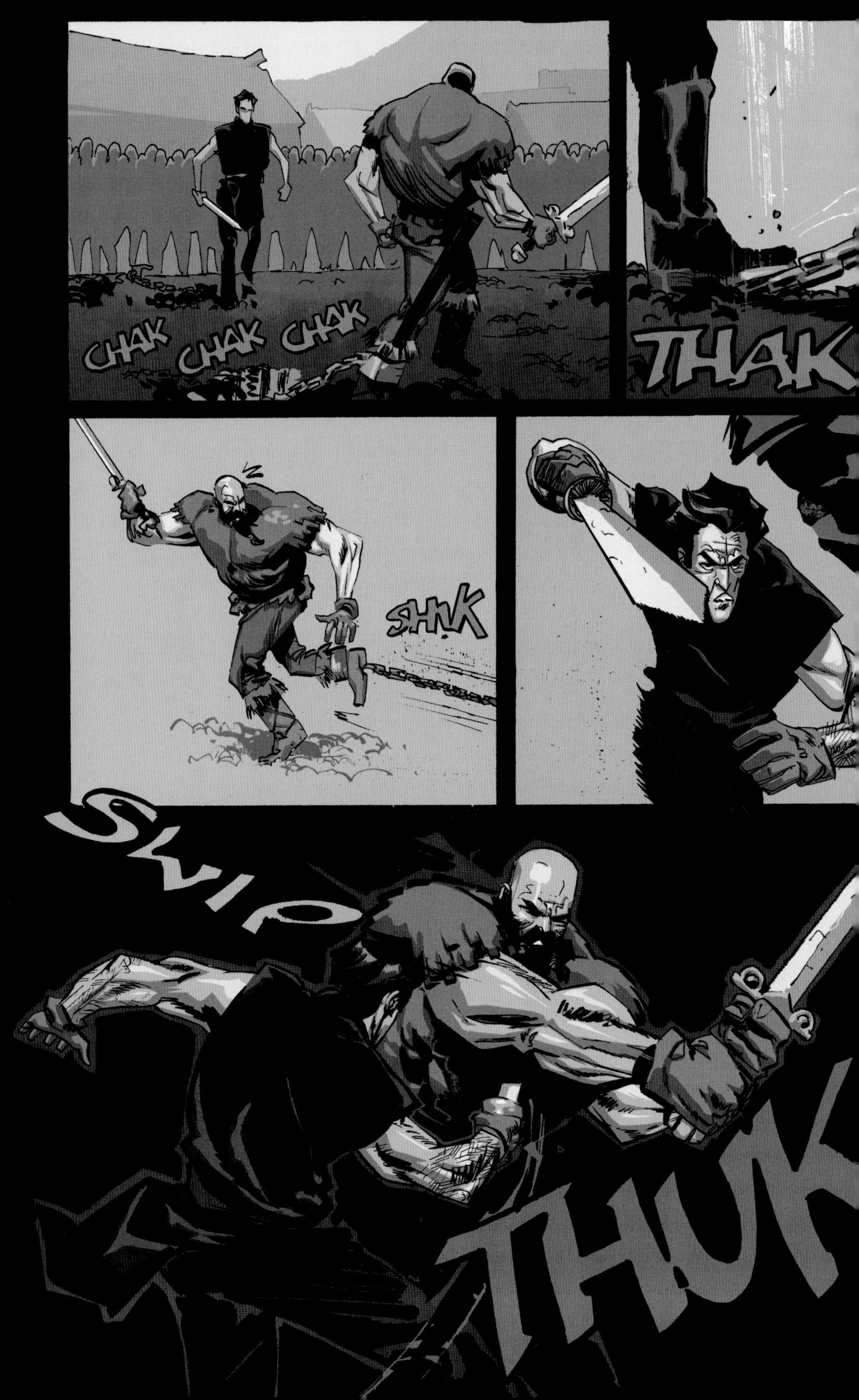
CHAK CHAK CHAK
THAK
SHNK
SWIP
THUK

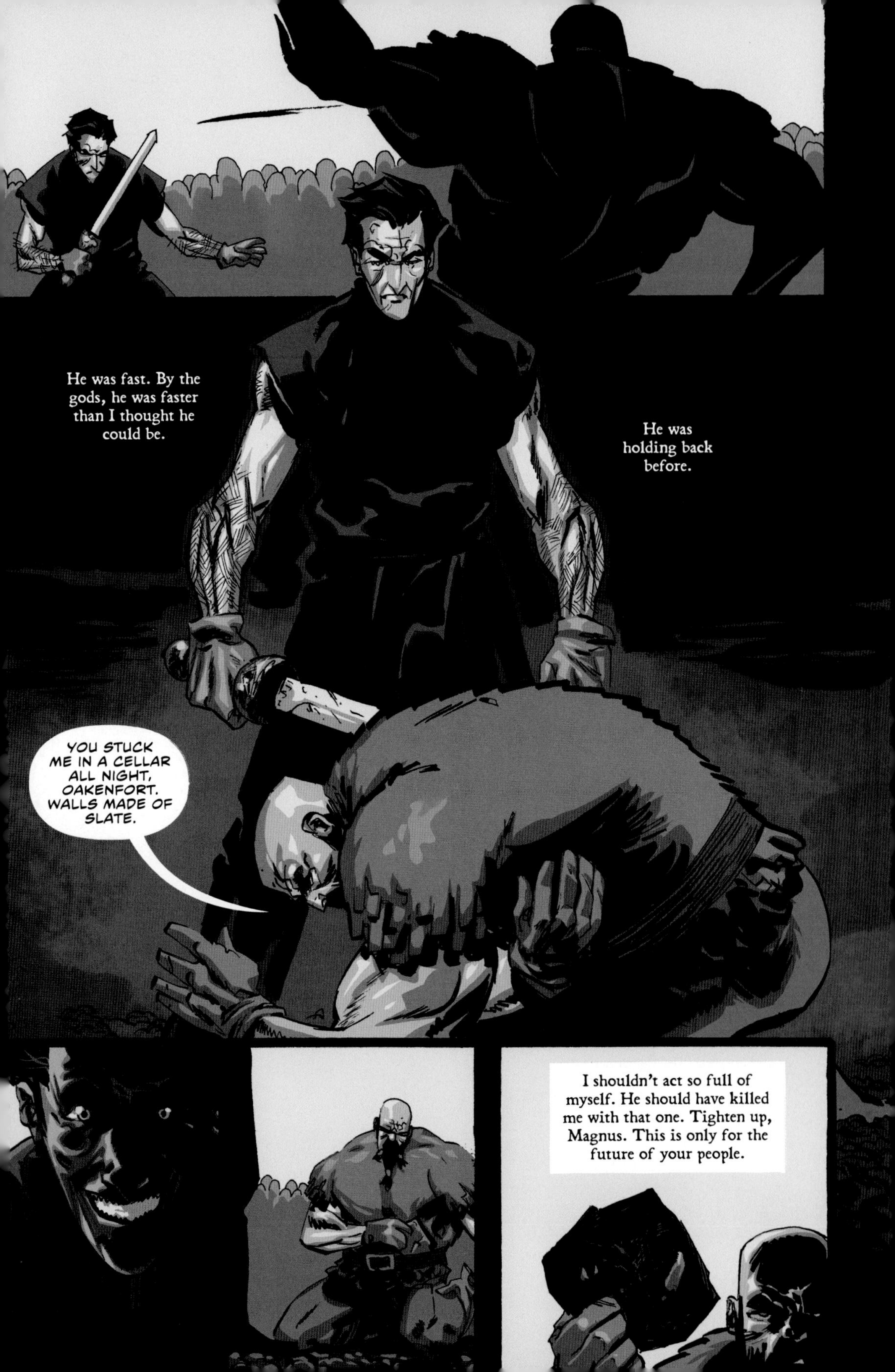
He was fast. By the gods, he was faster than I thought he could be.
He was holding back before.
YOU STUCK ME IN A CELLAR ALL NIGHT, OAKENFORT. WALLS MADE OF SLATE.
I shouldn't act so full of myself. He should have killed me with that one. Tighten up, Magnus. This is only for the future of your people.

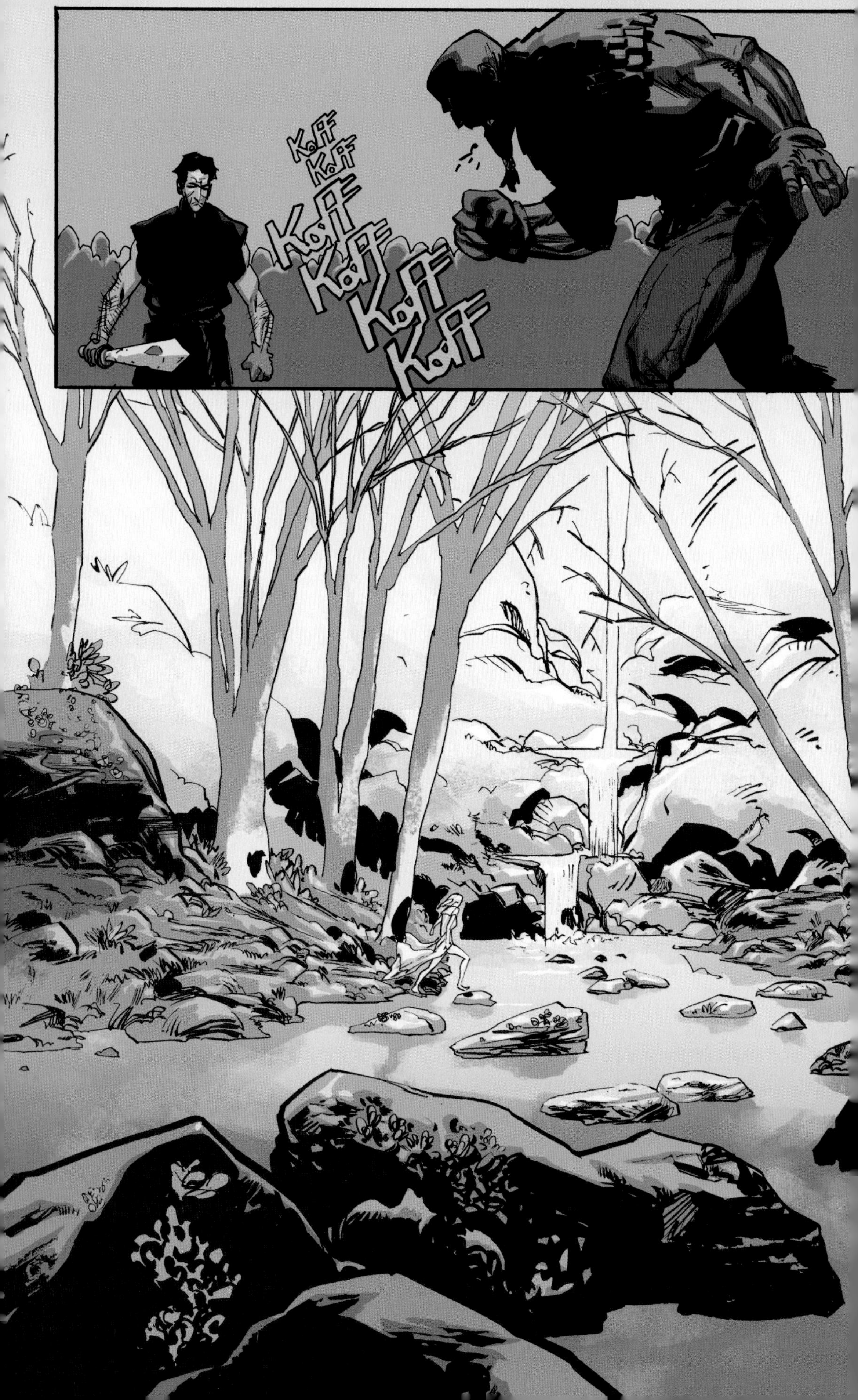
Koff
Koff
Koff
Koff
Koff
Koff

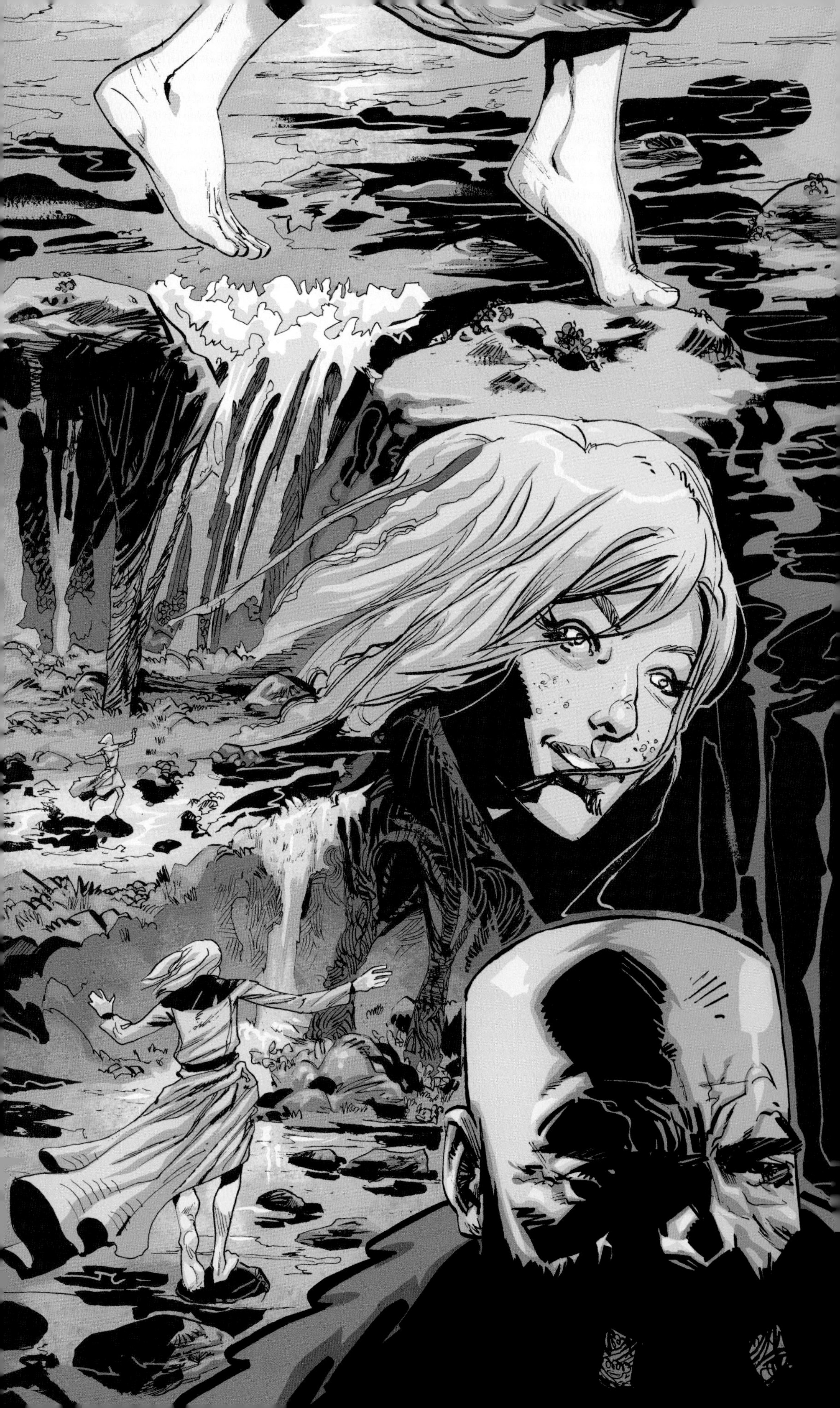

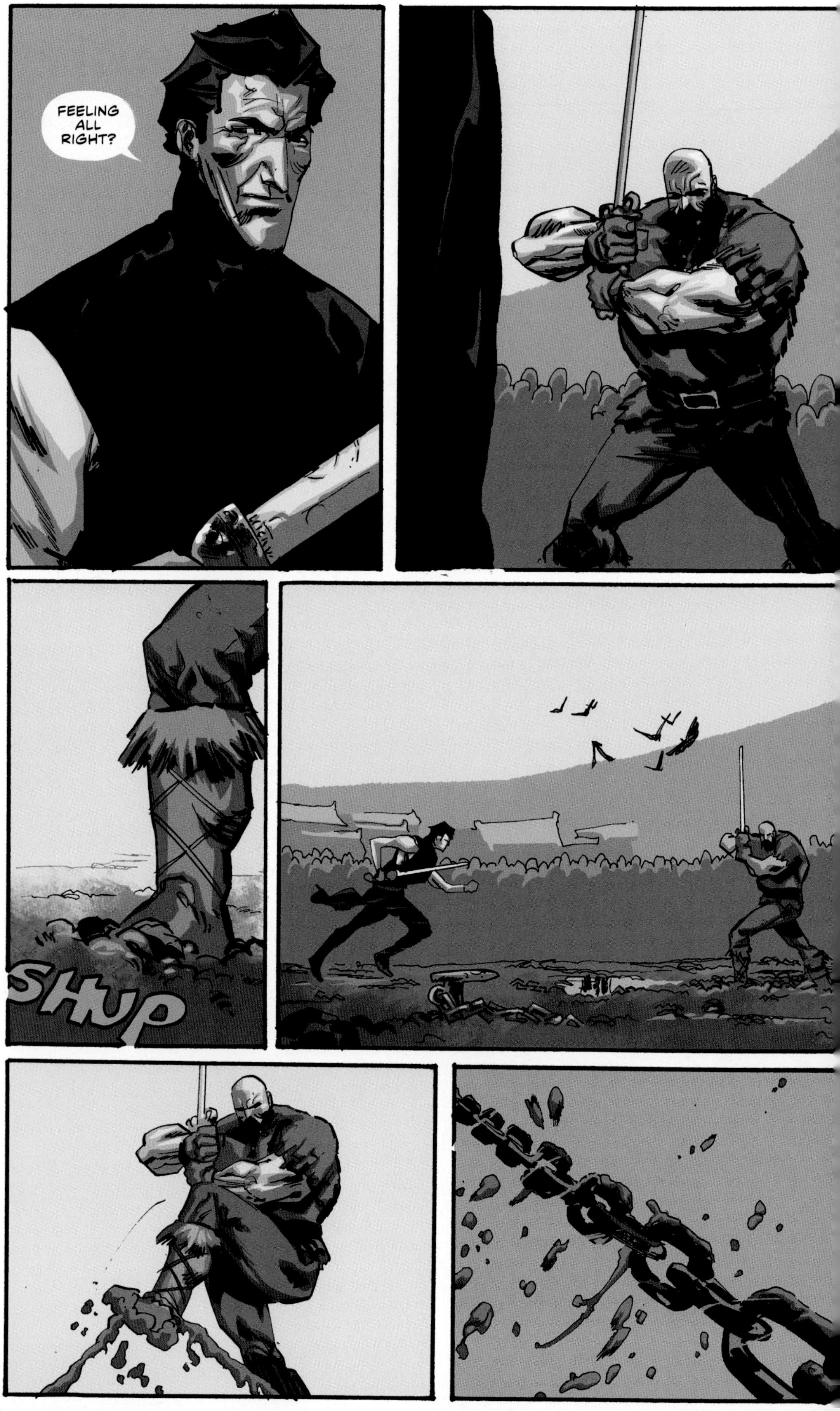
FEELING ALL RIGHT?
SHUP

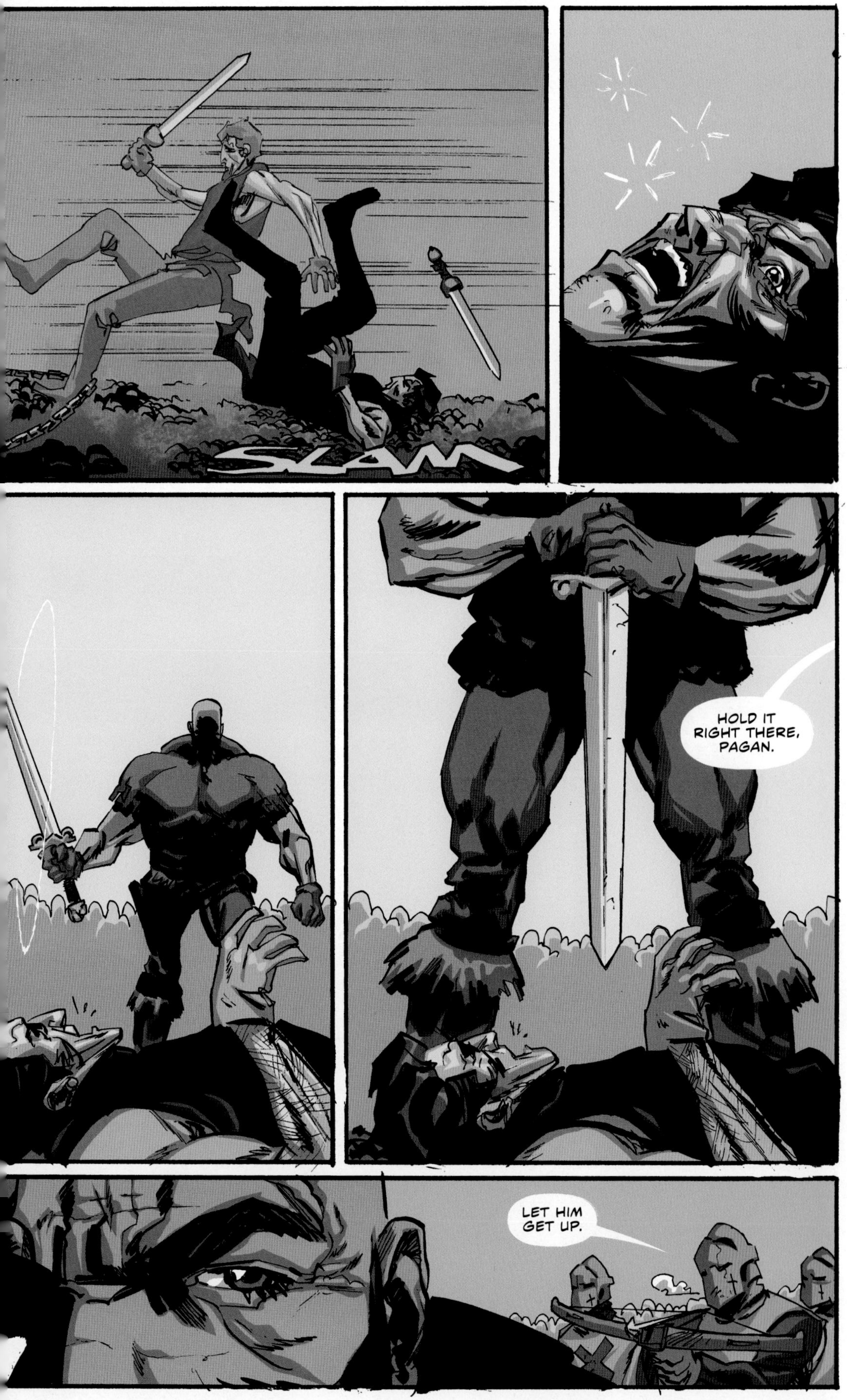
SLAM
HOLD IT RIGHT THERE, PAGAN.
LET HIM GET UP.

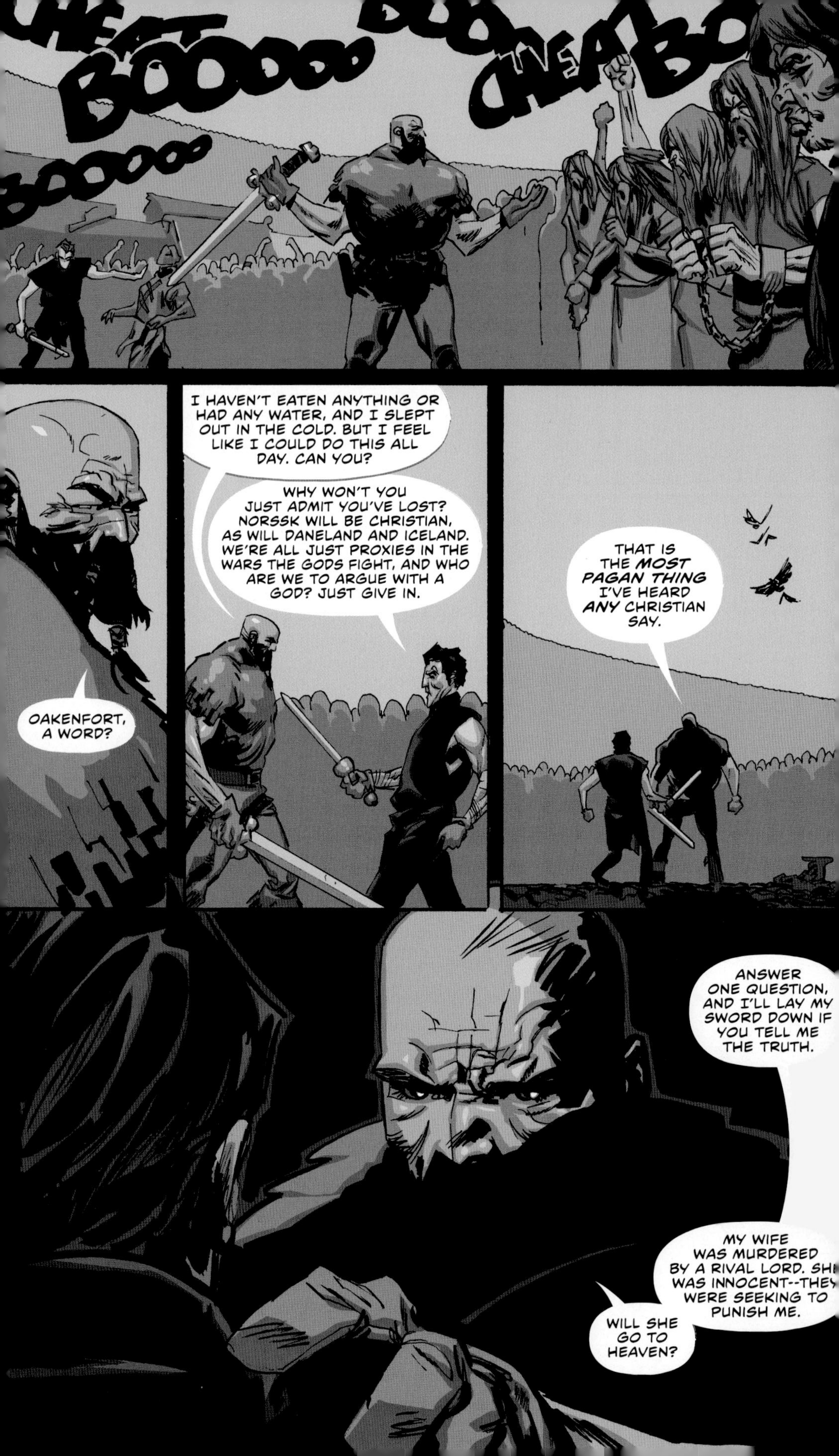
CHEAT
BOOOOOO
BOO
CHEAT
BOOOOOO
CHEAT
BO
OAKENFORT, A WORD?
I HAVEN'T EATEN ANYTHING OR HAD ANY WATER, AND I SLEPT OUT IN THE COLD. BUT I FEEL LIKE I COULD DO THIS ALL DAY. CAN YOU?
WHY WON'T YOU JUST ADMIT YOU'VE LOST? NORSSK WILL BE CHRISTIAN, AS WILL DANELAND AND ICELAND. WE'RE ALL JUST PROXIES IN THE WARS THE GODS FIGHT, AND WHO ARE WE TO ARGUE WITH A GOD? JUST GIVE IN.
THAT IS THE *MOST PAGAN THING* I'VE HEARD *ANY* CHRISTIAN SAY.
ANSWER ONE QUESTION, AND I'LL LAY MY SWORD DOWN IF YOU TELL ME THE TRUTH.
MY WIFE WAS MURDERED BY A RIVAL LORD. SHE WAS INNOCENT--THEY WERE SEEKING TO PUNISH ME.
WILL SHE GO TO HEAVEN?

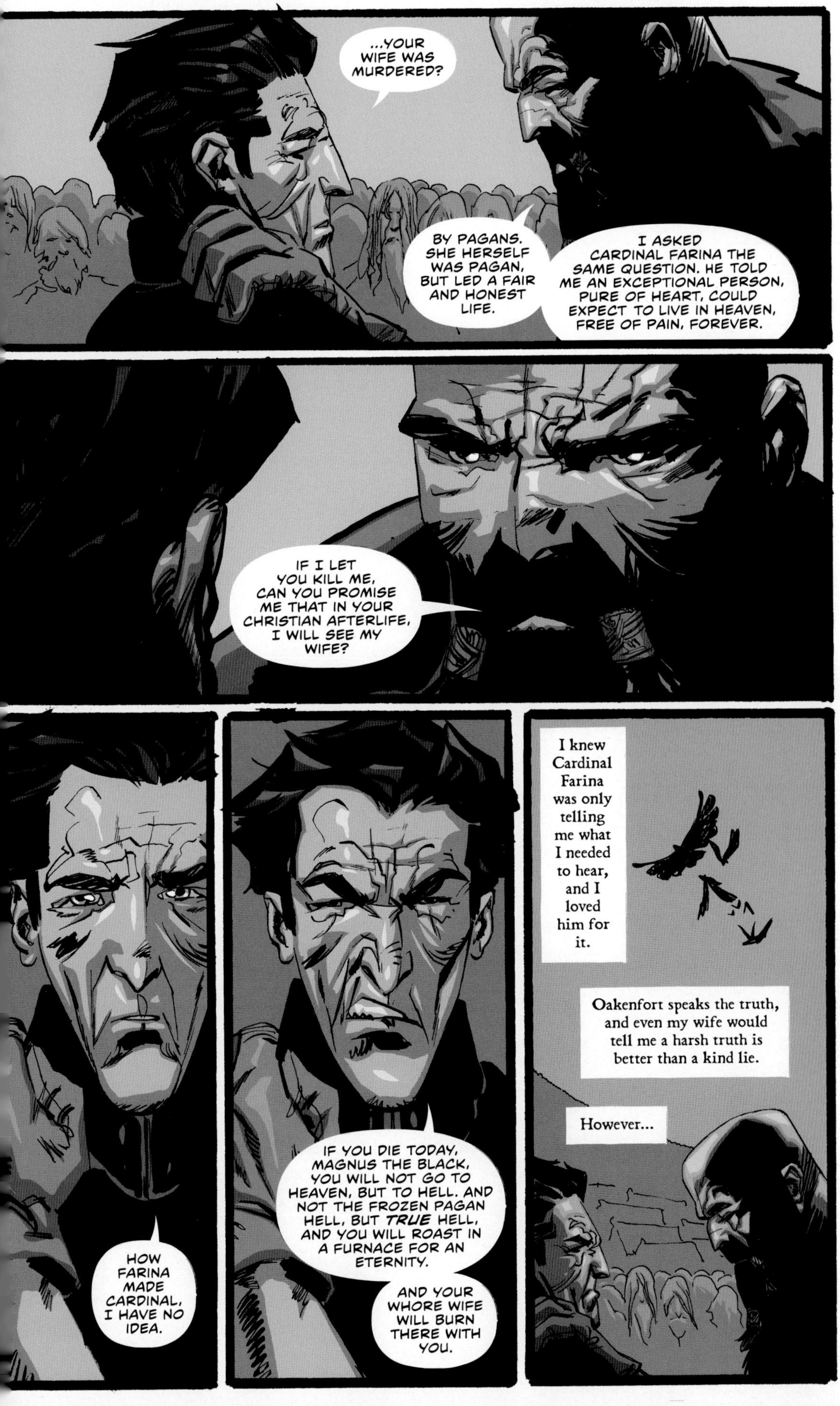
...YOUR WIFE WAS MURDERED?
BY PAGANS. SHE HERSELF WAS PAGAN, BUT LED A FAIR AND HONEST LIFE.
I ASKED CARDINAL FARINA THE SAME QUESTION. HE TOLD ME AN EXCEPTIONAL PERSON, PURE OF HEART, COULD EXPECT TO LIVE IN HEAVEN, FREE OF PAIN, FOREVER.
IF I LET YOU KILL ME, CAN YOU PROMISE ME THAT IN YOUR CHRISTIAN AFTERLIFE, I WILL SEE MY WIFE?
HOW FARINA MADE CARDINAL, I HAVE NO IDEA.
IF YOU DIE TODAY, MAGNUS THE BLACK, YOU WILL NOT GO TO HEAVEN, BUT TO HELL. AND NOT THE FROZEN PAGAN HELL, BUT TRUE HELL, AND YOU WILL ROAST IN A FURNACE FOR AN ETERNITY.
AND YOUR WHORE WIFE WILL BURN THERE WITH YOU.
I knew Cardinal Farina was only telling me what I needed to hear, and I loved him for it.
Oakenfort speaks the truth, and even my wife would tell me a harsh truth is better than a kind lie.
However...

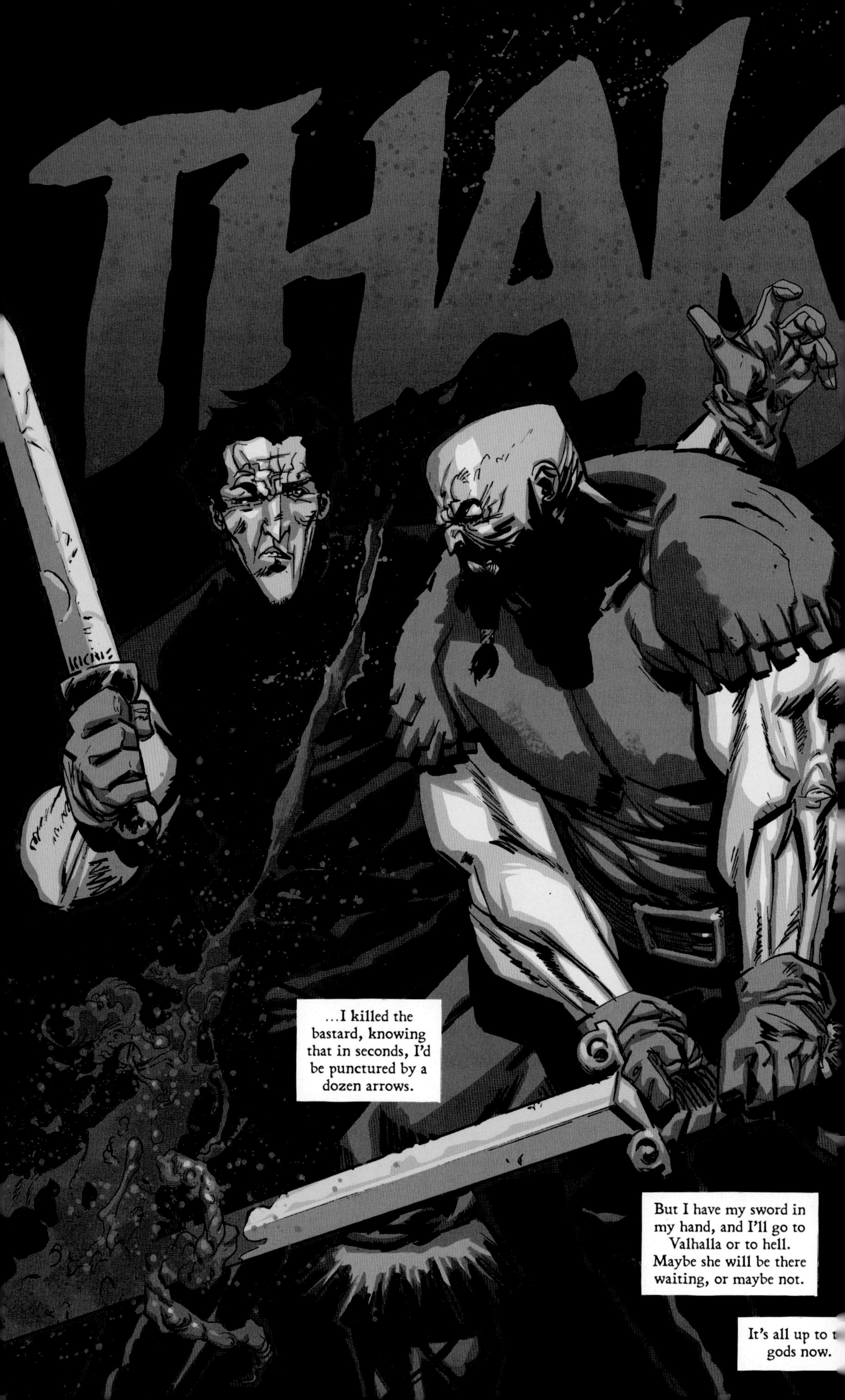
THAK
...I killed the bastard, knowing that in seconds, I'd be punctured by a dozen arrows.
But I have my sword in my hand, and I'll go to Valhalla or to hell. Maybe she will be there waiting, or maybe not.
It's all up to t gods now.

A MAGNUS THE BLACK MYSTERY

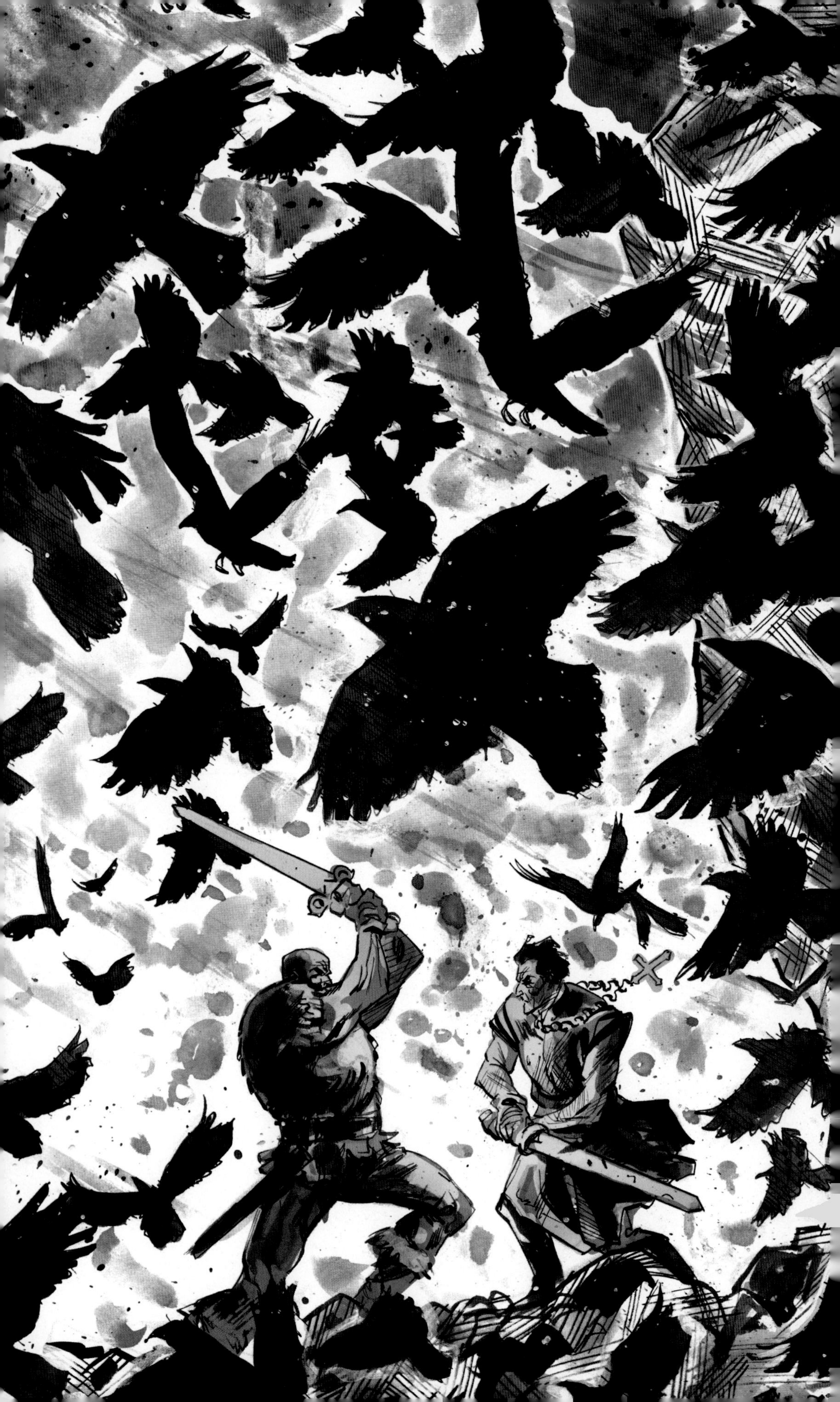

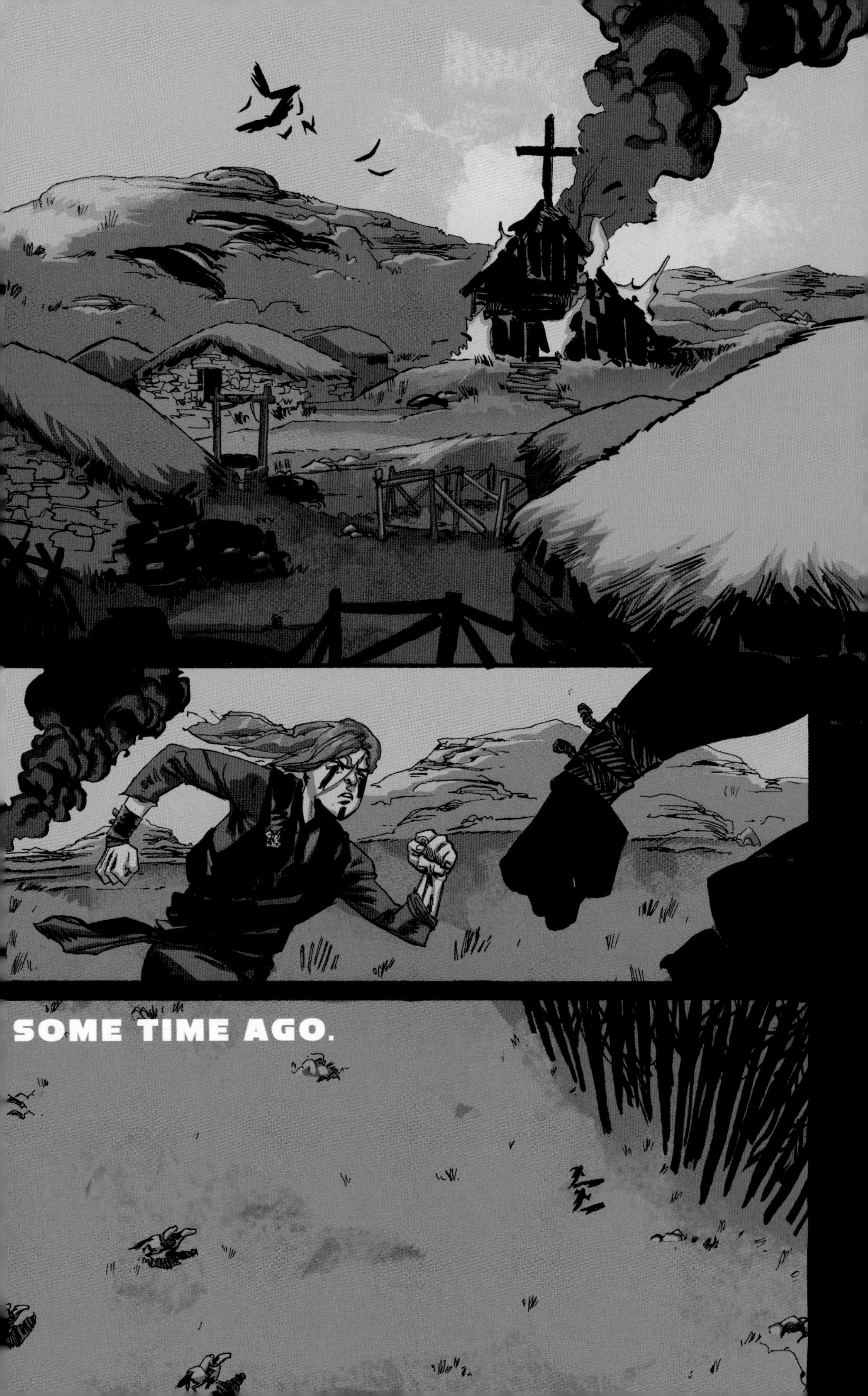
SOME TIME AGO.

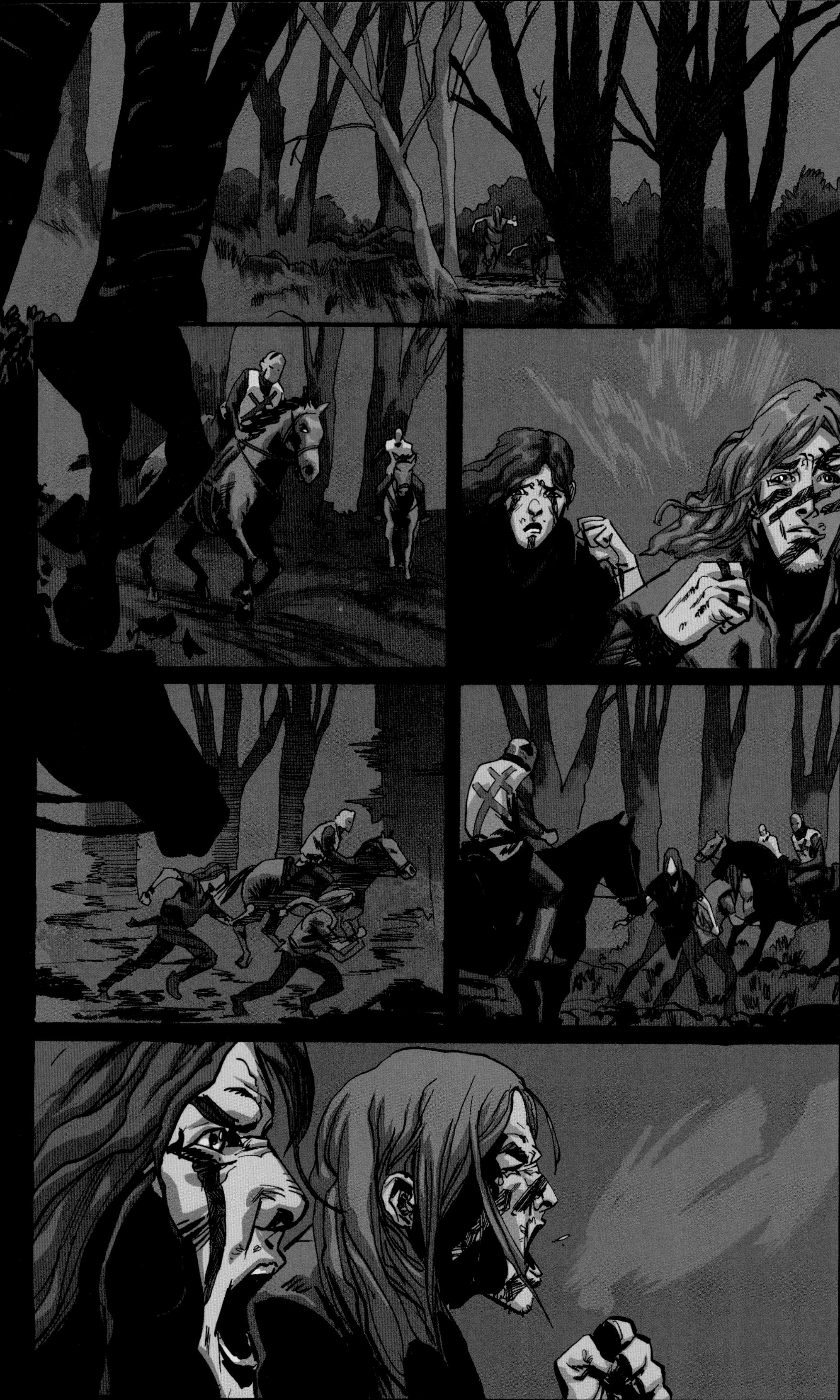

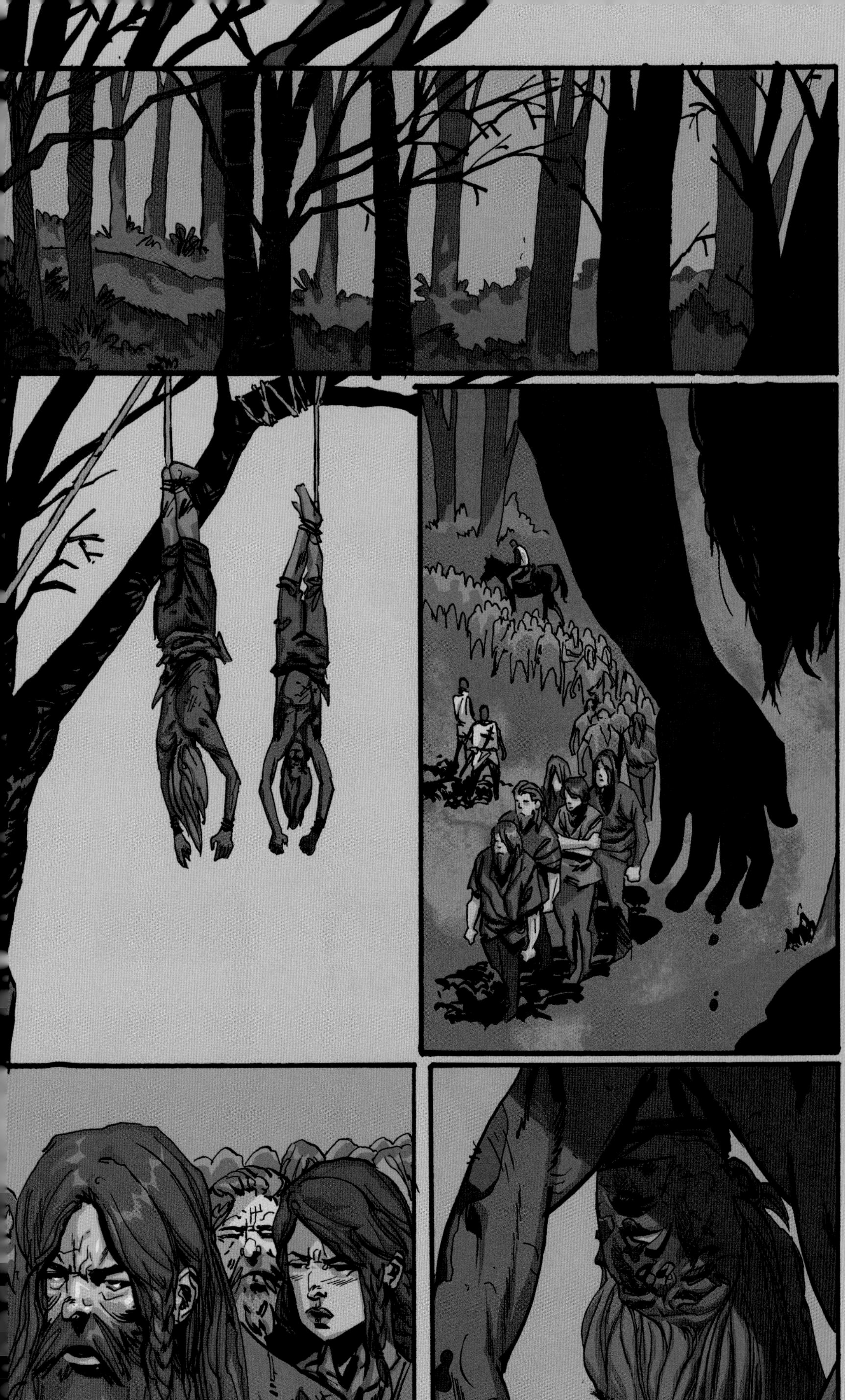

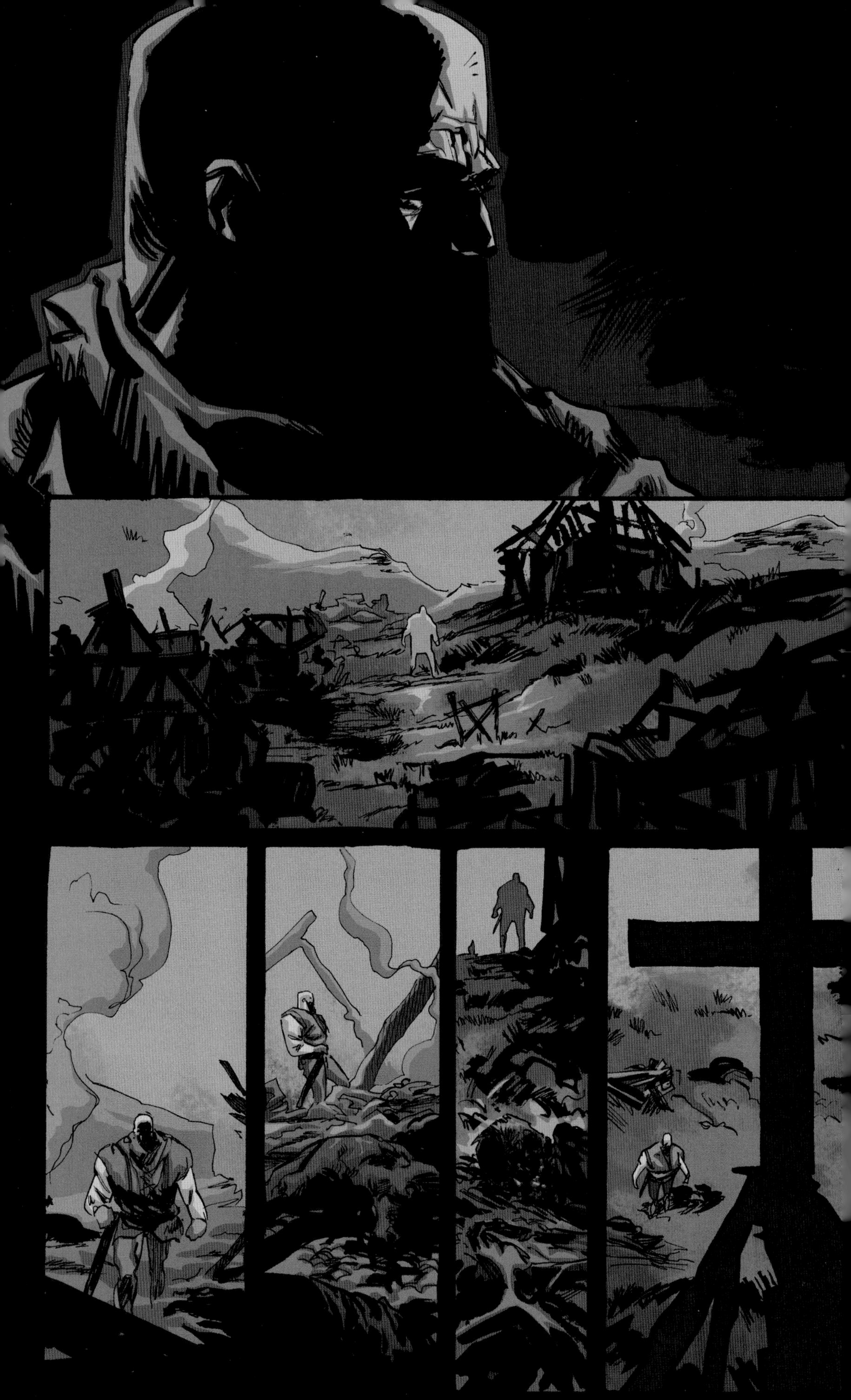

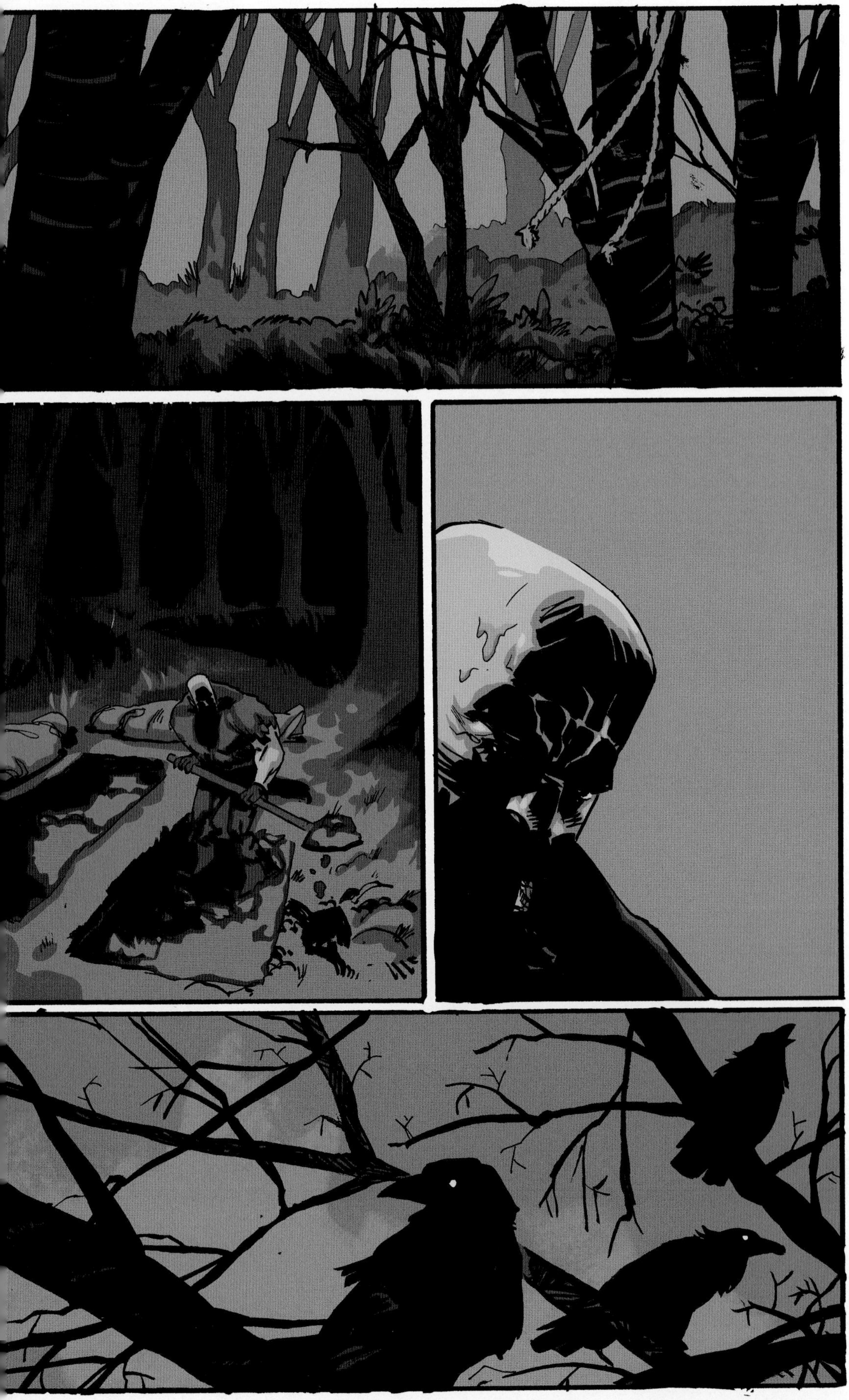

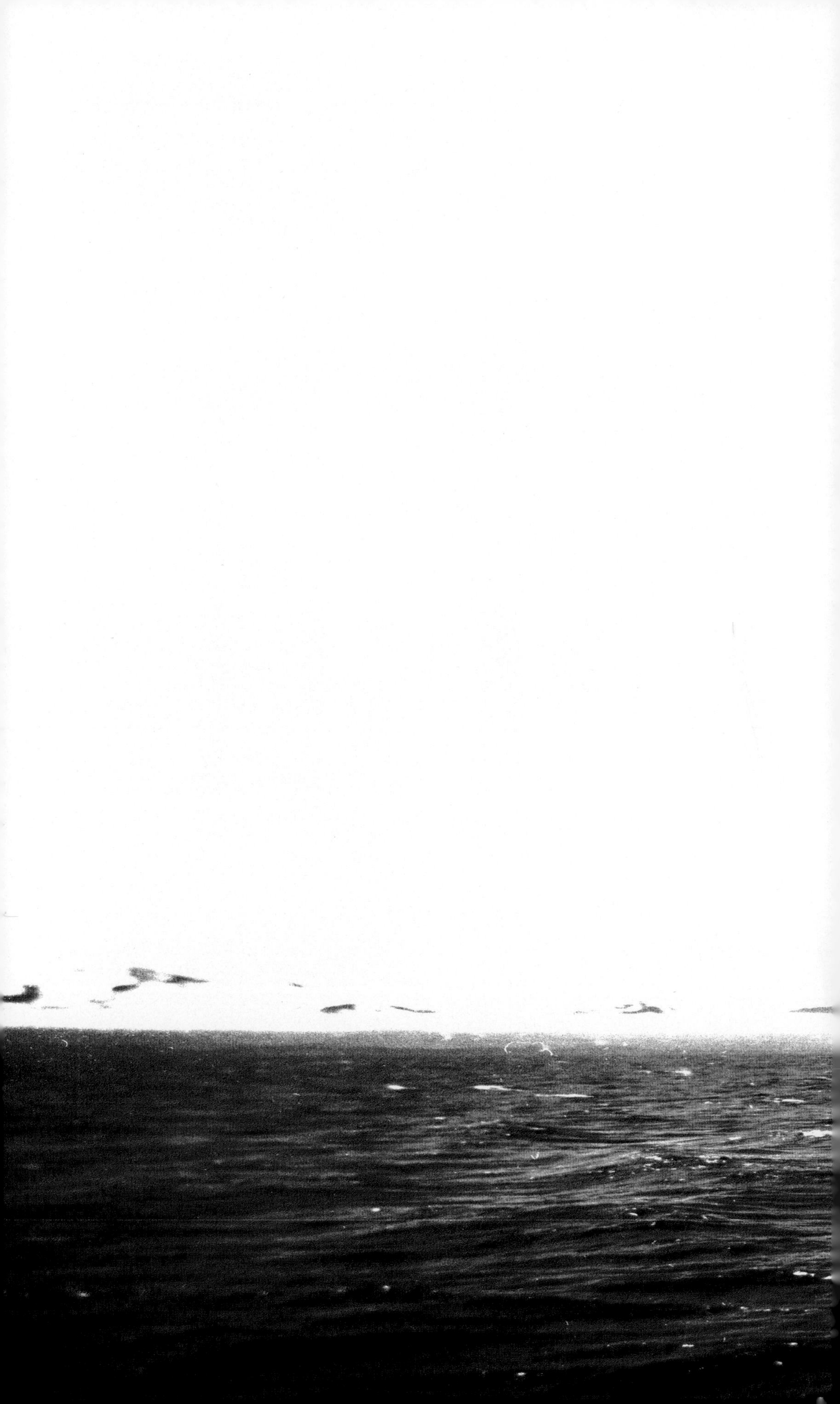

BRIAN WOOD / GARRY BROWN / DAVE McCAIG / STEVE WANDS

BLACK ROAD

#9 - "SHATTERPOINT"

A MAGNUS THE BLACK MYSTERY

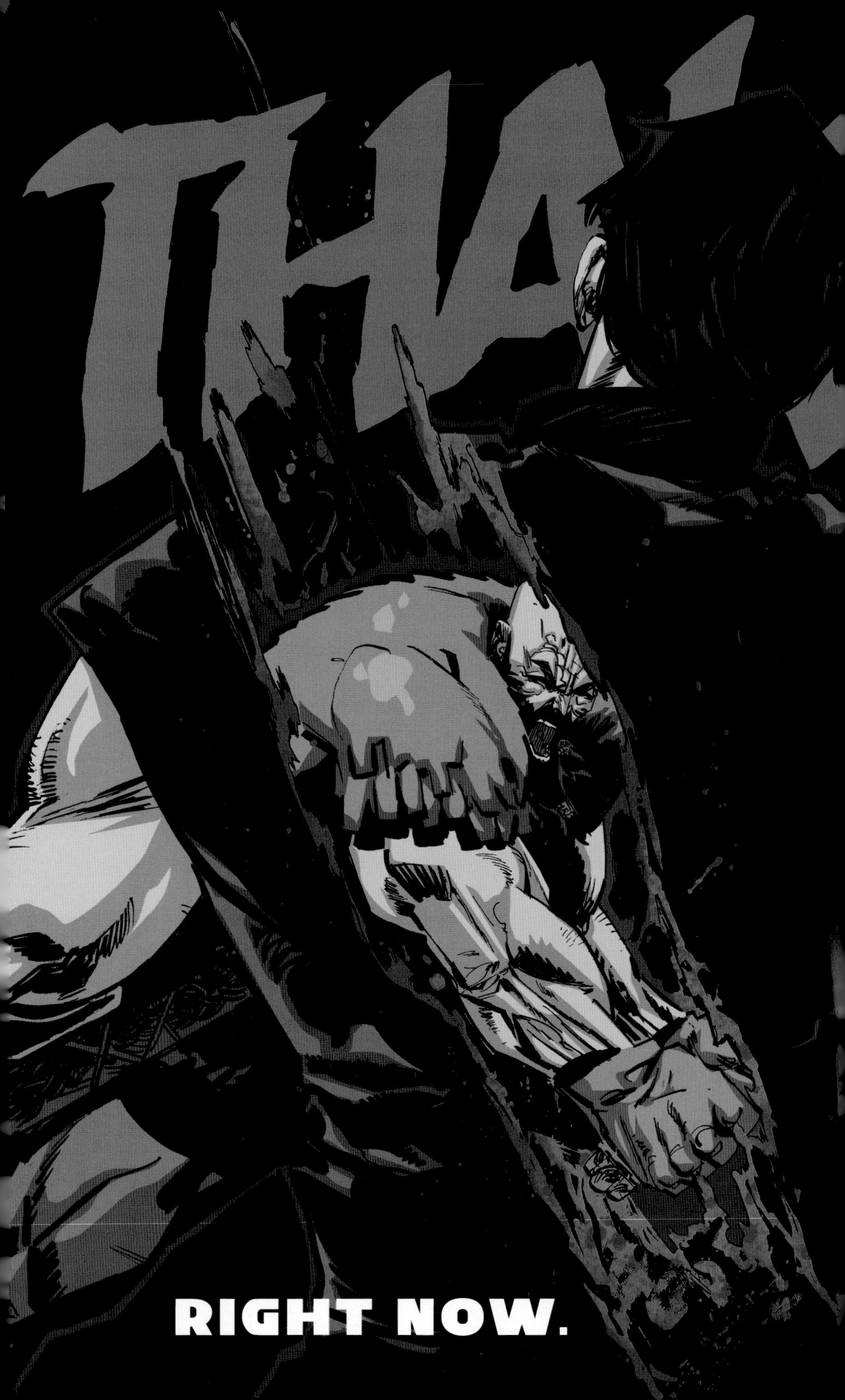
THA
RIGHT NOW.

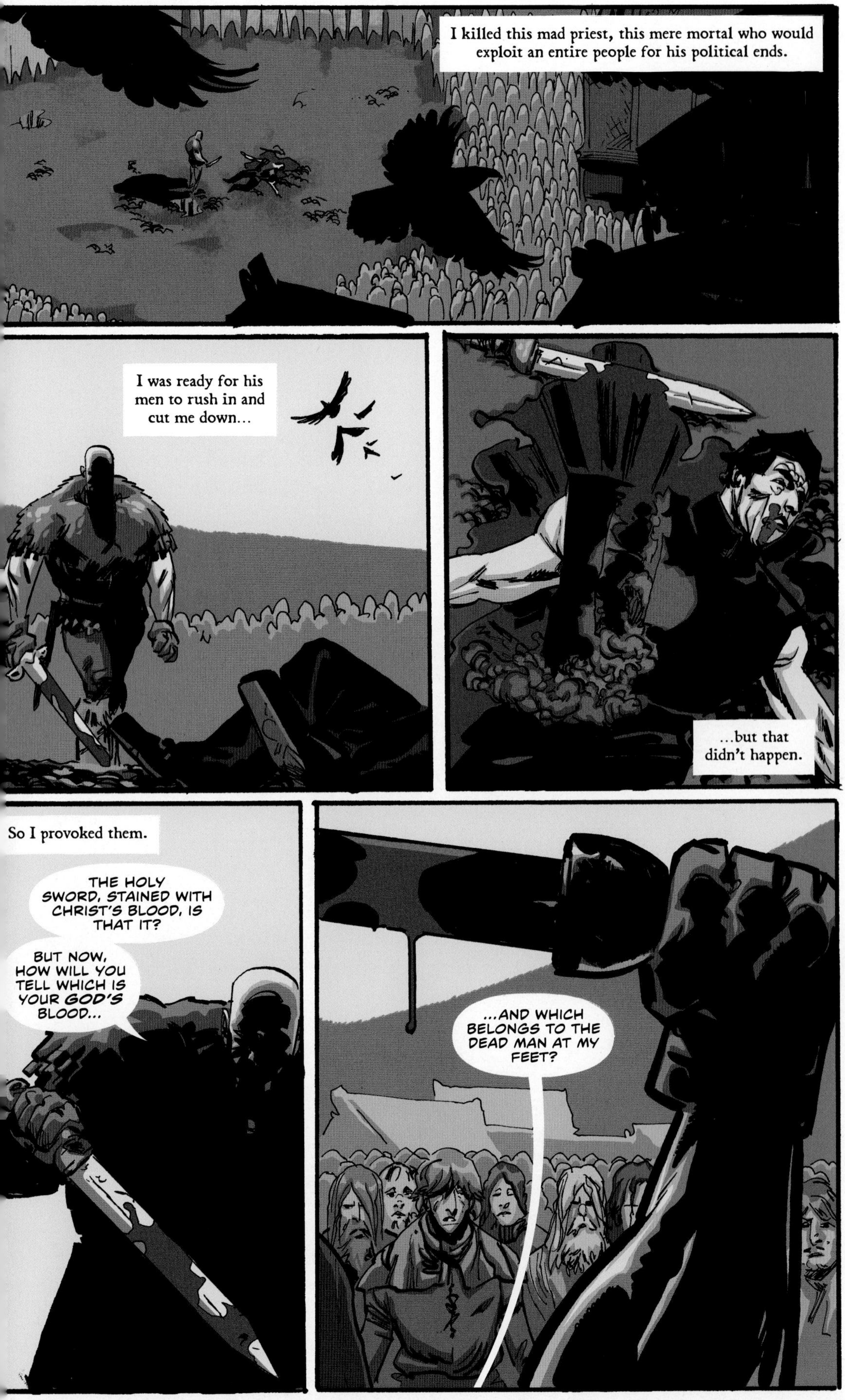

I killed this mad priest, this mere mortal who would exploit an entire people for his political ends.
I was ready for his men to rush in and cut me down…
…but that didn't happen.
So I provoked them.
THE HOLY SWORD, STAINED WITH CHRIST'S BLOOD, IS THAT IT?
BUT NOW, HOW WILL YOU TELL WHICH IS YOUR GOD'S BLOOD…
…AND WHICH BELONGS TO THE DEAD MAN AT MY FEET?

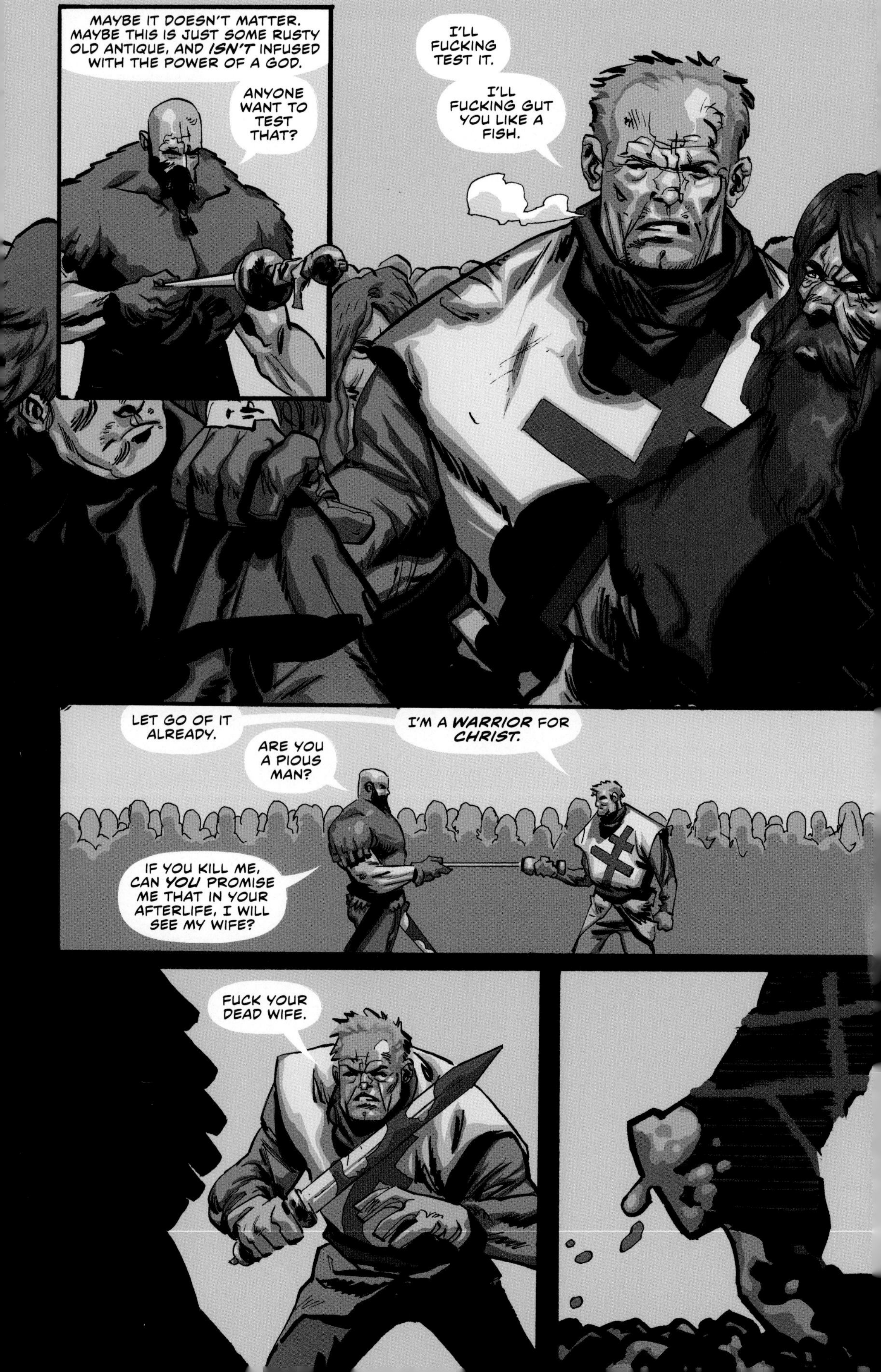

MAYBE IT DOESN'T MATTER. MAYBE THIS IS JUST SOME RUSTY OLD ANTIQUE, AND ISN'T INFUSED WITH THE POWER OF A GOD.
ANYONE WANT TO TEST THAT?
I'LL FUCKING TEST IT.
I'LL FUCKING GUT YOU LIKE A FISH.
LET GO OF IT ALREADY.
ARE YOU A PIOUS MAN?
I'M A WARRIOR FOR CHRIST.
IF YOU KILL ME, CAN YOU PROMISE ME THAT IN YOUR AFTERLIFE, I WILL SEE MY WIFE?
FUCK YOUR DEAD WIFE.

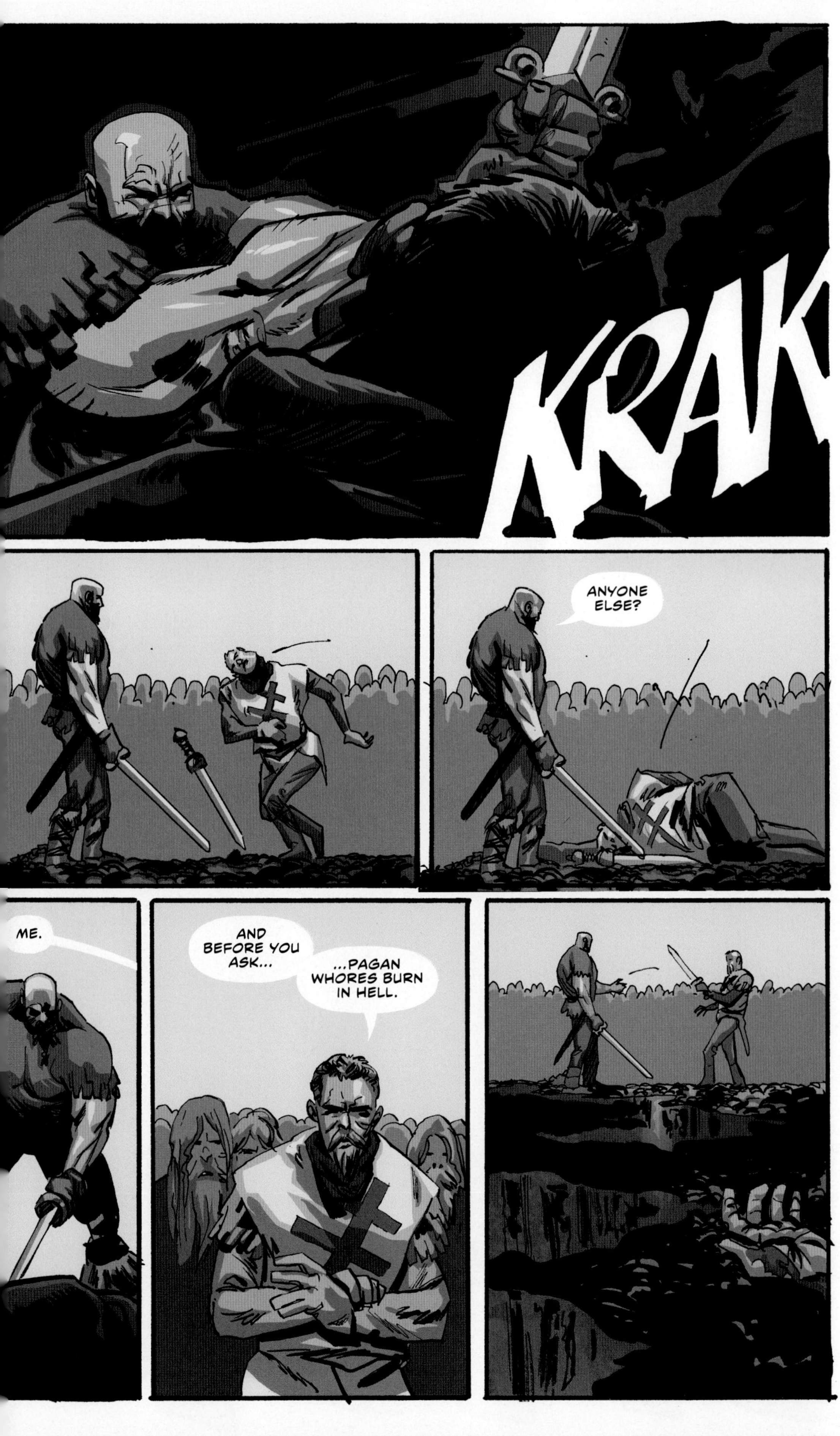
KRAK
ANYONE ELSE?
ME.
AND BEFORE YOU ASK...
...PAGAN WHORES BURN IN HELL.

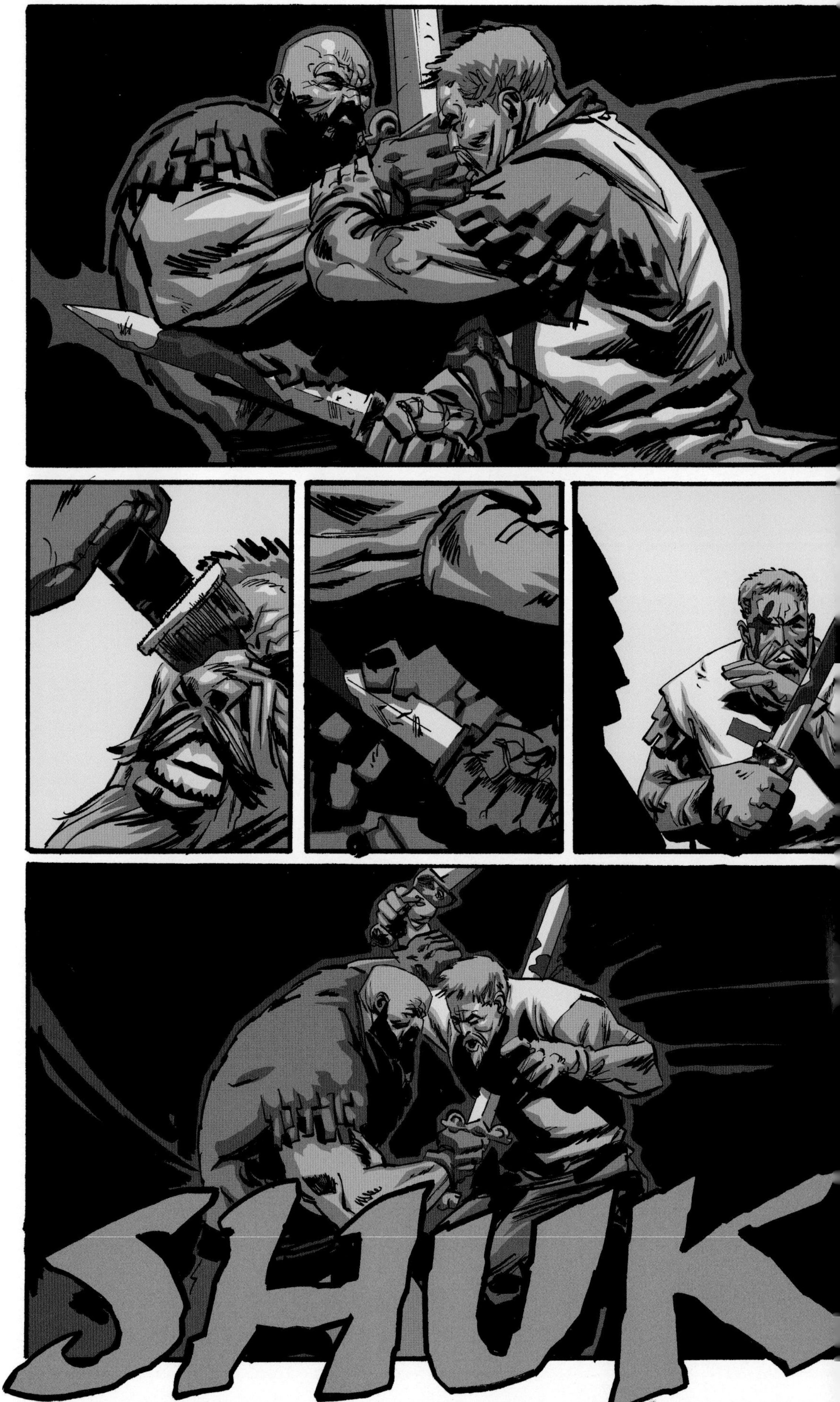
SHUK

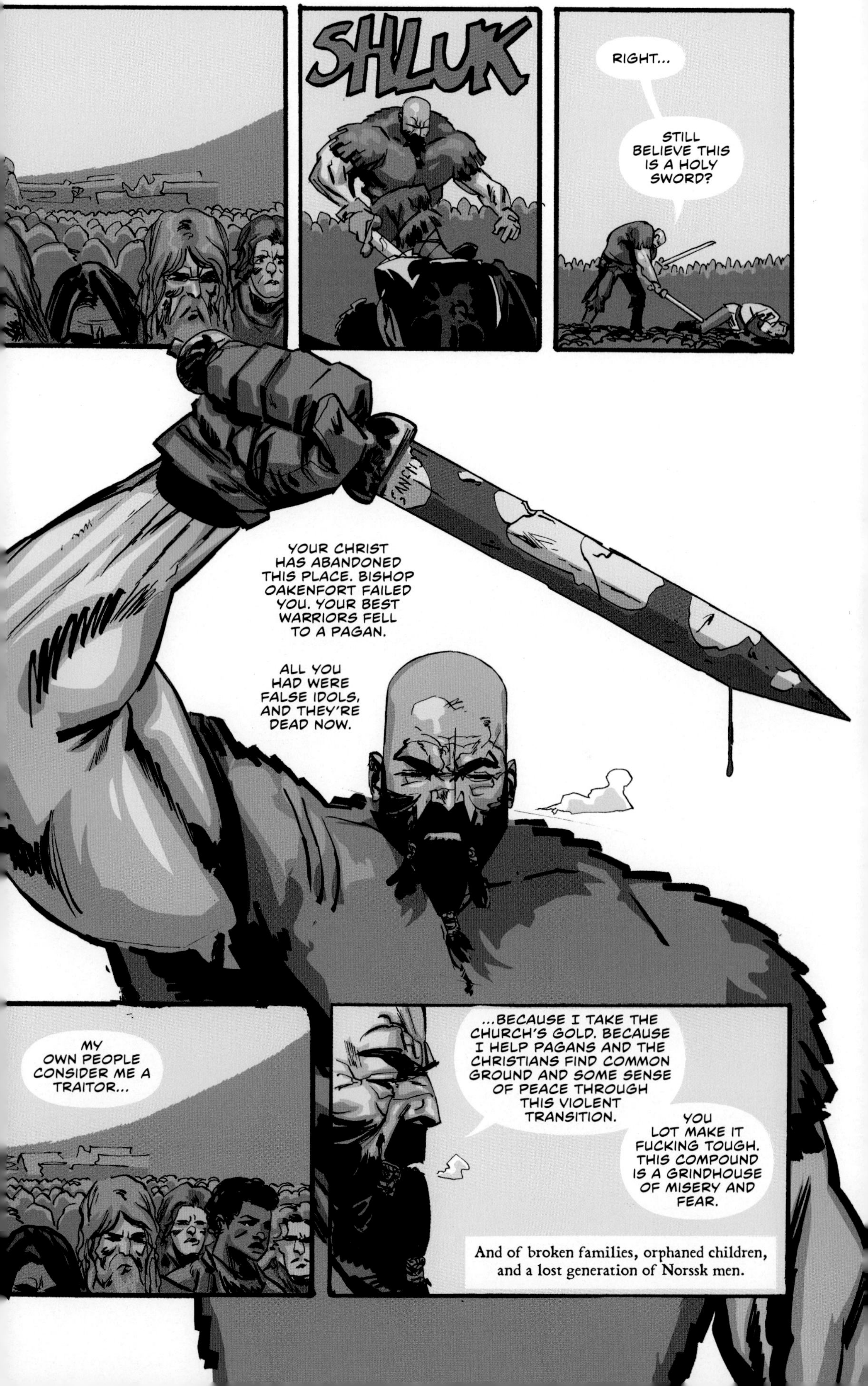
SHLUK
RIGHT...
STILL BELIEVE THIS IS A HOLY SWORD?
YOUR CHRIST HAS ABANDONED THIS PLACE. BISHOP OAKENFORT FAILED YOU. YOUR BEST WARRIORS FELL TO A PAGAN.
ALL YOU HAD WERE FALSE IDOLS, AND THEY'RE DEAD NOW.
MY OWN PEOPLE CONSIDER ME A TRAITOR...
...BECAUSE I TAKE THE CHURCH'S GOLD. BECAUSE I HELP PAGANS AND THE CHRISTIANS FIND COMMON GROUND AND SOME SENSE OF PEACE THROUGH THIS VIOLENT TRANSITION.
YOU LOT MAKE IT FUCKING TOUGH. THIS COMPOUND IS A GRINDHOUSE OF MISERY AND FEAR.
And of broken families, orphaned children, and a lost generation of Norssk men.

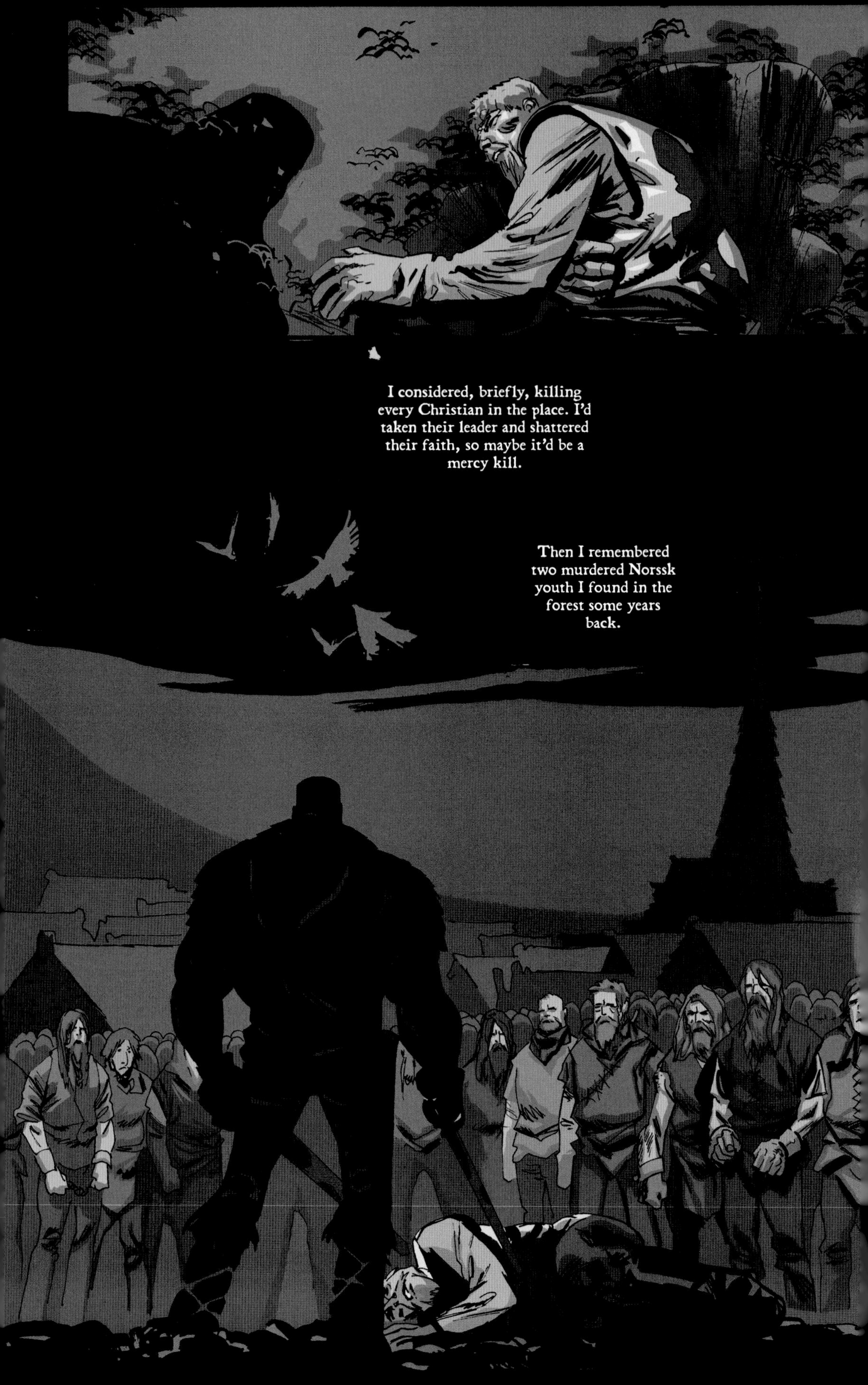
I considered, briefly, killing every Christian in the place. I'd taken their leader and shattered their faith, so maybe it'd be a mercy kill.
Then I remembered two murdered Norssk youth I found in the forest some years back.

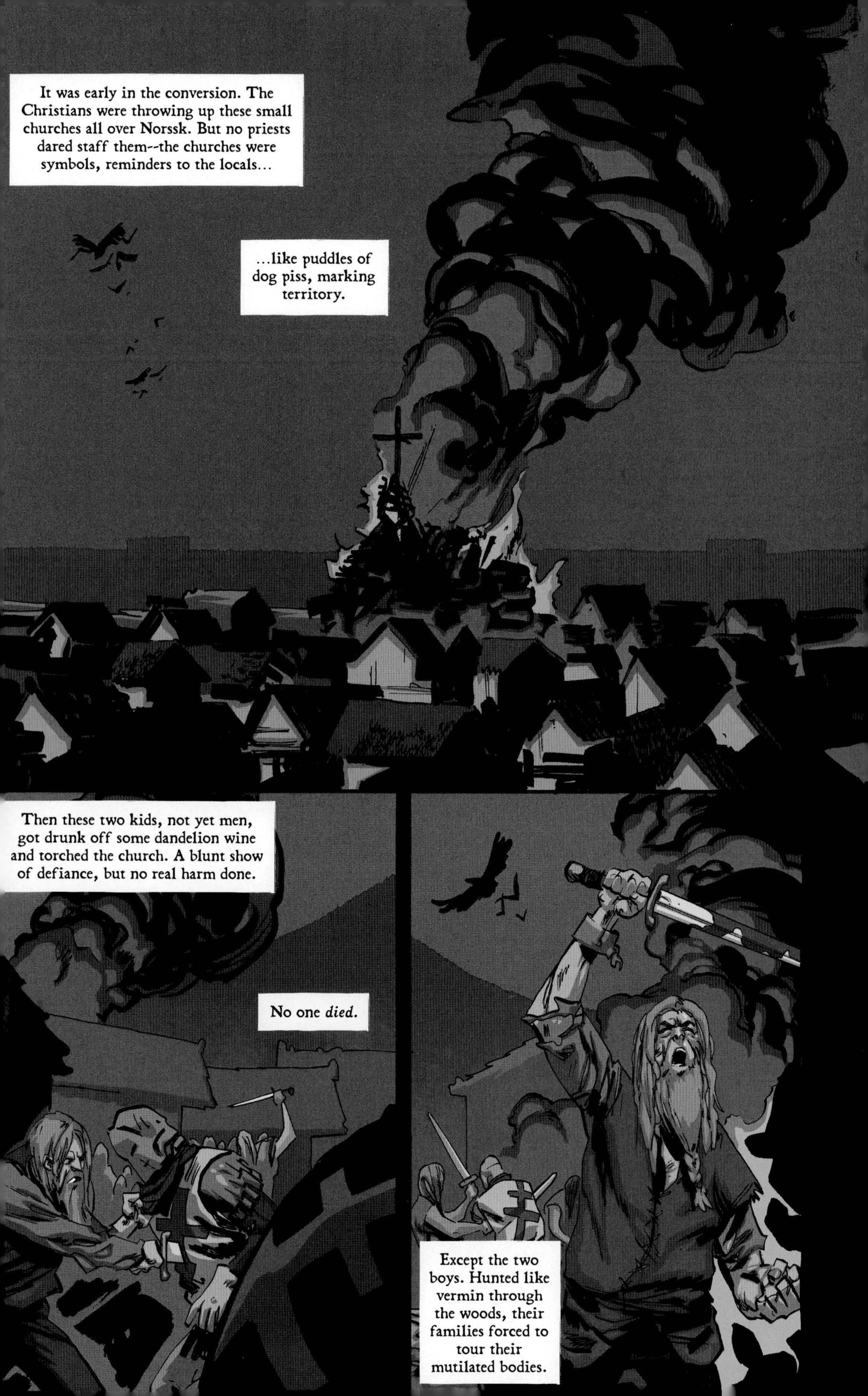
It was early in the conversion. The Christians were throwing up these small churches all over Norssk. But no priests dared staff them--the churches were symbols, reminders to the locals...
...like puddles of dog piss, marking territory.
Then these two kids, not yet men, got drunk off some dandelion wine and torched the church. A blunt show of defiance, but no real harm done.
No one *died.*
Except the two boys. Hunted like vermin through the woods, their families forced to tour their mutilated bodies.

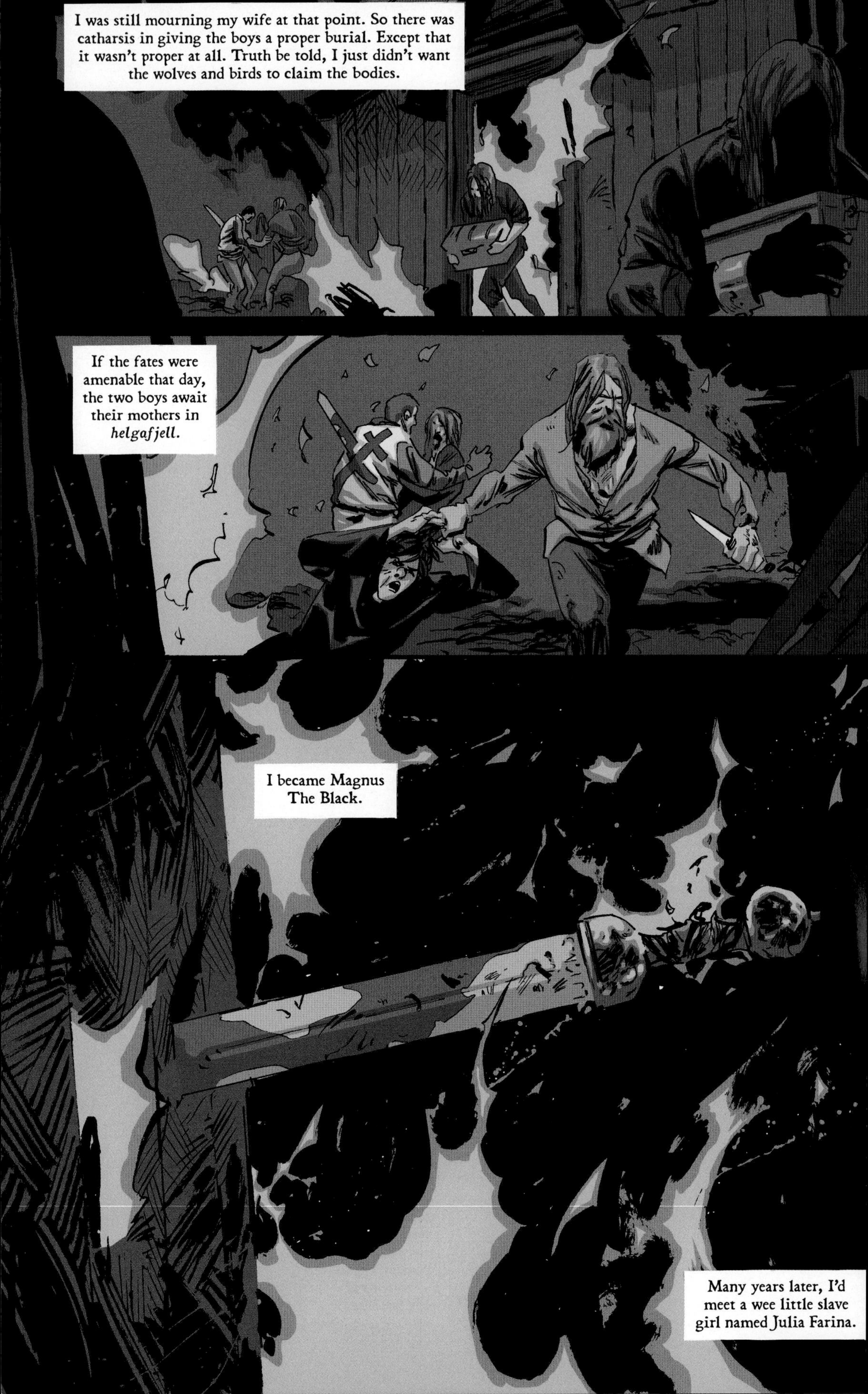
I was still mourning my wife at that point. So there was catharsis in giving the boys a proper burial. Except that it wasn't proper at all. Truth be told, I just didn't want the wolves and birds to claim the bodies.
If the fates were amenable that day, the two boys await their mothers in *helgafjell*.
I became Magnus The Black.
Many years later, I'd meet a wee little slave girl named Julia Farina.

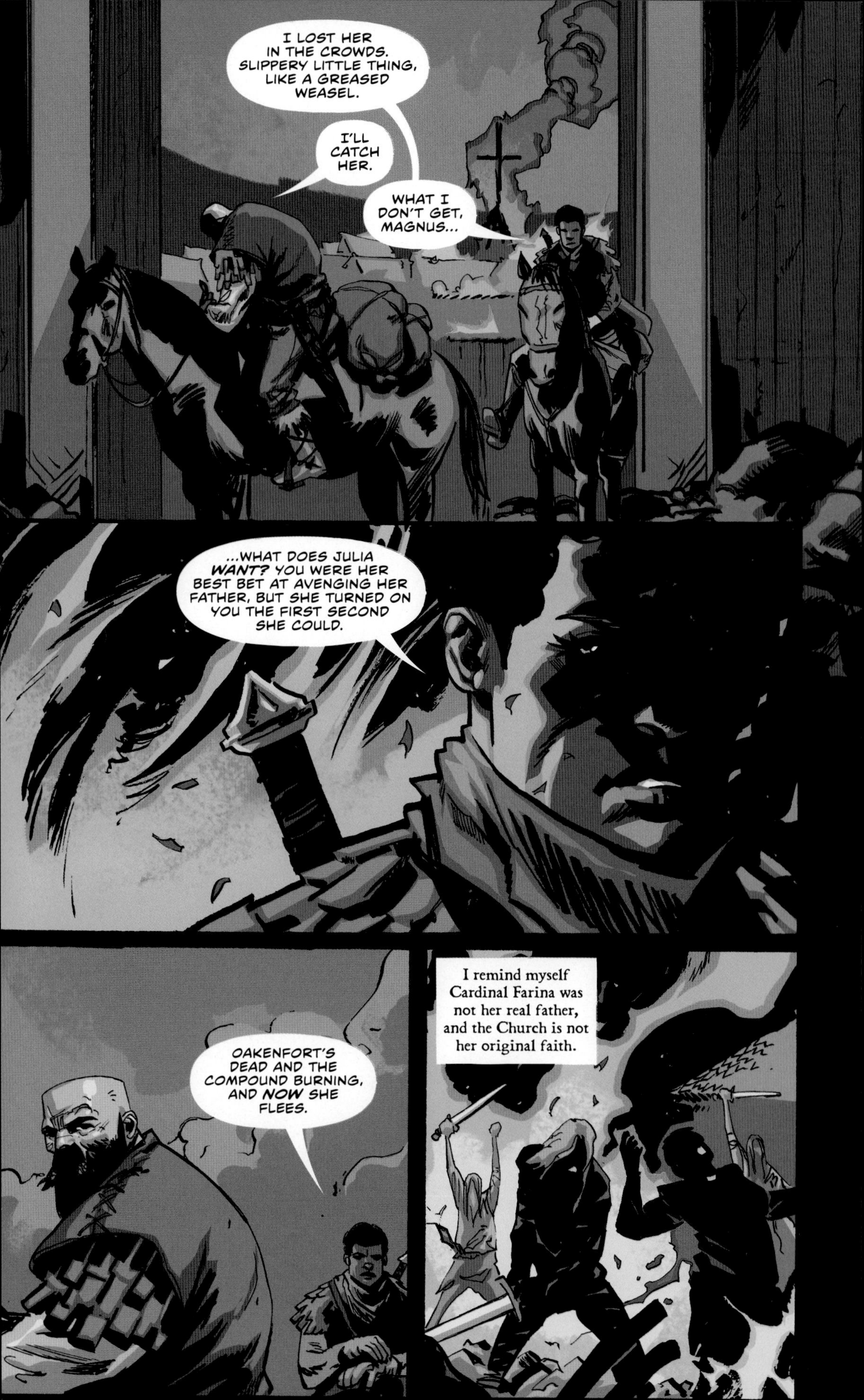
I LOST HER IN THE CROWDS. SLIPPERY LITTLE THING, LIKE A GREASED WEASEL.
I'LL CATCH HER.
WHAT I DON'T GET, MAGNUS...
...WHAT DOES JULIA *WANT?* YOU WERE HER BEST BET AT AVENGING HER FATHER, BUT SHE TURNED ON YOU THE FIRST SECOND SHE COULD.
OAKENFORT'S DEAD AND THE COMPOUND BURNING, AND *NOW* SHE FLEES.
I remind myself Cardinal Farina was not her real father, and the Church is not her original faith.

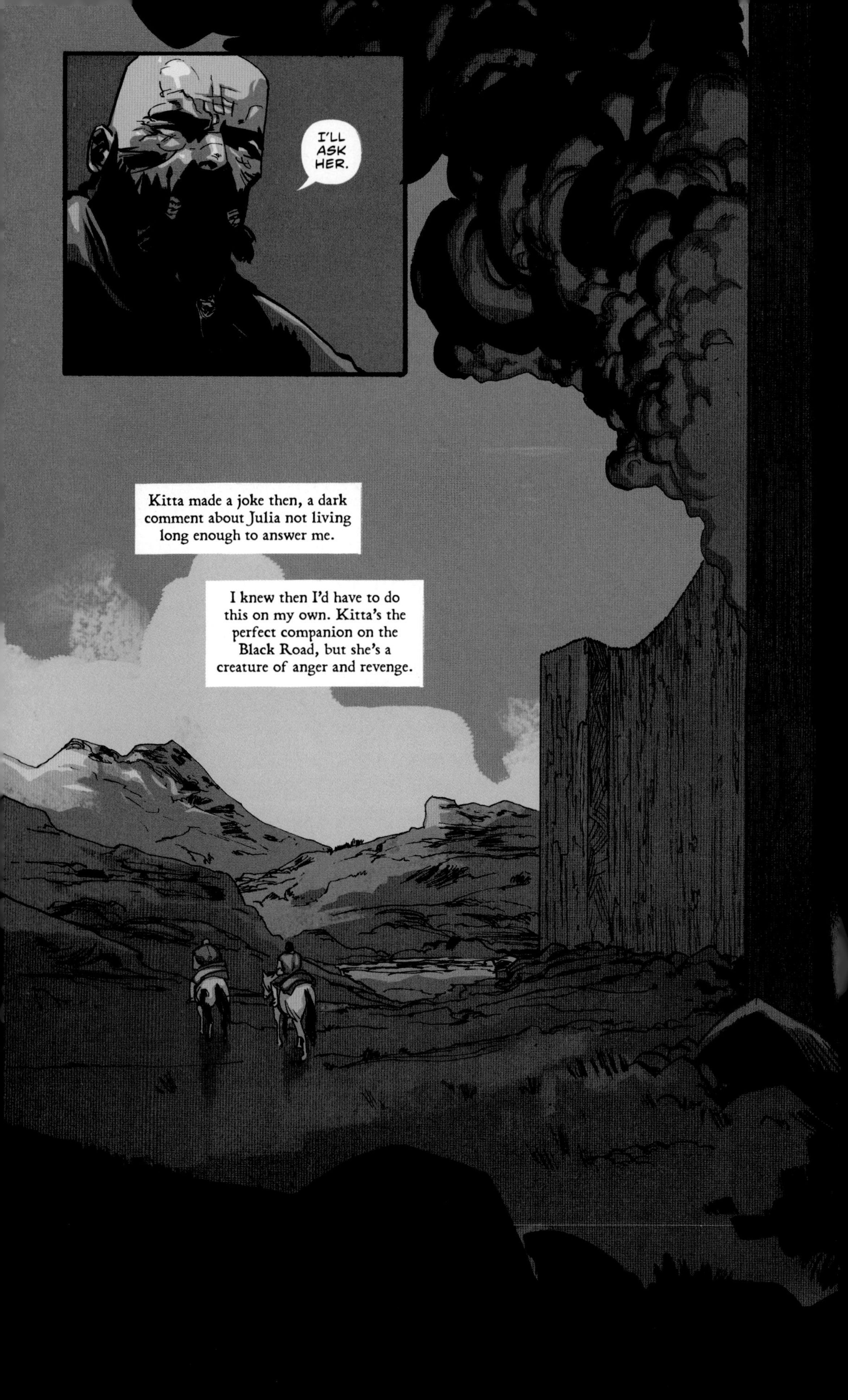
I'LL ASK HER.
Kitta made a joke then, a dark comment about Julia not living long enough to answer me.
I knew then I'd have to do this on my own. Kitta's the perfect companion on the Black Road, but she's a creature of anger and revenge.

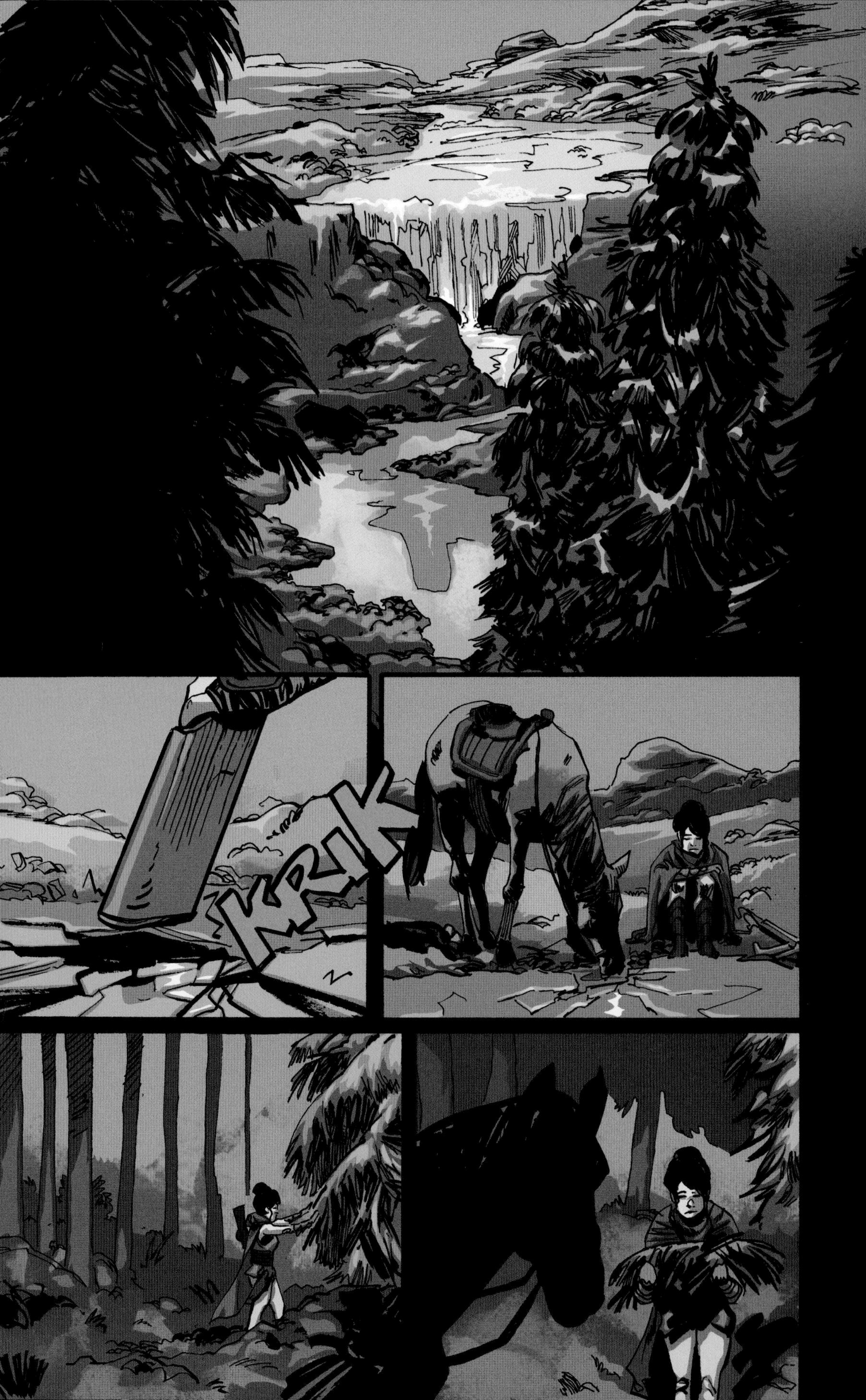
KRIK

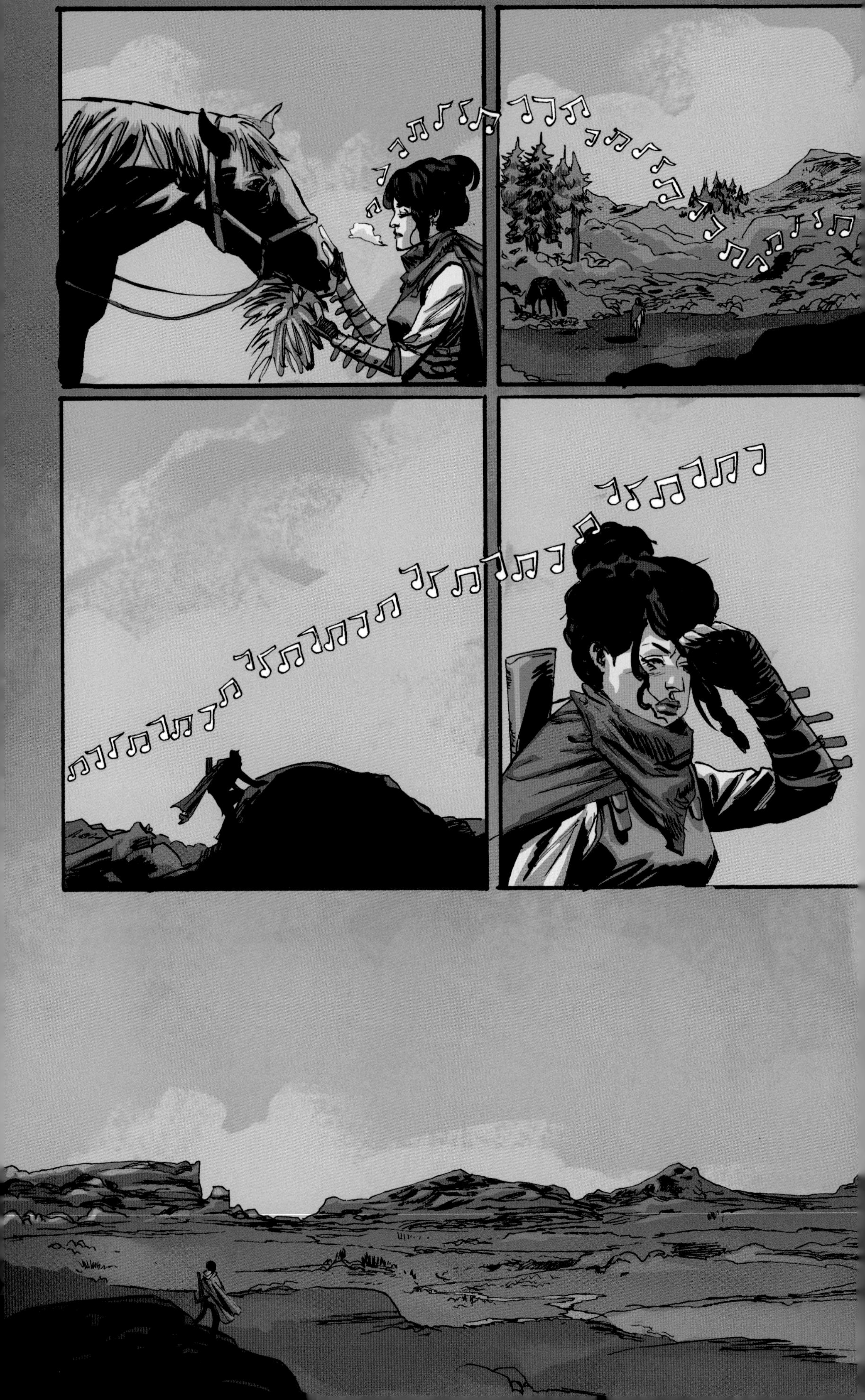

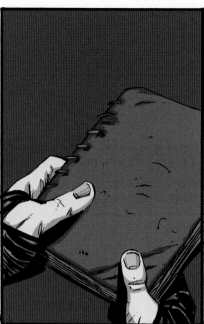

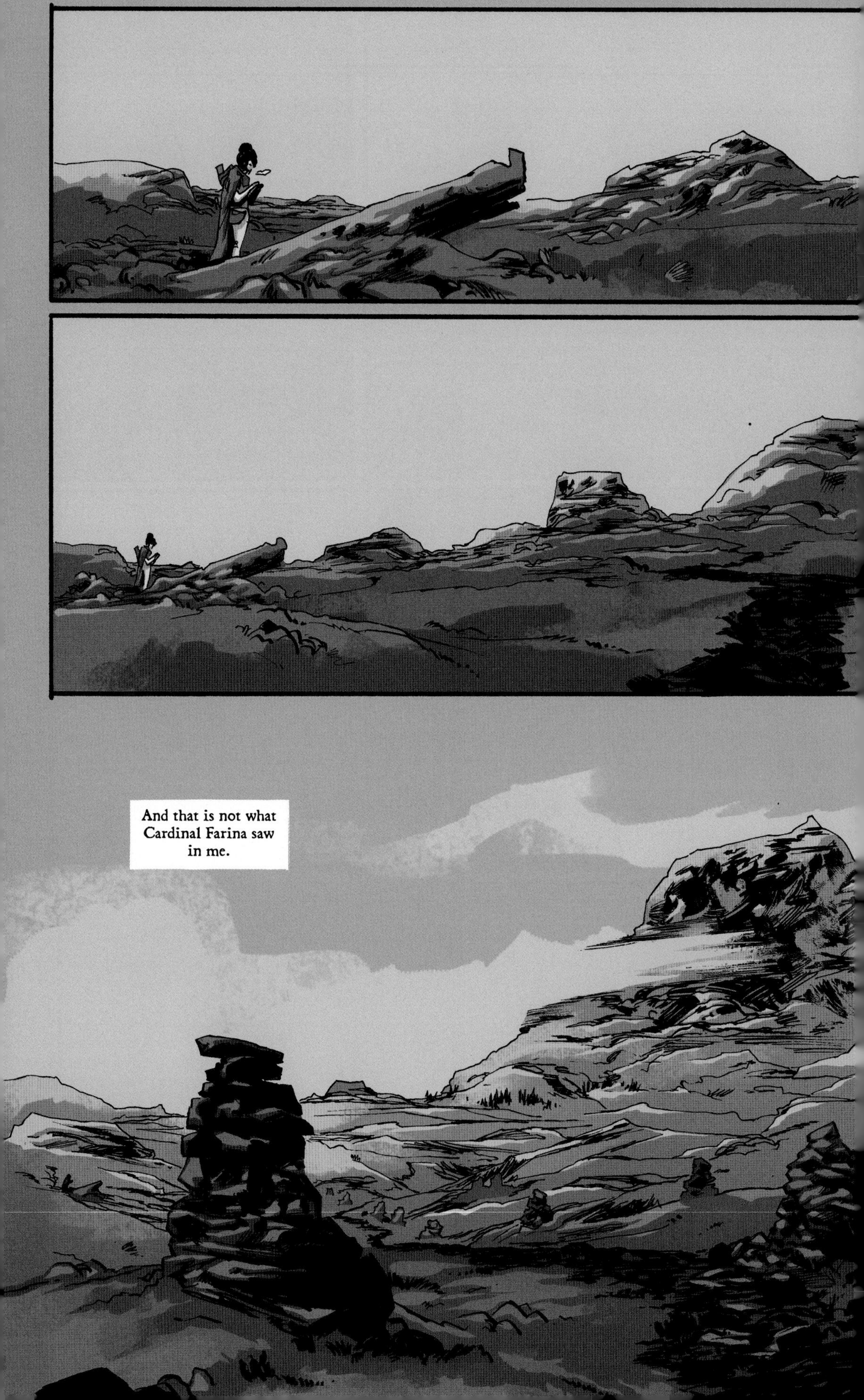
And that is not what Cardinal Farina saw in me.

A MAGNUS THE BLACK MYSTERY

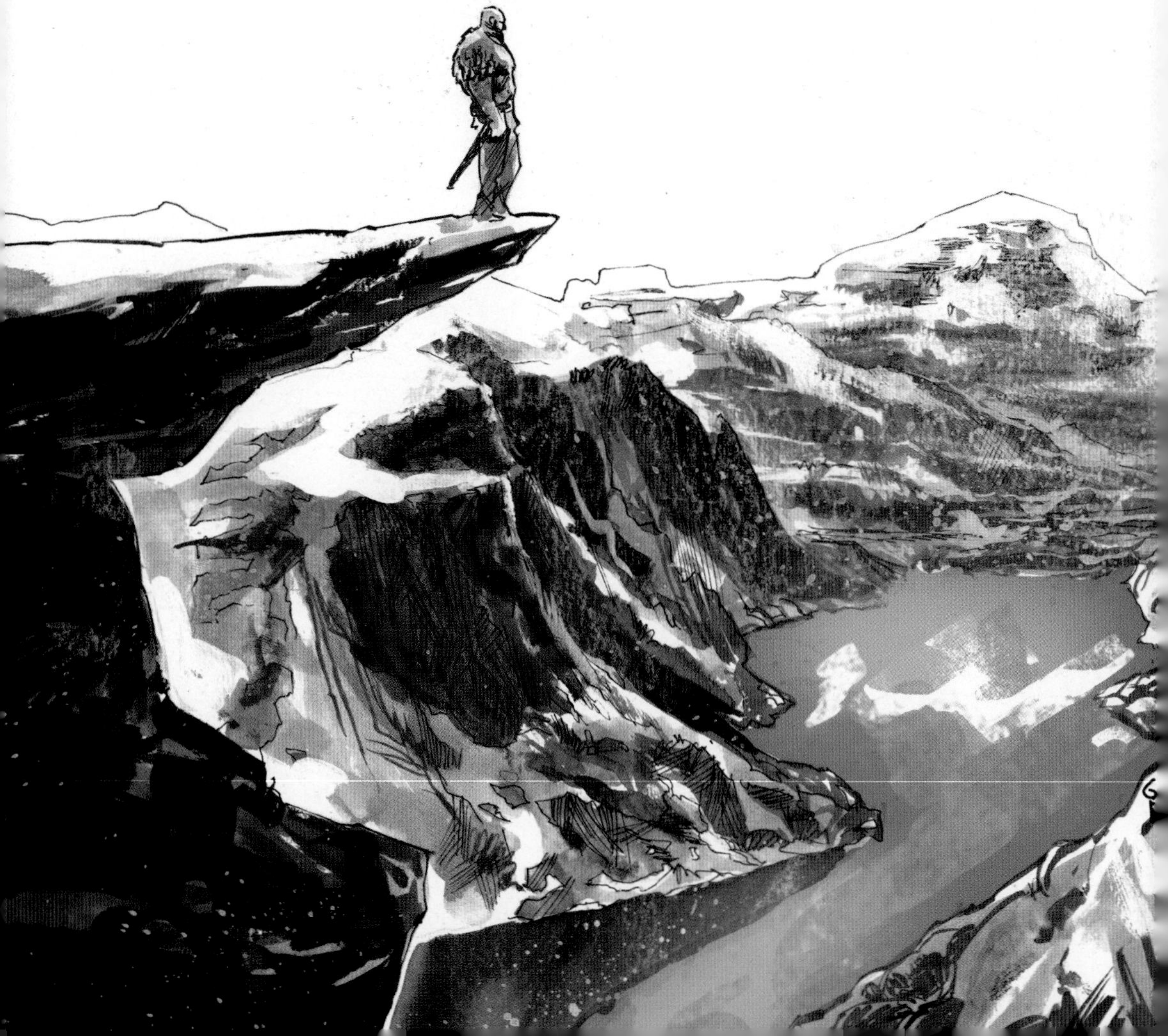

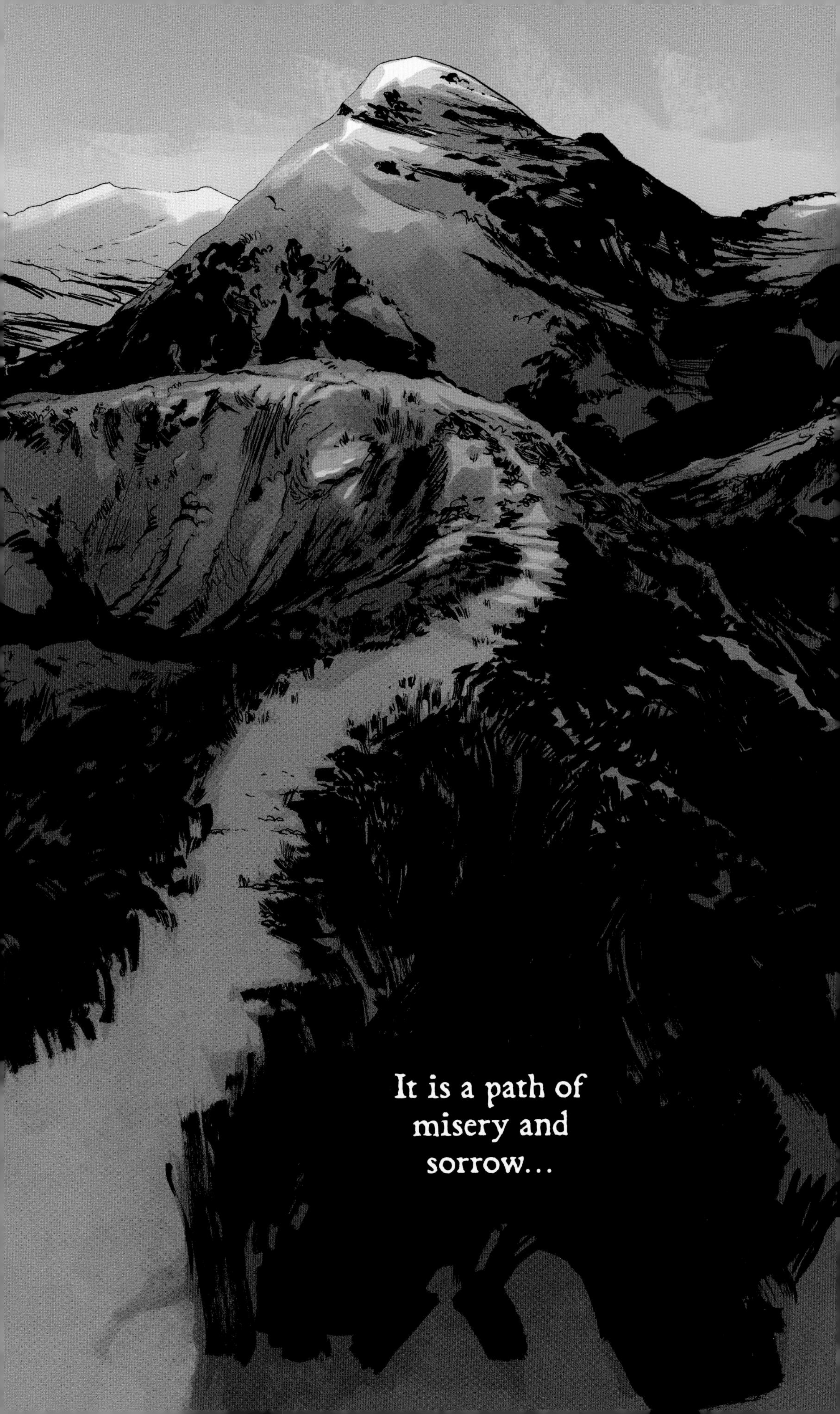
It is a path of misery and sorrow...

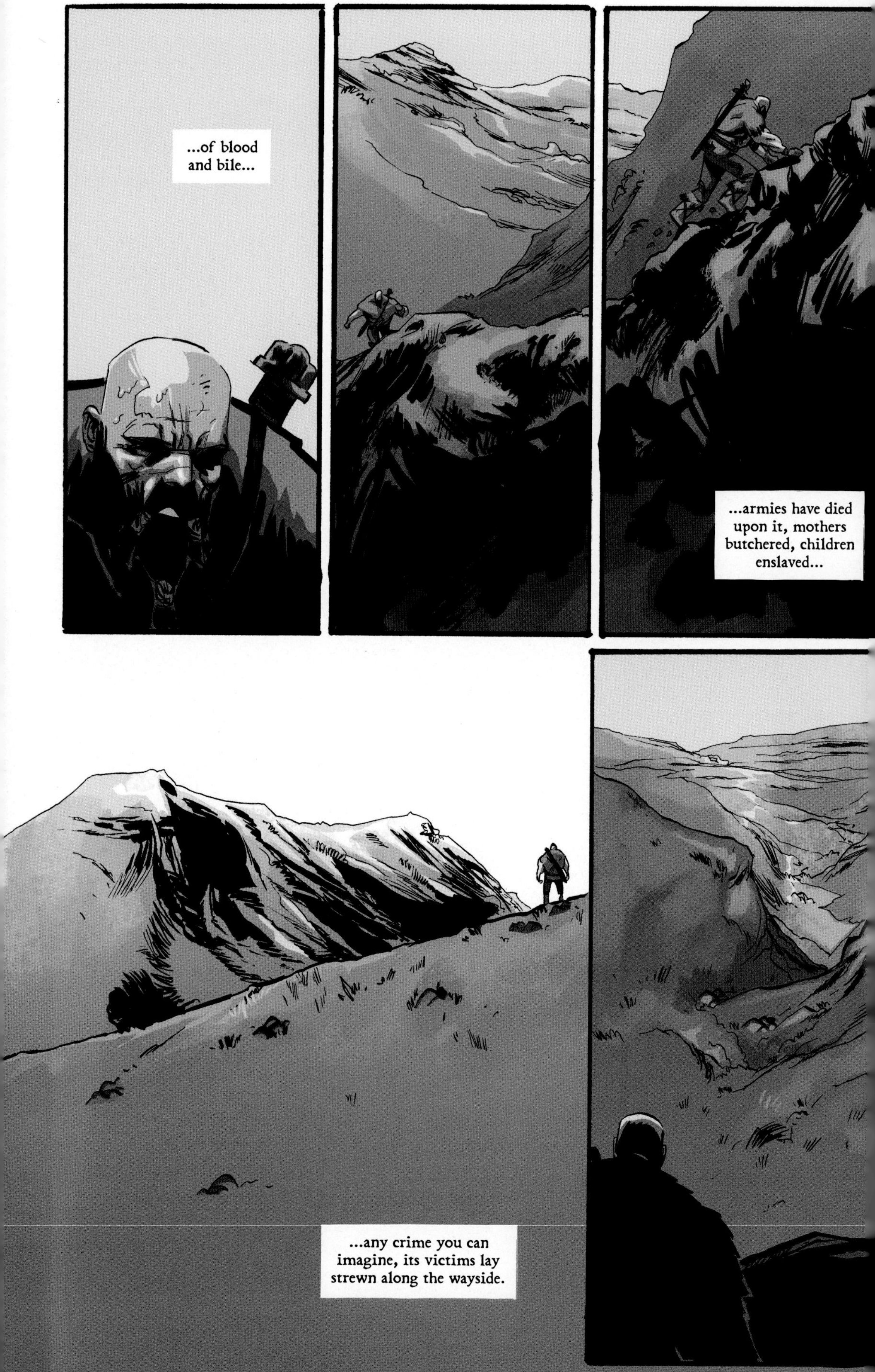
...of blood and bile...
...armies have died upon it, mothers butchered, children enslaved...
...any crime you can imagine, its victims lay strewn along the wayside.

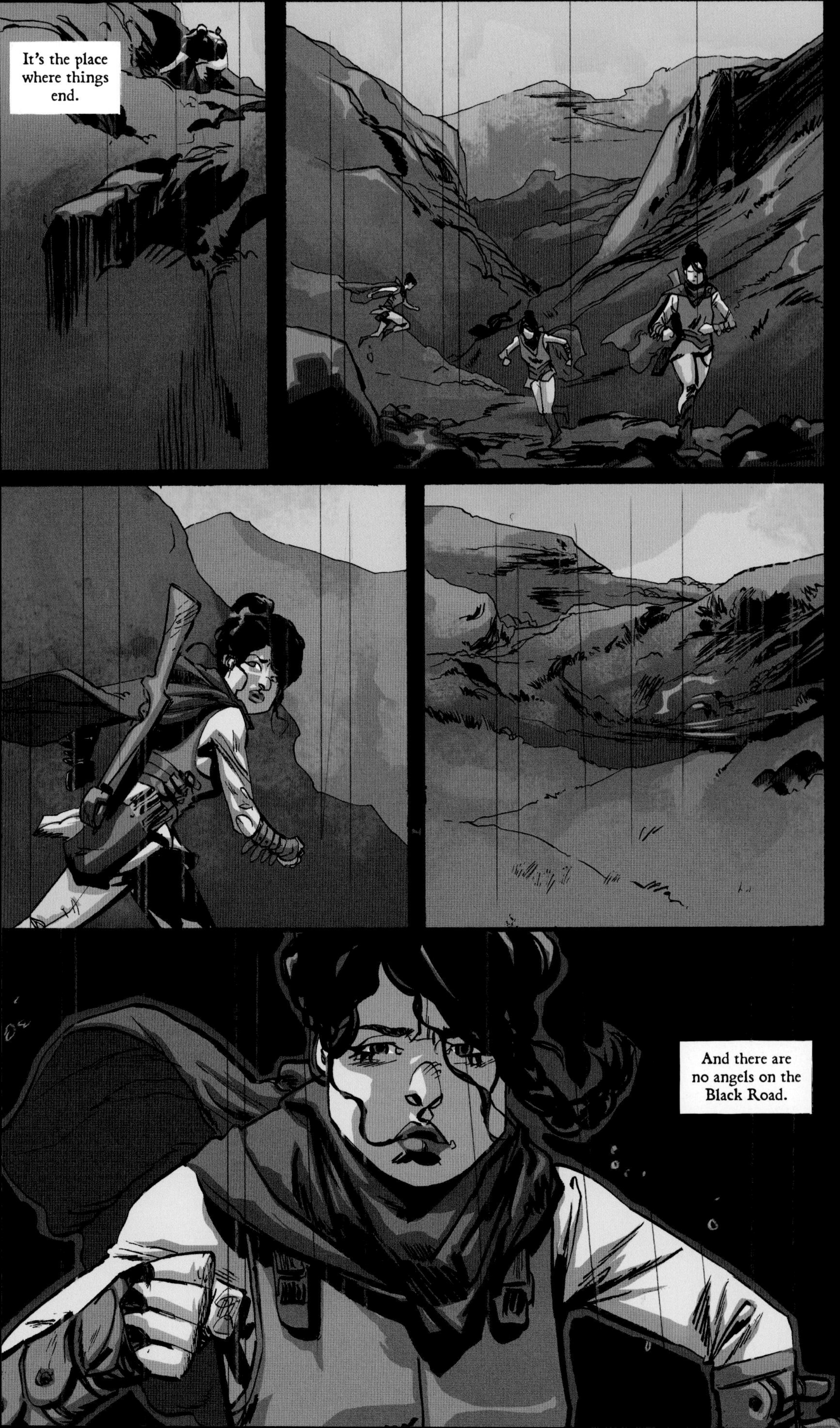
It's the place where things end.
And there are no angels on the Black Road.

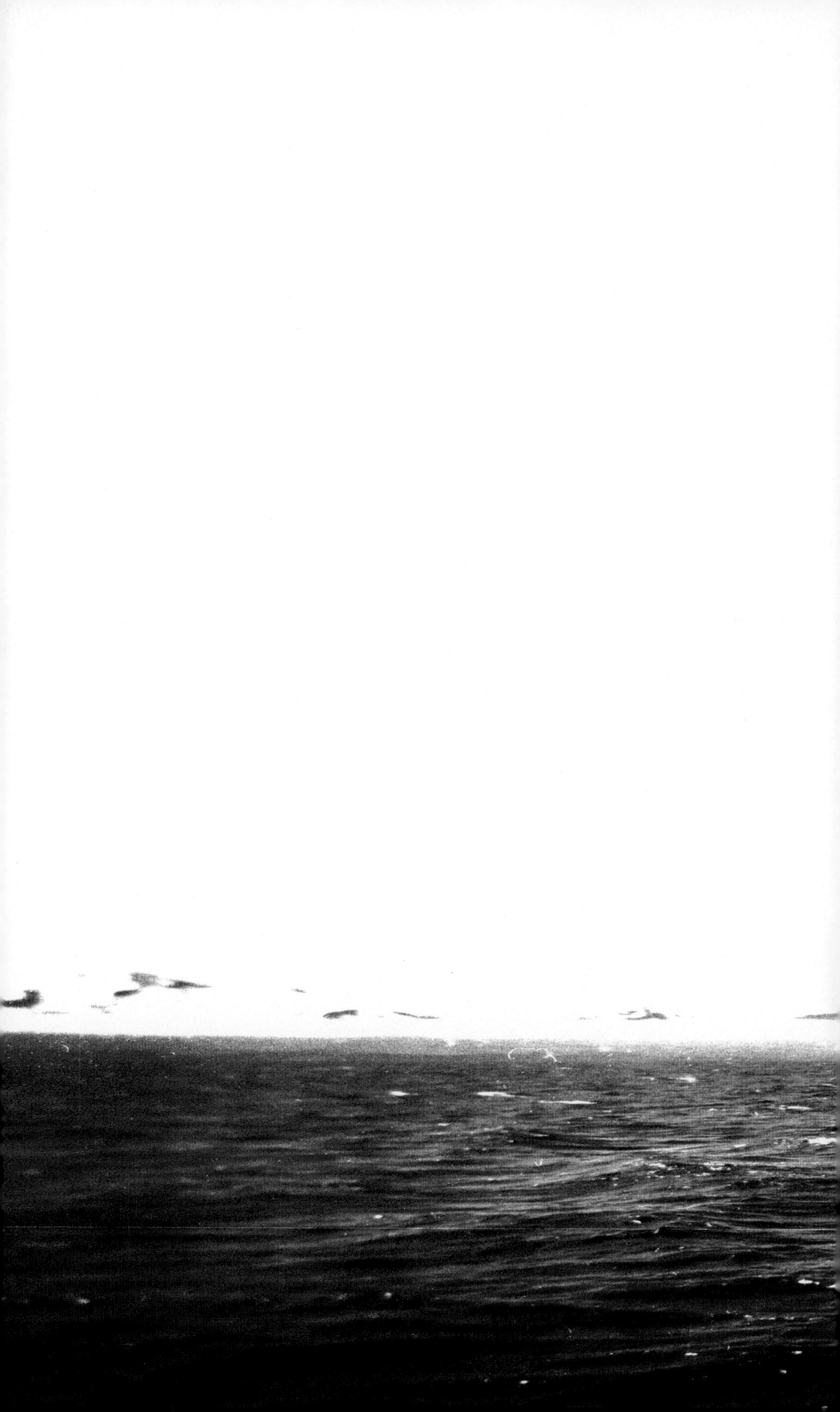

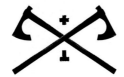

BRIAN WOOD / GARRY BROWN / DAVE McCAIG / STEVE WANDS

BLACK ROAD

#10 - "MAGNUS THE BLACK"

A MAGNUS THE BLACK MYSTERY

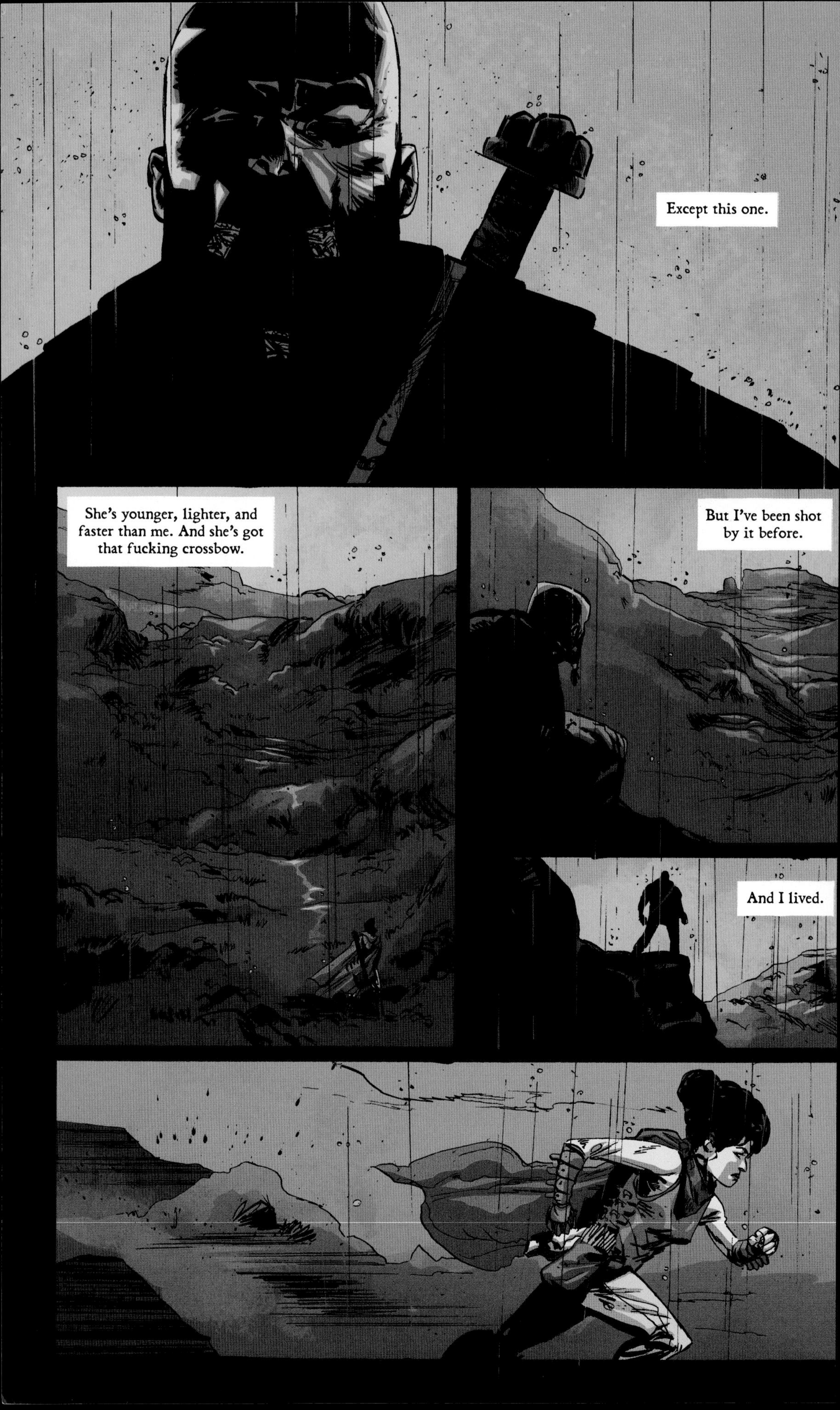
Except this one.
She's younger, lighter, and faster than me. And she's got that fucking crossbow.
But I've been shot by it before.
And I lived.

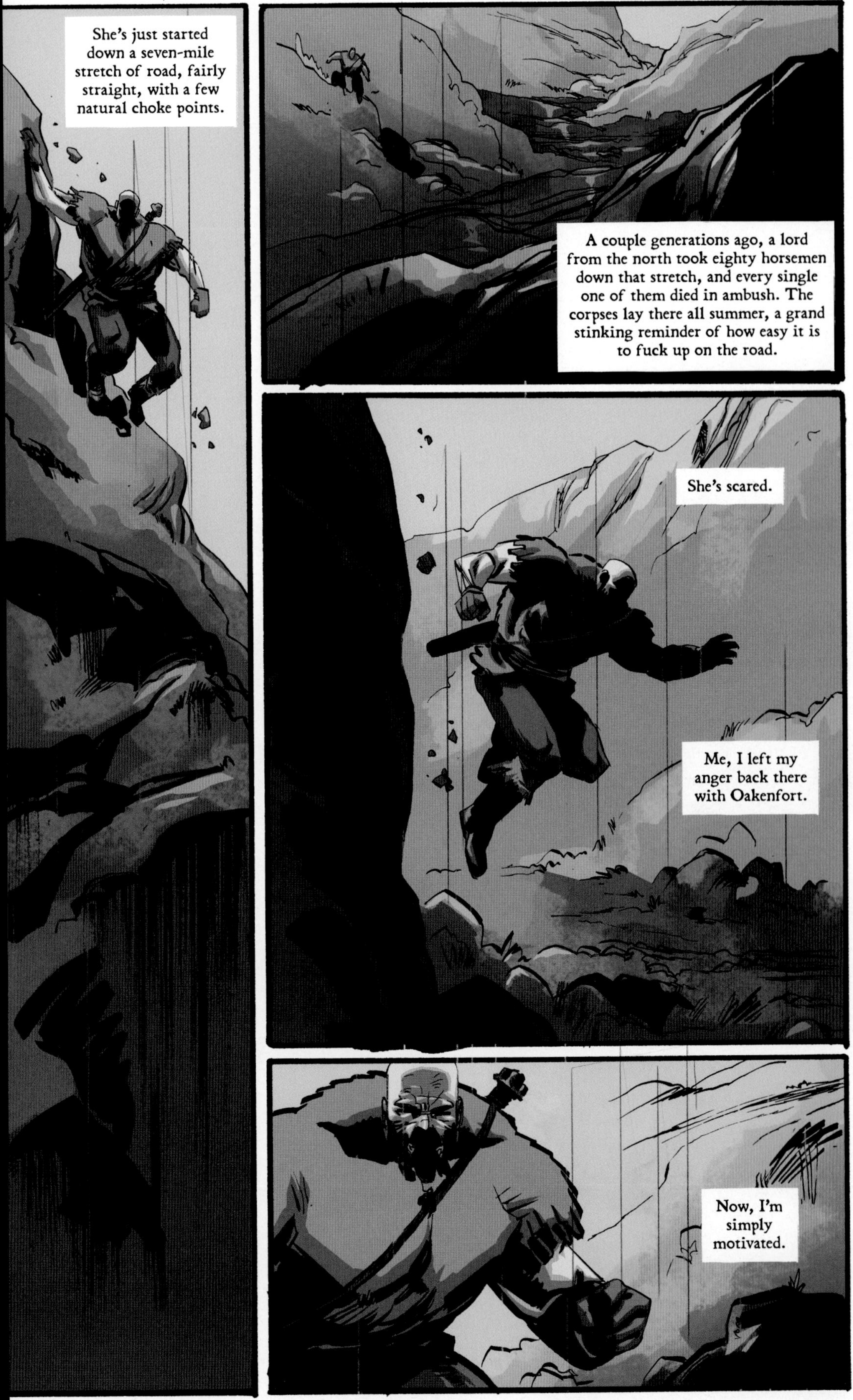
She's just started down a seven-mile stretch of road, fairly straight, with a few natural choke points.
A couple generations ago, a lord from the north took eighty horsemen down that stretch, and every single one of them died in ambush. The corpses lay there all summer, a grand stinking reminder of how easy it is to fuck up on the road.
She's scared.
Me, I left my anger back there with Oakenfort.
Now, I'm simply motivated.

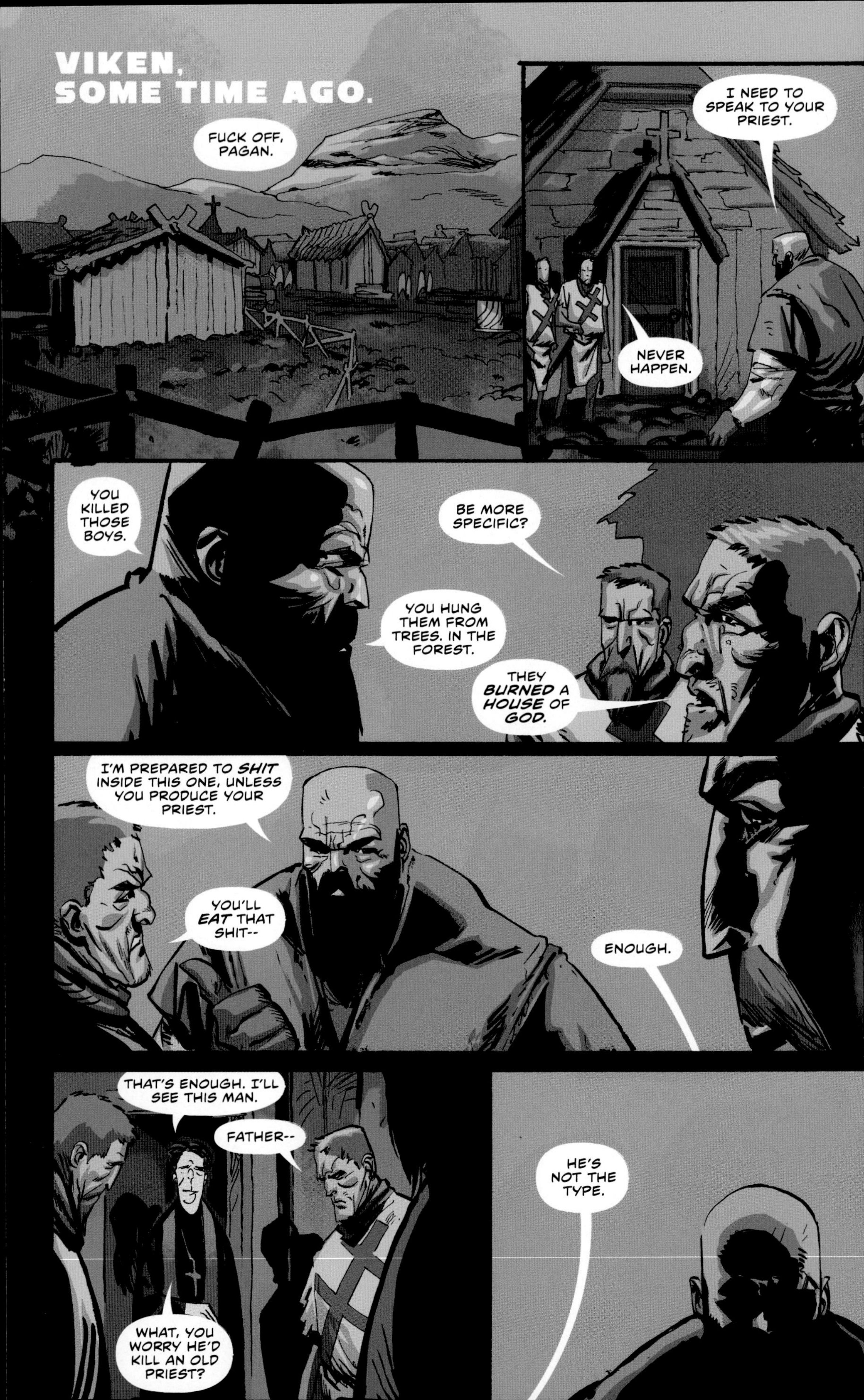
VIKEN, SOME TIME AGO.
FUCK OFF, PAGAN.
I NEED TO SPEAK TO YOUR PRIEST.
NEVER HAPPEN.
YOU KILLED THOSE BOYS.
BE MORE SPECIFIC?
YOU HUNG THEM FROM TREES. IN THE FOREST.
THEY BURNED A HOUSE OF GOD.
I'M PREPARED TO SHIT INSIDE THIS ONE, UNLESS YOU PRODUCE YOUR PRIEST.
YOU'LL EAT THAT SHIT--
ENOUGH.
THAT'S ENOUGH. I'LL SEE THIS MAN.
FATHER--
WHAT, YOU WORRY HE'D KILL AN OLD PRIEST?
HE'S NOT THE TYPE.

NOT MUCH TO LOOK AT, I KNOW.

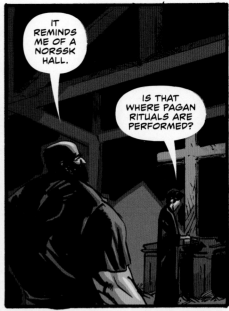

IT REMINDS ME OF A NORSSK HALL.

IS THAT WHERE PAGAN RITUALS ARE PERFORMED?

WE DON'T NEED A SPECIAL BUILDING TO TALK TO OUR GODS, PRIEST. OUR GODS ARE EVERYWHERE.

AS THEY SHOULD BE.

HERE WE ARE.

WHAT'S THAT FOR?

RESTITUTION. FOR THE FAMILIES OF THE BOYS. THAT'S WHY YOU CAME, ISN'T IT?

One fucking silver coin.

Maybe I *could* kill a priest.

THEY *DID* BURN DOWN A CHURCH.

AND THAT CARRIES A *DEATH SENTENCE,* IN ANY PART OF CHRISTENDOM YOU CAN NAME.

PRIEST, I'M A SWORD-NORSSK, NOT A POLITICIAN OR A RELIGIOUS MAN. BUT I'M ALSO NOT AN IDIOT.

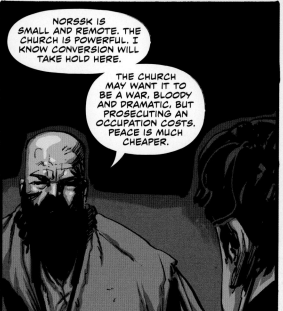

NORSSK IS SMALL AND REMOTE. THE CHURCH IS POWERFUL. I KNOW CONVERSION WILL TAKE HOLD HERE.

THE CHURCH MAY WANT IT TO BE A WAR, BLOODY AND DRAMATIC, BUT PROSECUTING AN OCCUPATION COSTS. PEACE IS MUCH CHEAPER.

WHAT DO YOU PROPOSE?

AN ALLIANCE.

YOU AND I, FOR STARTERS. LET'S SEE NO MORE CHURCHES BURNED, AND NO NORSSK HANGING FROM TREES. LET PEOPLE ADJUST, LET THEM COME TO GRIPS WITH THEIR CHANGING WORLD.

ROME IS FAR FROM HERE, AND MY CONSULTING WITH A PAGAN WILL GO UNNOTICED. BUT YOU...

...YOUR PEOPLE WILL CALL YOU A TRAITOR.

I CAN LIVE WITH THAT.

BUT I NEED ONE THING FROM YOU FIRST.

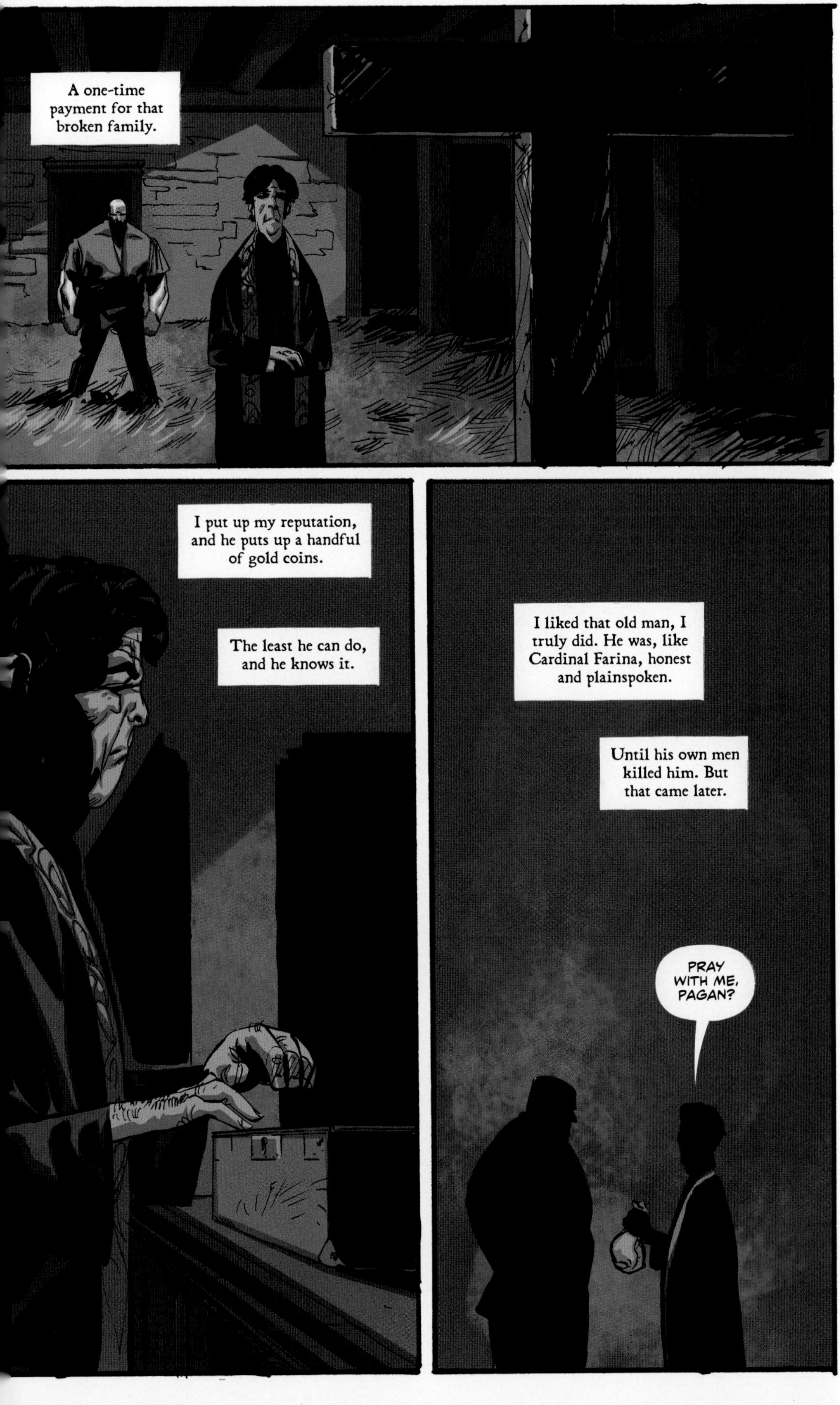
A one-time payment for that broken family.
I put up my reputation, and he puts up a handful of gold coins.
The least he can do, and he knows it.
I liked that old man, I truly did. He was, like Cardinal Farina, honest and plainspoken.
Until his own men killed him. But that came later.
PRAY WITH ME, PAGAN?

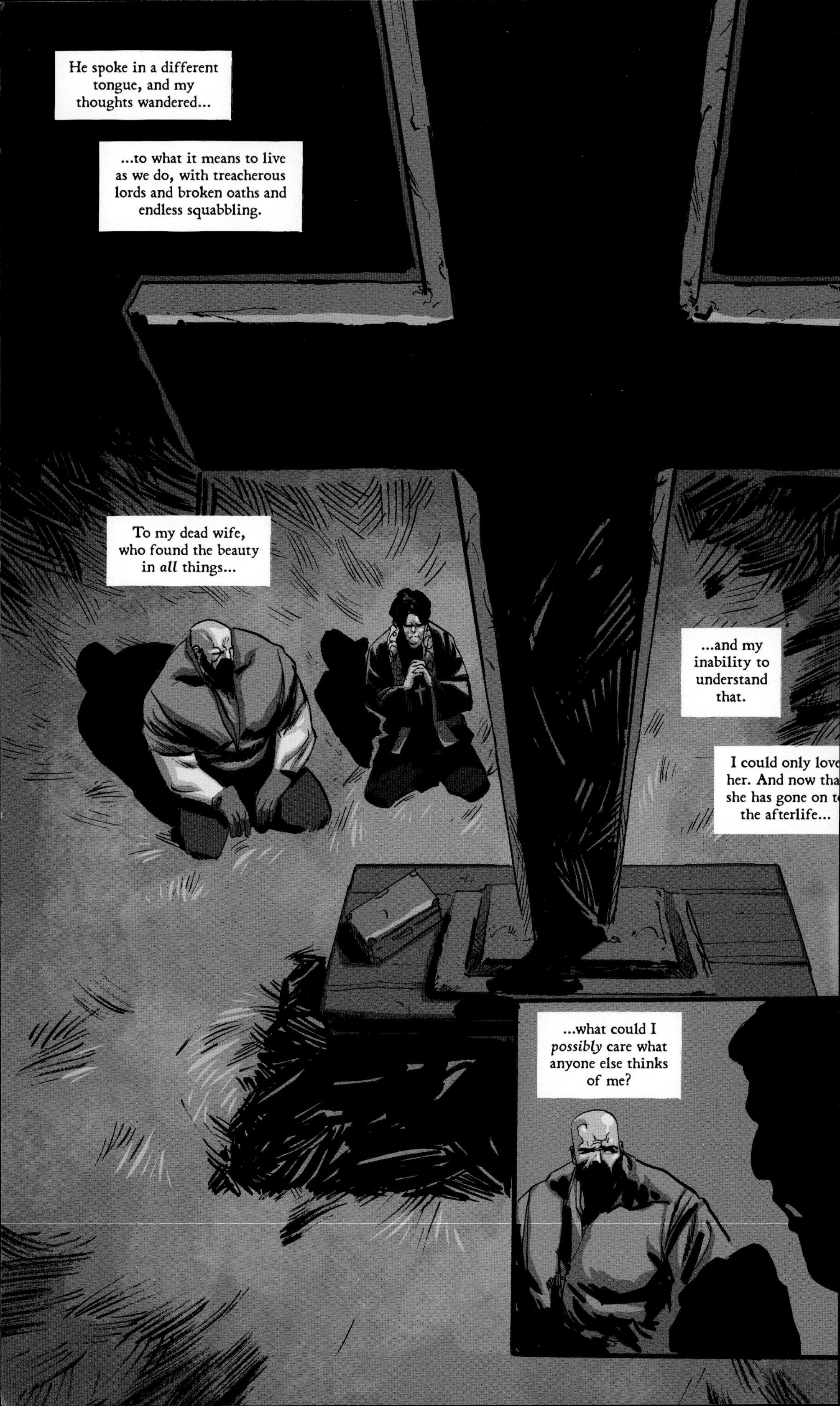
He spoke in a different tongue, and my thoughts wandered...
...to what it means to live as we do, with treacherous lords and broken oaths and endless squabbling.
To my dead wife, who found the beauty in *all* things...
...and my inability to understand that.
I could only love her. And now that she has gone on to the afterlife...
...what could I *possibly* care what anyone else thinks of me?

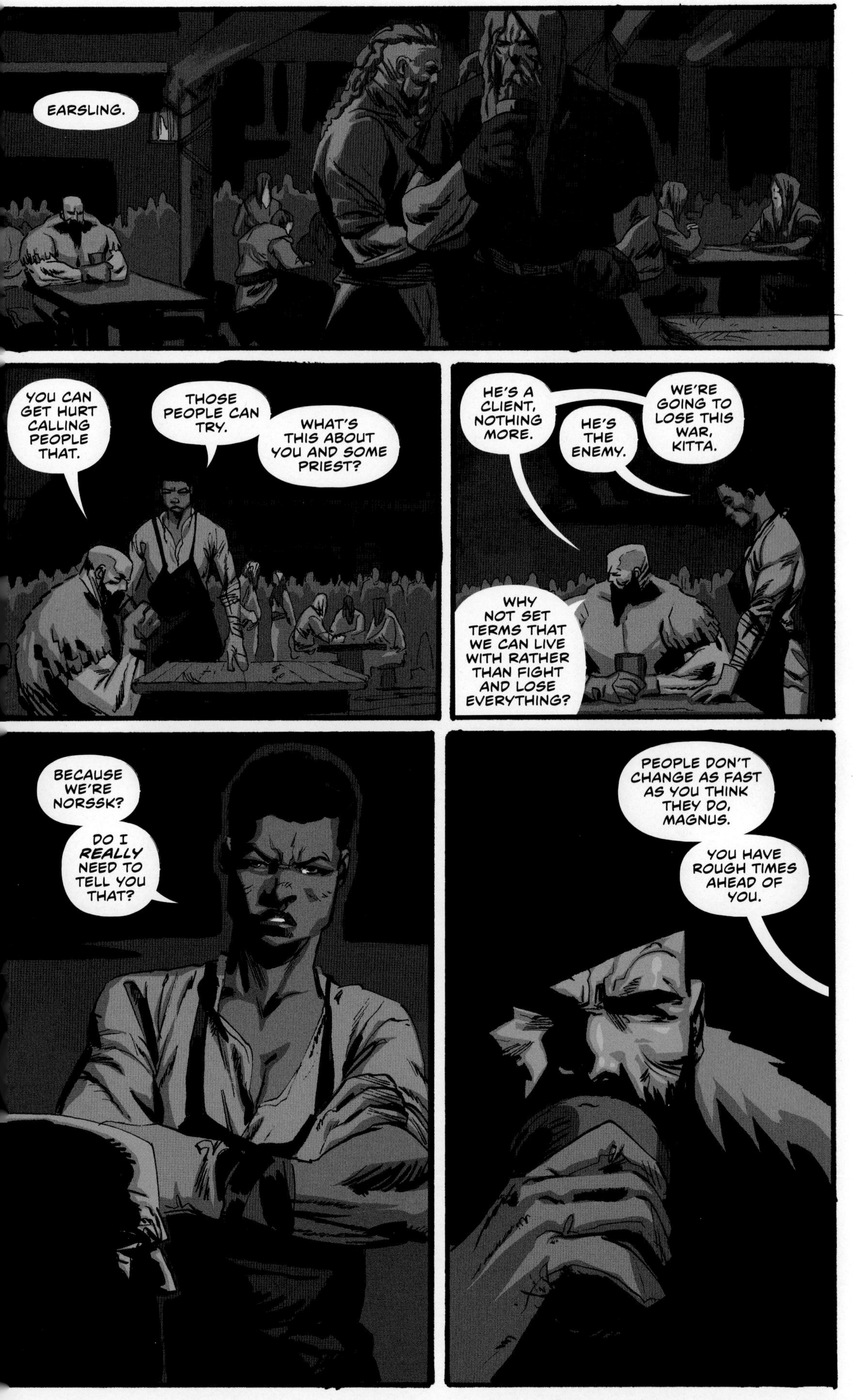
EARSLING.
YOU CAN GET HURT CALLING PEOPLE THAT.
THOSE PEOPLE CAN TRY.
WHAT'S THIS ABOUT YOU AND SOME PRIEST?
HE'S A CLIENT, NOTHING MORE.
HE'S THE ENEMY.
WE'RE GOING TO LOSE THIS WAR, KITTA.
WHY NOT SET TERMS THAT WE CAN LIVE WITH RATHER THAN FIGHT AND LOSE EVERYTHING?
BECAUSE WE'RE NORSSK?
DO I *REALLY* NEED TO TELL YOU THAT?
PEOPLE DON'T CHANGE AS FAST AS YOU THINK THEY DO, MAGNUS.
YOU HAVE ROUGH TIMES AHEAD OF YOU.

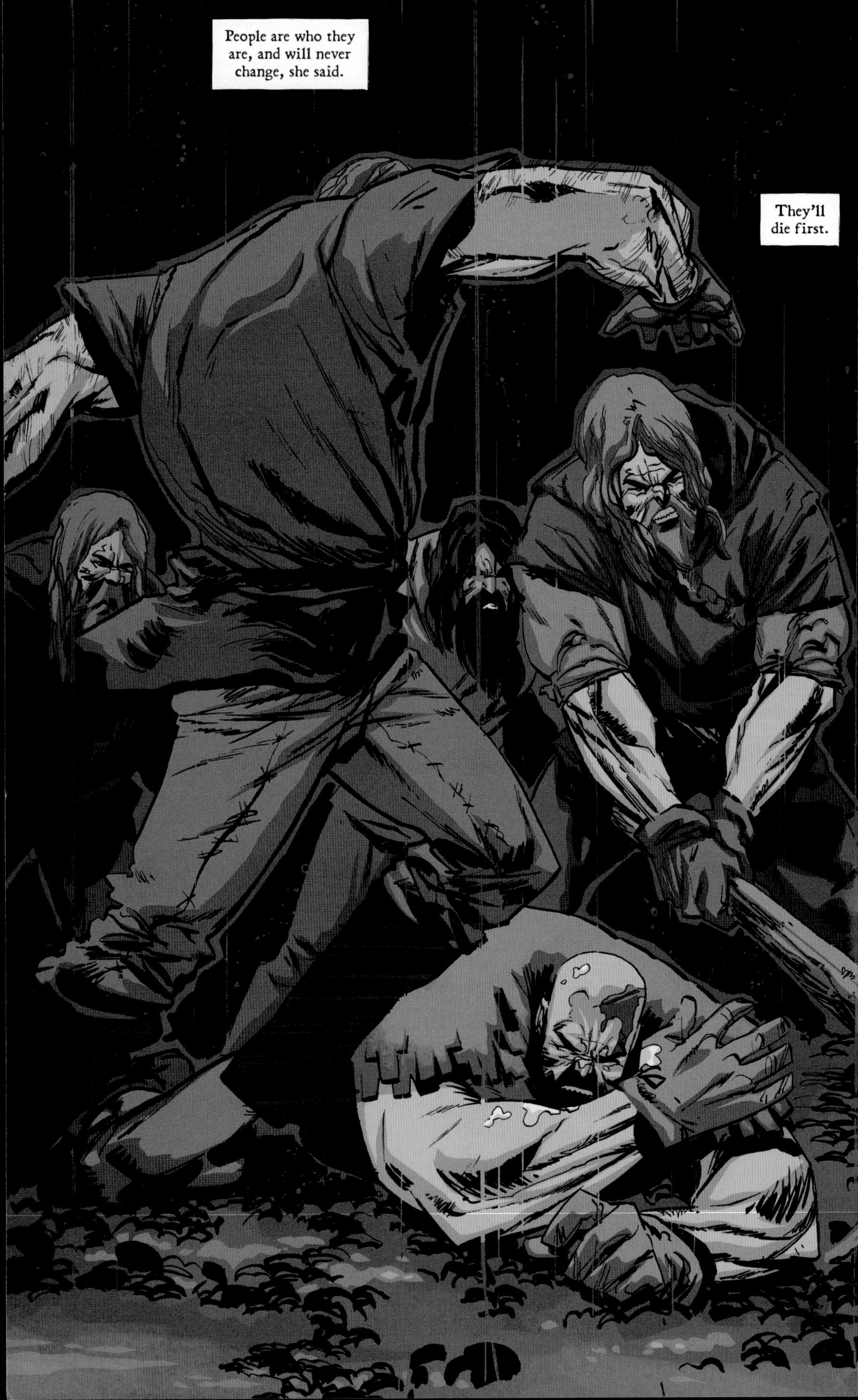
People are who they are, and will never change, she said.
They'll die first.

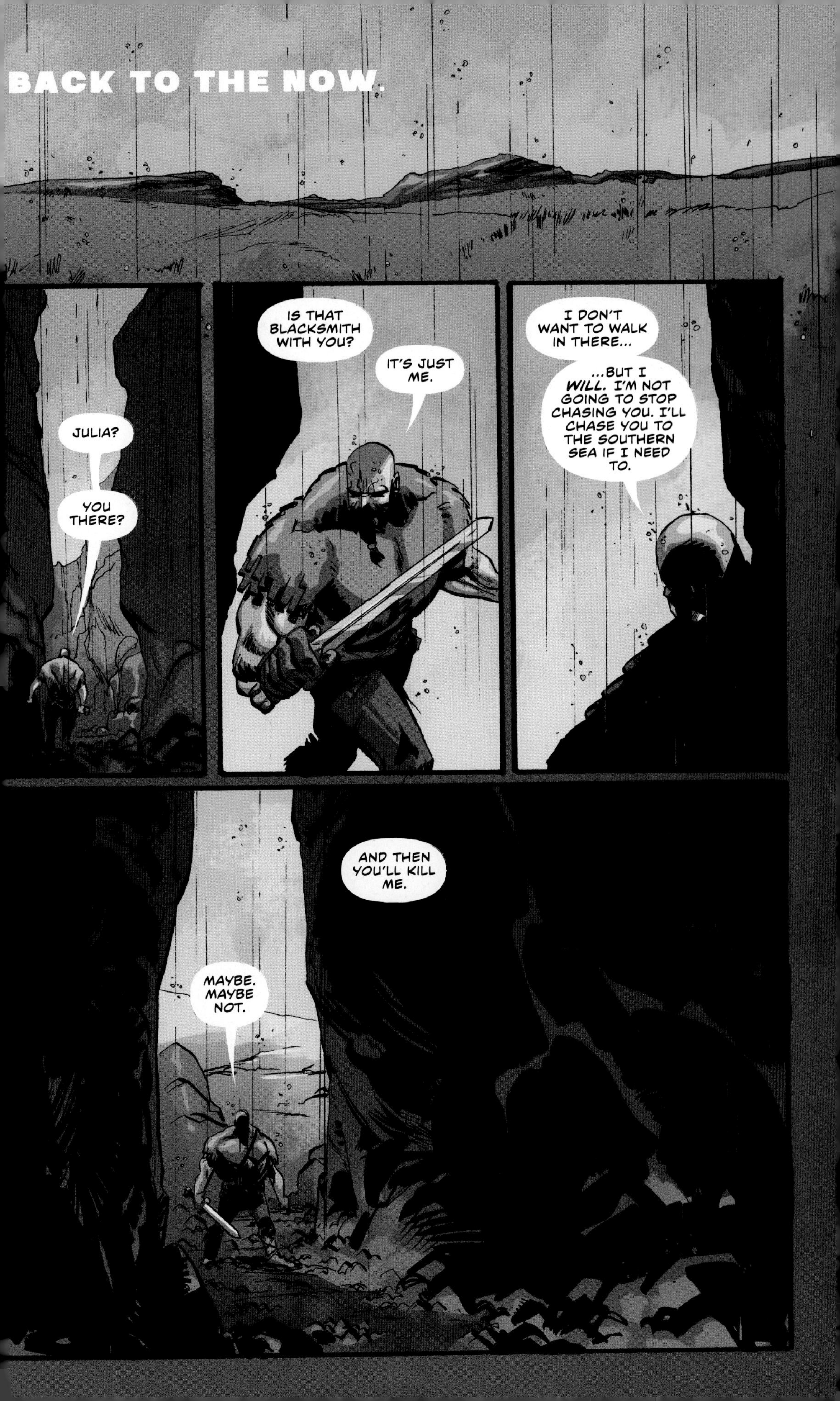
BACK TO THE NOW.
JULIA?
YOU THERE?
IS THAT BLACKSMITH WITH YOU?
IT'S JUST ME.
I DON'T WANT TO WALK IN THERE...
...BUT I *WILL*. I'M NOT GOING TO STOP CHASING YOU. I'LL CHASE YOU TO THE SOUTHERN SEA IF I NEED TO.
AND THEN YOU'LL KILL ME.
MAYBE. MAYBE NOT.

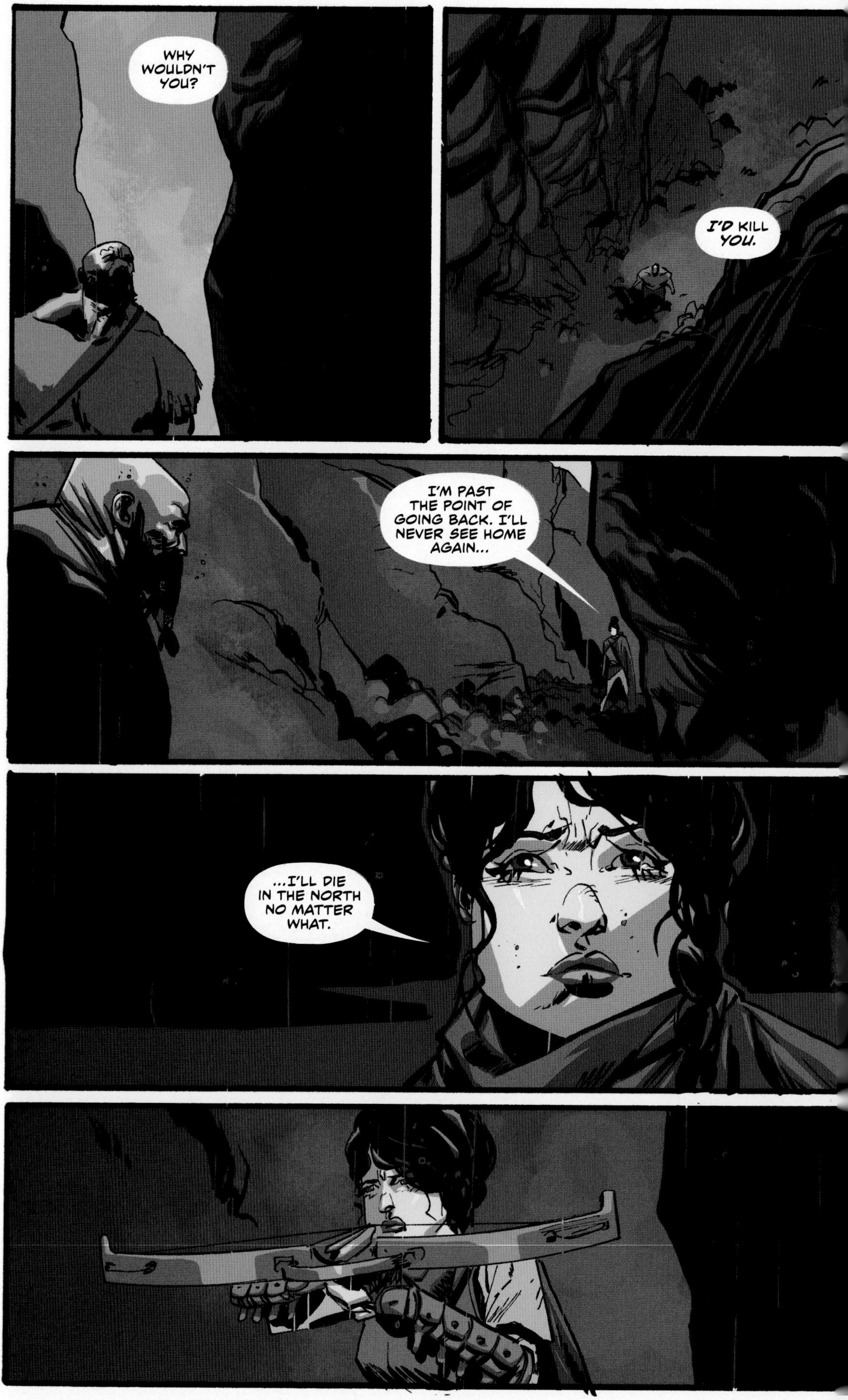
WHY WOULDN'T YOU?
I'D KILL YOU.
I'M PAST THE POINT OF GOING BACK. I'LL NEVER SEE HOME AGAIN...
...I'LL DIE IN THE NORTH NO MATTER WHAT.

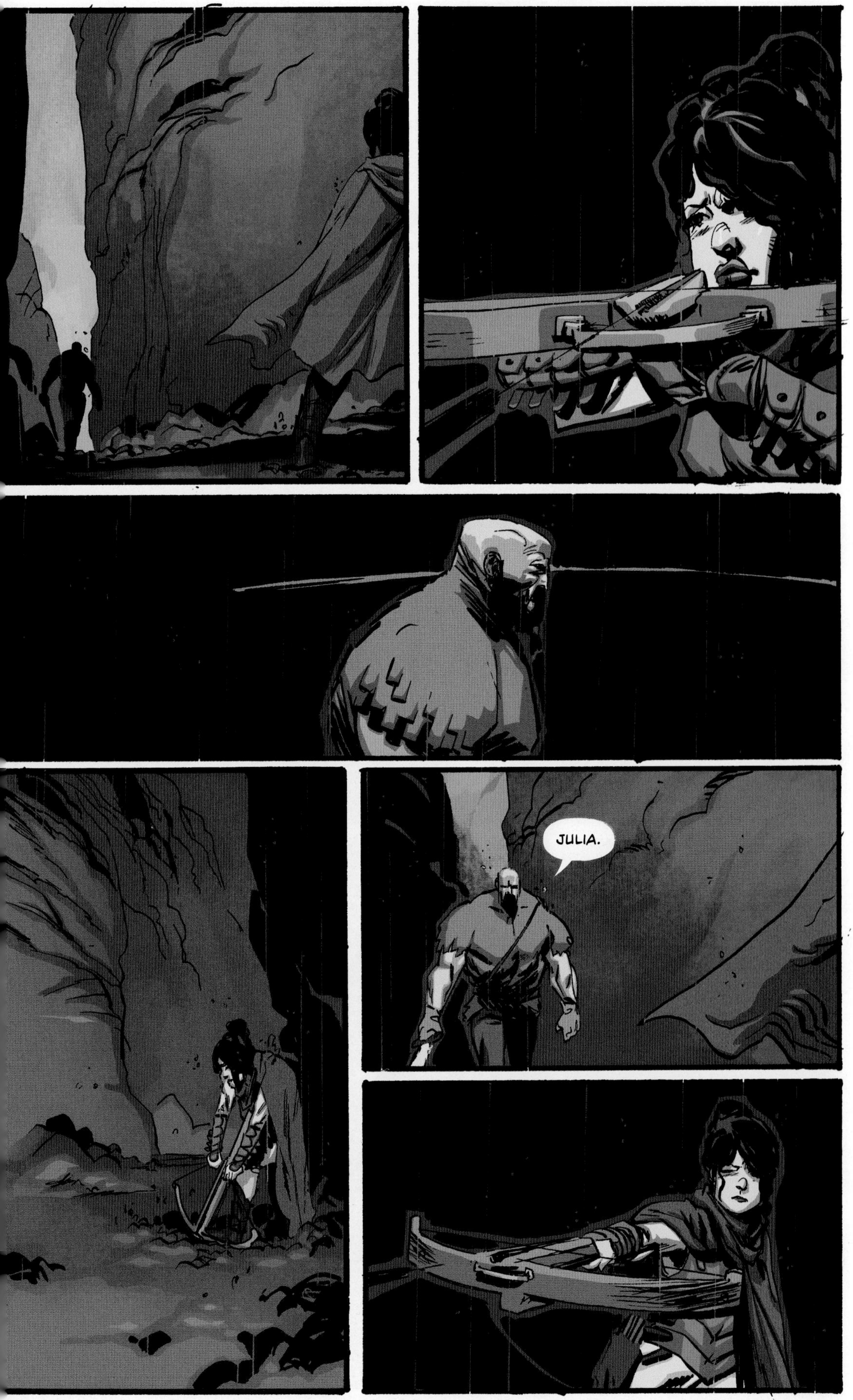
JULIA.

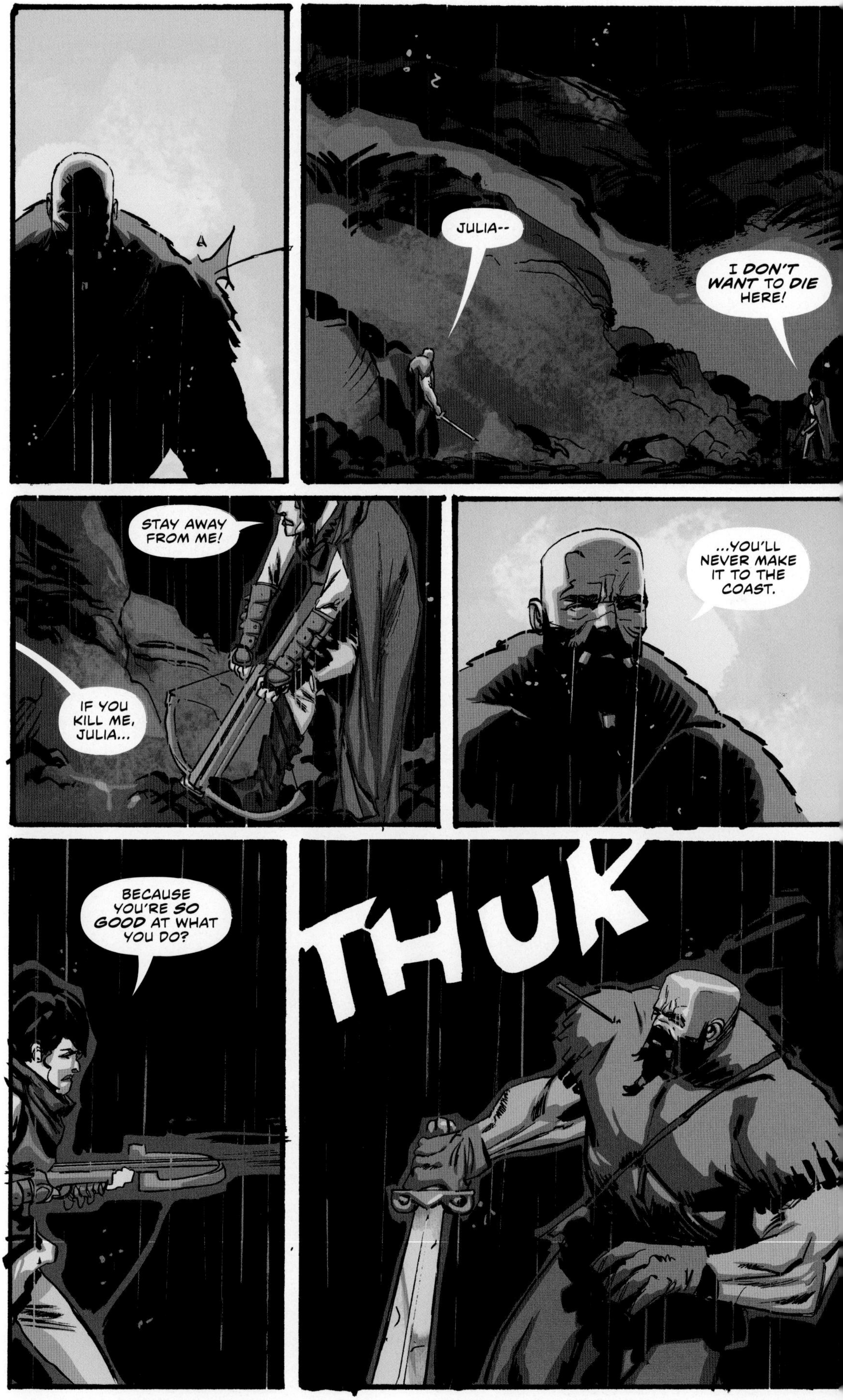
JULIA--
I DON'T WANT TO DIE HERE!
STAY AWAY FROM ME!
IF YOU KILL ME, JULIA...
...YOU'LL NEVER MAKE IT TO THE COAST.
BECAUSE YOU'RE SO GOOD AT WHAT YOU DO?
THUK

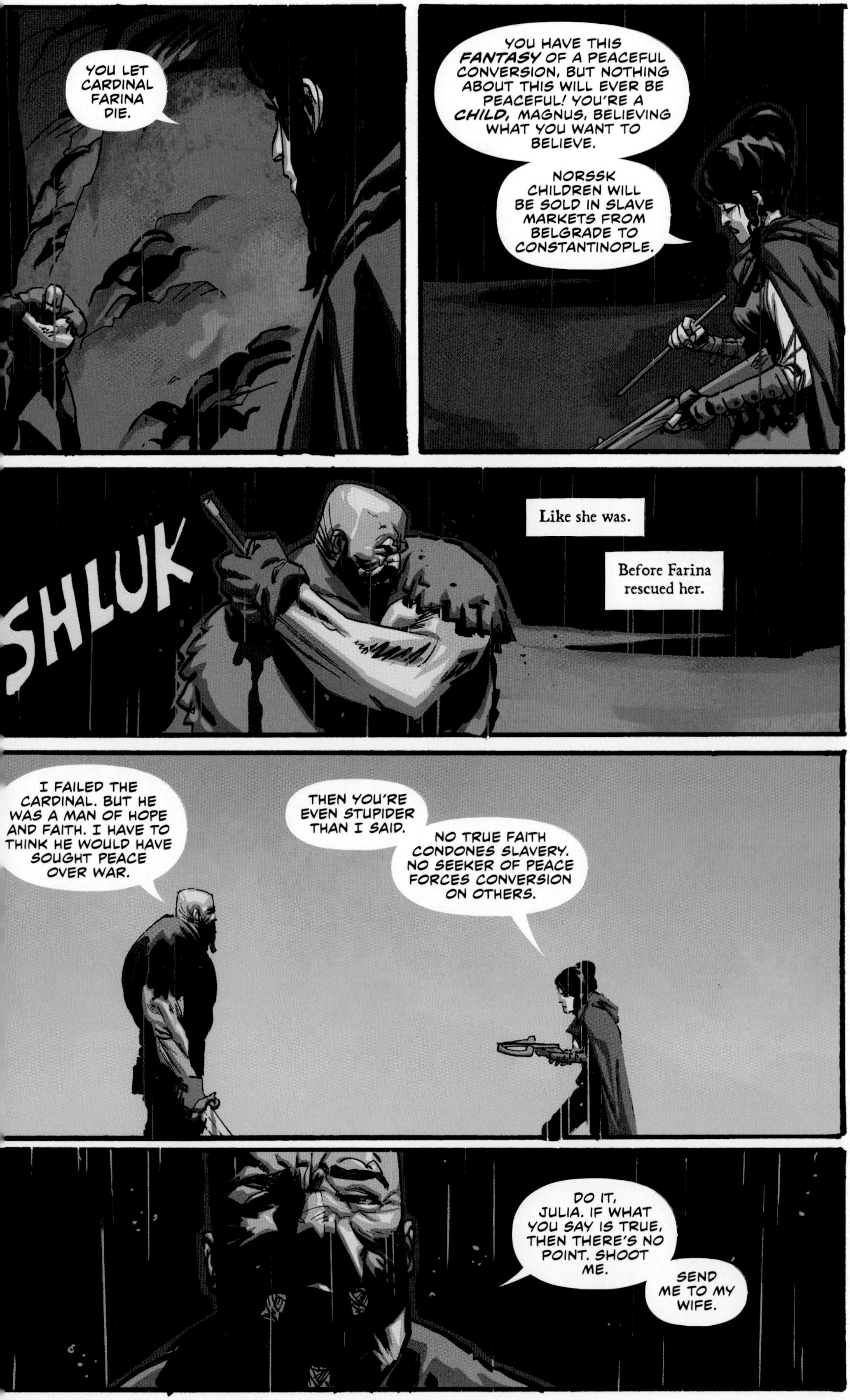
YOU LET CARDINAL FARINA DIE.
YOU HAVE THIS FANTASY OF A PEACEFUL CONVERSION, BUT NOTHING ABOUT THIS WILL EVER BE PEACEFUL! YOU'RE A CHILD, MAGNUS, BELIEVING WHAT YOU WANT TO BELIEVE.
NORSSK CHILDREN WILL BE SOLD IN SLAVE MARKETS FROM BELGRADE TO CONSTANTINOPLE.
SHLUK
Like she was.
Before Farina rescued her.
I FAILED THE CARDINAL. BUT HE WAS A MAN OF HOPE AND FAITH. I HAVE TO THINK HE WOULD HAVE SOUGHT PEACE OVER WAR.
THEN YOU'RE EVEN STUPIDER THAN I SAID.
NO TRUE FAITH CONDONES SLAVERY. NO SEEKER OF PEACE FORCES CONVERSION ON OTHERS.
DO IT, JULIA. IF WHAT YOU SAY IS TRUE, THEN THERE'S NO POINT. SHOOT ME.
SEND ME TO MY WIFE.

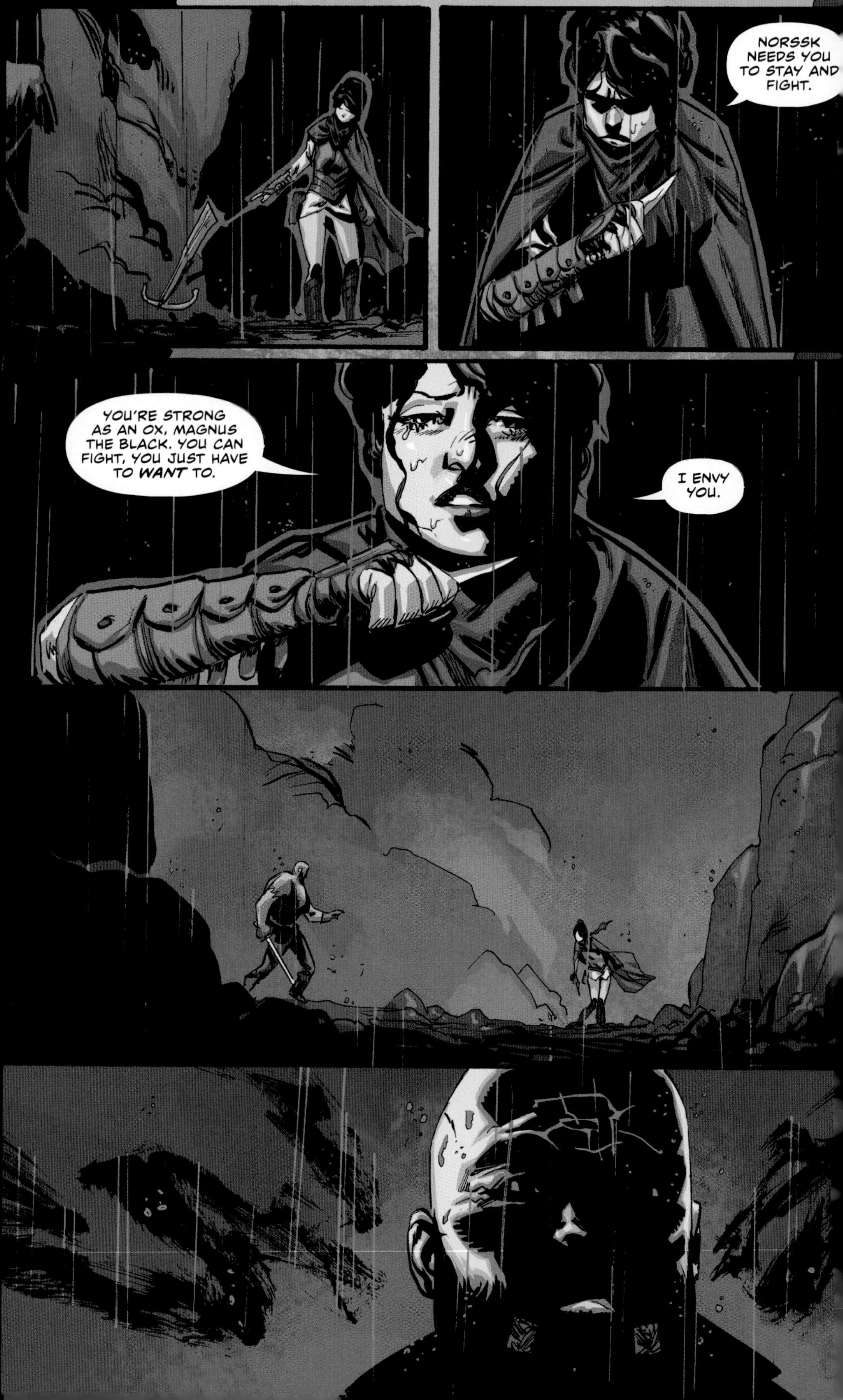
NORSSK NEEDS YOU TO STAY AND FIGHT.
YOU'RE STRONG AS AN OX, MAGNUS THE BLACK. YOU CAN FIGHT, YOU JUST HAVE TO *WANT* TO.
I ENVY YOU.

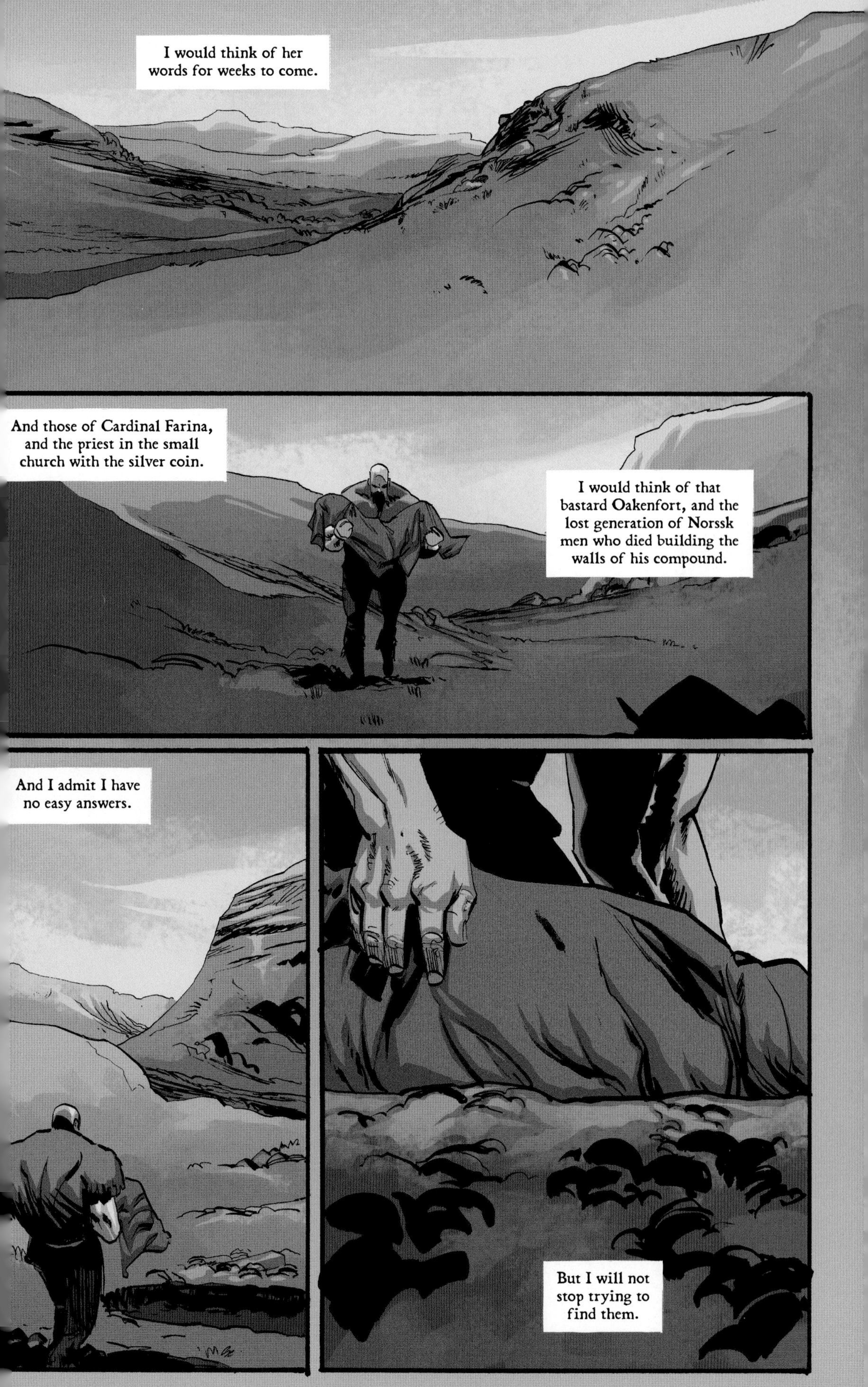
I would think of her words for weeks to come.
And those of Cardinal Farina, and the priest in the small church with the silver coin.
I would think of that bastard Oakenfort, and the lost generation of Norssk men who died building the walls of his compound.
And I admit I have no easy answers.
But I will not stop trying to find them.

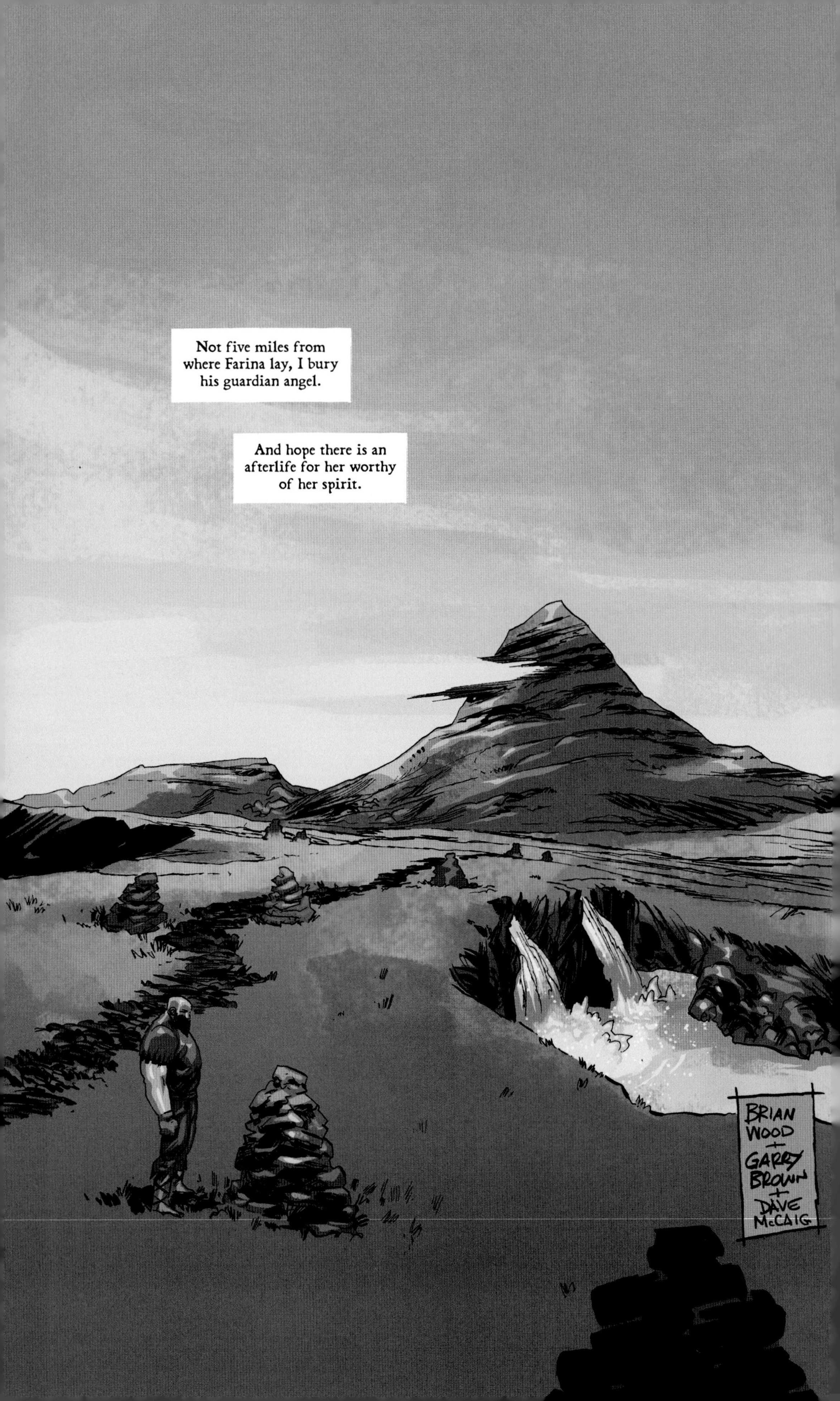
Not five miles from where Farina lay, I bury his guardian angel.
And hope there is an afterlife for her worthy of her spirit.
BRIAN WOOD + GARRY BROWN + DAVE McCAIG

THE
END

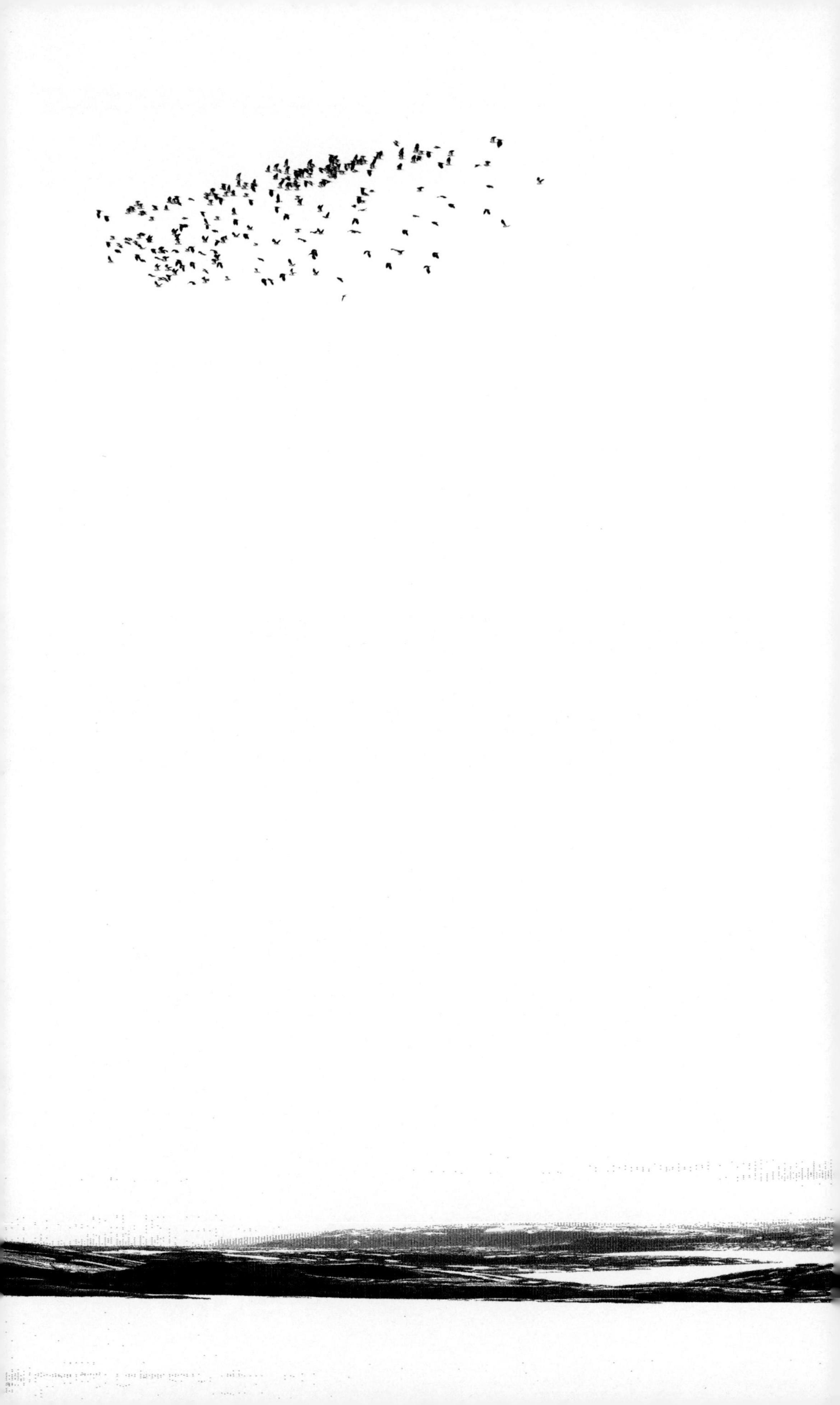

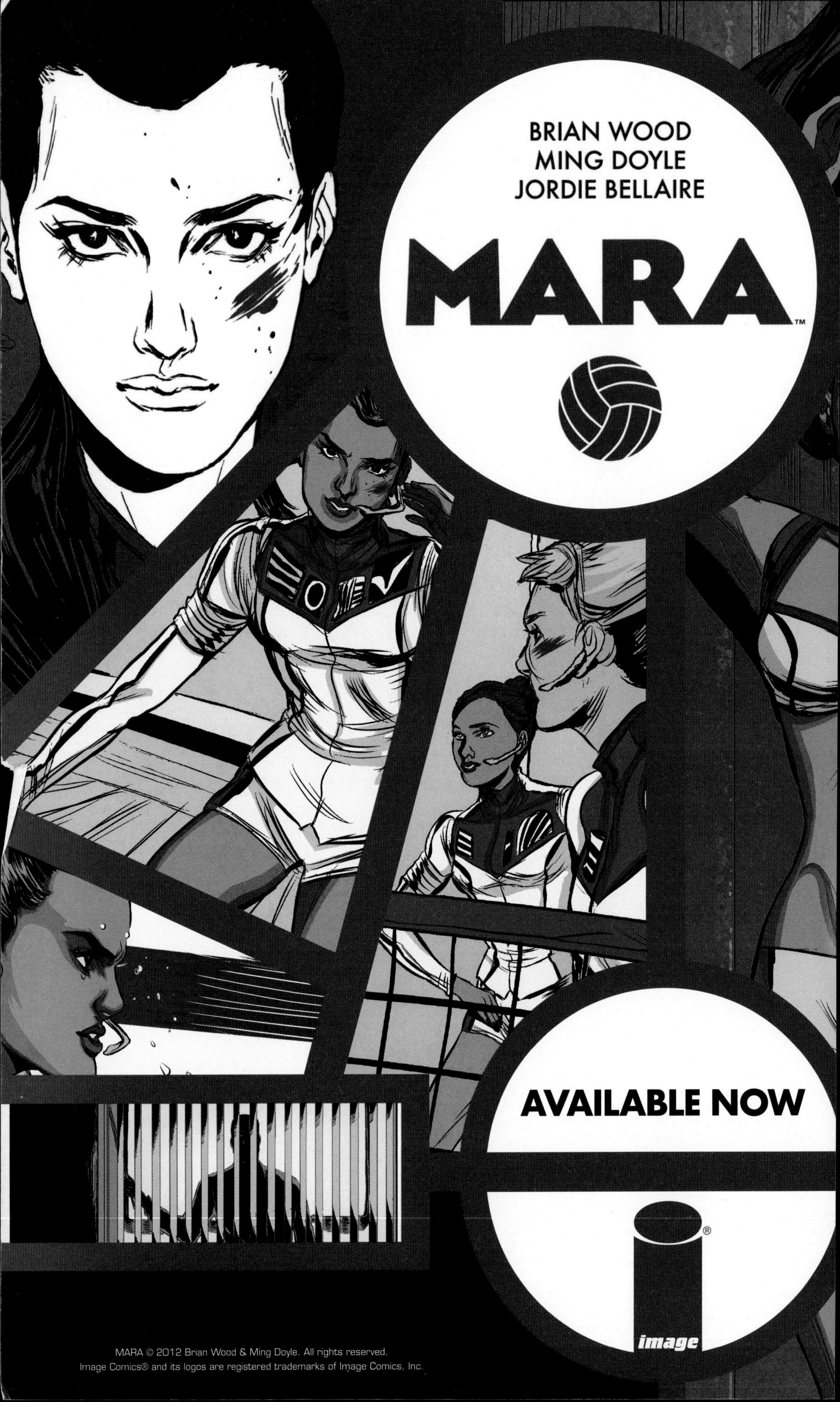

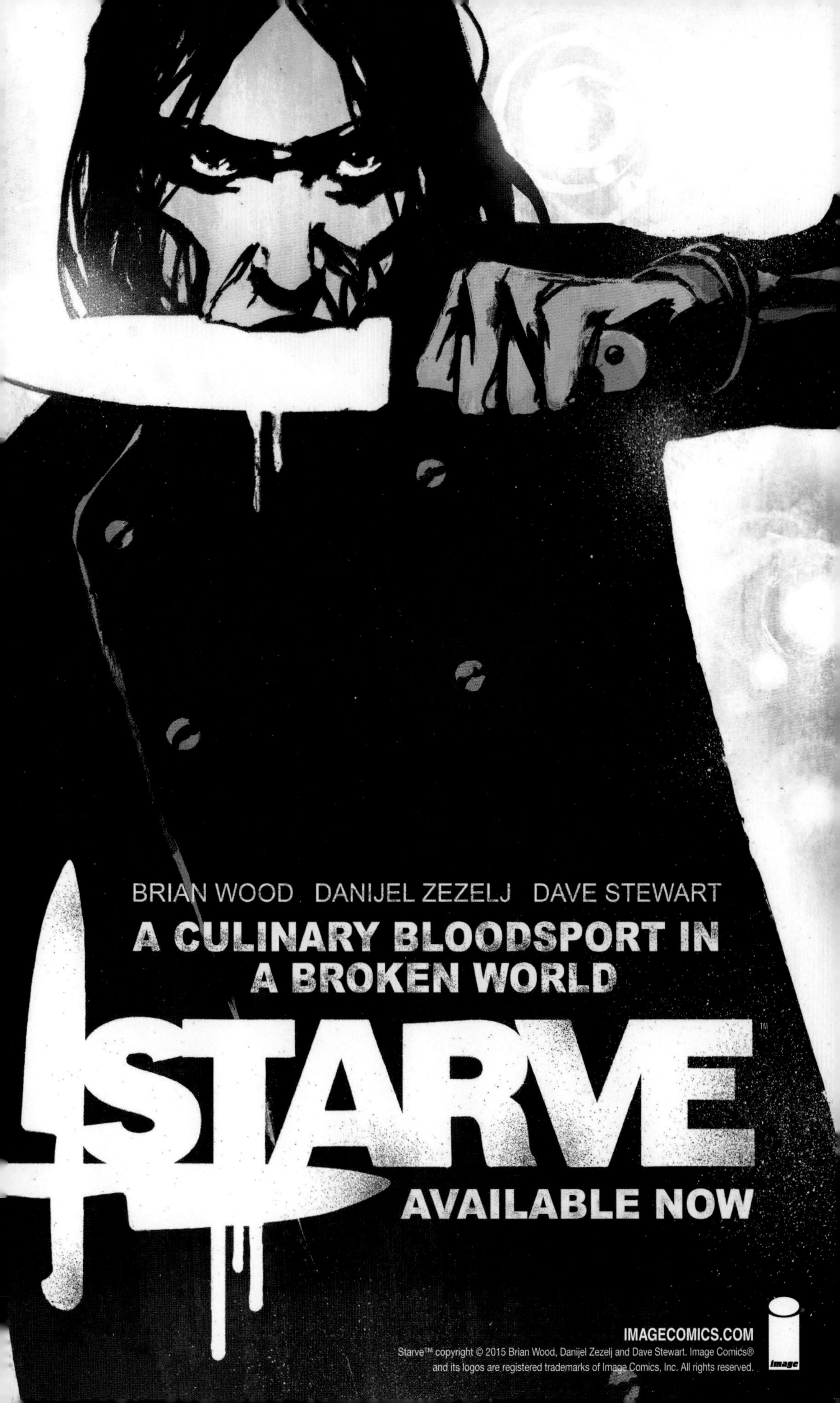

BRIAN WOOD DANIJEL ZEZELJ DAVE STEWART
A CULINARY BLOODSPORT IN A BROKEN WORLD
STARVE™
AVAILABLE NOW
IMAGECOMICS.COM
Starve™ copyright © 2015 Brian Wood, Danijel Zezelj and Dave Stewart. Image Comics® and its logos are registered trademarks of Image Comics, Inc. All rights reserved.
image